TITUS CROW

Volume Two

THE SHADOW OVER DYLATH-LEEN...

I remembered Atal's warning "not to watch," but was unable to turn away. I was rooted to the spot, and as the screams from the city rose in unbearable intensity, I could but stare into the darkness with bulging eyes. Then . . . *It* came!

It came, rushing from out the bowels of the terrified town, bringing a black and stinking wind that bowled over its fleeing enemies as if they had no weight at all. And God help me, I *saw* it! Blind but all-seeing—without legs yet running like flood water—the poisonous mouths in the bubbling mass—the fly-the-light beyond the wall. The sight of the thing was mind-blasting.

And what it *did* to the pitiful Leng-creatures!

TITUS CROW

Volume Two

◆

THE CLOCK OF DREAMS

SPAWN OF THE WINDS

BRIAN LUMLEY

A TOM DOHERTY ASSOCIATES BOOK/NEW YORK

TITUS CROW: VOLUME TWO

This book is an omnibus edition, consisting of *The Clock of Dreams*, copyright © 1978 by Brian Lumley, and *Spawn of the Winds*, copyright © 1978 by Brian Lumley.

This book is printed on acid-free paper.

A Tor Book
Published by Tom Doherty Associates, LLC
175 Fifth Avenue
New York, NY 10010

www.tor.com

Tor ® is a registered trademark of Tom Doherty Associates, LLC.

ISBN 0-312-86868-5 (pbk)

First Tor Hardcover Edition: July 1997
First Tor Trade Paperback Edition: October 1999

Printed in the United States of America

D 10 9 8 7 6 5 4 3 2 1

CONTENTS

THE
CLOCK OF
DREAMS

◆

For Barzai
the Not-So-Wise,
who proved—however
involuntarily—that what
goes up need not
necessarily
come down
again.

Introduction

Myself, I've never been much of a dreamer, never traveled far past Ulthar; but I have watched caravans fording the Skai, and I have sat in the smokeroom of the Inn of a Thousand Sleeping Cats and listened to the tales of my betters. I suppose most dreamers have. It's true, though, that there seem to be fewer of us around these days. Time was when a man of the waking world could guarantee that if he boarded at an inn in the land of Earth's dreams, sure enough he would find a fellow dreamer or two from the world of waking mortals; and wouldn't the tales fly thick and fast then? Yes, they surely would.

You would hear magical names of men and places—names to set your pulses pounding and your imagination tingling—and thrill to the telling of tales of heroic and fantastic deeds. And someone would be bound to mention Kuranes or Randolph Carter . . . or Richard Upton Pickman. And while you might shudder at the hinted fate of the latter, certainly you would also gasp in awe at the adventures of the others. Ah, those were the dreams . . .

Still, I suppose I shouldn't complain too bitterly, for when I come to think of it I heard two of my favorite tales quite recently, and as coincidence would have it I heard them at the Inn of a Thousand Sleeping Cats . . . in Ulthar.

The first was a strange tale and complicated, a tale of all the worlds of space and time, of strange dimensions and planes of existence beyond the ken of most men. A tale of motes in the multiverse swirling beyond barriers neither spacial nor temporal, nor of any intermediate dimension recognized by mortal man except in the wildest theories of science and metaphysics. A tale of paths between the spheres, dim corridors leading to equally dim and conjectural lands of elder myth . . . And yet all of these seemingly inaccessible places were just around the corner to the time-clock.

Indeed "time-clock," as Titus Crow had long since recognized the fact, was a completely inadequate misnomer for that—machine? A plaything of the Elder Gods come down the ages from lands beyond legend, from a time beyond time as men reckon it, the clock was a gateway on—on everything! It was a door to worlds of wonder, joy and beauty—but it was also a dark pothole entrance to caves of innermost, alien evil and shrieking, unnameable horror.

The first tale I heard was the story of how the clock came into Henri-Laurent de Marigny's hands in the first place, and it is a tale already told. But for the sake of the unacquainted I will briefly reiterate it before taking up the second of the two stories proper. Before even that, however, I had better tell what little is known of the time-clock itself.

Certainly the clock's history is strange and obscure enough to whet the mental appetite of any lover of mysteries or would-be sounder of unfathomable wonders (which you must be, else you would not be reading this). First, tracing the existence of the weird—conveyance?—back as far as possible in the light of incomplete knowledge, it seems to have belonged to one Yogi Hiamaldi, an Indian friend of the ill-fated Carolina mystic Harley Warren. Hiamaldi had been a member, along with Warren, of a psychic-phenomenist group in Boston about 1916–18; and he had sworn before all other members of that group that he alone of living men had been to Yian-Ho, crumbling remnant of eons long lost, and that he had borne away certain *things* from that grim and leering necropolis.

For reasons unknown, the Yogi had made a gift of the clock to one Etienne-Laurent de Marigny (perhaps the greatest ever American occultist and the father of one of the heroes of the story to follow), who kept it at the New Orleans retreat where his studies of the arcane sciences formed his primary purpose in life. How much he discovered of its secrets remains unknown, but after the elder de Marigny died the clock was sold, along with many another antique curiosity, to a French collector.

Here there is a gap in the history, for while many years later Titus Crow bought the clock at an auction of antique furniture in London, all of his subsequent attempts to discover the whereabouts of its previous Parisian owner were doomed to failure; it was as though the man had simply vanished off the face of the Earth.

Now then, of Titus Crow himself—a man with a positive genius for the discovery of dark lore, lost legends, and nighted myth-patterns, who will also feature prominently in my tale—much is known; but for now suffice it to mention that his protracted studies of the clock over many years of his life were such that the device became something of an obsession with him. Often in his earlier years Crow would sit in his study in the night, his chin in his hands as he gravely pondered the enigma of the peculiar, coffin-shaped, oddly ticking monstrosity in the corner of the room; a "clock," of sorts, whose four hands moved in patterns patently divorced from any chronological system known or even guessed at by man, and his eyes would rove over the strange hieroglyphs that swept in intricate designs around the great clock's face.

When he was not at work on less baffling cases, always Titus Crow would return his attentions to the clock, and though usually such studies were in vain, they were not always complete failures. Often he believed himself on the verge of a breakthrough—knowing that if he were right he would finally understand the alien intricacies governing his "doorway on all space and time"—only to be frustrated in the final hour. And once he actually had the doubtful privilege of seeing the clock opened by two men of equally doubtful repute and intent, whose affairs in the world were fortunately soon terminated . . . but then at long last there came a genuine clue.

It was while he was working for the Wilmarth Foundation—a far-flung body of erudite men whose sole avowed intent and purpose was to rid the world, indeed the entire universe, of all remaining traces of an aeon-old evil, the surviving demonic forces and powers of the Cthulhu Cycle of Myth—that Titus Crow visited Miskatonic University in Arkham, Massachusetts. There, in one of the carefully guarded, great old occult volumes in the university's world-renowned library, he finally recognized a sequence of odd glyphs which at first he was startled, then delighted to note bore a striking resemblance to the figures on the dial of his huge clock. Moreover, the book bore translations of his own hieroglyphed passages in Latin!

Armed with this Rosetta-Stone knowledge, Crow had returned to London, where soon he was at work again disinterring many of the clock's centuries-buried mysteries. And he had been right, for that incredible device was indeed a vehicle: a space-time machine of sorts with principles more alien than the centers of stars, whose like we may at least conjecture upon.

Of his work on the clock at this time, he wrote to his friend and colleague, Henri-Laurent de Marigny: "I am in the position of a Neanderthal studying the operational handbook of a passenger-carrying aircraft—except I have no handbook!" And Henri was unable to assist his learned friend, for while his father had once owned the selfsame clock, that had been when he was a boy, and he could remember nothing of it. Titus Crow, however, was never a man to be denied anything once he set his mind after it, and so he had persevered.

And little by little he discovered all of the clock's peculiar secrets. He learned how to open its frontal panel, without suffering any of the many possible consequences, allowing the strange lights that invariably illumined its interior to flood out in eerie shades that dappled his study with alien hues. He knew how to attune himself "telepathically" to the device's sub-ethereal vibrations: how to "make himself one," as he had it, with the clock. He was aware of the nature of the "commands" he must give to the clock to guide it on its journeyings through temporal and spacial voids, so that the time soon came when he believed he might attempt his first flight in the weird vehicle.

All of this knowledge came to Titus Crow in the very nick of time, for no sooner was he physically ready to test his theories than just such a test was forced upon him. It happened when he and his young friend de Marigny (also a member of the Wilmarth Foundation) were staying at Blowne House, Crow's sprawling bungalow home on Leonard's Heath in London.

The two of them had grown to be very painful thorns in the sides of the deities or demons of the Cthulhu Cycle, and at last the prime member of that cycle, dread Cthulhu himself, had discovered a way to strike back at them. Dreaming hideously in R'lyeth, his "house" drowned somewhere in the vast Pacific, Cthulhu worked his evil plot through Ithaqua the Wind-Walker, Lord of the Snows. For while Ithaqua himself was unable to go abroad beyond barriers immemorially imposed by the Elder Gods—that is, while he was restricted in his movements to the Arctic Circle and its adjacent environs, and to strange Boreal starlanes and alien worlds—nonetheless he was still undisputed master of all the world's winds. And now he sent elementals of the air from the four corners of the sky to attack Titus Crow's home.

Left with no choice but to risk the doubtful sanctuary of the time-clock—as eerie shapes of evil formed beyond the shattering windows, monstrous forces that pounded at the shuddering frame of his bungalow retreat until Blowne House fell about his ears—Crow stepped beyond the open front panel of his vehicle and bade de Marigny follow him. And when that "freak localized storm" had expired and the house was discovered in ruins, perhaps not surprisingly no trace could be found of the two friends; neither of them, nor of the weird clock.

Well, to cut a long story short, Titus Crow made good his escape from those monstrous minion winds of Ithaqua into the far future, traveling almost to the End of Time itself before finally he mastered the clock's many intricacies to control its flight. But as for de Marigny, he was not the adept that his friend was. Barely was their craft "out of port," as it were, before de Marigny was "washed overboard" into terrible temporal tides—to be fished from the Thames more dead than alive *ten years later!* Though the flight in the time-clock had seemed to last mere seconds, and while Crow's younger friend had aged not at all, nevertheless ten years had sped by; which caused de Marigny to wonder *just how far* his friend had finally traveled—and was he perhaps still traveling?

It was not long before he was to learn the answers to these and to other questions.

Upon recovering from his fantastic ordeal, de Marigny went back to his old London home, and there one night a short time later Titus Crow also returned to the world of men. Ah, but this was a much-changed Titus Crow, for he had undergone a transition. Younger, stronger, wiser (though de Marigny found the latter hardly credible), the new Crow had seen marvels beyond belief, had traced his own lineage back to the very Elder Gods themselves. And now he had returned to Earth for one reason only: to offer Henri-Laurent de Marigny the opportunity to join him in Elysia, the home of the Great Gods of Eld. As an inducement, if such were needed, this is how Crow had told his friend of his adventures:

". . . I've been trapped on the shores of a prehistoric ocean, Henri, living on my wits and by hunting great crabs and spearing strange fishes, dodging the dinosaurs which in turn hunted me. And a billion years before that I inhabited a great rugose cone of a body, a living organism which was in fact a member of the Great Race that settled on Earth in unthinkable aybsses of the past. I've seen the cruel and world-spanning empire of Tsan-Chan, three thousand years in the future, and beyond that the great dark vaults that loom at the end of time. I've talked telepathically with the super-intelligent mollusks of soupy Venusian oceans, which will not support even the most primitive life for another half-billion years; and I've stood on the bleak shores of those same seas ten million years later when they were sterile, after a great plague had destroyed all life on the entire planet . . .

"Why, I've come close to seeing the very birth of the universe, and almost its death!—and all of these wonders and others exist still just beyond the thin mists of time and space. This clock of mine sails those mists more bravely and surely than any Viking's dragonship ever crossed the gray North Sea. And you ask me what I mean when I talk of another trip, one involving yourself?

"When I return to Elysia, Henri, to the home of the Elder Gods in Orion, there will be a place for you in my palace there. Indeed, you shall have a palace of your own. And why not? The Gods mated with the daughters of men in the old days, didn't they? And won't you only be reversing the process? I did, my friend, and now the universe is mine. It can be yours, too . . ."

Soon after that Titus Crow took his departure from Earth yet again, but this time he used the time-clock more properly as a "gateway," passing through it but yet leaving it behind until de Marigny should make up his mind one way or the other. If he decided to brave the machine's dark unknown, the way would not be easy. De Marigny knew that. But visions previously undreamed of had opened in his mind, and wonders beckoned and enticed him more magnetically than ever the Sirens lured Ulysses.

For de Marigny was a lover of mysteries no less than you, the reader, and as such could he possibly refuse the proffered challenge? Could you?

Part One

♦

I

The Call of Kthanid

De Marigny had first flown the time-clock two weeks earlier under Titus Crow's expert tutelage. Now Crow was gone—back to Elysia and the incredible girl-goddess he loved there, Tiania—and de Marigny had decided to follow him, alone.

Crow had done a marvelous job of instruction during the brief flights he had shared with his friend in the clock, and de Marigny was by no means lost in regard to controlling that fantastic machine. It was simply a matter of "meshing oneself" with the thing, so that the clock became an extension of its passenger's body and mind, an extra limb or sixth sense . . . or both.

Thus, while half the world slept and darkness covered the land, Henri-Laurent de Marigny set out to prove himself worthy of a new and higher life in Elysia; and he did so in the only way open to him, by pitting himself and his vessel against all the currents of space and time. The world, all unawares, dwindled behind him as he cruised out into the void in his strangely hybrid craft, his almost "human" machine, and a wild enthusiasm and exhilaration filled him as he piloted that vessel in the direction of Orion. Somewhere out there—somewhere in the distant void, behind invisible hyperdimensional barriers—he knew that faerie Elysia waited for him, and it seemed only reasonable to de Marigny that since Elysia lay "adjacent" to Orion, that star should mark his starting point.

On one thing de Marigny had already and irreversibly made up his mind: though Titus Crow had told him that in the event of insurmountable difficulties he could always contact him through the clock, he would not do so unless his life itself were threatened. From what he knew of it there seemed to be only one way into Elysia for a creature not born to it, and that was the way of peril. Only those who deserve Elysia may ever enjoy her elder wonders, and de Marigny did not intend to be dependant upon Titus Crow for his—birthright?

His birthright, yes—Elysia *was* his birthright, Crow had hinted as much. What was it his friend had said to him? "Lover of mysteries you are, Henri, as your father before you. And I'll tell you something, something which you really ought to have guessed before now. There's that in you that hearkens back into dim abysses of time, a spark whose fire burns still in Elysia. And one more thing you should know.

"Those places of fantasy and dream I've mentioned—they're all as real and solid in their way as the very ground beneath your feet. The Lands of Dream, after all, are only dimensions lying parallel to the Worlds of Reality. Ah, but there are dreamers and there are dreamers, my friend, and your father was a great dreamer. *He still is—for he is a Lord of Ilek-Vad, Counselor to his great friend Randolph Carter, who is himself a just and honored king!*

"I intend to visit them there one day, in Ilek-Vad deep in Earth's dreamland, and when I do you can be with me . . ."

Musing on these things that Crow had told him, physically and emotionally weary now that the initial stage of his flight was successfully completed and the journey safely underway, de Marigny lay back and watched with his mind's eye—which was now a part of the time-clock's equipment, a mental "scanner" of sorts—as the stars visibly moved in the inky blackness about him, so tremendous was the velocity of his craft as it hurtled through the airless, frozen deeps.

"As real and solid as the very ground beneath your feet," Crow had said of dreams. Well, if Titus Crow said it was so, then it was so. And hadn't Gerhard Schrach hinted much the same thing back in the thirties, and other great thinkers and philosophers before him? Certainly they had. De Marigny could remember Schrach's very words on the subject:

". . . My own dreams being particularly vivid and real—to such an extent that I never know for sure whether or not I am dreaming until I wake up—I would not like to argue which world is the more vital: the waking world or the world of dream. Certainly the waking world appears to be the more solid—but consider what science tells us about the atomic make-up of so-called solids . . . and what are you left with?"

And with thoughts such as these swirling in his head, and the fascinating panoply of vasty voids sprinkled with a myriad jewels in his mind's eye, de Marigny bade the clock speed on and drifted into a sleep; a sleep which seemed eagerly to open its arms to him, and one which was far from dreamless.

Beyond the slightest shadow of a doubt the slumbering de Marigny's dreams were not natural ones, and but for his previous knowledge of Elysia, passed on to him through Titus Crow—particularly of the Hall of Crystal and Pearl, wherein Kthanid the Elder God Eminence had his seat in an inviolable sanctuary beneath a great glacier—certainly he must have considered himself the victim of a vilest nightmare. For the thing upon which he suddenly found himself gazing was a shape of primal horror, the blasphemous shape of Cthulhu himself—except that it was not Cthulhu but Kthanid, and where the former was black as the pit the latter shone with the light of stars.

Thus, while his subconscious body hurtled through the star-voids within the spacetime-defying matrix of the great clock, de Marigny's dreaming mind was present in that very Hall of Crystal and Pearl which Titus Crow had described to him in so much detail. And he saw that Crow had painted an almost perfect picture of that magnificently alien palace beneath the ice of Elysia's "polar" regions.

Here was the massive high-arched ceiling, the Titan-paved floor of great hexagonal flags, the ornate columns rising to support high balconies which glowed partially hidden in rose-quartz mists and pearly hazes. And everywhere were the white, pink, and blood hues of crystal, strangely diffused in all those weird angles and proportions that Crow had spoken of. Even the hall's centerpiece—the vast scarlet cushion with its huge, milky crystal ball—was just as Crow had described it. And of course, Kthanid was there, too . . .

Kthanid the Eminence, Elder God and cousin to Great Cthulhu—indeed of the same strain of cosmic spawn that bred the Lord of R'lyeh—moved massively in the Cyclopean hall. His body was mountainous! And yet his folded-back, fantastic wings trembled in seeming agitation as Kthanid paced the enormous flags, his great octopoid head, with its proliferation of face-tentacles, turning this way and that in what was plainly consternation.

But for all that this Being was alien beyond words, what might easily have been horrific was in fact magnificent! For this great creature, bejeweled and glittering as though dusted with diamonds, stared out upon the hall through huge eyes that glowed like molten gold; eyes filled with compassion and love—yes, and fear—almost impossible to imagine as existing within so terrible a fleshly house. And those eyes returned again and again to peer intently at the lustrous crystal upon its scarlet cushion.

It was because of Kthanid's eyes that de Marigny knew—was certain—that there was nothing to fear here, and he knew too that this was much more than merely a dream. It was as if he had been called into the Elder God's presence, and no sooner had this thought occurred to the dreamer than the Eminence turned and stared straight at him where his disembodied being "stood" invisible within the vast subterranean vault.

"Henri-Laurent de Marigny," a rumbling but infinitely kindly voice spoke in the dreamer's mind. "Man of Earth, is it you? Yes, I see that it is. You have answered my summons, which is good, for that was a test I had intended to set you before—before—" The mental voice faded into uncertain silence.

"Kthanid," de Marigny spoke up, unsure as to how to address the mythical Being, "I see that you are . . . disturbed. Why have you called me here? Has the trouble to do with Titus Crow?"

"With Titus, yes, and with Tiania, whom I love as a father. But come," the great voice took on urgency, "look into the crystal and tell me what you see."

Disembodied, nevertheless de Marigny found that he was capable of movement. He followed Kthanid to the edge of the great cushion, then moved on across its silken expanse to the center. There the huge, milky crystal ball reposed, its surface opaque and slowly mobile, as a reflection of dense clouds mirrored in a still lake.

"Look!" the Eminence commanded yet again, and slowly the milky clouds began to part, revealing . . .

The dreaming de Marigny gazed upon a scene that filled him with icy dread, a scene he could understand even less than he could believe it. The crystal on its scarlet cushion now burned with red fires of its own, and dark shadows danced as flames leaped high above four hugely flaring, blackly-forged flambeaux. These torches stood at the corners of a raised dais or altar, atop which a great reddish mass—a living, malignant jewel at least three feet across—pulsed evilly as it reflected the ruddy light of the torches. The thing seemed to be an impossibly vast ruby; and guarding it, patroling the round-cobbled square in which the dais stood, were several squat, strangely turbaned figures with awful wide-mouthed faces. At their belts these guardsmen wore viciously curving scimitars, and as they moved about the foot of the raised altar de Marigny saw that they paused occasionally to torment two ragged figures whose limbs were roped to irons hammered into the steps of the dais.

The horror and sick shock that de Marigny experienced had its source in these two figures; for one of them was certainly his great friend of olden adventures, Titus Crow, while the other—ruddily illumined in the light of the flaring flambeaux, fantastically beautiful even in her present distress—must be the girl-goddess Tiania, late of Elysia. Then, as suddenly as it had come, while de Marigny tried desperately to commit all the vision's details to memory, the milky clouds rolled back across the crystal's surface and all was gone.

Away in the time-clock, still hurtling through the star-voids half a universe away in space and time, de Marigny's recumbent form sweated, tossed and turned; while in the great Hall of Crystal and Pearl his disembodied subconscious turned imploringly to Kthanid the Eminence to ask: "But what does it mean? Where are they? And how did this—"

"Hold!" The great Being turned abruptly and for a moment his huge eyes were slits, glittering with something other than compassion or love. Kthanid was every inch a God, and de Marigny sensed that for a moment he had been very close to witnessing the release of awesome energies. The Elder God's frustration was a living force that the dreamer felt as surely as his waking body would feel the warmth of sunlight or the chill of a bitter wind. Then the golden eyes blinked rapidly and Kthanid's towering form trembled violently as he fought to bring his emotions under control.

"Hold, de Marigny," the mental voice finally rumbled again, this time less forcefully, "and I will explain all. But understand that every wasted moment increases their peril . . ."

Then the great voice seemed almost to become resigned, as if giving a telepathic shrug. "Still, what other way is there? I must tell you as much as I know, for of course you are their one hope of salvation. Indeed, you will be the *instrument* of that salvation—if you are able. Have you the strength, de Marigny? Are you the man Titus Crow believes you to be? Would you really presume to enter Elysia? I tell you now, I am not unjust—but I love those two. Bring them back to me, and I will welcome you to Elysia as a son. Fail me, and—" again the mental shrug, "and you remain a child of Earth all your days—*if* you live through your ordeal!"

"Whatever needs to be done to help Titus Crow—yes, and his Tiania—I'll try to do it," the dreamer fervently answered. "Wherever I need to go, I'll go there."

"You will need to do more than merely try, de Marigny, and indeed there is far to go. When I have told you all I am able to tell, then you must be on your way—immediately."

"And my destination?"

"Earth!"

"Earth?" the dreamer gaped. "But—"

"Earth, yes, for your own homeworld is the only safe stepping-stone to your ultimate destination, to the place where even now Titus Crow and Tiania face unknown terrors." For a brief moment Kthanid paused, then he turned his golden eyes in the dreaming de Marigny's direction. "Obviously your mind is receptive to telepathic attraction, man of Earth, else I could not have called you here to Elysia. But tell me, can you dream? Can you truly dream?"

"Can I dream? Why, I—"

"Your father was a great dreamer."

"Titus Crow has told me much the same thing, but—" de Marigny began, then paused as an astounding thought came to him. "Are you trying to tell me that Titus and Tiania are—"

The great Being nodded: "Yes, they are trapped in Earth's dreamworld, de Marigny. To find them, free them, and return them to Elysia unscathed, that is your quest. One man against all Earth's dreamworld—which is also the land of her nightmares!"

II

Dreams of Doom

"There is a way," the Eminence continued, "by means of which I can rapidly impress upon your mind all that I know of your . . . destination. It may be unpleasant in that you could be left with a headache, but other than that it is not dangerous. There is also a way to speed the process up immeasurably, and . . . But no, I fear your mind is not ready for that. It would probably destroy you."

"Crow has told me how you—*revealed*—certain things to him," de Marigny answered. "Right here in this hall, I believe. I am ready for whatever it is you have to do to me."

"Titus Crow's capacity was unbelievably high, even taking into account the fact that the strains of Eld ran strong in his blood. With him the process was very quick, almost instantaneous, but I would not dare to attempt such a process with you. That is not to belittle you, de Marigny: it is simply that if you are incapacitated, then nothing can save Titus Crow and Tiania. But in any case, your education will not take too long; my knowledge of Earth's dreamland is regrettably limited. The reason for this will soon become amply clear to you. Now come to me . . ."

As the dreamer drifted toward the alien Eminence, so that great Being's face-tentacles seemed to reach out to touch his disembodied mind. "Steel yourself," came Kthanid's warning in the instant before contact was made.

. . . *And immediately gates of strange knowledge opened in de Marigny's mind, through which streamed fantastic visions of nighted myth and legend, released from Kthanid's mental storehouse of lore concerning Earth's dreamland. And though it was perfectly true that the Eminence knew comparatively little of that subconscious dimension, still it seemed to the disembodied Earthman that the Elder God must surely be omniscient in the ways of human dreams.*

For as rapidly as his mind could accept it, de Marigny became heir to a wealth of information previously known only to certain seasoned travelers in dreamland, a dimension whose very fabric existed for and was sustained only by the minds of Earth's dreamers. He saw the con-

tinents, hills and mountains, rivers and oceans of dream, her fabulous countries, cities, and towns, and he saw the peoples who inhabited those ethereal regions. Amazingly, he even recognized some of the places he saw, remembering now adventures believed forgotten forever in olden dreams, just as the night is forgotten in the light of dawn's rays.

And so knowledge passed from the mind of the great Being into the mind of Henri-Laurent de Marigny. He was shown the Cavern of the Flame where, not far from the gates of the waking world, the bearded, pshent-bearing priests Nasht and Kaman-Thah offer up prayers and sacrifices to the capricious gods of dream that dwell in the clouds above Kadath. Yes, and an instant later, whirled away to the Cold Waste, he even glimpsed Kadath itself, forbidden to men, but was offered no guarantee of that hideous region's location. Not even Kthanid knew for certain in which area of spacetime Kadath lay.

Snatched away from Kadath in the space of a single heartbeat, de Marigny traversed the seven hundred steps to the Gates of Deeper Slumber; and beyond those steps the Enchanted Wood with its furtive Zoog inhabitants was made known to him. He was given to understand how the Zoogs—small and brown and indeterminate as they were—might be very important to his quest, for they were not unintelligent and their knowledge of Earth's dreamland was prodigious. Moreover, the Zoogs were reputed to have access even to the waking world, knowing the two places where the dimensions of dream and reality merge; though mercifully, in consideration of their doubtful appetites, they could not journey far beyond the mysterious places of their own dimension.

Then the Enchanted Wood and its burrow-dwelling Zoogs were gone, and de Marigny was shown the resplendent city of Celephais in the valley of Ooth-Nargai beyond the Tanarian Hills. And he knew that Kuranes, himself once a legendary dreamer, reigned in Celephais, and that King Kuranes was renowned in all the lands of dream as the only man ever to transcend the star-gulfs and return sane. Gazing down upon Celephais from on high, de Marigny saw the glittering minarets of that splendid city and the galleys at anchor in the blue harbor, and Mount Aran where the ginkgos swayed in the breeze off the sea. And there was the singing, bubbling Naraxa with its tiny wooden bridges, wending its way to the sea; and there the city's *bronze gates, beyond which onyx pavements wound away into a maze of curious streets and alleys.*

But de Marigny was given precious little time to study Celephaïs, for no sooner had he glimpsed the city and its surroundings than he was whirled away, high over the Cerenarian Sea, whose billows rise up inexplicably to the heavens. There, among fleecy clouds tinted with rose, he was shown sky-floating Serannian, the pink marble city of the clouds, builded on that ethereal coast where the west wind flows into the sky; and he marveled at dream's wonders as he saw below, through breaks in roseate clouds, hills and rivers and cities of a rare beauty, dreaming gorgeously in brilliant sunshine.

And once again the scene quickly changed—so rapidly, indeed, that de Marigny was thrown in an instant from daylight into darkness—and now he knew that the land below him was none other than the icy desert plateau of Leng, and he saw the horrible stone villages whose balefires flared up so evilly. Then, coming to him on an icy wind that seemed to freeze his very soul, he heard the rattling of strange bone instruments and the whine of cursed flutes, while a distant chanting of monstrous implications chilled him further yet.

For a moment, peering down in starkest horror, he thought he saw some inhuman thing writhing and blazing upon a stake in the heart of one of these balefires, while in the red shadows around, monstrous figures jerked and cavorted to the hellish, wind-whipped music. De Marigny knew that the thing in the fire—whatever it was—screamed hideously as it roasted, and he was glad that the icy, howling wind kept those screams from him; and more glad when suddenly he was rushed away once more to other, less terrible visions.

Now he was relieved to behold the templed terraces of Zak, abode of forgotten dreams, where many of his own youthful dreams lingered still, gradually fading as all dreams must in the end. But before he could look too long or wistfully at Zak's dim visions, he felt himself borne irresistibly onward, to pass beneath twin headlands of crystal which rose up to meet high overhead in a resplendent arch; and then he found himself above the harbor of Sona-Nyl, blessed land of fancy. But since it could not have been deemed too important that he should look long upon Sona-Nyl, once again he was snatched away, without pause, on across the Southern Sea toward the Basalt Pillars of the West.

Now, some say that splendid Cathuria lies beyond the spot where those black columns tower from the ocean; but wiser dreamers are sure that the pillars are only a gateway, one which opens to a monstrous cataract where all dream's oceans fall abysmally away into awful voids outside the ordered universe. De Marigny knew these things at once, and he might have had the answer to the enigmatic problem had he not found himself once more suddenly and without warning whirled away to the Enchanted Wood. Patently there was something else in that dark place that Kthanid would appraise him of, for now he found himself in an exceptionally unfrequented part of the wood, where even the Zoogs rarely ventured . . . and he was soon given to understand the reason for their caution.

Here the great squat oaks were very much thinned out, all of them dead or dying, and the whole area seemed covered with unnaturally luxuriant fungi, springing up from the dead ground and the mush of fallen, rotten trees. And there was a twilight and a silence here such as might have existed since time began; and in a sort of clearing a tremendous slab of stone lay on the forest's floor, bearing in its center a Titan iron ring all of three feet in diameter.

As de Marigny was shown the strange moss-obscured runes graven into the vast slab's surface, so the timeless quiet and oppressiveness of the place seemed to swell beyond endurance. He gazed upon those graven runes and, finally understanding, shuddered; for while one set of the glyphs was patently designed to keep something down beneath the slab, a second rune seemed to have the power to cancel out the first.

Then de Marigny's very soul shrank down within him, as if some monstrously alien symbol had been held out to it. And now he seemed to hear his own voice repeating a warning couplet from Abdul Alhazred's abhorrent Necronomicon: *"That is not dead which can eternal lie, and with strange aeons even death may die . . ." And he knew that there must be something singularly evil and damnable here, a connection between this hideous slab lost in an ensorcelled wood . . . and all the dread demons of the Cthulhu Cycle of Myth!*

De Marigny was already more than well-acquainted with the CCD (the Cthulhu Cycle Deities, so designated by the Wilmarth Foundation) and now in an instant, faster than Kthanid might have implanted such knowledge in his mind, there flashed through his memory the pantheon as he knew it:

First there was dread Cthulhu, prime member of the CCD, prisoned in drowned R'lyeh somewhere in the vast and unknown depths of Earth's inscrutable Pacific. Then there was Yogg-Sothoth, the "all-in-one-and-one-in-all," a creature hideous beyond imagining—so monstrous indeed that his true shape and aspect are forever hidden, behind a mask or congeries of iridescent globes—who inhabits a synthetic dimension created by the Elder Gods to be his eternal prison. Since Yogg-Sothoth's prison dimension lies parallel to both time and space, it is often obscurely hinted of him that he is coexistent with the entire span of the former medium and coterminous in all the latter.

Then, high and low in the ranks of the CCD and their minions, there were the following: Hastur the Unspeakable, an elemental of interstellar space and air, and allegedly half brother of Cthulhu; Dagon, an ancient aquatic survival worshipped once in his own right by the Philistines and the Phoenicians, now lord and master of the suboceanic Deep Ones in their various tasks, chiefly the guarding of R'lyeh's immemorially pressured tombs and sunken sepulchers; Cthylla, Cthulhu's "secret seed," his daughter; Shudde-M'ell, Nest-Master of the insidious Cthonian Burrowers Beneath; the Tind'losi Hounds; Hydra and Yibb-Tstll; Nyogtha and Tsathoggua; Lloigor, Zhar and Ithaqua, and many, many more.

The list was a long one and contained, along with these actual, physical representatives of Cthulhu's cycle, several purely symbolic figures endowed with equally awe-inspiring names and attributes of their own. Chiefly, these were Azathoth, Nyarlathotep, and Shub-Niggurath, which symbols the Wilmarth Foundation had explained away thus:

Azathoth, the "supreme father" of the cycle and described as a "blind idiot god"—an "amorphous blight of nethermost confusion blaspheming and bubbling at the center of all infinity"—was in fact the devastating power of the atom. It was nuclear fission, particularly the great atomic explosion that changed the perfect peace of the primal NOTHING into a chaotic and continuously evolving universe: Azathoth—the Big Bang!

Nyarlathotep—as his imperfectly anagrammatical name had early suggested to Titus Crow (albeit that this fact was entirely coincidental) was none other than the power of telepathy, and as such was known as the "Great Messenger" of the CCD. Even after the rampaging members of the Cthulhu Cycle were put down and "imprisoned" or "banished" by the Elder Gods, Nyarlathotep had been left free to carry the messages of the CCD one to the other between their various prisons. How may one imprison purely mental power, telepathic thought?

Shub-Niggurath—known in the pantheon as a god of fertility, the "black goat of the woods with a thousand young"—was in fact the power of miscegenation inherent in all the CCD since time immemorial. For in the old days did not the gods come down to mate with the daughters of men?

So, de Marigny saw again in his mind's eye all of these things and knew the truth of them, these and many other facts concerning the CCD. And he knew, too, why Titus Crow had braved the trans- or hyper-dimensional voids between Elysia's and Earth's dreamworlds— a voyage undertaken in the past only by two great seekers after knowledge and one fool, of which trio only one returned sane—for Crow's errand had been of the utmost importance. It had been to put an end to Cthulhu's incursions into the dreams of men. For since men first walked the Earth as true men they had dreamed and peopled the parallel dimension of dream with their own imaginings; and Cthulhu, seizing early upon his opportunity as he lay in dark slumbers of his own in sunken, blasphemous R'lyeh, had achieved a certain mastery over dreams long before man mastered the mammoth.

But from the start Earth's dreamland had proven alien to Lord Cthulhu and had resisted him; for his were dreams of outer voids beyond the comprehension of men, and as such could invade human dreams only briefly. Also, many of dreamland's inhabitants—not the human dreamers themselves but the living figments of their dreams— were friendly toward men of the waking world and abhorred those concepts Cthulhu would introduce into their strange dimension of myth and fancy.

So the Lord of R'lyeh cloaked his schemes concerning Earth's dreamland in mysteries and obscurities, patiently going about his aeon-devised plan in so devious a fashion as to wear away the barriers of men's dreams, even as great oceans wear away continents. In this way he gradually introduced many utterly inhuman concepts into the dreamland, nightmares with which to intimidate the subconscious minds of certain men in the waking world. Thus, while Cthulhu himself could enter the dreamlands briefly, the evil concepts of his minion dreams would fester there forever; his, and those of his likewise "imprisoned" cousins of the same dreadful cycle.

All of these things concerning Cthulhu and the CCD flashed through Henri-Laurent de Marigny's mind in a split second, but in the next instant he was snatched away yet again to visions just as strange if not so fearsome. And yet these, too, were fearsome enough.

He saw Ngranek's peak, and the great face carven in the mountain's gaunt side. He saw the hideously thin and noisome outlines of horned bat-shapes with barbed tails, flapping not altogether vaguely about the mountain, and he knew that these were the night-gaunts that guard Ngranek's secret. Then, as some of them flew closer, he saw that which made him shudder horribly: they had no faces!

But the bat-shapes did not acknowledge his presence, and before they could draw too close he was rushed away again over the Peaks of Throk, whose needle pinnacles are the subject of many of dream's most awful fables. For these peaks, higher than any man might ever guess or believe, are known to guard the terrible valleys of the Dholes, whose shapes and outlines are often suspected but never seen. Then he soared down, down, and down, until his ears were filled with a vast rustling of Dholes amidst piles of dried-out bones . . . He knew then that this place he had swooped down to was none other than the Vale of Pnoth, into which ossuary all the ghouls of the waking world throw the remains of their nighted feastings; and he trembled violently as the rustling ceased momentarily—almost expectantly—just as the chirruping of crickets ceases at the tread of human feet.

But now the things de Marigny was experiencing were hastening one after the other through his mind at a dizzy pace, blurring as they went down upon his memory in fragmentary, erratic fashion. He was snatched up and out of the Dhole-infested Vale of Pnoth and away across dreamland in a frantic rush. In rapid procession he saw the oaken wharves of Hlanith, whose sailors are more like unto men of the waking world than any others in dreamland—and ruined, fearsome Sarkomand, whose broken basalt quays and crumbling sphinxes are remnant of a time long before the years of man—and the mountain Hatheg-Kla, whose peak Barzai the Wise once climbed, never to come down again. He saw Nir and Istharta, and the charnel Gardens of Zura where pleasure is unattainable. He saw Oriab in the Southern Sea, and infamous Thalarion of a thousand demon-cursed wonders, *where the eidolon Lathi reigns. He saw all of these places and things and many more . . . and then there came a terrific, sickening whirling of his soul*—following which de Marigny found himself dizzy and utterly disoriented back in the throneroom of Kthanid the Eminence in Elysia.

III

Journey Into Dream

"But why?" de Marigny asked the great Being. "Why did Crow go into Earth's dreamland, and how? And what possessed him to take Tiania with him? And where *exactly* are they? I need to know these things if I'm to—"

"Hold, man of Earth," Kthanid cut him off. "As to your first question: I had thought to make that amply clear in what I have shown you, but obviously I failed. Crow went into Earth's dreamland to put an end to Cthulhu's insidious fouling of the dreams of men. He went where it was his birthright to go, just as it was his birthright to enter into Elysia. He went because the Lords of Elysia—which you know as Elder Gods, of which I am one—cannot go there themselves. We would be just as alien in your dreamland as is Cthulhu, and for that reason we will not enter it. If ever the time arrives when we we *must* enter it, then the visit will be as brief possible—as brief and unobtrusive as we can make it. There are reasons other than those I have mentioned, and one of them is this: the gateway between Elysia and the world of Earth's dreams has two sides. If we entered from Elysia, who can say what might or might not follow us back through the gate when we returned?

"As to why Titus Crow took Tiania with him, she would not let him go without her! And it will be to my eternal sorrow if aught of evil befall them, for it was I laid them to sleep here, and I assisted their dreaming minds across nightmare voids to your Earth and its dreamland." As he spoke, Kthanid moved across the great hall to a small and curtained alcove. He drew aside the drapes to show de Marigny the forms of a man and woman where they lay in crystal containers, their heads resting upon silken cushions.

As his spirit eagerly drifted forward, it was as much of a "physical"

shock as it could be to the disembodied de Marigny to gaze upon the
recumbent form of the man with whom he had shared so many
strange adventures . . . and upon that of Titus Crow's woman, the girl-
goddess Tiania. Despite the fact that he knew what he had seen of
them in Kthanid's crystal was only a dream manifestation of the two,
nevertheless it was an eerie experience to see their living, breathing
bodies here in the Hall of Crystal and Pearl. Recovering himself, he
moved closer.

Crow's handsome, leonine face and his form were well enough
known to de Marigny, but Tiania was very new to him, a stranger. He
looked upon her, awed. Kthanid felt the awe of de Marigny and understood the emotions the Earthman must feel. He knew that no
mortal man could look upon Tiania and not be moved. And he was
right. Tiania's figure and face were indescribably beautiful. Her eyes
were closed now in dreams that brought troubled lines to her pale-
pearl brow, but de Marigny was almost glad that she slept this uneasy
sleep. He felt sure that to gaze into her eyes would be to drown quite
helplessly. He knew that he could never forget her, that he would
know her wherever and whenever he saw her again.

Her hair was a lustrous emerald ocean, cascading down the spun
golden strand of her cape, and her mouth was a perfect Cupid's bow
of pearl-dusted rose, lips parted slightly to show the whitest teeth de
Marigny had ever seen. The girl's face formed a slender oval in which
arcing emerald eyebrows melted into the verdure of her temples. She
had elfin ears like petals of rare blooms, and a nose so delicate as to go
almost unnoticed. She radiated a distillation of the very Essence of
Woman, human and yet quite definitely alien. She *was* a woman, yes,
and not a goddess—but certainly the stuff of the Gods was in her. And
she was the same woman he had glimpsed in Kthanid's crystal, helplessly staked out on the steps of the ruby altar in the distant world of
Earth's dreamland. And just as she lay here now in this strange casket,
so she had lain on those basalt steps—side by side with Titus Crow.

De Marigny turned suddenly to Kthanid to implore: "But why
don't you just wake them up? Surely that would get them out of
there?"

Seeming quite human now, or as human as he could in his alien
form, the great Being shook his head. "No, de Marigny, it cannot be
done. I have at my command every physical and psychical means by
which such a recovery could be attempted, but they cannot be awak-

ened. Do you think I have not tried? Something has them trapped
there in Earth's dreamland, a force which defies every attempt I make
to recall them. Here their subconscious bodies lie, rapt in evil dreams
from which I am powerless to rouse them. The problems are many, de
Marigny, and they are rare. First there is this unknown force that
binds them to Earth's dreamland. Then there is the fact that they are
separated from Elysia by vast alien voids of dream and all the horrors
such voids harbor, and finally—"

"Yes?"

"We do not know their exact location. The same force that binds
them to dream prevents detailed observation. I cannot name the region in which they are trapped. And Earth's dreamland is vast, de
Marigny, wide-ranging as all the dreams of men have made it."

"Then where do I begin?" de Marigny asked, perplexed. "When?
How?"

"Do not be too eager, Earthman. And, yes, perhaps I myself am
too fearful for the safety of Tiania and your friend. What you saw in
the crystal was a possible future, a possible occurrence yet to come. It
has not gone so far, but in all the worlds of probability it will. I have
searched the possible futures of Earth's dreamland as far as I dare, but
only that one future ever presents itself for my viewing, and that one
future draws ever closer. It is most certainly the same force that binds
Titus and Tiania in dream that threatens their very existence."

"Their very existence? But how can any real physical harm come
to them when their bodies are here? I don't understand."

Again (sadly, de Marigny thought) Kthanid shook his head. "You
seem to understand very little, Earthman."

"You have to remember, Kthanid, that I'm not a great dreamer."

"No, you are not," the Eminence answered, again sadly. Then the
great Being's thoughts brightened. "But your father was; indeed he
still is. And I believe that one day you will be, too."

"That's all very well—and I thank you for your faith in me—but
with all due respect, it doesn't help us much right now, does it? Look,
you keep mentioning my father. I don't remember a great deal of him,
but if it's true that he lives on in Earth's dreamland, well, surely he
would be able to help me."

"Etienne-Laurent de Marigny? Oh, yes, doubtless he would help
you. Indeed, I am certain he would find a way to go to the aid of your
friends—if he were able."

De Marigny waited for Kthanid to continue, then shook his head at the great Being's silence. "I still don't understand. My father is a lord in dreamland, surely. Trusted counselor to Randolph Carter, and—"

"Yes, that is so," Kthanid interrupted, "but there is a problem."

"A problem?"

Kthanid offered what de Marigny took to be a nod, then continued. "Ilek-Vad, where Randolph Carter wisely rules—and not only Ilek-Vad but Celephais and Dylath-Leen too—they are beyond my power to scan. This was not always so. Until quite recently, an Earth-year or so at most, I could look upon Ilek-Vad and Celephais in my crystal, but no longer. Dylath-Leen is different. For many years, there has been some sort of screen about Dylath-Leen. Of two of these forcefields—I suppose that is what they must be—those about Ilek-Vad and Celephais, I know only this: that nothing gets either in or out. I do not wish to alarm you, young man, but for all I know of those places their inhabitants are no more, they may well have been stricken from the dreams of men. As for the third city, Dylath-Leen, I believe that the same force which obstructs me in attempting to locate Titus Crow and Tiania is also responsible for my inability clearly to scan Dylath-Leen. Yes, perhaps there is a connection there, de Marigny. Perhaps—"

"Perhaps that's where they are, in Dylath-Leen."

"It would seem possible. You must look into it as soon as you can. Meanwhile, listen well to what I have to say. Remember that there are levels of dreaming, de Marigny, and that our lost friends must be in the very deeps of dream. A man might waken easily from the shallower levels, and he may be awakened even as he sinks into the abysses. But Titus and Tiania have penetrated to a region from which—for some reason as yet unknown, perhaps that *force* I have mentioned—they cannot escape unaided.

"In effect, this means that right now Earth's dreamland is more real to them than the waking world. Wherever they are you must find them; you must rendezvous with them there in the possible future that you saw in my crystal. It will not be easy."

"Then let's waste no more time. Tell me how to go about it."

"Yes, yes, in a moment. But before that there are certain things you must commit to memory. Firstly: in Ulthar there is a very ancient man named Atal. Seek him out and ask him what you will. He is wise almost beyond wisdom and good beyond goodness. Secondly: beware of manifestations of Cthulhu or his devil's brood that you may come across, and remember that in the dreamlands even purely symbolic concepts may take form. Be particularly wary of Nyarlathotep! Thirdly: remember that you have Crow's flying cloak, and you have the time-clock, too. These should prove to be great weapons against any terrors dream may confront you with. As for the clock: why, Titus Crow can use that device in ways that confound even me! Finally: never forget that while many things are far simpler in dream, others are maddeningly difficult, almost impossible. Now, do you think you can remember these things?"

"Yes, and everything else you've showed me."

"Good. As to how you may reach Earth's dreamland: first you must return to the time-clock, which you will then pilot back to Earth. I will of course assist you in your return to the time-clock, but from then on you will be on your own. I suggest you go into orbit about the planet Earth, after which . . . you will simply go to sleep. But as you drift into sleep you will command the clock to carry you *in the direction of dreamland!* Then you will sleep—and you will dream, de Marigny, you will dream."

The Eminence paused, and after a moment de Marigny asked: "And is that all?"

"That is all. Anything else would be a waste of time, superfluous, possibly dangerous. I do not know enough of your dreamland to say more. Now you must go back to the clock. Your quest begins, de Marigny. I wish you luck."

Suddenly the great Being's face-tentacles spread outward from his face like the rays of a bright sun, and the light of stars blazed in his eyes. De Marigny—or rather his Ka, or whatever it was of him that Kthanid had called to his glacier palace in Elysia's frozen regions— was instantly dazzled. When finally he could see again, the scene before him was rapidly shrinking, dwindling down to nothing, so that soon even Kthanid was only a tiny, alien, jeweled creature that finally shrank away and vanished. Then there was nothing but a rushing darkness that seemed to last forever; and yet he knew when the rushing stopped and he found himself once more within the matrix of the time-clock that his journey had taken less than a second. Indeed, it had been instantaneous.

Without wasting a single moment, he turned the clock about and raced back through the voids of space toward the world of his origin. His heart began to beat wildly and his head started singing with exhilaration as he thought of the quest before him, and the reward at quest's end—to enter Elysia! Not once did he contemplate failure . . .

Some time later, in the Hall of Crystal and Pearl, Kthanid stood where de Marigny had last seen him. Now, however, no bright fires lit his golden eyes, and the lighting of the vast chamber itself was greatly subdued. Within the Eminence an unseen battle raged, and he trembled violently as he sought to calm himself. Of course he had done the right thing . . . or had he? After all, he owed no loyalty to the Earthman de Marigny . . . but then, neither was the man an enemy. Nor was his willingness to be faulted. Yet, if the problem was looked at in the right perspective it was immediately apparent that in the great scheme of things Henri-Laurent de Marigny was utterly insignificant. On the other hand . . .

For what must have been the fifth or sixth time since he had sent the disembodied de Marigny back to his Earthly body in the time-clock, Kthanid went to the huge cushion with its milky crystal and peered into translucent depths that quickly cleared to his gaze. And as before he drew back from the scene which repeated itself within the crystal's all-scanning eye. It was that same cruel scene de Marigny had gazed upon earlier, at least in all the details of its background. But whereas before two figures had lain stretched out on the basalt steps of the ruby dais, now there was only one. Kthanid could see the man's face quite clearly, and once more he trembled mightily as the battle within him welled up again. The fear-filled yet grimly determined face in the crystal was that of Kthanid's most recent visitor—Henri-Laurent de Marigny!

Finally, something gave within the great Being's heart; a decision like none he had ever made before was made. He uttered a word which only the Elder God themselves might ever repeat or understand, then snatched his eyes from the scene in the crystal. And in the next instant his golden eyes blazed brighter as, tapping the tremendous sources of his body's alien energies, he sent his mind racing out on a Great Thought across strange transdimensional gulfs and light-years of space.

Straight to the time-clock where it raced in orbit around the Earth Kthanid's mind sped—but too late. De Marigny was already fast asleep in the warm womb of his weird vessel. And while that vessel registered his body's presence, Kthanid knew that the real de Marigny was somewhere else, inhabitant now of Earth's mysterious dreamland. It was as it should be, as Kthanid had planned it to be, and yet . . . What use to call him back from dream now?

Feeling within himself a treachery as alien to his emotions as they were to those of the Earthman he felt he had betrayed, the Elder God rushed in a fury back to Elysia. There he closed his palace and his mind to all would-be visitations and sat alone in the vast Hall of Crystal and Pearl.

IV

The Quest Begins

Night merged slowly into dawn in dreamland. To the east the very faintest of flushes tinted the sky gray, which was as well, for otherwise the night, except where it was studded with the bright jewels of fireflies, was of the very blackest.

At first de Marigny was disoriented, dazed; a lassitude was upon him. It was pleasant to do nothing but stand and admire the night and the first stirrings of a distant dawn. Then, as he drifted deeper into dream, he felt the night's chill and shivered at the luminous mist that began to swirl up eerily about his ankles. Then, he remembered his mission, and realized his supreme mistake. He was . . . alone! True, he still had Titus Crow's flying cloak about his shoulders, but where was the time-clock?

Suddenly complete realization of his plight filled him. He was lost in a nighted mist in some unknown region of Earth's vast dreamland, with only the fireflies for company and a ground mist that lapped at his ankles. And somehow he had lost his greatest hope of ever completing his mission; somehow he had left the fabulous time-clock behind him in the waking world.

How had it happened?

What was it Kthanid had said he must do? Yes, the Eminence had said: "Command the clock to convey you in the direction of dreamland." Well, he had done just as Kthanid had directed . . . hadn't he? Then, remembering, de Marigny groaned and cursed himself for a fool. The instructions he had given the clock had been wrong. He had simply ordered it to *transport* him to dreamland. And it had done just that. Without really knowing what he was doing, de Marigny had discovered Crow's method of using the clock more truly as a "gateway." For right now that alien vehicle was still in orbit around the Earth where he had left it, and de Marigny was stranded in dream just as surely as the friends he had come to rescue.

Perhaps if he had kept his head—if he had given the problem a little more studied thought—he might have seen a solution. For he was not yet too deeply drowned in dream to strike out for the surface, to waken himself up. Things are rarely perfectly clear in dream, however, and de Marigny was not an expert dreamer . . .

As the sky gradually lightened and the fireflies blinked out one by one, the adventurer found himself at the top of a great flight of steps that went down into a sea of mist. De Marigny knew those steps from older dreams forgotten until now, and more recently from his telepathic session with Kthanid. They were the seven hundred steps to the Gate of Deeper Slumber, beyond which lay the Enchanted Wood and those regions of dream which he sought.

De Marigny gritted his teeth and pulled Crow's cloak more warmly about his shoulders. Somewhere down there, beyond that wood at the foot of the steps, somewhere in those dreamlands spawned of the fantasies of a million dreamers, Titus Crow and Tiania of Elysia were or would soon be in desperate need of help, in peril of their very lives. There was only one course of action open to him.

Cautiously de Marigny descended the seven hundred steps and passed through the Gate of Deeper Slumber, and as the mist began to disperse and dawn grew more strongly beyond the trees, he set out through the groves of great gnarled oaks toward the far side of the Enchanted Wood, where he knew that the Skai rushed down from Lerion's slopes to Nir and Ulthar on the plain. Often as he pushed on through the wood, de Marigny heard the sounds that Zoogs make, but he saw not a one and was glad for that.

Often, too, he stumbled upon places where the trees were fallen into decay, and the ground was soggy with its burden of rotten oaks and alive with phosphorescent fungi. He would skirt these diseased areas, knowing that in one of them a massive slab of stone set with an iron ring of fantastic girth stood sentinel over nameless Cthonian things of hideous connections.

The wood was a fearsome place indeed, but while de Marigny was tempted again and again to use his flying cloak to climb above its suspected but unseen terrors, he refrained from doing so. He could not say what eyes might be watching him; he did not wish it known that a dreamer with a strange and wonderful flying cloak had entered dreamland. In any case, the sun was up now and the fears of the dark wood were disappearing along with the last wisps of mist.

It was a bright morning when he finally, wearily came out of the wood and set off across the rolling plains for Ulthar. He skirted Nir late in the morning, and as the sun approached its zenith crossed the Skai by means of an ancient wooden bridge. Hungry now, he was tempted to stop and rest at one of the many farms that dotted the plain; he had little doubt but that the friendly folk of these parts would find a meal for him. He did not stop, however, for the urgency of his mission was driving him relentlessly onward. And he did not know how long he had to effect the rescue of Titus Crow and the girl-goddess Tiania.

And so Marigny came to Ulthar, the City of Cats, where an ancient ordinance has it that no man may kill a cat. It was quite obvious to the dreamer that this was indeed Ulthar, for even the outskirts were crowded with felines of every variety. Sleek females sunned themselves atop sloping roofs; young, careful-eyed toms kept cool while guarding their territories in shaded doorways; kittens tumbled comically in the long grass of the ornate gardens of rich personages. He paused very briefly in the suburbs to watch some of the kittens at their play; but then, having questioned a shopkeeper as to the whereabouts of the Temple of the Elder Ones, he hurried on into the city proper.

The Temple of the Elder Ones stood round and towering, of ivied stone, atop Ulthar's highest hill; and there, just within the temple's vast outer door, de Marigny was politely questioned by three young priests as to his purpose at the temple. He answered that he was from the waking world, that he sought audience with Atal the Ancient on very important matters. And when, in answer to further questioning, he told them his name the young priests grew wide-eyed indeed. One of them went hurriedly off into the dim and mysterious heart of the temple to seek an audience for de Marigny with the ailing high priest.

Finally the dreamer was taken to an inner sanctum where in a bed of finest silks lay the frail and weary shell of dreamland's wisest and oldest inhabitant. Now the younger priests departed, bowing themselves from the presence of their master and his visitor. Atal very gently propped himself up on his pillows to beckon de Marigny closer. When he could see the man from the waking world more clearly, he smiled feebly to himself, nodding in silent acknowledgment.

Eventually the ancient spoke, and his voice was like the rustle of late autumn leaves. "Yes, yes—you are truly the son of your father."

"You knew . . . you *know* my father?"

"Aye. Etienne-Laurent de Marigny, Lord of Ilek-Vad and Advisor in Chief to the king, Randolph Carter. He *is* your father, is he not?"

De Marigny nodded in answer, studying the trembling ancient where he lay. Atal's face was like a tiny wrinkled walnut; his head had a sparse crest of white hair; a long and voluminous beard like a fall of snow flowed down over the covers of his bed. And yet the eyes in the wrinkled face, faded as they were to the point of being colorless, had lit with an inner intelligence as they recognized the dreamer's lineage.

"Aye," Atal continued, "he came to see me once, your father, when first he entered dreamland to dwell here. A wise dreamer, and a fitting counselor to Randolph Carter. He came merely to see me, to honor me, but you—"

"I come to seek your help," de Marigny promptly answered, "in order to discover—"

"I know why you are here, my son," Atal whispered. "And I know who sent you. Am I not the high priest of the temple, and is this not the Temple of the Elder Ones? When the light of life flickers out in this old, old body, then it is my hope to move on to greater marvels, to immortality in Elysia, where I may continue to serve forever the elder Intelligences of my faith." The old man paused to peer again at de Marigny where he stood by his bed. "It is true that *They* sent you, those elder Beings, is it not?"

Once more de Marigny nodded, and when Atal spoke again his voice was very low, as if he wished to conceal his words even from the air of the room. "Aye, I knew you were coming—you, instrument of Kthanid, great Voice of all the Gods of Eld—and I know where your friends are!"

"Titus Crow and Tiania?" De Marigny leaned closer, his eyes intent upon Atal's, aware of the ancient's fragile and trembling form.

Now it was Atal's turn to nod, and when he spoke again his voice was a low, fearful, broken whisper. "They are on their way to Dylath-Leen, of which place I . . . I fear to speak. They are held prisoners of creatures whose very presence in dreamland is a blasphemy!"

"When will they get to Dylath-Leen? Is there a way I might intercept them en route? Who are these creatures that hold them captive, and where is Dylath—"

"I know much of Dylath-Leen." Atal's dry whisper cut him off. "But there is one who knows much more. He was once a dreamer, just like you, but now he is an inhabitant of Ulthar. He dwells here with his wife, two fine sons, and a daughter of great beauty. I can tell you where his house is—but, de Marigny—"

"Yes?"

"I have a feeling that time is running out quickly for your friends." For a second or two the ancient's eyes seemed to gaze through the dreamer, as if they looked upon distant things, but then they focused upon him once more. "Now you must eat. The food here at the temple is plain but wholesome. You are welcome to take a meal, but then you must be on your way. Please clap your hands for me; my own are not very strong."

De Marigny clapped his hands once, and almost immediately one of the young priests entered the room. Atal told him to arrange a meal for their visitor, then lowered himself down once more onto his pillow. The audience was over.

Then, as the dreamer began to follow the young priest out of the room, Atal called out: "Oh, de Marigny—I almost forgot. I have something for you, which you must take with you." He reached beneath his pillow to take out a small, strangely shaped vial.

"It is a very potent liquid brewed here in Ulthar, in this very temple. Unknown in the waking world, and rare enough here in dreamland, it has the property of awakening dreamers from even the deepest slumbers. One sip will return a dreamer to the waking world in seconds—aye, and all he brought through the gates of dream with him. To the true inhabitant of dream, however, the potion is a deadly poison; for of course it 'awakens' such inhabitants to the world in which they do not exist! It can be seen that they must quite simply . . . disappear."

For a moment de Marigny looked stunned as the implications dawned on him—then he cried out: "What? A potion to awaken dreamers? Then I could take a sip right away, return to the time-clock, and then—"

"No, my young friend." Atal held up a quieting hand. "The potion is not yet quite ready. It has to ferment. I had it brewed as soon as I knew you were coming, for it came to me in a vision that you would need it. But you must wait for at least another day and a half a day before it will be safe to use. By that time, if good fortune goes with you, you ought to have found your friends."

Later, as the first stars came out in the evening sky, de Marigny walked the cool streets of Ulthar to the house of Grant Enderby, late of the waking world. Enderby was the man who could tell him about Dylath-Leen, perhaps help him in his search for Titus Crow and Tiania.

Dylath-Leen . . . The very name conjured up strange pictures in the dreamer's mind, and as he walked the darkening streets and watched the lights coming on in friendly, small-paned windows, he wondered why Atal had been so loth to speak of the place. Well, before the night was out doubtless he would know well enough.

Following Atal's directions, de Marigny soon came to the path that led to Grant Enderby's house of red stone and dark oaken beams. And the red stone walls about the garden bore testimony to Enderby's calling here in dreamland, the fact that he was a quarrier, and his sons in his footsteps. The walls were broad and straight and strong, as was the man who built them.

And so the dreamer knocked upon the oaken door and was welcomed into the home of this one-time man of the waking world; and after his host's family were all to bed, de Marigny sat alone with Grant Enderby and listened until the wee hours to the following story . . .

Part Two

◆

Grant Enderby's Story, I: Litha

Three times only have I visited basalt-towered, myriad-wharved Dylath-Leen, three curious visits which spanned almost a century of that city's existence. Now I am glad that I have seen it for the last time.

I went there first in my late teens, filled with a longing engendered of continuous study of such works as *The Arabian Nights* and Gelder's *Atlantis Found* for wondrous places of antique legend and fable and centuried cities of ages past. And my longing was not disappointed.

I first saw the city from afar, wandering along the river Skai with a caravan of merchants from distant places, and at first sight of the tall black towers which form the city's ramparts I felt a strange fascination for the place. Later, lost in awe and wonder, I took leave of my merchant friends to walk Dylath-Leen's ancient streets and alleys, to visit the wharfside taverns and chat with seaman from every part of Earth's dreamland—and with a few, I fancy, from more distant places.

I never once pondered my ability to chatter in their many tongues, for often things are far simpler in dream, nor did I wonder at the ease with which I fitted myself into the alien yet surprisingly friendly scene; once attired in robes of dream's styling, my looks were not unlike those of many of her peoples. I was a little taller than average, true, but in the main Dylath-Leen's diverse folk might well have passed for those of any town of the waking world, and vice versa.

Yet there were in the city others, strange traders from across the Southern Sea, whose appearance and *odor* filled me with a dread loathing so that I could not abide to stay near where they were for long. Of these traders and their origin I questioned the tavern-keepers, to be told that I was not the first from the waking world whose instinct found in those traders traces of hinted evil and deeds not to be mentioned. Randolph Carter himself had once warned

Dylath-Leen's peoples that the traders were fiends not to be trusted, whose only desire was to spread horror and evil throughout all the lands of dream.

But when I heard Carter's name mentioned I was hushed, for an amateur at dreaming such as I was at that time could not dare aspire to walk even in the shadow of one such as he. Why, Carter was rumored to have been even to Kadath in the Cold Waste, to have confronted Nyarlathotep the Crawling Chaos, and to have returned unscathed from that place! How many could boast of that?

Yet loth though I was to have anything to do with those traders, I found myself one morning in the towering tavern of Potan-Lith, in a high barroom the windows of which looked out over the Bay of Wharves, waiting for the galley I had heard was coming to the city with a cargo of rubies from an unknown shore. I wanted to discover just what it was of them that so repelled me, and the best way to decide this, I thought, would be to observe them from a safe distance and location at which I, myself, might go unobserved. I did not wish to bring myself to the notice of those queerly frightening people of unguessed origin. Potan-Lith's tavern, with its ninety-nine steps, served my purpose admirably.

I could see the whole of the wharfside spread beneath me in the morning light; the nets of the fishermen drying, with smells of rope and deep ocean floating up to my window; the smaller craft of private tradesmen rolling gently at anchor, sails lowered and hatches laid back to let the sun dry out their musty holds; the thag-weed merchants unloading their strongly-scented, dream-within-dream-engendering opiates garnered in exotic Eastern parts; and, eventually appearing on the horizon, the sails of the black galley for which I so vigilantly waited. There were other traders of the same race already in the city, to be sure, but how could one get close to them without attracting unwanted attention? My plan of observation was best, I was certain, but I did not know just what it was I wished to observe—or why.

It was not long before the black galley loomed against the entrance of the bay. It slipped into the harbor past the great basalt lighthouse, and a strange stench driven by the South Wind came with it. As with the coming of all such craft and their weird masters, uneasiness rippled all along the waterfront as the silent ship closed with its chosen wharf, and its three banks of briskly moving oars stilled and slipped in through their oarlocks to the unseen and equally silent rowers within. I watched eagerly then, waiting for the galley's master and crew to come ashore, but only five persons—if persons they truly were—chose to leave that enigmatic craft. This was the best look at such traders I had so far managed, and what I saw did not please me at all.

I have intimated my doubts with regard to the humanity of those—men? Let me explain why.

Firstly, their mouths were far too wide. Indeed, I thought that one of them glanced up at my window as he left the ship, smiling a smile that only just fell within the boundaries of that word's limitations, and it was horrible to see just how wide his evil mouth was. Now what would any eater of normal foods want with a mouth of such abnormal proportions? And for that matter, why did the owners of such mouths wear such queerly moulded turbans? Or was it simply the *way* in which the turbans were worn? For they were humped up in two points over the foreheads of the wearers in what seemed especially bad taste. And as for their shoes: well, they were certainly the most peculiar footwear I had ever seen, in or out of dreams. They were short, blunt-toed, and flat, as though the feet within were not feet at all! I thoughtfully finished off my mug of muth-dew and wedge of bread and cheese, turning from the window to leave the tavern of Potan-Lith.

My heart seemed to leap into my mouth. There in the low entrance stood that same merchant who had so evilly smiled up at my window! His turbaned head turned to follow my every move as I sidled out past him and flew down the ninety-nine steps to the wharf below. An awful fear pursued me as I ran through the alleys and streets, making my feet fly faster on the basalt flags of the wider pavements, until I reached the well known, green-cobbled courtyard wherein I had my room. But even there I could not get the face of that strangely turbaned, wide-mouthed trader from beyond the Southern Sea out of my mind, nor his smell from my nostrils. So I paid my landlord his due, moving out there and then to head for that side of Dylath-Leen which faces away from the sea and which is clean with the scents of window-box flowers and baking bread, where the men of the taverns rarely venture.

There, in the district called S'eemla, I found myself lodging with a family of basalt quarriers who were such good, cheerful, charming folk that later, when I became an inhabitant of dream proper, I too chose quarrying for my trade. The head of the house was named Bo-Kareth, and he provided me with my own wide-windowed garret room, with a bed and a mattress of fegg-down; so that soon it was as though I had been born into the family, or might have seemed had I been able to imagine myself a brother to comely Litha.

Within the month I was firmly settled in, and from then on I made it my business to carry on Randolph Carter's work of warning, putting in my word against the turbaned traders at every opportunity. My task was made no easier by the fact that I had nothing concrete to hold against them. There was only the feeling, already shared by many of the folk of Dylath-Leen, that trade between the city and the black galleys could bring to fruition nothing of any good.

Eventually my knowledge of the traders grew to include such evidences as to make me more certain than ever of their evil nature. Why should those black galleys come into harbor, discharge their four or five traders, and then simply lie there at anchor, emitting their foul odor, showing never a sign of their silent crews? That there were crews seems needless to state; with three great banks of oars to each ship there must have been many rowers. But what man could say just who or what such rowers were?

Too, the grocers and butchers of the city grumbled over the apparent frugality of those singularly shy crews, for the only things the traders bought with their great and small rubies were gold and stout Pargian slaves. This traffic had gone on for years, I was told, and in that time many a fat black man had vanished, never to be seen again, up the gangplanks into those mysterious galleys to be transported to lands across uncharted seas—if, indeed, such lands were their destination!

And where did the queer traders get their rubies, the like of which were to be found in no known mines in all Earth's dreamland? Yet those rubies came cheaply enough, too cheaply in fact, so that every home in Dylath-Leen contained them, some large enough to be used as paperweights in the homes of the richer merchants. Myself, I found those gems strangely loathsome, seeing in them only the reflections of the traders who brought them from across nameless oceans.

So it was that in the district called S'eemla my interest in the ruby traders waxed to its full, paled, waned, and finally withered—but never died completely. My new interest, however, in dark-eyed Litha,

Bo-Kareth's daughter, grew with each passing day, and my nights were filled with dreams within dreams of Litha and her ways, so that only occasionally were my slumbers invaded by the unpleasantly turbaned, wide-mouthed traders from unknown parts.

One evening, after a trip to Ti-Penth, a village not far from Dylath-Leen where we enjoyed the annual Festival of Plenty, as Litha and I walked back hand in hand through the irrigated green valley called Tanta toward our black-towered city, she told me of her love and we sank together to the darkling sward. That night, when the city's myriad twinkling lights had all blinked out and the bats chittered thick without my window, Litha crept into my garret room and only the narg-oil lamp on the wall could tell of the wonders we knew with each other.

In the morning, rising rapidly in joy from my dreams within dreams, I broke through too many layers of that flimsy stuff which constitutes the world of the subconscious, to waken with a cry of agony in the house of my parents at Norden on the northeast coast. Thereafter I cried myself to sleep for a year before finally I managed to convince myself that my dark-eyed Litha existed only in dreams.

Grant Enderby's Story, II: The Ruby Horror

I was thirty years old before I saw Dylath-Leen again. I arrived in the evening, when the city was all but in darkness, but I recognized immediately the feel of those basalt flagstones beneath my feet, and, while the last of the myriad lights flickered out in the towers and the last tavern closed, my heart leaped as I turned my suddenly light feet toward the house of Bo-Kareth. But something did not seem right, and a horror grew rapidly upon me as I saw in the streets thickening groups of carousing, nastily chattering, strangely turbaned people not quite so much men as monsters. And many of them had had their turbans disarrayed in their sporting so that protuberances glimpsed previously only in books of witchcraft and the like and in certain biblical paintings showed clearly through! Once I was stopped and pawed vilely by a half-dozen of them. As they conferred over me in low, menacing tones, I tore myself free and fled. For they were indeed those same evil traders of yore, and I was horrified that they should be there in my City of Black Towers in such great numbers.

I must have seen hundreds of those vile creatures as I hurried through the city's thoroughfares; yet somehow I contrived to arrive at the house of Bo-Kareth without further pause or hindrance, and I hammered at his oaken door until a light flickered behind the round panes of blue glass in the upper sections of that entrance. It was Bo-Kareth himself who came to answer my banging, and he came wide-eyed with a fear I could well understand. Relief showed visibly in his whole aspect when he saw that only a man stood upon his step. Although he seemed amazingly *aged*—so aged, in fact, that I was taken aback (for I did not then know of the variations experienced by different dreamers, variations in the passage of time between the waking world and dreamland)—he recognized me at once, whispering my name:

"Grant! Grant Enderby! My friend—my old friend . . . ! Come in, come in . . ."

"Bo-Kareth," I burst out, "Bo, I—"

"*Shhh!*" He pressed a finger to his lips, eyes widening even further than before, leaning out to glance up and down the street before pulling me in and quickly closing and bolting the door behind me. "Quietly, Grant, quietly. This is a city of silence now, where *they* alone carouse and make their own hellish brand of merry—and they may soon be abroad and about their business."

"They?" I questioned, instinctively knowing the answer.

"Those you once tried to warn us of. The turbaned traders."

"I thought as much," I answered. "And they're already abroad. I've seen them. But what *business* is this you speak of?"

Then Bo-Kareth told me a tale that filled my heart with horror and determined me never to rest until I had at least attempted to right a great wrong.

It had started a number of years earlier, according to my host (I made no attempt to pinpoint a date; what was the point when Bo-Kareth had apparently aged thirty years to my twelve?) and had involved the bringing to the city of a gigantic ruby. This great gem had been a gift, an assurance of the traders' regard for Dylath-Leen's peoples, and as such had been set upon a pedestal in the city's main square. But only a few nights later the horror had started to make itself noticeable.

The keeper of a tavern near the square, peering from his window after locking the door for the night, had noticed a strange, deep, reddish glow from the giant gem's heart; a glow which seemed to pulse with an alien life all its own. And when the tavern-keeper told the next day of what he had seen an amazing thing came to light. All of the other galley-brought rubies in the city—the smaller gems set in rings, amulets, and instruments, and those larger, less ornamental, almost rude stones owned purely for the sake of ownership by certain of the city's richer gentlemen—had glowed through the night to a lesser degree, as if in response to the greater activity of their bulky brother. And with that unearthly glowing of the gems had come a strange partial paralysis, making all the peoples of the city other than the turbaned traders themselves slumberous and weak, incapable and unwanting of any festivity and barely able to go about their normal duties and business. As the days passed and the power of the great ruby and the less regal ones waxed, so also did the strange drowsiness upon Dylath-Leen's folks. And it was only then, too late, that the plot was seen and its purpose recognized.

For a long time there had been a shortage of the fat black slaves of Parg. They had been taken from the city by the traders faster than they came in, until only a handful remained; and that handful, on hearing one day of a black galley soon due to dock, had fled their masters and left the city to seek less suspicious bondage. That had been shortly before the horned traders brought the great jewel to Dylath-Leen, and since that time, as the leering, gem-induced lethargy had increased until its effects were felt in daylight almost as much as they were at night, so had the number of oddly-shod traders grown until the docks were full of their great black galleys.

Then, inexplicable absences began to be noticed; a taverner's daughter here and a quarrier there, a merchant from Ulthar and a thagweed curer and a silversmith's son. Soon any retaining sufficient willpower sold up their businesses, homes, and houses and left Dylath-Leen for Ti-Penth, Ulthar, and Nir. I was glad to learn that Litha and her brothers had thus departed, though it made me strangely sad to hear that when Litha went she took with her a handsome husband and two strong sons. She was old enough now, her father told me, to be mistaken for my mother; but she still retained her great beauty.

By this time the hour of midnight was well passed and all about the house tiny red points of light had begun to glow in an eerie, slumber-engendering coruscation. As Bo-Kareth talked, his monologue interrupted now with many a yawn and shake of his head, I tracked down the sources of those weird points of radiance and found them to be rubies.

The curse was just as Bo-Kareth had described it—rubies! Ten tiny gems were set in the base of an ornamental goblet; many more of the small red stones enhanced the hanging silver and gold plates; fire-flashing splinters of precious crystal were embedded in the spines of certain of my host's leather-bound books of prayer and dream-lore—and when his mumbling had died away completely I turned from my investigations to find the old man asleep in his chair, lost in distressing dreams which pulled his gray face into an expression of muted terror.

I had to see the great gem. I make no excuse for such a rash and headstrong decision (one does things in dreams which one would never consider for a moment in the waking world) but I knew I could make no proper plans nor rest easy in my mind until I had seen that great ruby for myself.

I left the house by the back door, locking it behind me and pocketing the key. I knew Bo-Kareth had a duplicate key, and besides, I might later need to get into the house without delay. The layout of the city was well known to me, and thus it was not difficult for me to find my way through labyrinthine back streets to the main square. That square was away from the district of S'eemla, far closer to the docks and quays, and the nearer I drew to the waterfront the more carefully I crept.

Why, the whole area was alive with the alien and evil traders! The wonder is that I was not spotted in the first few minutes; and when I saw what those hellish creatures were up to, thus confirming beyond a shadow of a doubt Bo-Kareth's worst fears, the possibility that I might yet be discovered—and the consequences such an untimely discovery would bring—caused me to creep even more carefully. Each streetcorner became a focal point for terror, where lurking, unseen presences caused me to glance over my shoulder or jump at the slightest flutter at bat-wings or scurry of mice feet. And then, almost before I knew it, I came upon the square.

I came at a run, my feet flying frantically, all caution thrown to the wind. For I knew now for sure what the horned ones did at night, and a fancy had grown quickly on me that something followed in the dark; so that when I suddenly burst from that darkness into a blaze of red firelight I was taken completely by surprise. I literally keeled over backwards as I contrived to halt my flight of fear before it plunged me into the four turbaned terrors standing at the base of the dais of the jewel. My feet skidded as I pivoted on my heels and my fingers scrabbled madly at the round cobbles of the square as I fell. In truth it could scarce be termed a real fall—I was no sooner down than up—but in that split second or so as I fought to bring my careening body under control those guardians of the great gem were after me. Glancing fearfully back I saw them darting rat-like in my wake.

My exit from that square can only properly be described as panic-stricken, but brief though my visit had been I had seen more than enough to strengthen that first resolve of mine to do something about the loathsome and insidious invasion of the traders. Backtracking, bounding through the night streets I went, with the houses and taverns towering blackly on both sides, seeing in my mind's eye that horrible haunting picture which I had but glimpsed in the main square.

There had been the four guards with great knives fastened in their belts, the dais with pyramid steps to its flat summit, four hugely flaring torches in blackly-forged metal holders, and, atop the basalt altar itself, a great reddish mass pulsing with inner life, its myriad facets catching and reflecting the fire of the torches in a mixture with its own evil radiance. The hypnotic horror, the malignant monster—the great ruby!

Then the vision changed as I heard close behind me a weird, ululant cry—a definite *alert*—which carried and echoed in Dylath-Leen's canyon alleys. In rampant revulsion I pictured myself linked by an iron anklet to the long chain of mute, unprotesting people which I had seen only minutes earlier being led in the direction of the docks and the black galleys, and this monstrous mental image drove my feet to a frenzied activity that sent me speeding headlong down the dark passages between the city's basalt walls.

But fast and furious though my flight was, it soon became apparent that my pursuers were gaining on me. A faint padding came to my ears as I ran, causing me to accelerate, forcing my feet to pump even faster. The effort was useless, if anything, *worse* than useless, for I soon tired and had to slow down. Twice I stumbled and the second time, as I struggled to rise, the fumbling of slimy fingers at my feet lent them wings and shot me out again in front. It became as one of those nightmares (which indeed it was) where you run and run through vast vats of subconscious molasses, totally unable to increase the distance between yourself and your ethereal pursuer; the only difference being, dream or none, that I knew for a certainty I was running for my life!

It was a few moments later, when an added horror had just about brought me to the verge of giving up hope, that I found an unexpected but welcome reprieve. Slipping and stumbling, panting for air, I had been brought up short by a mad fancy that the soft padding of alien feet now came from the very direction in which I was heading, from somewhere in *front* of me! And as those sounds of demon footfalls came closer, closing in on me, I flattened myself to the basalt wall, spreading my arms and groping desperately with my hands at the bare, rough stone; and there, beneath my unbelieving fingers—*an opening!*—a narrow crack or entry, completely hidden in jet shadows, between two of the street's bleak buildings.

I squeezed myself into the narrow opening, trying to get my breathing under control, fighting a lunatic urge to cry out in my terror. It was pitch black, the blackness of the pit, and a hideous thought suddenly came to me. What if this tunnel of darkness—this possible gateway to sanity—what if it were closed, a dead end? That would be a dead end indeed! Then, as if in answer to my silent, frantic prayers, even as I heard the first squawk of amazed frustration from somewhere behind me, I squirmed from the other end of the division to emerge in a street mercifully void of the evil aliens.

My flight had carried me in a direction well away from Bo-Kareth's house; but in any case, now that my worst fears were realized and the alarm raised, it would have been completely idiotic to think of hiding anywhere in the city. I had to get away, to Ulthar or Nir, as far as possible—and as fast as possible—until I could try to find a way to rid Dylath-Leen of its inhuman curse.

Less than an hour later, with the city behind me, I was in an uninhabited desert area heading in a direction which I hoped would eventually bring me to Ulthar. It was cool beneath a full, cloud-floating moon, yet a long while passed before the fever of my panic-flight left me. When it did I was almost sorry, for soon I found myself shivering as the sweat of my body turned icy chill, and I wrapped my cloak more tightly about me for I knew it must grow still colder before the dawn. I was not particularly worried about food or water; there are many water holes and oases between Dylath-Leen and Ulthar. No, my main cause for concern lay in orientation. I did not want to end up wandering in one of the many great parched deserts! My sense of direction in open country has never been very good.

Before long, great clouds came drifting in from a direction I took to be the south, obscuring the moon until only the stars in the sky ahead gave any light by which to travel. Then, it seemed, the dune-cast shadows grew blacker and longer and an eerie sensation of not being alone waxed in me. I found myself casting sharp, nervous glances over my shoulder and shuddering to an extent not entirely warranted by the chill of the night. There grew in my mind an awful suspicion, one which I had to resolve one way or the other.

I hid behind a dune and waited, peering back the way I had come. Soon I saw a darting shadow moving swiftly over the sand, following my trail—and that shadow was endowed with twin points at its top and chuckled obscenely as it came. My hair stood on end as I saw the creature stop to study the ground, then lift its wide-mouthed face to the night sky. I heard again that weird, ululant cry of alert—and I waited no longer.

In a passion of fear even greater than that which I had known in the streets of Dylath-Leen, I fled—racing like a madman over the night sands, scrambling and often falling head over heels down the sides of the steeper sandhills, until my head struck something hard in the shadow of a dune and I was knocked unconscious.

But it seems that I was not too deeply gone in dream to be shocked back into the waking world, and I was fortunate enough to wake up before my pursuer could find me. This time I was far from sorry when I leapt shouting awake at my home in Norden; and in the sanity of the waking world I recognized the fact that all those horrors of dream and the night had existed only in my slumbers, so that in the space of a few days my second visit to Dylath-Leen was all but forgotten. The mind soon forgets that which it cannot bear to remember . . .

Grant Enderby's Story, III: The Utterer of the Words

I was forty-seven when next—when last—I saw Dylath-Leen. Not that my dream took me straight to the basalt city; rather, I found myself first on the outskirts of Ulthar, the City of Cats. Wandering through the city's streets, I stooped to pet a fat tom as he lazed upon a doorstep, and an old shopkeeper seated outside his store beneath a shade called out to me in a friendly, quavering voice:

"It is good, stranger. It is good when a stranger pets the cats of Ulthar. Have you journeyed far?"

"Far," I affirmed. "From the waking world. But even there I stop to play when I see a cat. Tell me, sir, can you direct me to the house of Litha, daughter of Bo-Kareth of Dylath-Leen?"

"Indeed, I know her well." He nodded his old head. "She is one of the few in Ulthar with as many years to count as I. She lives with her husband and family not far from here. Until some years ago her father also lived at his daughter's house. He came out of Dylath-Leen mazed and mumbling, and did not live long here in Ulthar. Now no man goes to Dylath-Leen."

But the old man had soured at the thought of Dylath-Leen and did not wish to talk any longer. I took his directions and started off with mixed feelings along the street he had indicated; but only halfway up that street I cut off down a dusty alley and made for the Temple of the Elder Ones instead. It could do no good to see Litha now. What use to wake old memories—if indeed she were capable of remembering anything of those golden days of her youth? And it was not as though she might help me solve my problem.

That same problem of thirteen waking years ago: how to avenge the outraged peoples of Dylath-Leen, and how to rescue those of them—if any such existed—still enslaved. For there was still a feeling of yearning in me for the black-towered city and its peoples of yore. I remembered the friends I had known and my many walks through the high-walled streets and along the farm lanes of the outskirts. Yet even in S'eemla the knowledge that certain offensive black galleys were moored in the docks had somehow always sufficed to dull my appetite for living, had even impaired the happiness I had known with dark-eyed Litha, in the garret of Bo-Kareth's house, with the bats of night clustered thick and chittering beneath the sill without my window.

As quickly as the vision of Litha the girl came, I put it out of my mind, striding out more purposefully for the Temple of the Elder Ones. If any man could help me in my bid for vengeance against the turbaned traders, Atal, the Priest of the Temple, was that man. It was rumored that in the temple he had keep of many incredible volumes of sorcery. His great knowledge of the darker mysteries was, in fact, my main reason for seeking his aid. I could hardly hope to engage the forces of evil controlled by the hell-traders with physical means alone.

It was then, as I left the little green cottages and neatly fenced farms and shady shops of the suburbs behind me, as I pressed more truly into the city proper, that I received a shock so powerful my soul almost withered within me. It is a wonder that I was not driven to seek refuge in the waking world, but a vision of vengeance made me cling desperately to dreamland.

I had allowed myself to become interested in the old peaked roofs, the overhanging upper storeys, numberless chimney pots, and narrow, old cobbled streets of the city, so that my attention had been diverted from the path my feet followed, causing me to bump rudely into someone coming out of the narrow door of a shop. Of a sudden the air was foul with shuddersome, well remembered odors of hideous connection, and my hackles rose as I backed quickly away from the strangely turbaned, squat figure I had chanced into. The slightly tilted eyes regarded me curiously and a wicked smile played around the too wide mouth.

One of *Them!* Here in Ulthar?

I mumbled incoherent apologies, slipped past the still evilly grinning figure, and ran the rest of the way to the Temple of the Elder Ones. If there had been any suggestion of half-heartedness to my intentions earlier there was certainly none now! It seemed obvious to me the course events were taking. First it had been Dylath-Leen, now an attempt at Ulthar. Where next? Nowhere, if I had anything to say of it.

I found the patriarch I sought, Atal of Hatheg-Kla, Atal the Ancient, in the Room of Ancient Records low in the great tower that houses the Temple of the Elder Ones. He sat, in flowing black and gold robes, at a centuried wooden bench, fading eyes studiously lost in the yellowed pages of a great aeon-worn book, its metal hasps dully agleam in a stray beam of sunlight striking in from the single high window.

He looked up, starting as if in shock as I entered the musty room with its tall bookshelves. Then he pushed his book away and spoke:

"The Priest of the Temple greets you, stranger. You *are* a stranger, are you not?"

"I have seen Ulthar before," I answered. "But, yes, I am a stranger here in the Temple of the Elder Ones. I come from the waking world, Atal, to seek your help."

"Huh!" He was calmer now. "You are not the first from the waking world to ask my aid, nor the last I fancy. How are you named and in what manner might I assist you?—*if* I choose to assist you!"

"My name is Grant Enderby, Atal, and the help I ask is not for myself. I come in the hope that you might be able to help me rid Dylath-Leen of a certain contagion; but since coming to Ulthar today I have learned that even here the sores are spreading. Are there not even now in Ulthar strange traders from no clearly named land? Is it not so?"

"It is so." He nodded his venerable head. "Say on."

"Then you should know that they are those same traders who brought Dylath-Leen to slavery—an evil, hypnotic slavery—and I fancy that they mean to use the same black arts here in Ulthar to a like end. Do they trade rubies the like of which are found in no known mine in the whole of dreamland?"

Again he nodded: "They do—but say no more. I am already aware. At this very moment I search for a means by which the trouble may be put to an end. But I work only on rumors, and I am unable to leave the temple to verify those rumors. My duties are all important, and in any case, these bones are too old to wander very far . . ." He paused for a moment, then continued.

"Truly, Dylath-Leen did suffer an evil fate, but think not that her peoples had no warning. Why, even a century ago the city's reputation was bad, through the presence of those very traders you have mentioned. Another dreamer before you saw the doom in store for the city, speaking against those traders vehemently and often; but his words were soon forgotten by all who heard them and people went their old ways as of yore. No man may help him who will not help himself.

"But it is the presence of those traders here in Ulthar which has driven me to this search of mine. I cannot allow the same doom to strike here—whatever that doom may be—yet it is difficult to see what may be done. No man of this town will venture anywhere near Dylath-Leen. It is said that the streets of that city have known no human feet for more than twenty years, nor can any man say with any certainty where the city's peoples have gone."

"I can say!" I answered. "Not *where*, exactly, but *how* at least. Enslaved, I said, and told no lie. I had it first from Bo-Kareth, late of Dylath-Leen, who told me that when those traders had taken all the fat black slaves of Parg for those evil stones of theirs, they brought to the city the biggest ruby ever seen—a boulder of a gem—leaving it on a pedestal in the main square as a false token of esteem. It was the evil influence of this great jewel that bewitched the people of Dylath-Leen, bemusing them to such a degree that in the end they, too. became slaves to be led away to the black galleys of the traders. And now, apparently, those traders have . . . *used up* . . . all the peoples of that ill-omened city and are starting their monstrous game here! And Bo-Kareth's story was true in every detail, for with my own eyes—"

"A great ruby . . . hmmm!" Atal musingly cut me off, stroking his face and frowning in concentration. "That puts a different complexion on it. Yes, I believe that in the *Fourth Book* there may be a mention! Shall we see?"

I nodded my eager agreement, and at Atal's direction lifted down from a corner shelf the largest and weightiest tome I had ever seen. Each page—pages of no material I had ever known before—glowed with burning letters which stood out with firefly definition in the dimness of the room. I could make out nothing of the unique ciphers within the book, but Atal seemed thoroughly familiar with each alien character, translating easily, mumbling to himself in barely discernible tones, until suddenly he stopped. He lurched shakily to his feet then, slamming the priceless volume shut, horror burning in his ancient eyes.

"So!" he exclaimed, hissing out the word. "It is *that!* The Fly-the-Light from Yuggoth on the Rim, a vampire in the worst meaning of the word—and we must make sure that it is never brought to Ulthar!" He paused, visibly taking hold of himself before he could continue.

"Let me tell you:

"Long ago, before dreams, in the primal mist of the predawn Beginning of All, the great ruby was brought from distant Yuggoth on the Rim by the Old Ones. Within that jewel, prisoned by light and the magic of the Old Ones, lurks a basic avatar of the prime evil, a thing hideous as the pit itself! Understand, Grant Enderby, it is not the stone that induces the hypnotic weariness of which you have spoken, but the thing *within* the stone, the evil influence of the Fly-the-Light from dark Yuggoth on the Rim. Few men know the history of that huge jewel and its monstrous inhabitant, and I do not consider myself fortunate to be one of the few.

"It is told that it was discovered after coming down in an avalanche from the heights of forbidden Hatheg-Kla—which I can believe for I know much of that mountain—discovered and carried away by the Black Princess, Yath-Lhi of Tyrhhia. And when her caravan reached her silver-spired city it was found that all Yath-Lhi's men at arms, her slaves, even the Black Princess herself, were as zombies, altered and mazed. It is not remembered now where Tyrhhia once stood, but many believe the centuried desert sands to cover even its tallest spire, and that the remains of its habitants lie putrid within their buried houses.

"But the ruby was not buried with Tyrhhia, more's the pity, and rumor has it that it was next discovered in a golden galley on the Southern Sea twixt Dylath-Leen and the Isle of Oriab. A strange ocean is the Southern Sea, and especially between Oriab and Dylath-Leen; for there, many fathoms deep, lies a basalt city with a temple and monolithic altar. And sailors are loth to pass over that submarine city, fearing the great storms which legend has it strike suddenly, even when there is no breath of wind to stir the sails!

"However, there the great jewel was found, aboard a great golden galley, and the crew of that galley were very beautiful even though they were not men, and all were long dead but not corrupt! Only one sailor, mad and babbling, was later rescued from the sea off Oriab to gibber pitifully the tale of the golden galley, but of his fellow crewmates nothing more is known. It is interesting to note that it is further writ how only certain people—horned people who dance to the evil drone of pipes and the rattle of crotala in mysterious Leng—are unaffected by the stone's proximity!" Atal looked at me knowingly. "And I can see you have already noticed how strangely our traders wear their turbans . . .

"But I digress. Again the jewel survived whatever fate overtook the poor seamen who rescued it from the golden galley, and it was later worshipped by the enormous dholes in the Vale of Pnoth, until three leathery night-gaunts flew off with it over the Peaks of Throk and down into those places of subterranean horror of which certain dim myths hint most terribly. For that underworld is said to be a place litten only by pale death-fires, a place reeking of ghoulish odours and filled with the primal mists which swirl in the pits at Earth's core. Who may say what form the inhabitants of such a place might take?"

At this point Atal's eyes cleared of their faraway look and turned from the dark places of his tale to the present and to me. He placed his rheumy hands on my shoulders, peering at me earnestly.

"Well, so says legend and the *Fourth Book of D'harsis*—and now, you say, the great ruby is come again into the known places of Earth's dreamland. I believe it, for over the years there have been vague rumors. Now hear you, Grant Enderby, I know what must be done—but how may I ask any man to take such risks? For my plan involves not only the risk of destruction to the mortal body, but the possible eternal damnation of the immortal soul!"

"I have pledged myself," I told him, "to avenge the peoples of Dylath-Leen. My pledge still stands, for though Dylath-Leen is lost, yet are there other towns and cities in dreams which I would dream again—but not to see them corrupted by horned horrors that trade in fever-cursed rubies! Atal—tell me what I must do."

Atal then set himself to it, and there was much for him to be about. I could not help him with the greater part of his work, tasks involving the translation into language I could understand of certain tracts from the *Fourth Book of D'harsis*. Even though many things are simpler in dream, those passages were not meant to be read by any man, neither awake nor sleeping, who did not understand their importance.

Slowly but surely the hours passed, and Atal labored as I watched, putting down letter after letter in the creation of pronounceable syllables from the seemingly impossible mumbo-jumbo of the great book from which he drew. I began to recognize certain symbols I had seen in allegedly "forbidden" tomes in the waking world, and even began to mumble the first of them aloud—*"Tetragammaton Thabaite Sabaoth Tethiktos"*—until Atal silenced me by jerking to his feet and favoring me with a gaze of pure horror.

"It is almost night," he remonstrated, striking a flint to a wax candle, his hands shaking more than even his extreme age might reasonably explain, "and outside the shadows are lengthening. Would you call *That* forth without first having protection? For make no mistake, distance is of no consequence to this invocation, and if we wished we could call out the Fly-the-Light even from here. But first you must cast a spell over Dylath-Leen, to contain the thing when you release it from the ruby; for certainly unless it is contained it will ravish the whole of dreamland. And you, the caller, the Utterer of The Words, would be one of the first to die—horribly!"

I gulped my apologies and sat silently from then on, listening attentively to Atal's instructions even as my eyes followed his scratching pen.

"You must go to Dylath-Leen," he told me, "taking with you the two incantations I now prepare. One of them, which you will keep at your left, is to build the protective Wall of Naach-Tith about the city. To work this spell you must journey around Dylath-Leen, returning to your starting point and crossing it, chanting the words as you go. This means, of course, that you will need to cross the bay; and I suggest that you do this by boat, for there are things in the night sea that do not take kindly to swimmers.

"When you have crossed your starting point the wall will be builded. Then you may use the other chant, spoken only once, to shatter the great gem. You should carry the second chant at your right. This way you will not confuse the two—a mistake which would prove disastrous! I have used inks which shine in the dark; there will be no difficulty in reading the chants. So, having done all I have told you, your revenge will be complete and you will have served all the lands of dream greatly.

"No creature or thing will ever be able to enter Dylath-Leen again so long as the Wall of Naach-Tith is there, nor leave the place, and the Fly-the-Light will be loosed amongst the horned ones. One warning though, Grant Enderby—*do not watch the results of your work!* It will be as was never meant for the eyes of men."

Grant Enderby's Story, IV: The Wall of Naach-Tith

I came through the desert toward Dylath-Leen at dusk, when the desert grasses made spiky silhouettes atop the dunes and the last kites circled high, their shrill cries telling of night's stealthy approach. Night was indeed coming, striding across dreamland in lengthening shadows which befriended and hid me as I tethered my yak and made for the western point of the bay. I would start there, making my way from shadow to shadow with the wall-building Chant of Naach-Tith on my lips, to the opposite side of the bay; and then I would see about crossing the water back to my starting point.

I was glad that the moon was thinly horned, glad the desert was not more brightly illumined, for I could not be sure that there were no sentries out from the unquiet city. Whatever joys Dylath-Leen may once have held for me, now the place was unquiet. No normal lights shone in its streets and squares; but, as night came more quickly, there soon sprang up many thousands of tiny points of evil red, and in one certain area a great morbidly red blotch glowed in strange reminiscence of Jupiter's huge eye-like spot, glimpsed often in my youth through a friend's telescope. Empty though the city now was of all normal life, that poisoned jewel in the main square still filled the town with its loathsomeness, a terror ignored by the abnormal traders as the statues of past heroes are ignored in saner places.

Halfway round the city's perimeter there came to my ears the strains of music—if such evilly soul-disturbing sounds warrant placing in any such category—and leaping fires sprang up in Dylath-Leen's outer streets, so that I could see and shudder at the horned figures that leapt and cavorted round those ritual hellfires, observing disgustedly the way their squat bodies jerked and shook to the jarring cacophony of bone-dry crotala and strangled flutes. I could neither bear to hear nor watch, and so passed quickly on, chanting breathlessly to myself and feeling about me a weird magic building up to a thrill of unseen energies in the night air.

I was more than three-quarters towards the eastern side of the bay when I heard far behind me a sound that stiffened the short hairs on the back of my neck and brought a chill sweat to my brow. It was the terrified cry of my yak, and following that single shrill scream of animal fear there came another sound—one which caused me to quicken my pace almost to a run as I emerged from the dunes to the washed pebbles of the shore—the horrid, ululant cry of alarm of the horned ones!

Stranded on the beach, its bottom festooned with barnacles, was a small one-man craft as used of old by the octopus fishers of Dylath-Leen. Frail and unsafe though this vessel looked, beggars cannot be choosers, and thus thinking I leapt within its tar-planked shell, offering up a prayer of thanks to the night skies when I found that the craft still floated. I found the old round-bladed paddle and, still chanting those mad words of Atal's deciphering, made strongly for the black outline of the far side of the bay. And, ungainly though my craft had at first looked, it fairly cleft the dark water as I drove furiously at the paddle.

By now there were squattish outlines on the shore behind me, dancing in anger at my escape to the sea, and I wondered if the horned ones had a means of communication with which more orthodox creatures such as men were unfamiliar. If so, then perhaps I would find monstrous welcomers awaiting my beaching on the western point.

Halfway across the bay things happened to make me forget the problem of what might wait for me on landing. I felt a tug at my paddle from the oily water and a dark mass rose up out of the depths before my boat. As that unknown swimmer came alongside and the thin moonlight lit on its sharp teeth, I lashed out with my paddle—taking a very deep breath when the horror turned slowly away and silently submerged.

I continued then with my frenzied paddling and chanting until the western point loomed out of the dark and the shallow keel of my boat bit sand. Leaping overboard into shallow, night-chilled water, I imagined soggy gropings at my legs and ploughed in an agony of terror for the pebbles of the beach—and in that same instant, as I touched dry land, there loped out of the dark from the direction of the city the squat forms of a dozen or so of those foul, horned creatures whose brothers dwell in nighted Leng! Before they could reach me, even as their poisonous paws stretched out for me, I raced across my starting point and there came a clap of magical thunder that hurled me down face first into the sand. I leapt up again, and there within arm's length, clawing at an unseen barrier—the merciful Wall of Naach-Tith—were those thwarted horned ones of elder dreams. Hateful their looks and murderous their strangled intent as they clawed with vile purpose at thin air, held back by the invisible spell of Naach-Tith's barrier.

Without pause I snatched out the second of those papers given me by Atal and commenced the invocation of the Fly-the-Light, the spell to draw forth the horror from the ruby. And as the first of those weird syllables passed my lips the horned ones fell back, unbelievable terror twisting their already awful features.

"*Tetragammaton Thabaite Sabaoth Tethiktos—*" As I chanted on, by the dim light of that thin-horned moon, the snarls of those creatures at bay turned to pleading mewls and gibbers as they began to grovel at the base of the Wall of Naach-Tith. And eventually I spoke the last rune, and there came a silence which was as that quiet that rules at the core of the moon.

Then, out of the silence, a low and distant rumble was born, growing rapidly in volume to a roar, to a blast of sound, to an ear-splitting shriek as of a billion banshees—and from the heart of Dylath-Leen a cold wind blew, extinguishing in an instant the hellfires of the horned ones. And all the tiny red points of light went out in a second, and there came a loud, sharp crack, as of a great crystal disintegrating. And soon thereafter I heard the first of the screams.

I remembered Atal's warning "not to watch," but found myself unable to turn away. I was rooted to the spot, and as the screams from the dark city rose in unbearable intensity I could but stare into the darkness with bulging eyes, straining to pick out some detail of what occurred there in the midnight streets. Then, as the grovelers at the wall broke and scattered, *It* came!

It came—rushing from out the bowels of the terrified town—bringing with it a wind that bowled over the fleeing creatures beyond the invisible wall as though they had no weight at all . . . and I *saw* it!

Blind and yet all-seeing—without legs and yet running like flood water—the poisonous mouths in the bubbling mass—the Fly-the-Light beyond the wall. Great God! The sight of the creature was mind-blasting! And what it *did* to those now pitiful things from Leng. . . .

Thus it was.

Three times only have I visited the basalt-towered, myriad-wharved city of Dylath-Leen—and now I am glad that I have seen that city for the last time.

Part Three

◆

I

Shadow Over Dreamland

"And it is still your intention to enter Dylath-Leen? Deliberately, despite all I have told you?" Grant Enderby's voice showed his incredulity. He stood up to pace the floor of the room wherein he and Henri-Laurent de Marigny had so firmly cemented their friendship through the hours of darkness. Enderby's tale had taken until the wee hours in the telling, and since then the two men had talked of a variety of things. Their discourse had covered many subjects, some of them centering upon de Marigny's quest, others touching upon the general air of malaise, of a strange impending doom that seemed to hang like a dark shadow over most of dreamland.

"Yes," de Marigny answered, "I must enter Dylath-Leen; my friends are there and they are in trouble."

"But, Henry, if the Elder Gods themselves are incapable of helping your friends, then what can a mere man do?"

"You ask me that? And you, a 'mere man,' once built the Wall of Naach-Tith about Dylath-Leen, destroying all of the horned traders in the city?"

"I was lucky," the older man grunted. "Without Atal's help I could have done nothing."

"But I, too, have been helped by Atal," de Marigny pointed out. "And I have my flying cloak."

"Huh!" Enderby grunted grudgingly. "Still, you do not know what you go against, Henri."

"Oh, but I do. You have told me what I go against, Grant, for which I am grateful. There is something further, however."

"Oh?"

"Yes. You explained how you built the Wall of Naach-Tith about Dylath-Leen, but you said nothing about its removal. How can you be sure that things are once more as they were—that Dylath-Leen again suffers the contagion of the horned traders?"

Enderby shrugged. "There are reasons. Travelers have strayed too close to the city, never to be seen again; others have been lucky enough to escape. It is rumored that two such men have stumbled away from the city in the last five years, two out of dozens lost forever. Then there is the vision you saw in Kthanid's crystal: the square in the center of Dylath-Leen, where once again the horned ones have set up a great ruby which doubtless pulses out its evil, debilitating radiations even now . . .

"As to how the horned ones regained Dylath-Leen—how they chained the Fly-the-Light from Yuggoth on the Rim, prisoning it again within this new ruby they have brought to the city from across the Southern Sea—of these things I can only guess. And anyone's guess is as good as mine. Remember, Henri, that there was a rune to build the Wall of Naach-Tith, and another to splinter the great ruby and free the Fly-the-Light. Why not a third to remove Naach-Tith's barrier, and yet another to prison the horror from Yuggoth?

"It is after all a Fly-the-Light, which, during the hours of day, must find a dark sanctuary or perish beneath the sun's rays. If man—or monster—knew the correct runes, it would be an easy task to trap the vampire during the hours of daylight."

Wearily de Marigny stroked his forehead. "Whichever way it is," he answered, "I'll find out soon enough for myself." He stood up and stretched, and his host immediately apologized.

"I fear I've kept you up talking too long, my friend. Let me show you to your room now. You have come a long way and will probably need all the strength you can muster. When will you tackle Dylath-Leen?"

Following Enderby upstairs to the tiny guestroom, de Marigny answered. "I intend it to be tomorrow night, and of course I will fly into the city. That way the journey will be one of minutes, a half hour at most. With luck I should be in and out of Dylath-Leen before your horned traders even suspect that I am there. I won't need much more equipment than I have already: a rope—a sharp knife, perhaps—a little blacking for my face."

"Ah, well, Henri, go to your bed now," his host answered. "We'll talk again tomorrow, when you are fully rested. If only I were a young man again, I—"

"No, no—you've done enough already, Grant, and I am extremely grateful."

"My boys, too," Enderby nodded, ushering the man from the waking world into the guestroom. "If you were going afoot, I would find it difficult to dissuade them from going with you. You will understand why I am glad you are flying to Dylath-Leen."

De Marigny nodded. "Of course I understand, but in any case it's best I go it alone. Goodnight, Grant."

"Goodnight, my friend. And may your dreams within dreams be pleasant ones."

The following evening, as twilight deepened and the first suggestions of stars began to glow dimly in the sky over Ulthar, de Marigny set out. People who saw his shadow and the shape that cast it flitting high over the rooftops would later talk of a great bat; or perhaps it was a night-gaunt—though night-gaunts were extremely rare in these parts.

As the dreamer passed swiftly through the darkening sky he retraced in his mind's eye the comprehensive map of Dylath-Leen which Grant Enderby had drawn for him. It was of the utmost importance that he remember all of the routes from the square of the ruby dais to the outskirts of the city, and from the outskirts to the desert. It would not be too difficult to reach that square, where by now Titus Crow and Tiania might well be suffering the none too tender attentions of the squat horned ones. But it could very well be a different story again to escape from the place.

De Marigny had upon his person a stout rope with a noose, a sharp knife in a leather sheath, and the precious vial given him by Atal. Nothing more. He hoped that nothing more would be necessary, for he dared not weigh himself down too much.

Out in the desert he paused briefly to alight and tie his rope to a boulder that must have weighed as heavy as two men. With the other end of the rope fastened to the harness of his cloak, he attempted an ascent into the night. His spirits dropped when, as he had feared, he found the cloak incapable of lifting the additional weight. He found a second boulder only half so great as the first and repeated the experiment, feeling a little of his confidence returning as the cloak bore its burden slowly but surely up into dark skies.

The cloak could manage two people without being taxed beyond its capabilities, but not three. That was more or less as de Marigny had expected, but he had hoped—

No, he checked himself, hope was nothing without strength and determination. He untied the smaller boulder and wound the rope about his body once more. Then, slitting his eyes against a wind that blew high above the desert, following the winding course of a river of stars reflected in the night-dark Skai, he once more headed for Dylath-Leen.

Fires surrounded the city, spaced out to form a horse-shoe pattern whose mouth was the bay of Dylath-Leen, where the land met the currents of the Southern Sea. Seeing these fires from afar, de Marigny rose higher in the sky until he could plainly make out the shape they formed. Then he flew up higher still so that there could be no chance of his being observed as he soared above the watchers who kept those fires burning.

There were other lights in the city, but they were not the healthy, welcoming lights of any normal town. There was no physical warmth in them for all their redness, and de Marigny knew that these crimson glow-worms were only smaller versions of the great malignancy in the central square, the horror which even now pulsed out its red rays, glowing like the evil eye of an alien Cyclops. And seeing from on high that great unwinking glow, de Marigny believed he knew now for sure the source of all the unease in dreamland.

II

Rescue

To the three squat creatures whose task it was to guard the two dreaming humans spreadeagled upon the steps of the ruby dais, the night was a welcome, beautiful thing. Most of their fellows were asleep now, for there were no longer any of the normal inhabitants of dreamland left in Dylath-Leen with which to amuse themselves. It had been thus for many a year, unless one cared to count the occasional unwary wanderer who might stumble mistakenly upon Dylath-Leen from out of the desert. This night, however, should prove a rare diversion—in the shapes of these two very important intruders from the waking world of men.

The grotesquely alien trio that formed the nightguard about the dais of the ruby would have to be patient, though, waiting until they could be sure that they would not be disturbed in their pleasures. Lots had been drawn for their "duty" this night, and the trio had been the winners. The prize must surely be enjoyed to the full, and it would be a pity if the cries of these two captives should attract jealous-minded colleagues to spoil their amusements.

The male captive would provide hours of sport, though he must not be *too* severely damaged. Nyarlathotep, emissary of Great Cthulhu himself, was coming to dreamland to speak with Titus Crow personally. It would not be meet if the Crawling Chaos should find the man a babbling idiot before he could question him—though doubtless he would be just such an idiot by the time the interrogation was over! As for the female . . . Ah! But *there* was a thought . . . They would have her one at a time, right there upon the dais steps, where her male companion could see and hear all that occurred. And later, before the morrow, they would have her again, perhaps all three at once!

As night deepened and the city grew quieter still, the three horned ones joked of such things and ensured that their captives overheard them—never knowing that upon a high, nearby rooftop a third party also heard them, nor that the unseen stranger grew livid with rage at their vileness!

The figures of the two captives tied to the dais steps were pitiful in their helplessness. Titus Crow, normally so proud and leonine—with eyes that spoke the secrets of strange ways walked unafraid, a man whose deeds had rocked the seats of the Great Old Ones themselves before taking him to the home of the Elder Gods in Elysia—now lay like a man already dead, naked and ready for the shroud. The ridges of the basalt steps bruised his back and cut into his flesh; his head lolled drunkenly; the only spark glowing behind his eyes was one of horror and shame. Shame that he was helpless now to protect the incredibly beautiful girl-goddess whose love for him had led her to this hideous place, this unthinkable fate.

The two gazed at each other, and for a moment their love blazed through all the misery. "Oh, Titus," the wondrous girl's equally wondrous voice, weak now and terrified, spoke to her Earthman. "Is this really how it is all to end?"

"Tiania," Crow's own voice plumbed the depths of wretchedness and shame, "I would not have—"

"Hush, my Titus," she shook her head, "for I would have it no other way. If we are to suffer and die, then we suffer and die together. Do you think I would even want to live without you?"

Before Crow could answer, the rattling, rasping tones of one of the squat, alien guardsmen crackled harshly in the still air. "Hah! The two lovers converse! See how they gaze upon one another and mumble their sweet nothings!" The speaker turned to his comrades. "What do you say, brothers? Is it not time we found ourselves a morsel of pleasure with these two?"

"Indeed," one of the two he addressed grated impatiently, "if you two had listened to me we'd have been at it an hour ago. I want the girl—and I want her now!" The great wide mouth in the speaker's evil face widened even further in a ghastly grin as he stared at the writhing figure of Tiania upon the basalt steps.

Hearing this horned one's words, Titus Crow struggled wretchedly, helplessly with his bonds, gasping: "By God, I'll—"

"You'll what, dreamer?" With his scimitar, the same horned one carelessly drew a thin red line down Crow's rib cage.

"Hold!" cried the third of the aliens. He approached Tiania and reached out a vile paw to snatch away the tattered square of silk which alone covered her perfect breasts. "We haven't yet decided who's to be first with the girl, have we?" He took from his belt a pouch, and from this removed a ten-sided die. "Highest score takes her first, lowest last. Agreed?"

His two companions nodded, at which he flipped his gamestone into the air. It fell, bounced, and the three horned ones crowded about it where it lay. "Ten!" crowed the thrower, delighted with his luck.

The next guardsman threw only a four, at which he grunted a low curse. But the third also threw a ten. To break the tie, the first thrower took up the die a second time, at which his opponent said:

"Throw it higher this time. I don't trust you and your die."

"High as you like," chortled the other, flinging the gamestone into the air. It did not return to earth.

The three looked up into the night for a little while, shading their eyes against the lurid glow of the great ruby, then peered puzzledly at each other and frowned uncertainly. And in this moment of indecision a noose snaked down out of darkness and settled about the shoulders of the lost gamestone's owner.

The noose swiftly lifted and tightened about the guardsman's fat neck, drawing him inexorably up from the ground. He disappeared into the sky, choking and gurgling and kicking wildly. Stunned, his companions gaped at one another—for a second or two only. Then, before they could make a move, the now inert body of their hanged comrade crashed down again from a great height, dashing one of the two remaining horrors to the ground with a broken back.

At that, the legs of the third member of that loathsome trio were galvanized into frantic activity. It seemed to the astounded, delighted, almost disbelieving pair tied to the dais steps that the remaining alien tried to turn in at least three directions at one and same time. But then, before the lone survivor of the unknown vengeance from the night sky could even cry out, as finally he made to bolt from the cobbled square, down swooped a great black-faced bat-shape that struck him from his feet and was upon him, knife glinting redly, all in one fluid motion. A second later, it was all over. De Marigny had acted with a murderous efficiency born of utter horror and loathing. He felt not the slightest repugnance at the fact that he had so ruthlessly destroyed these three abominations of darkest dream.

Without pause the avenging dreamer leapt to the steps of the dais, where it was the work of seconds to cut the captives loose. All this time Titus Crow had spoken not a word. His mouth hung half open in amazement and his eyes were wide in disbelief. Finally, as de Marigny helped the two to their feet, averting his eyes as best he could from Tiania's nakedness, Crow blurted: "Henri! De Marigny! It's you under that blacking! But how? You, here in dreamland? God! But I've never been more—"

"Later, Titus," de Marigny cut him off. "Heaven knows we've little enough time right now. I'll take Tiania first—the cloak can't manage three—but I'll be back for you immediately. Better grab yourself one of those scimitars in case more of these beasts come on the scene. I'll be as quick as I can." With that he turned to Tiania, who in turn looked to Crow for guidance.

"Trust de Marigny, Tiania," the bruised and bloodied man told her. "He is the greatest friend a man ever had." He gave the girl into his friend's care, and the latter, more than ever aware of Tiania's nakedness and unearthly beauty, wrapped her quickly in a wing of his cloak. Without further pause he took firm hold of her and flew up into darkness. They sped quickly to a tall unlighted tower about a mile from the dais of the ruby, and there de Marigny quietly deposited Tiania behind the balcony of the flat roof. Before he could fly off again she caught him by the arm.

"Titus has told me much of you, Henri-Laurent de Marigny," she whispered. "I understand now why he left me alone in Elysia to return to your green Earth. Friends such as you are singularly rare. He loves you as a brother, and from this time on so do I."

She leaned forward and kissed de Marigny lightly upon his mouth. A moment later, as he soared off again into the night, his heart also soared within him. And de Marigny knew that come what may he had already been rewarded fully for whatever risks he was taking here in Earth's dreamland.

A minute or so later de Marigny picked up Titus Crow from the square of the ruby dais, and then it became obvious to him just how much the latter's ordeals had taken out of him; scimitar grasped in one hand, Crow was barely capable of hanging on as they flew up into the night. De Marigny asked his strangely fatigued friend how long he and Tiania had languished upon the steps of the dais.

"Since noon, Henri, but we were weak enough before ever we got to Dylath-Leen. They brought us to the city in one of their vile black galleys, and never a bite to eat in three days. I was drugged and only half-conscious all of that time, but even wide awake I could never have eaten the unnameable slop they offered us! And don't forget that we've been tied beneath that monstrous abnormality in the square for nigh on eleven hours. That alone has robbed me of more energy than the three days spent in that galley rolled into one.

"Tiania is amazing. There's more of the Elder Gods in her than you'd ever guess—even taking into account her unearthly beauty— and I fancy that's what saved her from being greatly affected by proximity to the great ruby. As for me, all I need is a bite of plain, decent food, a little rest, and I'll soon be my normal self again. Or my *ab*normal self, if you will. I don't suppose you brought a bottle of brandy with you, Henri! By God, that would cheer me up no end!"

In spite of all his worries, de Marigny had to grin. This was typical of the Titus Crow he knew, a far cry from the forlorn and desperate figure so recently tied fast to the steps of the ruby dais. Indeed, Crow had not been understating that vast jewel's debilitating influence, and as the distance between the flyers and the ruby increased, so something of Crow's former strength and zest began to return. De Marigny knew that when that strength had returned fully, then indeed would Titus Crow be a force to reckon with, and it would certainly be a dark hour for the evil influences at present operating in Earth's dreamland.

And de Marigny understood what his friend had meant by referring to himself as being "abnormal." During his adventures in space and time, on his way to Elysia, Crow had crashed the time-clock into an alien world. Rescued from oblivion by a robot doctor, T3RE, Crow had been rebuilt from the pulp of his human body by a science beyond anything even guessed at by the doctors and scientists of his mother world. He was immensely strong and fast; he could stay underwater without mechanical aids for indefinite periods; his skin was impervious to all but the most corrosive atmospheres; and, perhaps most amazing of all, he had been built in the image of himself as he had been twenty to twenty-five years earlier! Even Crow's mind had been altered! He had found himself able to do completely inexplicable and unbelievable things with the time-clock, using it in ways never conceived of by its original builders, the Elder Gods themselves.

De Marigny banished all such thoughts and memories from his mind as he caused the cloak to drop them down to the roof of the tower. With a little cry of relief Tiania threw herself into Crow's arms. He stroked her for a moment, then turned to their rescuer:

"Well, Henri, what do you have in mind now? We're not out of the fire yet, my friend."

"I know that, but—" de Marigny began, then paused and put a finger to his lips as suddenly sounds of activity began to drift up from the nighted city. Below, some distance away, freshly lighted torches flared redly. The man in the flying cloak turned a wide-eyed look to his companions. "That sounds like trouble. It looks like they've discovered your escape!"

III

Night-Gaunt

"They'll soon alert the whole city," de Marigny continued in haste as he tried to rearrange his plans. "Titus, how many of them are there in Dylath-Leen?"

"A thousand, possibly more," Crow answered. "We saw a regular fleet of their black galleys in the harbor."

"Then we've no time to lose. Same as last time, I'll take Tiania first and see if I can get her to a safe place beyond the watchfires at the perimeter of the city. Then I'll be back for you. Lie low, Titus, until I get back."

Crow clapped his friend on the back and wished him luck, then squatted down behind the tower's parapet wall. A second later de Marigny was once again airborne, with Tiania wrapped in a wing of his cloak. As they flew on high, looking down at the squares and rooftops of nighted Dylath-Leen, they could see that indeed the horned horrors from Leng were beginning to throng the city's streets.

With the fingers of his free hand upon the studs that controlled the cloak's antigravitic forces, and his other arm wrapped firmly around Tiania's tiny waist, de Marigny coaxed the cloak up higher still into the night air. The girl clung tightly to him, but though the swift-flowing air was chill, their height above the ground fearful, and the tension increasing with each passing moment, not once did she tremble.

He believed she must be thinking about Titus Crow, left behind now atop the tower in the middle of an unquiet city, and to divert her mind from any morbid train of thought, he said: "You're a brave girl, Tiania."

She immediately turned her head toward him and smiled through the rush of dark air, and de Marigny believed he could see the worry and fear swiftly fading from her lovely, almost luminous face. "I'm not really brave," she said. "In the care of two such as you and Titus, what can there be to fear?"

It was de Marigny's turn to smile; but a second later he frowned, asking: "Why in the name of all that's wonderful didn't you two bring flying cloaks with you to dreamland? I should have thought that—"

"But we did bring cloaks," she cut him off, "and would have brought a time-clock, too, except that it would give the game away. Our cloaks were taken from us by those horned beasts when they trapped us. The fools, they threw them away with the rest of our clothes!"

"They didn't know what they were?"

"No. Creatures such as they are could never dream of flying. Their very souls are earthbound."

"And how were you trapped in the first place?" de Marigny asked, noting that the watchfires were slowly falling away to the rear. He stared ahead into darkness, hoping to find a good place to alight.

"That is a long story, but I will try to be brief . . .

"When first we came here there were many things we should have done. We ought first to have visited Atal the Wise, and perhaps Kuranes of Ooth-Nargai beyond the Tanarian Hills. But there seemed so many wonders to see—almost as many as one might find in Elysia— and it was the first time I had ever been in an alien world, even a dream world. Also, I wanted Titus for myself for a little while. And so I persuaded him to spend just a day or two in idle wandering from town to town, spending the nights at tiny inns and taverns. To me it was just a game, you see. I did not know . . .

"Anyway, Titus agreed to my silly ideas, saying it would be a good way to acclimatize ourselves, to get the feel of dreamland. We used our cloaks very discreetly, usually traveling in the hours immediately before dawn. Thus, distance was no problem.

"Those first two days were wonderful; then in Ath—

"Ath is an unpleasant little place bordering on Istharta. Neither Titus nor I liked it much and we did not stay there long. But while we were there Titus was given a lead to follow. It was a false lead, but we did not know that then. We were told by a man of dreamland—a traitor, in league with the dark forces of nightmare, a dupe of powers unnatural in dream who must have somehow known who we were and why we were here—that we should go to the Isle of Oriab, across the Southern Sea. He told us to go to Baharna, the great seaport, where we would find a black galley whose captain would be able to tell us all we needed to know of the troubles besetting dreamland, perhaps even how to deal with those troubles.

"We went to Baharna, arriving late in the evening when the

wharves were all in darkness. The captain of the black galley, a squat little man who kept himself in the shadows, told us to go to a certain tavern, that he would meet us there upon the morrow. The tavern was a wharfside place, none too clean and somehow depressing, where furtive figures seemed to hide in dark corners. But our room was the best in the house, and the food and wine seemed excellent . . . The food, the wine too—they were drugged! We woke up captives of the black galley, and . . . but the rest you know."

De Marigny nodded. "Well, it's all over now. And look there!" he pointed sharply down into the darkness. "That's it, that white rock there. It's not too high or steep for you to climb down from should . . . should anything happen. And it's a landmark I can't miss when I return with Titus. Down we go, Tiania."

He caused the cloak to drop them gently down to a wide ledge halfway up the peak that jutted stark and white from the desert's sands. There he deposited Tiania, telling her that it would not be long before he brought Titus to her, and then that they would all three be in Ulthar in time for breakfast. It was not to be so, but de Marigny could not know that.

To Titus Crow, waiting behind the parapet wall of the tower only a mile from the unquiet center of Dylath-Leen, it seemed an inordinately long time indeed before de Marigny came silently winging down once more out of the night to alight beside him like some great bat. "Henri," Crow whispered, "is all well?"

The low hush of his voice was not unwarranted. The streets below were alive with torch-bearing search parties, so that Dylath-Leen was a maze of redly flickering flames and leaping shadows—and now from all directions could be heard the hideous, ululant alert-cries of the horned ones from nighted Leng. Indeed the sound of hurrying footsteps even echoed up to them from the street directly beneath their tall refuge.

"So far so good," de Marigny breathlessly answered. "Tiania is safe for the moment. I think we're just about in the clear, Titus. This flying cloak of yours must take all the credit, though. Without it I could have done nothing."

"The cloak is yours now, Henri—you've earned it. Here, tuck this sword into your belt. Now, just let me get a firm grip. Right, up we go!"

More slowly this time, feeling the burden of Titus Crow's greater weight, the flying cloak lifted the two friends into the night air over Dylath-Leen, and both men were greatly relieved when the flickering torchfires had dimmed and fallen away below and behind them. It was not long then before other fires sprang up in red relief to their front, and soon after that they were flying high above the watchfires at the rim of the city.

"A mile, perhaps two miles more," said de Marigny. "There's a jagged fang of white rock sticking up out of the desert. That's where I left Tiania. We'll be there in another minute or so."

"And what then, Henri—a series of short hops to Ulthar?"

"Something like that, I think, yes."

"Good. And as soon as we've rested up a little and found safe lodging for Tiania, then we're off to Ilek-Vad. I want to know just exactly what's going on there. Yes, and you might even find time to tell me what the devil you're doing here in Earth's dreamland, when by all rights you should be well on your way to Elysia."

"I *am* on my way to Elysia, Titus. This is the only way I'm ever likely to get there. Kthanid asked me to come, telling me that you and Tiania were in trouble. I'll tell you the whole story later. As for Ilek-Vad: yes, I, too, would like to know what's going on there. After all, that's where my father is. I don't remember a great deal about him, but—"

"There's your white rock dead ahead!" Crow suddenly cried, cutting his friend off short. He pointed eagerly. "And there's Tiania, I can see her waving. Oh, well done, Henri. You're not an inch off course!"

Controlling the cloak's descent, de Marigny brought them drifting down toward the ledge where the girl-goddess waited. She waved again, reaching out her arms to them as they approached out of the darkness.

It was only then—as the two men felt a rushing blast of air, a buffeting gust much stronger and quite different from any normal draft they might expect to meet during their steady flight above the desert—that they realized something was greatly amiss. The freakish, turbulent eddy tossed them to one side, so that they crashed shoulders-on into the sheer wall of the rock at a point some thirty feet to one side of Tiania. Here the drop was sheer to the desert's floor, and de Marigny had to manipulate the cloak's studs to draw back from the white rock's jagged face. As he did so he heard Crow's sharp intake of breath, and following his friend's horrified gaze he saw and recognized a huge gray shape that passed noiselessly by, circling the rocky spire on membrane wings.

"Night-gaunt!" cried de Marigny, fighting to regain control of the cloak as it was caught again in the wash of the creature's wings. "A great gray gaunt!"

"Put me down on that ledge, quick!" Crow shouted. "That damn thing must be after Tiania! Look—here it comes again!"

For the third time they felt the turbulence of the huge night-gaunt's wings as they flapped in leathery sentience, suspending their rubbery owner directly over the girl who now crouched terrified on the ledge of the white rock. Now they were able to get a reasonably clear view of the thing, better by far than de Marigny's previous look at such creatures received through Kthanid's telepathic knowledge-imparting.

The horror, while being twice as big as any of its loathsome species viewed before, was nevertheless endowed with the same noxiously thin outline as lesser gaunts and wore precisely the same aspect. Horns sprouted from its faceless head; it was barb-tailed and bat-winged; its skin looked rubbery, cold and damp—and, possibly worst of all, it was utterly silent.

Then de Marigny was rushed abruptly aloft as Crow let go his hold on the cloak's harness to leap to the ledge close to Tiania. Yet again struggling to bring the cloak under his control, de Marigny all but missed what followed next. As it was he heard Crow's cry of rage and horror . . . and he saw the gray shape of that giant among night-gaunts as it lifted skyward on silently beating pinions, bearing aloft the wriggling, shrieking, slender form of Tiania grasped in prehensile paws!

IV

Atal's Elixir

On the wide ledge of the white rock's peak high above the desert, Titus Crow raged silently in the night and shook his scimitar at the diminishing gray shape that flapped away against a background of strange constellations. By the time de Marigny had landed beside

him, however, the naked giant had recovered his equilibrium sufficiently to cry out in a half-choked voice: "Quickly, man, out of the
cloak! Hurry, Henri, I must get after that monster!"

Seeing instantly how useless and time-consuming it would be to
argue—aware that the cloak was designed to operate at maximum efficiency with only one passenger and that it was Titus Crow's preroga-
tive to pursue the huge night-gaunt and rescue Tiania, if such was at
all possible—de Marigny immediately unfastened the cloak's harness
and helped Crow into it. Then without another word spoken, Crow
grabbed his friend around the waist with one arm, his other hand flying to the collar studs that controlled the cloak. Another moment saw
de Marigny deposited none too gently on the desert's sandy floor.

Rising again into the night, Crow called: "Can you find your way
back to Ulthar, Henri?"

"I know the way," de Marigny shouted back. "Five miles or so
from here I pick up the Skai and simply follow the river. No need to
worry about me, Titus. I'll see you in Ulthar . . . both of you! Good
luck!"

"Thanks. I fancy I'll need all the luck I can get," Crow's answer
came back from the heights. "Take care, Henri." For a moment or two
he was a vague batshape against the blue crystal stars, then he was
gone.

Half and hour and a little more than two miles later, as he strode out
over the desert dunes in the direction of Ulthar, led on by the sweet
scent of night-blooming flowers on the banks of the Skai, de Marigny
glanced for the tenth time apprehensively over his shoulder. It was his
imagination, of course, but for the last twenty minutes or so, since
shortly after he set out from the foot of the white rock pinnacle, he
had had the feeling that he was being followed. Yet each time he
looked back there was nothing to be seen, only the low dunes and occasionally the rock jutting starkly against the night-dark sky.

Climbing to the top of a high dune, he glanced back yet again and
this time spied in the distance the darkly looming basalt towers of
Dylath-Leen. No healthy lights showed in the city, only a dull glow
from the watch fires at its rim. It shocked de Marigny to be reminded
how close he still was to that nightmare-cursed city, and he determined there and then to increase his distance from it as rapidly as hu-

manly possible. It did not seem likely that the horned ones could be on his trail already, and yet—

He shuddered and felt the short hairs rise at the back of his neck, a reaction not alone engendered of the desert's chill, and turned once more toward friendly Ulthar; but even as he turned he saw a movement in the corner of his eye. Something had slipped silently from shadow to shadow less than a hundred yards to his rear. Now he remembered something Grant Enderby had told him—about how expert the horned ones were at tracking their prey—and he shuddered again.

Quickly de Marigny slid down the side of the dune and looked about for a vantage point. He ran for a boulder that lay half-buried in the sand and hid behind it. As he went to his knees in the shadows he heard a distant but distinct wail rising in the night air. The cry reached its highest note, quavered inquiringly, then died into eerie silence. It was almost immediately answered by a second call, from a point de Marigny judged to be just beyond the tall dune; and while these were not the ululant alert cries with which he was now familiar, nevertheless the dreamer knew that they were given voice by those same horned horrors from Leng!

Now de Marigny shot frantic glances to left and right, his eyes searching the desert's starlit gloom for areas of deeper shadow that might hide his onward flight toward the river. And as he did so there came to his ears many more of the inquiring cries—except that now certain of the creatures who uttered those hideous bayings obviously flanked him! Indeed, one of those cries had seemed to come from somewhere *behind* where he crouched, from the direction of the Skai itself. And this cry had been different in that it had seemed somehow—triumphant?

So intent was he upon gauging the exact directions whence these latter sounds had issued that he almost failed to hear the soft footfalls in the sand. Too late, he did hear them, and he turned with a single gasp of horror in time to see only the jeweled hilt of a scimitar in the instant before it struck him between the eyes . . .

When de Marigny regained consciousness he believed for a moment that he had somehow returned through the barriers of dream to the waking world. But not so. Though the sun stood at its zenith and hurt his eyes behind his fluttering eyelids, the dreamer knew that indeed he was still a prisoner of dreamland; more than ever a prisoner, for the buildings and towers that loomed blackly upwards before him, and the steps that sent knives of pain lancing into his spine where he was tied to them were a basalt quarried in dreamland. This could only be Dylath-Leen; and sure enough, if he tilted his head right back at an angle he could see—the great ruby!

"Ah, our friend from the waking world of men has finally returned to us—with a very sick head, no doubt!" The squat speaker leaned carelessly on the hilt of his scimitar, its point digging into the rough grain of the steps and its blade curving uncomfortably close to de Marigny's rib cage. The coarse black silk of the horned one's baggy breeches was stained and grimed, the red sash at his waist festooned with knives. He wore huge rubies in the rings of his fat fingers and an evil grin upon his face, in which veiled, slightly slanted eyes regarded de Marigny almost hungrily.

And suddenly the dreamer was aware of his pain. His skin felt completely dehydrated, baked dry under the noon sun; his back, which through long hours of unconsciousness had lain across the sharp corners of three of the dais steps, felt as though it might break in pieces at any moment; his head ached abominably and felt grotesquely swollen. Naked, his entire body was bruised from being brutally dragged across miles of desert sands; his lips, tongue, and throat were parched, and leather thongs cut into his wrists and ankles where they were tied.

"Dreamer, we are going to kill you!" This time the speaker emphasized his words by idly kicking de Marigny's bruised ribs. De Marigny barely held back the cry of agony that sprang to his lips, managing at the same time to lift his head up high enough to see that he was ringed by perhaps twenty of the horned ones. Their leader, the speaker, wore no shoes, and de Marigny knew that the extreme pain he had felt when his tender ribs were kicked was due to the fact that this torturer had hooves instead of feet.

"We are going to kill you," that monstrous being said again, "but it is entirely up to you how we do it. You can die slowly, very slowly, losing first your hands, then your feet, and your so-called manhood. Then your ears, your eyes, your tongue at the very end. It would take at least a day, perhaps two. *Or you could die the hard way!*"

He paused to let that last sink in, then continued: "On the other hand, we could be merciful."

"I doubt," de Marigny groaned, "if your sort know the meaning of mercy."

"Ah, but we do! For instance, it would be merciful to lop off your head with a single stroke—but before you are granted that boon, there are several things I want to know."

The horned one waited expectantly but de Marigny made no answer.

"If I have your eyes propped open with slivers of wood, and your head tied back, you would very quickly, very painfully go blind. The sun is singularly unkind to those who stare so at her. But before that becomes necessary—"

"—You want to know something."

"Correct! You have been listening to me. That is good. There are several things I wish to know, yes. One: how did you come into Dylath-Leen so secretively, and manage to kill three of our colleagues so efficiently before they could even raise the alarm? Two: how were you able to smuggle your friends so cleverly, so swiftly away, when you yourself were later caught? Three: where are your friends now, for we must bring them back here in order that they may keep an important appointment. And finally, four: what is in this vial, which was all you carried other than your knife and a length of rope?"

The elixir! De Marigny gasped involuntarily as his questioner mentioned Atal's elixir. He had forgotten about the vial until now. The horned one heard the dreamer's gasp and was quick to note how his eyes had widened fractionally, however momentarily. "Eh?" he grunted. "Something I said? About this strange little bottle of liquid, perhaps?" He held the vial out, between thumb and forefinger, where de Marigny could see it.

"A man, with no food, no water, coming out of nowhere with nothing but a knife, a rope, and this—and yet you somehow succeeded in rescuing your two friends. Amazing! And such a little thing, this vial, to sustain the three of you across the desert to Ulthar. What does it contain?"

De Marigny's brain whirled as he sought an advantageous way to answer the horned one's question. "A . . . a *poison*," he finally offered. "It contains a deadly poison."

His questioner lifted his scimitar, allowing its point to scrape slowly up the line of de Marigny ribs, and peered intently at its shiny blade. For a long moment he was silent, then: "Oh, no, no, no, my friend." His voice was low now, oily, deadly; his eyes glittered dangerously. "That will never do. A little vial of poison—no more than a dozen or so drops—to murder an entire city?"

De Marigny writhed both physically and mentally, like a great intelligent moth pinned to some entomologist's card. He had hoped that his interrogator would make him drink his own "poison"—which by now should have properly fermented—but the ruse had not worked. Then, like a flash of lightning illuminating the dark clouds of the dreamer's mind, there came a scene remembered from his youth. From a book, perhaps, or a cartoon viewed in some movie house of childhood. It was the picture of a rabbit: Br'er Rabbit! And suddenly de Marigny believed that there might after all be a way out. He could but try.

"If I tell you what is in the vial—if I reveal the secret of the magical potion it contains—will you swear to set me free unharmed?"

The horned one pretended to give de Marigny's proposal some consideration, fooling the dreamer not at all, then grated: "Agreed. After all, it is not you we want but the two you stole from us. If what you have to tell us has some bearing on their present whereabouts, then we will set you free."

Now it was de Marigny's turn to feign deliberation. Finally he said, "It is an elixir to increase one's strength tenfold. One sip of the potion—one drop—and a man may leap the tallest dune at one bound, stride over the desert to Ulthar in the space of a single hour, fight like ten men to overcome tremendous odds, aye, and never once feel the effort."

The horned one folded the vial carefully in his fat fist and stared at de Marigny intently. "Is this true?"

"How else do you suppose I came out of the night, without provisions, defeating your three guardsmen like so many children to be tossed aside? How else do you explain the utter absence of the two I rescued, gone now like the wind over the desert? Doubtless they are even now in Ulthar, at the Temple of the Elder Ones, where Atal—"

"*Atal!*" hissed his interrogator. "What do you know of Atal?"

"Why, it was Atal gave me the elixir, to speed me on my quest!"

A murmuring swelled in the crowed of horned ones standing about, mutterings of hatred, of awe and amazement—of greed for the magic elixir, if elixir it was. Now de Marigny's questioner opened his fist once more to stare lustfully at the tiny bottle it contained. Then his expression grew very sly.

"No, I do not believe you. I think that after all it is perhaps a poison, and that you would trick me into tasting it. If so, then—" He quickly unstoppered the vial and thrust it toward de Marigny's face. The dreamer, expecting that this might happen, lifted up his head and opened his mouth wide, straining his neck to reach the tiny bottle.

Immediately the horned one snatched back his arm. He grinned evilly. "So your story *is* true! It . . . must be." His grin was quickly replaced by a look of strange anticipation. He licked his wide lips and his hand actually trembled as once more he studied the vial with wide eyes.

"Let me try it, Garl," came a guttural rasp from one who stood behind the leader.

"No, me," another voice demanded.

"Hold!" Garl held up his hand. "There is still one question unanswered." He turned his gaze once more to de Marigny's face. "If indeed you tell the truth, how was it we caught you so easily? Why did you not escape, like your friends, by leaping away over the dunes and speeding to Ulthar?"

"Simple." De Marigny attempted to shrug as best he could. "I neglected to heed Atal's warning."

"Which was?"

"Too much of the elixir affects a man like too much wine, slowing him down and dulling his senses for a while. After freeing the other two dreamers, thinking to make myself stronger and faster still, I took a second sip of the elixir. Before I knew it—"

"We caught you. Hmm! I believe you, yes. And I also believe that with the aid of your elixir we might even recapture the ones you freed. But first the elixir's powers must be tested."

"I'll test it, Garl," came a concerted babble of cries from the crowding horned ones.

"Me!"

"No, let me be the one, Garl!"

De Marigny's inquisitor turned on his colleagues. "What? You'd all like to be stronger than Garl, would you?" He laughed and shook a fat finger at them. "None of that, my lads. The elixir is far to precious to waste on fools and hotheads. Later, perhaps, I'll handpick a raiding party—and tonight we'll look for certain absent friends in Ulthar—but right now I myself will test the illustrious Atal's elixir! Stand back, all of you!"

Though the sun blazed high overhead, it was not the heat of that golden orb that brought fresh streams of sweat to de Marigny's brow but the slow and deliberate way in which Garl of Leng lifted one hand up to his alien face—that and the way his other hand lifted high his scimitar.

"If you have lied to me, dreamer, then at least you'll have earned yourself a quick death. That is the only bonus such lies will bring you, however. And now—" He barely touched his lips to the rim of the tilted vial.

First a look of puzzlement changed the horned one's features, then a frown. "A not unpleasant taste," he began, "though somewhat—" Then he reeled drunkenly backward down the dais steps, his scimitar falling with a clatter from a suddenly spastic hand that clawed its way to his throat. He swayed at the foot of the dais for a second only, bulging eyes fixed upon the vial still clenched in one shaking hand.

Then his outline wavered; he seemed to puff outwards as his flesh became a mist; finally his clothes fell in a silken rain to the cobbles of the square. The vial fell too, cushioned by the coarse silks. Hanging in the air, all that remained of Garl was a rapidly diminishing echo, a thin squeal of outrage and horror!

Then de Marigny's hoarse laughter broke the stunned silence. Hearing the derision in the dreamer's voice, the awed crowd of horned ones was galvanized into activity. As one of them stooped to snatch up the fallen vial and others fought over the remaining silks, the rest ringed de Marigny on the steps. Scimitars whispered from scabbards and flashed in the sun, and for a moment the dreamer thought that he was done for. Then —

"Hold, lads!" shouted the one who had snatched up the vial. "I, Barzt, now lead you—and I claim the right to avenge Garl myself. But first there is something I must know." He tickled de Marigny's throat with the point of his scimitar. "You, man from the waking world, dreamer. Where have you sent Garl with your dark magic?"

"He's gone to a hell worse than anything even you could imagine," de Marigny chuckled. "Worse by far than any torture you could apply to me. You see, the 'elixir' was a poison after all, the key to a gate

which opens to the blackest hells. Even now Garl screams in eternal
agony, where he will curse me in his torment forever; but I am safe
from him here in dreamland. Kill me now, if you will, for I am satisfied that Garl has paid for the deaths of my two friends from the waking world. They, too, drank of the poison rather than suffer the
indignities of your vile paws. Kill me—kill me now!" He offered up his
throat. "Only—"

De Marigny paused, as if biting his tongue, feigning sudden horror. Then, to the crowding horned ones, it seemed as if he attempted
to cringe into himself upon the dais steps. "No!" he forced a strangled
cry from parched lips. "No, not . . . not *that!*"

"Wha—?" began the frowning Barzt. Then he noticed how de
Marigny's terrified eyes had fastened upon the vial he held so gingerly
away from his vile body. And Barzt's eyes lit at once with a fiendish delight.

"So!" he cried. "Garl will curse you in his torment forever, will he?
Well then, go to this hell you speak so eloquently of, dreamer, where
you, too, may suffer its eternal torments—*and* Garl's tender mercies!"
So saying, standing on the dreamer's hair to hold his head still, he
stooped and touched the vial to de Marigny's lips.

But no sooner was the oddly shaped bottle at his lips than he
licked its moist rim with a darting tongue. Barzt sensed that he had
been fooled, but it was too late. In the space of another second or so
de Marigny seemed to fill out like a limp balloon suddenly inflated
with air, and even as his form wavered and disappeared the horned
ones noted the look of glad triumph that lit in his eyes.

And in the wake of his vanishing they heard the echoes of joyous
laughter.

Part Four

◆

I

Beyond the Peaks of Throk

Subduing his raging fury as best he could, yet totally incapable of curbing the sick feeling of horror that lay thick in his stomach like bile—horror for Tiania in the clutches of that flying beast-thing that soared somewhere ahead in the darkness over the desert—Titus Crow leaned into the wind and rode his cloak like a great bat through the night. He followed the occasional shriek from Tiania, dread draining him every time he heard her cry out, until at last he realized that she was deliberately screaming, creating a trail by means of which he could follow the flightpath of the great night-gaunt.

And it dawned on him too that, plucky girl though she was, she might save some of her breath for later—when perhaps they might both have more need of screaming. Indeed, the flight of the night-gaunt seemed arrow-straight, and Crow's instinct told him where the beast was headed. Then, as its outline momentarily obliterated a great whorl of stars hanging low in the sky ahead, he caught a glimpse of the thing and knew he had been correct. Unlike its cousins, the common gaunts, by virtue of its gigantic size, nevertheless this faceless terror of the night made for a region of dreamland where Titus Crow knew that the lesser gaunts proliferated. He put on a burst of speed to shorten, if possible, the monster's lead.

Out over the southern Sea sped the great gaunt, and far below Tiania could see all the stars of the night sky reflected in black mirror waters. Normally she would have found such a sight beautiful indeed, but now, dangling from the rubbery paws of this clammy creature as it soared silently through the upper air of dreamland, she shuddered and cried out yet again. She knew that Titus Crow must be some-where behind the great night-gaunt, knew too that her cries must eventually guide him to her; for while the gaunt could not fly on for-ever, Crow's cloak was utterly tireless.

Behind her now, Tiania could make out the dim lights of small towns spread along the coast of the southern sea, and briefly from far below there came drifting the song of a lone fisherman at the helm of his night-becalmed vessel. Doubtless he was singing to ward off the dark spirits of the night waters, which legend had it walked on the glassy surface of the deep when the nights were calm.

Then, far to the east, Tiania saw the first thin gray line of light curving on the distant horizon. True dawn was still hours away, but the promise of a new day was already aborning. She wondered what the new day would bring, and she thought with longing of faerie Elysia, many dimensions away in space and time. Love of Elysia was strong in Tiania, but love of Titus Crow was stronger. Though she was no longer afraid, she cried out yet again in the darkness, praying that her voice would ride back to her Earthman on the night wind. He would not an-swer, dared not alert the monstrous creature that carried her high above the Southern Sea of his presence, but as certain to Tiania as the beating of her own pure heart was the knowledge that he was there.

Thus the hours sped by, until chilled and weary, utterly depleted by her adventures, the girl-goddess fell asleep in the grip of the great gaunt. And perhaps fate smiled at Tiania in her innocence, for a warm wind from far exotic lands found her there where she lay between the night-gaunt's clammy paws, lulling her into dreams within dreams which were not at all nightmarish.

Titus Crow, too, saw the thin gray light on the horizon, and he urged still more speed from his cloak and streamlined himself to cleave the air more cleanly. He believed that with the dawn the huge night-gaunt would find a cave or crevice in which to sleep and while away the hours of daylight, like less fabulous nocturnal beasts of the waking world. And he wanted to be in view of the creature when it went to ground.

For some time now he had listened intently for Tiania's cries com-ing back to him on the wind, but in vain, and while he was fairly cer-tain of the direction in which the great gaunt headed, nevertheless he would dearly love to hear the girl's golden voice confirming his guess. Then, as dawn turned the horizon into a gray mist, he spied the vapor-wreathed Isle of Oriab ahead, and against the pale of dawn a nightmare shape that fell down and down toward far Ngranek.

Crow's spirits immediately revived. He had been right, then. The great gaunt's destination was indeed Ngranek, haunt of all the lesser gaunts of night. Now he flew more carefully, keeping his presence secret, for he was closer to the monster than he had dared hope. Down toward Ngranek's peak spiraled the gaunt, with Titus Crow behind it, down toward the mouths of certain caves that opened to the cavernously honeycombed interior of that mountain.

Now Crow could see the strange face cut in vast outlines on that side of the peak forever hidden to Oriab's peoples, the face carved more in the likeness of a strange god than a man. And looking down from on high he saw far beneath those carven features the sterile lava abysses which marked the wrath of the Great Gods of Eld . . . even here in Earth's dreamland! Now, seeing for himself this proof positive of a mighty battle long forgotten and beyond the meager imagination of men, he knew indeed that Ngranek was a peak ancient beyond words.

But Titus Crow had little enough time to study these things or ponder their import. He had seen the great gaunt settling on high-arched wings toward a black cave mouth, and now he flew his cloak as swiftly as he could in that direction. Around and about this cavern entrance flew a flock of lesser gaunts in apparently aimless circles, and for all that they were more than twice the size of a man they scattered in terror as Crow hurtled through their midst. Then, after he had passed by, they hung in the brightening dawn air in sleepy, faceless bewilderment. And down, down into Ngranek's inner darkness went Titus Crow, flying blind now and of necessity more slowly, following only the muffled throb of vast and leathery wings.

It seemed to the cloaked dreamer that he flitted down through inconceivable gulfs of night; but then, as his eyes grew more accustomed to the gloom, he saw that the dark air was semiluminous with a gray phosphorescence. Moments later he descended into reeking clouds of mist that may well have had their origin in Earth's core.

And now, high above, a monstrously vast ceiling of stalactites stretched away into dim distances, while below marched the ominous needles of spires which could only be the fabulous Peaks of Throk.

Down and down, ever deeper the cloak carried Crow into this under-world of dream, until the stark gray Peaks of Throk reached up im-mense and ageless on all sides. And then the needle tips of those peaks were lost in legendary heights and their feet in darkest depths, so that it seemed to the dreamer he fell between numberless pillars going down to infinity. And always he followed the throb of tremen-dous, rubbery wings.

Then, for what seemed an interminable time, there came buffet-ing, howling winds that blew Crow far off course; and struggle as he might against this unexpected maelstrom of air, he could do nothing but pray that he would not be hurled against the granite pillars that loomed on all sides. Now, too, he found his view obscured by clouds of sulphurous ash and smoke; but at last the winds calmed down, the smoke cleared, and far away the dreamer saw the Peaks of Throk re-ceding into flickering, pale-blue death-fires. Then there was only dark-ness and a distant, weary-sounding throbbing of monstrous wings.

Knowing that by now he could only be in the fabled Vale of Pnoth, where the enormous dholes dig their burrows and pile their cairns of bones, Crow felt something of the unreasoning terror that all dream-ers know in the face of nightmare. For this was that place where all the ghouls of the waking world are reputed to throw the remains of their graveyard feasts. Titus Crow desired to meet neither ghouls nor dholes, and so he put on a burst of speed in the direction of the now fading throbbing.

Again he was flying blind, in near-solid darkness, but his instinct did not desert him; and as he rushed through reeking ebony vaults he reminded himself over and over again that many things are far sim-pler in dream. But then he uttered a short, harsh sardonic bark of self-derision as he wondered why, if this were really so, he was finding things so difficult!

Beneath him now as he flew he could hear a dry rustling, which he guessed must be the sound that dholes make in their singular bone-heaping occupations; and once he brushed against something that loomed up vast and slimy in his path. Then ahead he saw a bright point of light that soon grew into a painful white glare. Approaching the source of this harsh illumination, he saw that it was a natural cave that led back into the face of a sheer wall of granite. A moment later a great gray shadow flitted eerily and silently along the path of white light to disappear into the cave beyond.

Titus Crow's mechanical heart seemed to give a great leap within him then, for at the last he had seen a limp, slender form hanging from the shadow's tiredly drooping paws! Now, reassuring himself, he fondled the hilt of his scimitar where it hung from the belt of his cloak's harness, and he allowed himself a low grunt of grim anticipation as he drove for the bright cave's entrance.

It was then, as he entered into a tremendously vast white cavern, that the disaster occurred. Fortunately for Titus Crow the thing came immediately after he cleared the cave's entrance, when he was flying only a few feet above the white sands that floored the fantastic cavern. If he had been at a greater height . . . it did not bear thinking about.

For without warning his cloak suddenly disappeared, vanishing utterly and without trace in an instant, leaving him prone in thin air, diving forward in a downward curve that could only end in the white sand! A second later came the shock of impact and momentary oblivion, then painful consciousness. He spat out sand and picked himself up; shaken and awed, he stared all about. The cloak had quite definitely vanished, so useless to worry or wonder about the hows or whys of it—and anyway there were other, more important things to think about.

Staring across the desert of white sand, Crow's eyes narrowed as he picked out a vague movement in the middle distance. Instinct warned him that there were terrible dangers here, for himself as well as the girl-goddess, and if Tiania of Elysia was to be rescued unharmed from this unknown place, then he must face those dangers alone, naked and on foot . . .

II

Perchance to Dream

De Marigny came joyously awake in the time-clock, whirling in orbit high above the Earth. His awakening was instantaneous, without any of the usual transitory dullness of mind and physical sloth, so that he immediately remembered all that had happened. Indeed, his *removal* from dreamland to the waking world was so complete that its effect upon his senses was more a physical than a purely mental thing; for a few moments he felt that his body as well as his mind had been transported. Then the truth of the matter sank in, and as his somewhat shaky laughter terminated in a ringing shout of triumph, he realized that his ploy against the horned ones in Dylath-Leen had been completely successful.

It was only when this initial euphoria began to wear off that de Marigny saw the several rather less than pleasing circumstances of his escape. One: he was wearing the flying cloak, which could only mean that Titus Crow no longer wore it. Then he remembered what Atal had told him about the elixir—how one sip would immediately transport a dreamer back to the waking world, *along with anything he had brought into dreamland with him!* Knowing that in all likelihood Titus Crow depended upon the cloak for his own and Tiania's lives, de Marigny found this last train of thought too unpleasant to follow up. Instead he turned to problem number two: his main reason for wanting to wake up had been to return at once to dreamland, this time taking the time-clock with him. How might he do this now, when he had never felt more fully awake in his entire life?

Now, furious that everything he did seemed to be working out adversely, he cursed himself soundly. Atal's elixir, as far as Henri-Laurent de Marigny was concerned, had performed its function marvelously—but its effect now was that of a strong stimulant, and there seemed no guarantee at all that this effect would soon wear off. He cursed himself again. Of course, it could hardly have been foreseen, but it would have been so simple to ask Atal for something, some drug or "potion" with which he might return himself to dreamland.

Then de Marigny's eyes lit with inspiration and he snapped his fingers. A drug to return him to dreamland? Why, he knew of something that could do the job admirably. Alcohol!

He was not a great drinker, but he did enjoy a glass of brandy. A double invariably quickened his mind. Another, taken immediately after the first, usually made him tingle. A third would dull his senses considerably, and a fourth—

Half a bottle should see him back to dreamland almost as quickly as he could drink it! One of his few, hasty, last-minute provisions prior to setting out for Elysia had been to load the time-clock with three bottles of the very best cognac. These had been for Titus Crow, for good brandies were Crow's one weakness. Now he opened one of the bottles and took a long, deep draft, coughing and spluttering as the first 'bite' of the fluid inflamed his throat. Crow, he knew, would have called him a barbarian; but doubtless he would also have agreed that the deadly serious nature of the situation demanded a rapid solution, however drastic.

Halfway through the bottle, de Marigny felt his head begin to spin quite independently of the whirling timeclock (the motion of which, impossibly, he was beginning to believe he could now actually feel) and suddenly he found himself incapable of repressing a short burst of uproarious laughter. Also, a haze was definitely creeping over his brain, but much too slowly. He took another mouthful of the warming, heady fluid, and yet another. Then as he removed the bottle from his lips, he staggered.

Now, he knew that it was quite impossible for him to physically stagger inside the clock. While Titus Crow could use the machine both as a gateway into all space and time and as a vehicle proper, de Marigny simply was not yet adept enough for that. Indeed, his one effort in that direction had been completely involuntary, almost disastrous. Therefore he recognized the fact, however vaguely, that he had "staggered" mentally. In short, he knew now that he was very nearly drunk.

By this time only an inch or so of brandy remained in the bottle. De Marigny peered at it curiously for a moment, swilled it about—then yawned. No more than twenty minutes had elapsed since he started on his solitary binge, but he grinned lopsidedly and began to sing, finishing the bottle off between repeated bursts of the following four lines:

> *"Oh, carry me back to dreamland,*
> *That's the way to go, to go.*
> *Carry me back to dreamland,*
> *You space-time so-and so!"*

The minutes passed steadily and de Marigny's singing occasionally faltered, picking up intermittently as he struggled to keep the song going. Finally the bottle slipped from his fingers—but he was not aware of it.

Outside the clock, had there been someone to observe it, it would at that moment seem that the stars themselves blurred, if only for a moment, and that the disc of Earth trembled in its inexorable orbit of the mighty solar furnace. It might seem, for a moment, that the entire scene were viewed through smoke or warm, rising air—and that then, in the next instant, things were once more as they had always been.

But they were not . . .

III

Creatures of the Cave

White crystal sands shifted beneath Titus Crow's naked feet. He stood under a great white roof that formed a sky reflecting the whiteness of the desert. And the floor of the vast cavern surely was a desert. Miles of bleached sand stretched to the limits of vision in dunes and hills, and the only relief in this blinding monotony was a dark dot moving in the middle distance.

The dreamer had no idea where the blinding light of the place came from—that brightness which so garishly illumined every feature of what ought to have been one of the underworld's blackest pits—but in any case he was far more concerned about other things. One of those things, the one uppermost in his mind, was the agitated motion of the distant dot.

He found his scimitar where it had fallen from the belt of his disappearing cloak, then turned to face in the direction of the peculiar movements. He watched the disturbance grow with a startling swiftness. Soon the single moving shape split amoeba-like into two—one up and one down—and in only a few seconds more the two took on definite forms. Spiraling up from the lower form he could see regular white puffs of sand.

The hairs at the back of Titus Crow's neck suddenly stiffened. At first he had thought that the moving object must be that great gaunt which had carried off Tiania; now he could see how wrong he had been. There were in fact three—creatures? One flew, the second rode upon the Flyer's back, the third ran beneath . . . and all three were things of sheerest nightmare!

Of the three as they drew closer, Crow found the tripedal Runner the most fantastic. Though its two outer legs were thin and bent like those of some monstrous spider, nevertheless they were powerfully muscled; they acted as springs or pistons. The inner or center leg was three times as thick as the other two together, straight and horribly hammerlike. The Runner looked like a great freakish three-legged race, with its center leg slamming forward and down, to be hoisted up again and thrust forward by the springy power of its twin companions. The—foot?—at the end of that middle limb was awesome: hugely splayed and webbed, as wide at least as any ten normal feet, clublike. Why! That great foot would crush muscle and bone to pulp as easily and utterly as would a falling northern pine!

Tall though Crow was, the Runner stood at least half as tall again. It had short, stumpy arms—useless appendages to Crow's keen eyes—and a slender neck. But the *face* above that neck! The dreamer shuddered. He had seen similar things in nightmares as a boy; the red, bulging eyes, the dripping fangs in grinning, wide-slit mouths . . .

By now the creatures were much closer and slowing their pace, but still eagerly craning their necks in Crow's direction, obviously appraising him before a concerted attack. The Runner uttered a hideous cry—like the rasp of a file upon an edge of glass, or a giant chalk on a slate—before moving off to one side from beneath the Flyer and its Rider. Crow did not have to turn to follow the creature's movements; the thudding vibrations of the sand under his feet positioned the Runner exactly in his mind's eye. Instead he concentrated upon the other two.

The Flyer was a monstrous, slender worm, with no eyes that Titus Crow could see, just undulant body and gaping beak. Yet, somehow he knew that the thing sensed him keenly and knew of him as he knew of it. The Rider, seated to the rear of the bat-worm's wings, was worse still. A skull-like head set with glaring green eyes surmounted a thin and wiry body, scaled and mottled in squamous shades, with arms of fantastic length hanging like coiled whips at its sides.

Studying these beings of nightmare Crow tightened his grip on his sword. He was aware of their subtle, edging approach. He would have preferred them to come on at their original headlong pace, when he would have relied upon the superb reactions built into his semisynthetic body by the robot T3RE, but they had seemed to sense his tremendous speed and strength and were wary. Indeed, Crow's strength had returned, and now it redoubled as he reconciled himself to battle. It seemed that this was to be the only way he could get on with his pursuit of the great gaunt and Tiania: first, to do battle with these three creatures of the white cavern.

The Flyer and its Rider were still twenty feet or so from the dreamer when he had his first taste of the fight to come. The Rider took first blood when, catching Crow off guard, a razor-clawed tentacle lashed out like the tongue of a chameleon, cutting his cheek. The cut almost touched his eye and caused him to cry out in outrage at the unexpected pain. The tentacle was withdrawn well out of range before he could even bring his scimitar into the defensive position.

Instantly, at sight of the red blood on Crow's cheek, the Rider began to laugh: "*Rhee, rheee, rheee-eee-eee!*" And as the hair of Crow's neck again reacted to this hellish sound, so he sensed the rapid approach of the Runner—from the rear!

Second blood, with a lightning stroke of the scimitar, went to the embattled dreamer. For having perceived the Runner's cowardly rear attack through the shuddering of the sand underfoot, Titus Crow turned and made a headlong dive to one side. And as the Runner pounded by mere inches away, so the scimitar leaped up in Crow's hand to sever at the knee the creature's right outer leg.

The rest of the fight was chaos and nightmare combined. All three of the hideous guardians of the cavern were screaming, particularly the pain-crazed, crippled Runner. The latter was now slewing mindlessly about on its own axis in a welter of gray ichor and white sand. Half blinded by his own blood and that of the Runner, Crow flailed about with his sword, knowing from the deafening cries of the Flyer and its razor-tentacled rider that they were near at hand. He felt his sword arm suddenly caught in a tentacular grip and wrenched at an odd angle, felt the scimitar fly from fingers part-numbed as his forearm almost broke. And then he took his strong square teeth savagely to work on the slimy tentacle coiled crushingly round his arm.

With his free arm he protected his head, all the time working at the tentacle with his teeth and feeling upon his shoulders and back the agony of ripping cuts from the Rider's second vicious appendage. But suddenly, as his mouth filled with a vile fluid from the rubbery limb, he felt himself jerked off his feet and dashed down in the sand. The movement had been convulsive and he guessed that his teeth had found a ticklish nerve. But he had lost his sword.

Free now, he rolled automatically—feeling the burning sting of sand in his torn back, groping for his sword, not knowing where or even in which direction it lay—until his hand came into contact with something solid. He clenched his fingers about the unknown object and rolled onto his back.

There, immediately above him, lancing down, came the vicious beak of the blind Flyer. Just how the awesome bat-worm knew his exact position he could never have guessed, and he had no time for guessing. He jerked up the object grasped in his hand and thrust it between himself and the descending beak. He saw then that his shield was nothing less than the shorn leg of the Runner, which the Flyer at once tore from his grasp and tossed to one side.

Yet, even as Crow gave up his gristly shield he came to his feet, swinging one fist in a deadly arc to smack shatteringly against the side of the lunging beak. The "bones" of Crow's arms and hands were shaped mainly of an incredibly tough plastic, but the bat-worm's beak, however effective as a weapon, was only of shell-like bone. That great beak cracked open like a hammered egg, and marrow and yellow juices slopped out to further drench the bloodied dreamer.

The Flyer went mad then, shrieking in its excruciating agony, worm-body coiling and whipping, flinging its harshly gibbering Rider down onto the white sand. Crow had but a second to collect his scattered senses as the dazed and suddenly silenced Rider climbed to its feet, but in that second he saw his sword sticking pommel-up from a patch of slimed sand.

The weapon lay directly in the path of the Runner, which was again heading, in an erratic and lumbering fashion, for the gorespattered dreamer. Crow saw the thing's approach as a last desperate effort to bring him down before the seepage of its vile life's juices stilled it forever; he saw, too, the possible destruction of his sword beneath that lopsidedly pounding hammer-leg.

Without the scimitar he was done for, and so he hurled himself frantically across the sand, fingers stretched wide and reaching. Even as his hand grasped the hilt of the curving sword, Crow knew he had run out of time. The huge, pounding leg of the Runner was already in the air, its own thrust compensating for the missing outer member. Down came that great hammer toward his head—and then, a miracle!

With a bubbling shriek something shot over Crow's spread-eagled body on tortured wings to smack blindly into the towering Runner. Bat-worm and Runner alike crashed down onto the sand as Crow rose with the scimitar in his hand, unable to believe that he still lived. The Runner lay there—mad fangs gnashing in its hideous face, its remaining outer leg limp but its hammer continuing to pound away at the air—and the half-crippled Flyer flopped mindlessly about on the sand, its fractured beak dripping evil-smelling liquid.

The dreamer knew suddenly the means by which that bat-worm had known his whereabouts during the fight. The thing had somehow been guided by its Rider—that Rider which held the reins *in its mind* rather than in its hand! The two had existed in a weird symbiosis. But now, without its Rider, the Flyer was truly blind! No wonder the tentacled Rider was even now crying out harshly to the wounded monster, trying the while to climb once more onto its back.

"To hell with that!" Crow roared, leaping forward to swing his sword in an awesome blow that cut into and through the neck of the bat-worm, sending its evil head flying to spatter the already fouled sand. Yet again the half-mounted Rider fell as the body of his beast-brother commenced its last, convulsive spasm and fell to sprawl on the white sand beside the now motionless Runner.

And now the Rider saw that he was indeed on his own. With an alien cry of rage and hatred he sprang to his feet, uncoiling his tentacular arms, drawing them back whiplike onto the sand behind him. Crow knew that in another moment those viciously claw-tipped weapons would be at him; his superb reactions took over almost unbidden. In one lithe movement he leaned forward, throwing the scimitar like a knife straight at the Rider's black heart.

The point ran home and the weight of the curving blade carried it through the Rider's thin body. Surprise grew like a pale stain on the creature's face, then his tentacular arms wrapped themselves spastically around the length of his body, head to toe. The hideous form trembled violently for a moment and gave one final shriek of hatred and frustration before falling slowly over backward onto the churned and stained sand. In a count of ten, bar the dreamer's hoarse shout of triumph, the white cavern was still again and silent.

For a few seconds more Titus Crow swayed over the bodies of the defeated trio, every flesh-and-blood muscle in his body aching and his arms like lead. Then he lifted his eyes to peer undaunted across the white waste. Somewhere here, somewhere in this glaring white nightmare, Tiania of Elysia was even now in dire need of him.

He had not a moment to spare.

IV

The Clock in Flames!

Three hours had elapsed in Dylath-Leen since Henri-Laurent de
Marigny's disappearance from the dais of the ruby. During the interval there had been some little turmoil in the city. Barzt, the new, self-
appointed leader of the horned ones, had himself very recently been
removed from power. His position had been disputed; a fight with
knives had decided the matter positively in favor of his opponent.
That opponent, Eriff, now licked his wounds and supped muth-dew
with his cronies in a rotting tavern near the seafront.

There was much for Eriff to consider now that he was a leader; a
good deal of thinking—an art for which he had no great aptitude—
was required. He was uncertain now, for example, whether or not his
usurping of Barzt's pretensions to leadership of the horned ones had
been a wise move. Nyarlathotep was coming to Dylath-Leen, expecting to interrogate (whatever form such interrogation might take) the
man and woman of the waking world. That prize pair, however, were
no longer here. Even the unknown dreamer who freed them had
made his escape, albeit into oblivion. On top of all this, disturbing reports were beginning to reach the horned ones in their basalt city, reports hinting that the insidious incursions of their agents into the
healthier cities of dreamland were being inexplicably checked, particularly in Ulthar, which had been their next objective.

No, Eriff was not at all happy with the situation, and what little he
knew of Nyarlathotep only went to increase his apprehension. Perhaps it were better, he was beginning to reason, that the ancient com-
pact between the horned ones of Leng and the prisoned Great Old
Ones of the Cthulhu Cycle had never been. Better, perhaps, if all of
Dylath-Leen's horned ones now took to their black galleys and sailed
away across the Southern Sea. Better for Eriff, certainly; for what had
he now to offer that mighty emissary of Cthulhu, the dread
Nyarlathotep? Utterly emptyhanded, how might he greet the Great
Messenger?

So Eriff grumbled over his muth-dew and nursed his bruises and
cuts. And this was the brooding, pensive mood he was in when they

came from the square of the great ruby to find him, bringing him the news that even now a strange, silent, enigmatic visitor stood in Dylath-Leen's central square on the cobbles opposite the ruby dais. The thing, they said, was tall and oddly figured, like a mummycase of olden Ohlmi. Of wood or a material like wood, it was very heavy and hard, and in its upper part four hands swung about a common center in wholly inexplicable motions. Would Eriff not come and say what must be done with this object, which had appeared as if from thin air?

In the heat of the afternoon Eriff left his cool drink and made his way with his retinue of cronies painfully to the square of the ruby dais. And it was just as he had heard it: there, facing the dais almost as if it scrutinized the monstrous ruby atop the basalt steps, stood the unknown object from another world. Eriff, for all his ignorance, saw one thing immediately: that indeed this thing was not fashioned of dreamland's skills. Staring at the time-clock, his unnatural features quickly took on a cautious, a suspicious look.

How did this thing get here? What was it? Why was it here in the square of the ruby? He had been told that it was of wood, and certainly it appeared to be. Well then, why take chances?

"Either carry it away, out of the city, or burn it!" he ordered. "Use old timbers, doors, and furniture from the city's houses. Build a pyre for the thing, whatever it is. I don't like it . . ."

"But Eriff, it appears to be a box of some sort!" one of his brothers protested.

"And what's inside it?" he asked.

"We don't know, but——"

"And can you open it?"

"Not yet, but——"

"Then burn it and be on the safe side!"

And so a pyre was built around the time-clock, of furniture from the old uninhabited houses and timbers from other habitations long fallen into ruin; and when the time-clock was completely obscured from view by the flammable materials thus heaped about it, then torches were brought and the fire lighted.

Within the clock, whose shell was impervious to all but the most incredible temperatures and pressures, in an indeterminate limbo which might best be described as the place where all the "corners" of space and time meet, Henri-Laurent de Marigny was ill. He was as drunk, more drunk than at any previous time in his entire life. That is not to say that he had never before consumed a whole bottle of brandy—he had, but in a civilized manner. Never in such barbarous haste!

And yet he knew that he had a mission . . . if only this dark universe would stop revolving long enough to allow him to remember what that mission was! It had to do with Titus Crow, and it had to do with Tiania . . . And with the time-clock.

The time-clock! De Marigny's mind fastened avidly upon that concept.

Time-clock! Of course! He was *inside* that peculiar device, that space-time vehicle, right now—in a warm womb between the worlds. He had only to reach out his mind, and—but that would be too much of an effort. It would be better simply to fight the flooding nausea within himself, the sickening spinning and whirling of vast black voids within and without him. Oh, yes—much better to sleep until the alcohol had burned itself out of his system.

Alcohol?

Sleep . . . ?

Alarm bells clamored distantly in de Marigny's inner being. Alcohol—sleep—*dream!* That had been his mission: to sleep and to dream. And he had slept, he knew that. Why, then, was he not dreaming?

The answer was obvious: he was not dreaming because as he had fallen drunkenly asleep he had released his mental contact with the time-clock. Where was the clock now? Had he in fact managed to pilot his fantastic vehicle to the desired destination?

Now he put himself to the effort so recently rejected, meshing his besotted mind with that of his machine—and instantly the scanners opened in his mind's eye.

An inferno—all the fires of hell blazing about the clock—the inner cone of some primeval volcano during an eruption—the fiery surface of the solar orb itself! *Where the devil was he?*

Panic clawed momentarily at de Marigny's insides as he instinctively threw up his arms to ward off the heat that he knew could never penetrate the clock's shell. Then, fleetingly through the flame and smoke, he glimpsed the ruby dais and the horned figures that cavorted around the bonfire in demoniac glee, and he knew where he was. He was back in Dylath-Leen, in Earth's dreamland. Now too, however drunkenly, he remembered what had gone before.

Then, fighting to hold the time-clock's scanners steady in his staggering mind, de Marigny attempted to focus his blurred thoughts on the horned ones, on their present activity. What were they doing now, these wide-mouthed monsters? Plainly, they were trying to burn the time-clock! Anger began to expand within de Marigny's breast. He glared at the creatures from Leng with a fiery hatred that burned in his veins to match the heat of the brandy.

These vile inhabitants of the forbidden plateau had perpetrated enough horrors in the lands of Earth's dreams. They, or their fathers before them, had brought down Dylath-Leen in the first place; they were responsible for the dissemination of much that was abominable in dreamland; they were the foul sores of Man's subconscious, in league with the Powers of Darkness, particularly with the prisoned Cthulhu spawn of the waking world. And on top of all this they had recently humiliated Titus Crow, Tiania, even de Marigny himself.

Tiania they would have violated—unthinkably. Crow would have been put to terrible tortures; indeed, de Marigny's friends would eventually have been handed over to Nyarlathotep, the Great Messenger of the CCD. And here in dreamland Nyarlathotep had been given monstrous form by the massed telepathic sendings of his immemorial masters. The more the dreamer's foggy mind dwelled on the CCD—and on the horned ones, their minions in dreamland—the more angry he became. And now those minions were trying to burn the time-clock, with de Marigny inside it!

His anger suddenly boiled over into a rage that drove back his alcoholic nausea and brought him into awesome action. It was high time these Leng-spawned horrors were taught a lesson, and one that would not be quickly forgotten . . .

V

Weapon from the Waking World

It was, of course, the habit of the horned ones of Leng—who were cannibals whenever the opportunity to eat the flesh of sentient beings presented itself—to leap and dance about their ritual fires. In this way in ages long lost they had thought to propitiate the elemental spirits. Therefore, the knowledge that an enemy—a thing alien to their monstrous conception of normalcy, in the shape of the time-clock—was burning in the center of their bonfire was sufficient to set them dancing. Had they been roasting a man, then they would have leaped in time to his screaming, invoking the spirits of the feast. In the case of the clock, they danced to thank the spirits of their fathers, which had delivered this enemy unto them.

Eriff, lightly wounded in his fight with the unfortunate Barzt, sat on the steps of the ruby dais and clapped his hands, accompanying the musicians who rattled chalk-dry crotala and played upon whining flutes. All the while, other horned ones darted in and out between the encircling dancers, feeding the flames with the looted furniture of olden Dylath-Leen.

Then there was an astounding occurrence: the strange, coffin-shaped object at the fire's core started to spin, fanning the flames of the fire outward.

Instantly the dancers backed away, the dreadful cacophony of the musicians faded, and Eriff stopped his clapping to stand up on the dais steps, his too-wide mouth falling open and his slanted eyes bugging. Faster the time-clock whirled, until a wind began to roar outward from it that hurled blazing brands in all directions. Now the horned ones broke and scattered, screaming and gibbering, many of them beating frantically at themselves as their coarse silken clothes caught fire.

And up rose the spinning clock from the blackened cobbles, the winds of its whirling bowling over the fleeing horned ones, hurling great timbers about like straws, its shrieking voice that of the storm-demon and its wild gyrations increasing from moment to moment. Then, high above the square, it tilted, seeming to aim itself directly at the basalt dais—at the massive ruby!

Finally Eriff, recovering his slow wits, made to flee from the steps of the dais—but too late. Such was the speed of the clock as it drilled down through tortured air to slam into, *through* the splintering jewel, that for a second it seemed simply to elongate itself.

Eriff was shredded as he tried to run from the steps, blasted into crimson pieces by the bombburst of ruby fragments; and the clock drove on, wildly slewing to one side, tearing a great hole in one of the square's buildings before coming to a shuddering halt in the debris. For a moment or two there was silence in the square of the dais.

Within the clock de Marigny fought down the rising tide of nausea within him, a sickness born not only of his alcoholic condition but also of the devastation he had wrought in the space of the last few seconds. For of course he had seen the results of his great anger, and drunk or sober such slaughter was not to de Marigny's liking. Not now that his original passion of rage was dying down. It was one thing to do away with such as the three who had so direly threatened Titus Crow and Tiania when they were tied to the dais steps, even coldbloodedly, but quite another to go unaffected by the scene in the square as it was now.

Corpses literally littered the smeared and slimed cobbles, many of them with limbs missing, torn like Eriff in the explosion of ruby shards; others lay in smoldering rags or trapped beneath still-burning timbers. And there were some who still lived, crawling across the square, mewling dementedly both in fear and in the agony of their wounds . . .

Finally, shakily, de Marigny took control of the clock once more, freeing it from the rubble of the collapsed wall and turning it toward the now empty dais. As he did so he saw several of the horned ones, apparently unharmed, climbing to their feet and backing away in utmost horror from the center of the square. At first he could not make out what it was that they so patently feared. It was not de Marigny's coffin-shaped weapon from the waking world; indeed, they appeared to be ignoring the time-clock completely. Then—

There atop the dais steps, shimmering faintly in the cleansing sunlight, a shape gathered. Even as he focused the clock's scanners upon the thing, its form began to solidify, its outline to fill in. And at last de Marigny knew what the thing was.

The Fly-The-Light from Yuggoth on the Rim—a vampire molded of the malignity of the Cthulhu Cycle Deities themselves—a thing of *Their* manufacture! In shattering the great ruby, he had freed the demon from that multifaceted prison, loosing it for the second time upon Dylath-Leen . . . except that this time the sunlight poured down upon it from a clear mid-afternoon sky, the blessed light from which it must either flee or die!

De Marigny saw the horror, but still could hardly believe his own eyes. He remembered Grant Enderby's ambiguous description and

knew now why the man had phrased it so. For how might one describe this monster except as Enderby had described it? Blind and yet
all-seeing—limbless and yet mobile as some vast, mercurial amoeba—
with poisonous mouths that gaped and drooled in its bubbling mass!
The only thing Enderby had left out of his tale was the thing's size. It
was *huge!*

And it was screaming—shrieking and writhing in agony under the
rays of the sun—melting and shrinking visibly as great black clouds of
smoke poured from it. Then it "saw" the half-dozen or so horned ones
that cringed sway from it as they tried to slink unseen from the
square. And it was just as Enderby had said: The Fly-the-Light moved
after them like flood water, pouring down the dais steps and soaking
them up in an instant. When the frantic, awful screaming had
stopped, finally the thing "saw" the time-clock.

By then its bulk was greatly reduced, despite the *sustenance* so recently and hideously derived from the six or seven horned ones, whose
bones now gleamed wetly in small heaps about the square. Black smoke
still roiled from it; its quakings were awful to watch; the screaming
sounds it made had risen so far up the sonic scale as to be almost in-
audible. And yet, when the horror suddenly made for the time-clock,
de Marigny sensed that it was far from done for. He sensed, too, that
the thing knew what the time-clock was, its fantastic function. The
vampire had purpose now, its movements were no longer hopeless; it
seemed to exude an essence of eager—anticipation!

Then an incredible suspicion set de Marigny's flesh to creeping.
What if this thing of blackest nightmare was capable of entering into
the time-clock? Suppose it could *come through* the clock's outer
shell? Titus Crow had told him that the Hounds of Tindalos could do
this quite effortlessly. Was it completely inconceivable that this thing
from the great ruby might possess the same power? De Marigny in no
way intended to put his suspicion to the test. He backed his vehicle
hurriedly away as the Fly-the-Light rushed upon him, lifting the vessel up high into the sunlight over the square in an effort to avoid contact with the horror.

He was astounded and terrified when the vampire flashed skyward after him! The thing did not recognize the restrictions of gravity!

By now it was much smaller—a pulsating fireball of greenly drool-
ing mouths that trailed a pall of foul black smoke. But it moved at a
lightning pace that de Marigny, still drunk and completely off guard,

found difficulty in matching. It was not that the clock could not out-
run the vampire, rather that the man within the clock was off guard,
by no means recovered yet from his overdose of alcohol.

Then, his dulled senses shocked into positive action, at last de
Marigny made to flee the Fly-the-Light's advances at full speed—only
to discover that the demon was not prepared to let him go! A numbness fell over his mind like an icy shroud; a great white fog obscured
his brain; and pouring from behind this awful mental mist, penetrating it, came the mind-commands of the thing from the ruby:

*"You will not flee. Stand and accept me. You have not the strength
to flee. You are weak, as all mortal creatures are weak, and I am
strong. Even now I am stronger than you but I will be mighty once
more. Therefore you must obey me. Stand—you may not flee—you
have not the strength to flee!"*

Over and over the message repeated in de Marigny's mind, and
while he was dimly aware of what was happening, still the dreadful
paralysis held him in an unbreakable embrace. This was that debilitating force with which the ruby-creature had whelmed Dylath-
Leen's peoples many years ago, the vampiric power that had drained
even Titus Crow of his strength. And now, freed from the prisoning
ruby, the former gem-dweller was concentrating that power in its last
bid for life.

The thing was depleted and quickly dying, but still the mental
sloth it generated gripped de Marigny's mind as it moved, carefully
now, toward the time-clock. And the paralyzed dreamer knew that indeed the clock would be the horror's salvation, for once inside the
weird vehicle—and as soon as its present master had been dealt
with—then the thing would be truly free to ravage among all the dark
dimensions of a limitless multiverse. That must never be.

As the horror closed with him, de Marigny groped for the clock's
controls with blunted senses. It was quite hopeless. He could find
nothing. The time-clock was completely immobilized. The Fly-the-
Light sensed this too, and thrust itself triumphantly upon its prey in
one last surge of waning strength. In that final moment, still desperately groping in vague, unfeeling abysses, de Marigny came across a
control which had absolutely nothing to do with the clock's mobility. It
was a trigger rather than a control proper, the trigger that powered a
weapon Titus Crow had brought back with him from Elysia!

De Marigny squeezed that trigger.

Instantly the alien numbness was flushed from his mind. The vampire dwindled in his scanners, dwindled and boiled as a beam of purest light flashed from the clock's dial to strike it squarely and thrust it back. The beam lengthened as it forced the shrinking horror away, until finally the dying thing was pinned by that shaft of light to the basalt dais amidst shards of shattered ruby.

There, at last, in a blaze of purest white light, the creature expired, became nothing. And still de Marigny played his weapon's beam upon the spot where it had been. Shortly the dais itself began to melt and bubble, the very basalt to run like water. Only then, when the dais was a misshapen hummock of glowing rock, did de Marigny release the mental trigger.

Wearily then, thankfully, the dreamer set the clock down in the silent, scorched square. And yet, exhausted as he now felt and still by no means sober, he remembered Titus Crow and Tiania. Indeed they were now uppermost in his thoughts. What terrors were they facing even now? And what was he doing, wasting his time here in Dylath-Leen?

He grasped his vehicle's controls with his mind and lifted it up, however tiredly, unsteadily, to the skies. But where to go? Where was Titus Crow now?

No sooner had the unspoken question passed through de Marigny's mind than the clock trembled and strained like a great hound tugging at its leash, and simultaneously a scene of startling clarity flashed upon the dreamer's inner eye. He saw Titus Crow, naked, pacing a great white sandy expanse, scimitar in hand, head hung low. The vision began to fade—but not before Crow had looked up startled, frowning and peering puzzledly about.

His face was dusted with white sand, caked at the corners of his mouth, and his weariness was plainly great. Even as the vision receded once more and vanished from de Marigny's mind, he saw Crow's lips form the question: "Henri! Is that you?"

And de Marigny *knew!*

Of course! There had always existed between the two men a strange psychic link—a connection which the time-clock had momentarily picked up and magnified. Indeed, this was how Titus Crow had found his way back to Earth from Elysia, by using de Marigny's mind as a beacon. Well, why shouldn't the method work just as well in reverse?

He released his mental grasp upon the clock's controls by all but the merest contact, then transmitted the following message to that vehicle of the Elder Gods: "You know where Crow is. He's here within my mind—within *our* minds!—and he's in trouble. It's up to you now. Go to him—*go to Titus Crow!*"

And like a great hound hearing its master's call, freed from the restraining leash, away the clock raced across the skies of dreamland . . .

VI

At the Pits of Nightmare

The white sand tugged at Titus Crow's naked feet; fine particles of white dust stung his eyes and clogged his nostrils. His scimitar seemed to weigh a ton and he felt as though he had walked a thousand miles. He allowed himself a derisive snort and cursed whichever fool had said that things were often far simpler in dreams. If that were really so, then it was high time things began working in favor of Titus Crow!

For hours now—or what seemed like hours—he had been making his way toward what looked like a continuous geyser of concentric rings of steam or vapor, rising, expanding, and dispersing high in the atmosphere of the great cave. He had first seen this phenomenon shortly after setting out across the desert and had automatically headed toward it. These distant smoke rings, rolling swiftly up at regular intervals from some unknown source, had been the only sign of life, however inorganic, in the entire cavern. His instinct told him that this was where he would find Tiania.

And at long last he had almost reached his destination. Just across a range of low dunes lay the source of these puzzling eruptions of vapor. The sand now transmitted to his naked feet a steady hammering as of massive subterranean sledges, and he saw that the rising rings of vapor soared skyward in perfect synchronization with these poundings. These were not, Crow was certain, purely natural phenomena. Then, mounting the crest, he saw how right his instinct had been.

The scene was alien and fantastic. Beyond the dunes a deep valley opened to Crow's eyes; in its center a crater, with sides of fused sand, went down like the mouth of some vast funnel into indeterminate abysses of earth. To one side of this gaping hole, from which issued the billowing smoke rings, a structure like some enormous asymmetrical birdcage stood, of intertwining metal bars half rotten with a leprous gray oxidization. Within the cage, which was open at its very top, a motley collection of dreamland's diverse peoples, men, women, and children, stood or reclined upon the sandy floor. Many of them were plainly distraught, wringing their hands and crying out in horror at their plight, beating frenziedly with bloodied hands at the metal bars of their prison. Others simply lay on the sand in attitudes of exhaustion, or sat blankly staring at nothing through eyes glazed with shock.

There were other . . . *things* . . . to be seen: the Keeper of the Cage, for instance, seated on a throne of boulders; and the great gaunt, perched now upon the Keeper's shoulder. But for the moment Crow's eyes sought elsewhere. They swept the crowded cage until finally they rested upon Tiania. And within the singular prison she was even now in danger of hideous outrage!

Two horned ones were trapped in the cage along with all the rest, and they were trying to dislodge Tiania from where she clung halfway up the cage's wall in the latticework of silver bars. They were climbing after her, laughing loudly and gutturally as they snatched at her naked feet to bring her down.

All common sense, all caution went out of Titus Crow then. Strength born of a raging bloodlust surged in his veins and the purr of his synthetic heart became a snarl deep within his chest. His cry of rage was almost animal; he saw nothing but blood—the blood of the horned ones from Leng—as he raced with all speed down the dune. He ignored utterly, as if they did not exist, the creatures that kept the cage. Skirting the crater, running like the wind, he came to the cage and put his terrible strength to bear upon the bars where they seemed most rotten. In a rending of rusted metal he was inside the cage, leaping the prostrate forms of weeping inmates and dodging the beseeching embrace of others as he raced across the sandy floor.

Another moment saw him directly beneath the horned ones who climbed after Tiania; and then, because he could not climb and carry his scimitar easily at the same time, he put down the sword and swung himself swiftly up into the framework of bars. By now the horned ones had seen him—Tiania, too.

"Be careful, Titus!" she cried.

Dodging a kick from the lower of the two horned ones, he

grabbed the creature's leg and hauled mightily. The thing from Leng gave a shriek and tried to hold on to the bars; Crow shook him like a hawk shakes its prey, tore him loose and threw him down to the floor fifty feet below. Then, hauling himself higher, he came face to face with the second of Tiania's tormentors.

The horned one had made himself fast in a secure position; he stabbed at Crow with a curved knife. Crow caught the creature's wrist, twisting until its snarls became cries of pain. Then he swiftly twisted the other way, slamming an elbow of hard flesh with a core of harder bone and plastic into the horned one's face.

That face was smashed in an instant. Teeth crunched and blood flew. The nose disintegrated, the wide mouth became a red gash, the slanting eyes glazed over. Crow released his grip on the horned one's wrist, caught him by his neck, and jerked him free of the bars into empty air. A moment later came the crunch of bones from below. Then Crow reached for Tiania where she clung naked to the bars just a few feet higher.

Before their hands could meet there came a buffeting of air and a shadow fell across them. Crow cried out a sick denial as the great gaunt soared down through the open roof of the cage to snatch the girl from her precarious position. Tiania screamed and struggled as she was lifted up, up and out of the cage, carried high into the white cavern's atmosphere. There the great gaunt found the thermal current rising from the crater and glided in wide circles in the rising air. Below the gaunt where it soared with its wriggling captive, the smoke rings went down in concentric circles to the crater-like vent that issued them; the thundering, as of massive, monstrous engines, pounded up through leagues of earth and sand to make the very air shimmer and vibrate.

With horrified eyes Titus Crow watched the circling gaunt, certain with every passing moment that the blank-faced bat-thing would drop Tiania into the throat of the mysterious vent. Then the Keeper of the Cage spoke:

"Come down from the cage, man of the waking world. Come and speak to me." The voice of the gigantic, manlike figure was loud to match its dimensions but flat and utterly void of life. It was as if some colossal zombie had spoken, a thing brought back from the dead against its will, without emotion.

Titus Crow dragged his eyes from the high-circling gaunt and stared at the Keeper where it sat upon its throne of huge boulders. It was as naked as Crow himself, hairless, with skin the color of death. Its eyes were lusterless yellow orbs that never blinked, through which it seemed to stare straight into Crow's very soul.

"I'll come down," Crow shouted his answer, clambering down the bars of the cage, "and I'll speak to you—but order your hideous pet to bring my woman down to safety!"

"Your woman? No, she is mine now, and when I am ready she will go down into darkness to fuel the nightmares of certain awful dreamers. You, too, are destined for the pits of nightmare. But not until I have spoken with you."

By then Crow had left the cage through the hole he'd made in its rotten bars. He ran to the feet of the Keeper of the Cage and waved his scimitar futilely up at the giant. "Why?" he shouted. "Why will you do these things?"

"It is my reason for being. It is why *They* put me here. Long and long ago I was a man of the waking world, like you. But I learned the mysteries of the Great Old Ones and became *Their* priest. Then, when I tried to use *Their* power to my own ends, *They* destroyed me on Earth and put me here to serve *Them* in Earth's dreamland. *They* gave me great size and amazing powers to command. Then, mockingly, *They* robbed me of my will, left me emotionless. I am almost omnipotent, almost immortal, and yet I am *Their* slave, powerless to do except as *They* will be done." Even saying these things the huge figure showed no emotion; the tone of his voice remained unvaried.

"If the Cthulhu spawn did these things to you, then Cthulhu is your enemy no less than mine," Crow cried. "Yet you have given yourself over into his service—you are his slave. I would sooner die than be slave to Cthulhu, but I'll fight as long as there's life in me!"

The Keeper answered: "Ah, but *They* thought of that, too. I might also fight, might also believe death preferable to this existence *They* plotted for me—had *They* not increased tenfold within me the human instinct for survival. All I have is an unquenchable desire to survive— and to survive I must obey."

With that the massive, white-fleshed creature leaned forward and scooped up Titus Crow in one hand before he could move. Crow struck time and again at the great hand that held him, but his blade drew no blood from the deathly flesh.

"Now," the Keeper continued, "stop your pointless striving and tell me who you are, why you are so different from other men. You are strong beyond belief for a mortal dreamer, and strange, too, I fancy."

"And if I tell you these things will you set the woman free?"

"No, no. You and she must both go down to nightmare. Down there in the pit, where the Engines of Horror pound, your souls will feed the darkest dreams of the Great Old Ones, and the nightmares *They* send to plague human dreamers will be that much more horrible."

"Then I'll not speak to you. I'll speak only to . . . Nyarlathotep!" Crow cried, desperately.

"Nyarlathotep?" No emotion but a certain hesitation entered into the Keeper's voice. "What do you want with Nyarlathotep—and what makes you think that the Great Messenger would want anything of you?"

"He wants to . . . to see us," Crow insisted. "I don't know why."

"If what you say is true, then I was right and you are indeed an extraordinary human being. I believe you." With that, the Keeper lifted up a great dead white arm and beckoned, and the circling gaunt immediately flew down and settled on his shoulder, still holding fast to the wriggling form of Tiania.

"I have the power," the Keeper continued, "to contact *Them* in *Their* immemorial slumbers. Perhaps *They* will send Nyarlathotep directly to see you."

"No!" Crow gasped.

"Oh? Were you after all lying, then?"

"No, but—"

"But you don't really want to see Nyarlathotep? I see. His plans for you are not to your liking, that is it. I will contact *Them*. But meanwhile my familiar must be about his work. See, you have freed all of my prisoners. They have escaped through the hole you tore in the cage's bars."

Crow saw that the Keeper was right. The last of the escapees was just hurrying over the crest of the sandhills out of sight. Again the Keeper gave a signal, and Tiania fell from the great gaunt's clutches and slid with a cry of alarm down over the Keeper's leprous chest and into his lap.

The Keeper placed Crow in his lap, too, and at that moment, as the great gaunt flapped aloft to soar after the fleeing people from the cage—then came an amazing diversion!

VII

Dreams of a Diseased Mind

Out of the sky, from above the white horizon of sandhills, a beam of purest white light struck at the great gaunt, shredding one wing into a swirling gray mist of fine particles. The beam was cut off instantly at its as yet unseen source, leaving the crippled gaunt to spin madly down, down the funnel of concentric smoke rings to where it struck the curving mouth of the pit, bouncing and tumbling like a bundle of rags before plummeting out of sight into the abyss. And not once did the creature voice its agony; no cry escaped it as it went down to the pits of nightmare.

"Whatever this is," said the Keeper, "plainly it is not intended to benefit me. Someone seeks perhaps to rescue you, or to destroy me, or both. If the intention is to rescue you, then your rescuer must first destroy me. Therefore I give your would-be rescuer no chance!" Even as the vast pale creature spoke—even as he snatched up Titus Crow and Tiania in one massive hand, holding them high over the throat of the great pit—so the white beam came again, lancing out of the sky to strike him square in his leprous chest.

The Keeper sprang to his feet and reeled at the edge of the pit. His strange eyes stood out huge and round in his face, and from his suddenly scarred and seared chest there came a deep and plainly audible wheezing. Now he slowly opened his outstretched hand, so that the dreamers had to scramble up onto his palm, clinging to each other above the vapor-belching pit.

"If he strikes me again, whoever or whatever he is, then he strikes all three of us," the Keeper said, pain in his voice but still no emotion. "For you will fall as surely as I, but you will fall into deepest purgatory. You see? It is my instinct for survival . . ."

By now the time-clock was plainly visible, racing in wide circles at some considerable height above the cage and its Keeper. Titus Crow knew that only Henri-Laurent de Marigny could be at the machine's controls, and hope sprang up in him as he watched its circlings. The Keeper followed Crow's eyes to the clock and he asked: "What kind of device is that?"

"Right now it's a weapon," Crow answered. "From the waking world. A weapon against all the Cthulhu Cycle Dieties and their minions!"

"You are . . . stranger than I thought, dreamer," the vast being said, his voice now faltering, an echoing croak that crackled like muted lightning. His great palm, upon which Crow and Tiania crouched, trembled mightily. They threw themselves down to lie prone across the huge fingers.

Suddenly the Keeper fell to his knees, the ground trembling as all the tons of his weight crashed down upon the sand. But still he held out his hand, palm up, above the great glassy abyss. Now the time-clock was stationary, poised threateningly on high, its dial turned toward the fantastic tableau below.

There at the lip of the infernal funnel, from whose nightmare throat those exhalations of obscene vapor puffed upward unabatedly, the Keeper kneeled, plainly injured. Crow and Tiania hung on grimly to his great fingers as his huge frame trembled, rocking to and fro. Beside him the now empty cage was an oddly woven lobster pot of gleaming metal and scabrous gray rust, and on all sides the white sand formed a dazzling, sterile backdrop to the entire scene. The time-clock fell from on high, moved closer, and became motionless again.

"It is my belief," came the Keeper's broken voice, drawing Crow's fevered gaze back from the time-clock, "that for all your woman's strange beauty you, dreamer, are far more important in the great scheme of things. That being so, I will now let her fall into nightmare, saving you until later. But unless you send your aerial weapon away, you will surely follow her."

"If you let her fall," Crow shouted, a conflicting mixture of horror, rage, and desperation in his voice, "I'll order your death immediately!"

"And your own?"

Crow knew what the Keeper meant: if the white ray struck him down, then Crow must fall from his hand into the pit. He answered, "And my own."

"Bluff." The Keeper's free hand moved out over the pit, thumb and forefinger reaching for Tiania. She threw her arms about her man.

"Wait!" Crow slashed uselessly at the threatening fingers with his scimitar. "Even if I were bluffing, what about Nyarlathotep? He wants to see us. Had you forgotten? Even if you escape with your miserable life—if my weapon from the waking world fails to kill you—how will you explain the woman's death, my death, to your masters?"

"Her death? Oh, but she will not . . . die, not immediately, not for a . . . long time. You do not . . . know as much as you . . . pretend, dreamer," the Keeper wheezed shudderingly on. "Nyarlathotep is . . . *Their* messenger, the Great . . . Messenger of my masters. Embodied or . . . disembodied, he is . . . *Their* messenger.

"Ask yourself who it is that carries Cthulhu's nightmares to . . . influence the dreams of mortals. It is . . . Nyarlathotep! You desired to . . . see him? So you shall—at the pits of nightmare. There your souls will fuel the engines of horror, for long and long before . . . you are . . . finished; and Nyarlathotep will disseminate all the . . . horror of your shrieking minds and souls among the dreams of . . . other mortals. But enough! The woman first!"

Suddenly Tiania, breathless and frightened but brave as ever, freed herself from Crow's arms to throw back her emerald hair in a defiant gesture. Her beautiful voice trembled almost unnoticeably as she spoke up in her own right.

"You would do this to Tiania of Elysia? Then you are surely doomed in this land of dream and in all others. You should know, creature, that I am beloved of the Elder Gods—beloved of Kthanid himself. Beware!"

"The . . . Elder Gods? Kthanid?" For the first time there was, or appeared to be, a trace of emotion—fear—in the Keeper's steadily disintegrating voice. "You are of . . . Elysia?"

The vast being's frame rocked more wildly yet, and for a moment his hand swung to one side, so that the pair huddled upon his palm suddenly found themselves above sandy ground and not the gaping maw of the glassy-throated pit. In one movement Crow grabbed Tiania and carried her into space in a coiled-spring leap; and in that same instant de Marigny, seizing upon his one opportunity, applied pressure to the mental trigger that controlled the time-clock's weapon.

Again the white ray reached blindingly, unerringly out, stabbing at the Keeper and striking him between the eyes. He fell back upon his haunches, clawing at his face and jerking spastically, toppling against the cage, which crumpled beneath his great weight.

Titus Crow hit the ground a second later, holding Tiania above him, deliberately cushioning her with his body as she fell upon him. It was a fall of at least thirty feet and would certainly have broken the bones of any normal man. Crow was not normal, however, and had fallen in a spot where the sand was soft and deep. Nevertheless, he was momentarily winded, so that it was several seconds before he drew himself to his knees to take the badly shaken Tiania in his arms. They had been lucky: a distance of only a few feet separated them from the smooth, curving lip of the pit, from which those regular exhalations went up inexorably as ever to the great cavern's roof. There, at the edge of the pit, clinging together, they saw a terrible sight.

The time-clock, flying in tight circles about the Keeper's gigantic, leprous, reeling form, was pouring a constant beam of white light down upon him, and wherever the ray struck his body oily black smoke gushed out from steaming pits to form darkly drifting cloudlets in the throbbing air.

It could not last for long. With one abrupt, flailing motion, the mortally wounded Keeper lurched to his feet. He glared from a single bulging eye—its twin now a gaping, blackly bubbling hole—and took a single, stumbling step after his aerial tormentor. Then he swayed to a halt. His mouth fell open and he spoke, signaling at last his recognition of doom, the fact that for all his instinct for survival, his lust for life even in the hell that Cthulhu had given him, he was done for.

"I know this . . . *power!*" he cried, his voice a monstrous bell with a cracked clapper, tolling a cacophony of horror. "I . . . know it. It is . . . that power which . . . even *They* fear. It is . . . the star of Mnar— the love of the . . . Elder Gods—the Good before which all Evil . . . flees. And it is . . . my . . . death!"

He staggered wildly, then spun about, throwing his arms wide to form an unholy cross. And again the beam of white light reached out. But this time de Marigny aimed it out of mercy. The beam played upon, passed *through* the Keeper's body, finally expending its potent energies harmlessly in the sand. The giant uttered one last incoherent cry; his arms fell uselessly to his sides; his head snapped back with a loud crack. He toppled forward, it seemed almost in slow-motion, crashing headlong down the glassy funnel to hell.

Titus Crow and Tiania, fleeing wearily toward the sandhills, were hurled flat by the hurricane rush of displaced air and stinging sand as the colossus fell. When they regained their feet again he was gone, and for several minutes there were no more rings of vapor rising over the white sands . . .

Cresting the dunes, they came to where de Marigny stood at the open door of the time-clock. He was deathly pale, trembling; he leaned unsteadily, balancing himself by holding onto the clock.

"Henri," Crow said, taking his arm. "Without you we were finished. You'll never know how I felt when . . ." His voice tapered off and a frown creased his brow. He put his face closer to de Marigny's and sniffed suspiciously. The frown deepened. "Man, I do believe you're drunk!"

"No, no, Titus," the other managed a sickly grin. "I'm almost sober now. But you should have seen me an hour or so ago! Here." He passed Crow an unopened bottle of brandy. "I don't care if I never taste a drop again."

"What? Brandy?" Crow turned to Tiania and hugged her, showing her the bottle. "Even in Elysia there's nothing quite like this, Tiania. What a man, eh? Twice he's rescued me in ten minutes!" Then his voice took on a more serious note. "But we'll celebrate later. Right now all I want to do is—"

At that moment there came a deep subterranean rumbling that shook the ground and made the trio stumble to keep their balance. It seemed suddenly darker, as though clouds had gathered to obscure the sun, though no such healthy orb illumined the great cavern. Again the ground shuddered, and they felt a series of dull detonations far below. A moment more and there came a roaring blast from the mouth of the pit, and almost simultaneously a huge black ring of smoke hurtled up into view—and with it the vilest stench imaginable.

"Right now," said de Marigny, finishing what Crow had started to say, "I reckon we ought to be getting out of here!"

Crow nodded in agreement, bundled de Marigny in through the clock's open panel and Tiania after him, looked once more upon the awful landscape of the white underworld, whose light was now visibly failing, then entered the clock himself.

As he took the vessel's familiar controls and lifted it up into the cave's atmosphere, Crow saw massive cracks opening in the floor of the desert. Dimly in the distance he perceived through the clock's scanners the impending death of this subterranean vault: the fall of great chunks of rock, stalactites and smaller debris from the shuddering ceiling. Of the diverse peoples so recently escaped from the Keeper's cage, there was no trace. Then, as the cavern grew darker yet and the pace of its disintegration accelerated, he raced the clock across the desert and out into the nighted places of deeper dream . . .

Later, high over the Southern Sea and under a sky that was beginning to fill with evening, as they sped for Ulthar and the haven that the City of Cats offered, de Marigny thought to ask of Crow: "What was it, that place?"

Tiania answered him. "It was one of those places where Cthulhu manufactures nightmares with which to terrorize dreaming mortals."

Crow nodded. "Yes, and there must be a number of places like it in dreamland. Factories where Cthulhu employs the Machineries of Horror to amplify his loathsome dreams before transmitting them to the minds of sensitive dreamers. Tiania and I almost became the raw materials such factories consume. Yes, we were very nearly part of it, Henri. *Aegri somnia vana!*"

"Dreams of a diseased mind," de Marigny translated with an involuntary shudder. "Ah, well—that's one factory I wasn't sorry to close down, Titus. No, not at all."

Part Five

◆

I

Ilek-Vad

After three days of somewhat crowded but contented recuperation at the home of Grant Enderby in Ulthar—three days of almost complete peace and quiet, marred only by the knowledge that soon they must once more be about the task in hand—Titus Crow, Henri-Laurent de Marigny, and Tiania of Elysia convened at the Inn of a Thousand Sleeping Cats, taking a secluded table in an alcove where they could talk in utmost privacy.

They were dressed now in rich robes of dream's styling. Tiania wore a low-cut flowing gown of mother-of-pearl whose mobile, greenly glowing tints matched her hair perfectly; Crow sported a short jacket of yellow silk, with matching Eastern-styled trousers supported by a wide black belt; de Marigny had chosen a single-piece suit of scarlet satin, throwing his black flying cloak carelessly about his shoulders. In their cool alcove they relaxed, toyed with their food, which at the Inn of a Thousand Sleeping Cats is the best in all dreamland, and sipped exotic liqueurs.

Eventually, almost reluctantly, Titus Crow opened the conversation. "Now, Henri, how did you get on the temple of the Elder Ones yesterday evening? Was Atal able to offer any more help?"

"Well," de Marigny began, "first of all I told him how well things had worked out: about our escape from Dylath-Leen, the destruction of the great ruby and the Fly-the-Light, the death of the Keeper and his—pets—and more or less everything else that happened in be-

tween. He was particularly pleased that his elixir had served me so
well.

"Then I told him how we planned to go to Ilek-Vad . . ." He
paused and shrugged. "I'm afraid I drew something of a blank there,
Titus. Atal could only repeat what Kthanid told me in the Hall of
Crystal and Pearl: that there is some sort of screen about Ilek-Vad,
one that lets nothing in or out."

"Drawn a blank, eh?" Crow repeated after a while. "Maybe, and
maybe not. I'm inclined to look on the bright side. Look at it this way:
a screen has two sides, Henri. True, it might have been built, this
screen, by enemies of dreamland, to keep people from knowing what
was going on in there. But on the other hand, might it not have been
built to keep Cthulhu's invasion forces out?"

"You think that perhaps Randolph Carter and my father—"

"That they built this screen? I think it's possible. As to what they're
doing behind it, in Ilek-Vad, that's another matter. It's something we'll
have to find out for ourselves. And there's really only one way to do
that."

"We're going to Ilek-Vad!" Tiania put in, excitement in her beautiful voice.

"No," said Crow, "not you, Tiania. Henri and I—*we* are going to
Ilek-Vad."

"Titus," she answered, "I'm not letting you out of my sight again,
not for a moment. There are too many terrors in this dreamland of
yours. What would I do if any harm befell you?"

"And what would I do if harm befell you, Tiania? No, you stay
here in Ulthar, at Grant Enderby's house. I'll know you're safe there.
It will only be for a day or two, until we know what's going on, then
we'll be back. And don't argue. You might be able to sway Kthanid,
but not me."

Tiania pursed her lips and sat back, eyes flashing angrily. De
Marigny coughed and hastily asked: "When do we set out?" He was already beginning to feel his stomach tighten as the Unknown loomed
once more before him.

"Tomorrow morning, at dawn," Crow answered. "We're known to
be here in dreamland now, so it's useless to attempt any sort of stealth.
We leave at first light, in the time-clock."

"Then you two will have to excuse me," said de Marigny, rising to
his feet.

"Oh? An early night, Henri?" Crow asked.

"No, I'm meeting with . . . someone."

"I have seen the way she looks at you!" Tiania laughed mischievously, her disappointment already forgotten.

"She?" Crow frowned. Then his face brightened. "Oh, you mean Litha, Grant Enderby's daughter." He too laughed, then warned: "But remember, Henri, that beautiful as she is with those huge dark eyes of hers, she's only a dream."

"I'll endorse that heartily," de Marigny answered, turning away to hide the sudden flush that suffused his face. "She is a dream, isn't she?"

And so Titus Crow and Henri-Laurent de Marigny set out at dawn's first light, leaving Tiania behind at the friendly house of Grant Enderby in Ulthar. And by midday they were well out over the twilight sea.

They could have traveled at a greater speed, certainly, but Crow was fascinated by the topography of dreamland. He had closely scanned all of the rivers, towns, lakes, islands, and villages as they passed in endless procession beneath the time-clock. Now he silently appreciated the calm, peaceful, scintillating surface of the twilight sea.

For the twilight sea is a vast island ocean (whose name derives from a perpetual serenity reminiscent of that of lonely lakes on calm summer evenings) far to the west of dreamland's third greatest continent. There, on a high promontory of volcanic glass that reaches far out over blue waters, stands Ilek-Vad—city of fabulous towers, domes, and turrets—once seat of a proud line of ancient kings, palace-city now of King Carter, late of the waking world.

Below the time-clock as it sped high over the wavelets, Crow and de Marigny could make out the coral-like labyrinths of the bearded and finny Gnorri, industrious dwellers in crystal depths. And it was as they scanned the marvelous intricacy of the Gnorri's incessant subaqueous labors, while yet Ilek-Vad lay a good ten miles distant, that the time-clock suddenly began to act very strangely indeed. Refusing to obey Crow's commands, the vessel veered to one side and began to fly in a wide circle which would eventually carry it *around* Ilek-Vad but no *closer* to that splendid city.

After a minute or so of wrestling with the clock's mind-controls,

Crow grunted: "Huh! Well, there's your screen, Henri, and a damned effective one at that!"

"That's amazing!" de Marigny replied. "It must be similar to the Wall of Naach-Tith that Grant Enderby told me about. An invisible, impenetrable wall. A force-screen. But how . . . ?"

"Science, Henri—or sorcery. Remember that this is Earth's dreamland, and men have been dreaming of such devices for a long, long time. In any case, what does it matter? The wall exists, and we're on the wrong side of it."

"Do you suppose," asked de Marigny, thoughtfully, "that the barrier goes down under the twilight sea?"

"We can soon find out," Crow answered, and he caused the time-clock to dive down, down into blue waters where the Gnorri swam and ogled and constructed their calcium caves and labyrinths. And there they once more came up against the invisible wall. But here there was a strange thing: the Gnorri were unobstructed in their submarine activities! For them the barrier did not exist, and they swam without hindrance to and fro across the invisible line.

"Well, now," Crow mused. "And I wonder how the birds fare?"

Up he took the clock and out of the calm waters with barely a splash. And there in the sky they waited until a cloud of white birds like geese, with a harsh, surprised gabble of inquiry, parted to fly around the clock and on through the invisible barrier.

"And the clouds themselves," said de Marigny, watching in the scanners the passage of fleecy clouds into regions where the clock was forbidden. "I don't understand . . ."

"I think I do," Crow said. "The Gnorri, the birds and clouds, they are all, well, *natural* things. They are the harmless, everyday, commonplace realities of dreamland, with no special allegiances to any powers, good or evil. The clock, on the other hand—yes, and its passengers—we are the aliens here."

"But Atal, and Kthanid before him, said that *nothing* could get in or out of Ilek-Vad," de Marigny protested.

Crow shrugged. "What would they know about birds or clouds or the Gnorri, Henri? No, Ilek-Vad is only forbidden to alien things and to things which would fathom her secrets. Forbidden to alien scanners on alien worlds, and to alien Elder Gods that use such scanners. Forbidden to the shew-stones of dreamland's magicians—black or white—because shew-stones are not natural but supernatural, alien.

Forbidden to the minions of the CCD, and to Nyarlathotep, *Their* messenger and agent."

"And to us," de Marigny added, "because of the clock, no doubt. A device of the Elder Gods and alien to dreamland."

"Oh, the clock is alien, all right," Crow nodded, a stubborn frown wrinkling his forehead. "It's damned ingenious, too. I don't think this barrier will stop us for too long, Henri."

"Titus, I don't see—"

"Listen, my friend. In this clock I've escaped from the awesome pull of a black hole in space, an omnivorous freak of nature from which not even light may flee. I did it not by going around the black hole but simply by moving . . . *away* from it! You see, the clock isn't only a space-time machine but a gateway between intermediary dimensions, too. The proof of that statement lies in the simple fact that the clock is here in dreamland right now, in that you yourself have used it to travel between dimensions, Henri. For dreamland after all is only a parallel dimension existing on a level compatible to the subconscious mind of man.

"But I didn't only escape from a black hole; I've also been safely into and out of the prison dimension of Yog-Sothoth, the Lurker at the Threshold, where not even one of Kthanid's Great Thoughts could follow. Yes, and from there into Elysia itself! Why, the clock slips between dimensions as easily as it flies through space and time!" He paused. "But there, we've wasted enough of the latter, now let's see just how resourceful the time-clock really is."

In the space of the next ten minutes Titus Crow piloted the clock into as many again parallel dimensions, using the semisentient machine in a way which might baffle even the Elder Gods themselves. De Marigny was astounded at the view the scanners gave him of these remarkable planes of existence. Some of them seemed darkly gaseous, nighted places, where vague shadowy shapes moved inexplicably; others were riots of primal color, to the apparent exclusion of all else. In two more there were definite geometric shapes, but Crow was quick to leave the latter planes; he was leery of the interest certain sharply angled shapes displayed in the time-clock.

What most surprised de Marigny, however, was the fact that in several of these parallel universes the barrier about Ilek-Vad—or rather, the barriers about corresponding areas in the alien spaces and times—was not only extant but visible. In one it showed in the scanners as a vast, silvery shimmering sphere, in another as an opaque pyramid of enormous proportions. But in all its various manifestations one thing about the barrier remained constant: to the time-clock it was impenetrable.

Then, as Crow switched dimensions yet again—to emerge in a scarlet glare through which thin bars of green light appeared to shoot in every conceivable direction without ever colliding—he gave a cry of triumph. "This is it, Henri, our gateway into Ilek-Vad. The barrier doesn't extend into this subdimension, the scanners show no trace of it. We simply move forward, in a physical sense, like this—" The alien universe outside the clock seemed momentarily to whirl. "And then we slide back through the intermediate dimensions to dreamland!"

There followed a kaleidoscopic confusion of weird colors, shapes, and motions as Crow returned the time-clock sideways through a dozen intervening planes of existence; and at last they emerged again above the twilight sea. All was as it had been, except that now they were moving forward, toward Ilek-Vad, and they were at last within the ten-mile boundary line of the invisible force-screen.

And there ahead and below was Ilek-Vad itself, fabulous city of towers, turrets, and domes rising up from the hollow glass cliffs wherein its foundations are housed, straddling the volcanic promontory beneath whose heights the Gnorri labor ceaselessly in the twilight sea. The afternoon sun shone down on Ilek-Vad, reflecting brilliantly from windows and bright metal statues, and in the city's squares and gardens brightly garbed crowds gathered to watch the approach of the weird aerial visitor.

As they drew even closer to the city, de Marigny's attention was drawn to what looked like a huge mirror at the very tip of the glassy promontory. At the base of this device, at what looked like a control bank, a pair of helmeted—soldiers?—busied themselves. Then, all around the rim of the city, many apertures appeared simultaneously in rampart walls, and out from these openings trundled more of the great mirrors.

"Titus," de Marigny began, "I don't think I quite like—" But before he could finish, suddenly Ilek-Vad seemed to disintegrate in a blinding flash of light that bloomed outward from the great mirrors. Actually the city had suffered no harm whatever, and as quickly as it had come the blinding glare died down—only to repeat a moment later as once more the vast mirrors hurled forth their incredibly bright beams of light.

The answer was now obvious, and Crow gave voice to de Marigny's unspoken thought:

"Those things are weapons, Henri!" he cried. "And damn it, *they're firing them at us!*"

II

Warlords of Dream

Half-a-dozen times at least the clock was caught in a crisscross of blinding rays from the projector-batteries about the city, before an astonished Titus Crow even thought to make a move to avoid them. By then such a move would have been superfluous; it was obvious that the beams of dazzling white light were neither damaging nor impeding the clock.

The troops manning the projectors saw this too, and moments later a second screen—this time a flickering, redly coruscating dome of purely physical energies—went up to enclose the city proper.

"No good, my friends," Crow grinned. "That's not going to keep us out either." He flew the time-clock forward and, as if the redly flickering screen did not exist at all, the vehicle of the Elder Gods passed through the curtain of energies without pause.

Into the heart of the city Titus Crow flew the clock, slowly and carefully now, not wishing to alarm Ilek-Vad's inhabitants more than was absolutely unavoidable. Finally, after hanging motionless for a few seconds over the gardens of the central palace itself, he set the clock down between tinkling fountains and exotic flowering shrubs.

Shortly thereafter a thousand soldiers, attired in lightly armored suits with shining metal helmets, emerged from new, barrack-like buildings in the outer gardens to surround the time-clock and take up defensive positions. They wore swords and carried shields which bore in their centers small versions of the mirror-like ray projectors. None of these troops came any closer to the time-clock than thirty or forty feet, and once they were in position behind their shields they made no further threatening move. Crow and de Marigny were content for the moment to remain in the complete safety of their vehicle and await developments—which were not long in coming.

Escorted by some two-dozen personal guardsmen, approaching on foot and dressed in splendidly opulent robes of silver and gold cloth, a strange, slender personage came from the direction of the palace itself. The soldiers around him were patently men of Ilek-Vad, and they had obviously been selected for their task. But while they were noticeably taller than the average inhabitants of dreamland, nevertheless the man they protected stood head and shoulders taller than the tallest of them.

"That man," said de Marigny. "He's as tall as I am. Is he young or . . . old? I can't quite make up my mind. And surely he's—"

"A man from the waking world?" Crow asked it for him; and answered: "Yes, he is, Henri. And unless I'm very much mistaken, we're singularly honored. Oh, yes, see? He recognizes the time-clock! And so he should, for he used it long before I even knew it existed."

"Randolph Carter!" De Marigny nodded his acknowledgment, awed in spite of himself. "King Carter of Ilek-Vad!"

Now the king waved his guardsmen back and came right up to the clock. His face was pale, slender, that of a young gentleman, but his shoulder-length hair was white and his eyes old with incredible wisdom. Amazement shone in those eyes now and, as Titus Crow had noted, recognition. He reached out his hands and touched the clock, saying:

"Whoever you are, please come out now. I know that you mean no harm, for if you did, then by now my city would be falling around me. You have my word that no harm will come to you in Ilek-Vad. See, I know your vehicle well . . ."

As King Carter's hands moved expertly along the clock's sides there came an odd clicking from some hidden mechanism. The tall man stepped nimbly back as the clock's front panel swung silently open beneath the weird, four-handed dial, and his eyes scrutinized the clock's passengers minutely as they emerged.

Then, plainly perplexed at some as yet unknown thing, after taking Crow's hand in a somewhat cursory greeting he grasped de Marigny's shoulders and stared hard at him. The frown deepened then on his own face and he shook his head in mystification.

"For a moment I thought that . . . you look so very much like . . . someone."

"I know who you are," answered the object of the king's scrutiny, "but I'm pretty sure we never met—or if we did I was only a very small child at the time. I am Henri-Laurent de Marigny, and this is Titus Crow."

Now the king's lantern jaw fell open in an unashamed gasp of astonishment. His grip tightened on the other's shoulders. "Then you *are* a de Marigny! By all the lands of dream, I should have guessed it! Who could possibly look more like his father than a son? Only a twin, I think, and believe me you *are* the twin of Etienne as he was . . . how long ago?

"But this is unforgivable of me. I have guests from the waking world—the son of my trusted friend and counselor, Etienne-Laurent de Marigny, and your friend here. Mr. Crow—and here we stand chatting in the garden! Forgive me, forgive me, and come with me please to the palace. There is much to talk about. I don't know why you're here, but I feel it's a good omen—and by the Sign of Koth, dreamland needs all the good omens she can get!"

"So," said the king much later, after they had dined and when he knew all about his visitors—from their initial encounters with the CCD, through Titus Crow's venturings in space and time and de Marigny's attempt to find Elysia for himself, right up to the present moment— "then I was right. It was an omen, your coming here. You could have chosen no more opportune time, for at this very moment we prepare for war against dream's minions of the CCD, against the nightmares of the Great Old Ones themselves.

"In you two we have powerful allies, and already you have struck telling blows against the evil in dreamland. Yes, great allies indeed! Why, you, Titus Crow, have seen Elysia, and for all my wanderings I never found my way there!"

"But your name is known there," Crow answered, equally gallant. "And as for encounters with the CCD: what other man has sought out, even confronted Nyarlathotep? And escaped sane!"

"That was long ago," the king modestly answered, "and I was by no means as great a dreamer as the stories have it. No, my adventures in dreamland were often ill-advised. I was lucky, believe me. Nyarlathotep will not let me go so lightly next time."

"And you think there may be a next time?" de Marigny asked.

"It seems more than possible," King Carter nodded. "There are warlords stalking dreamland even now, and war itself cannot be far behind."

"Warlords?" Crow questioned.

"Myself and Kuranes, yes, and others, too. And then, of course, there are also our enemies, the warlords of the CCD! Of the latter you know as much, possibly more than I do." He paused for a moment of contemplation, then went on:

"Like myself, Kuranes trains his generals; and in the sky-islands about cloud-floating Serannian he builds a great armada of sky-yachts and yearns for the day when he may once more return to the throne in timeless Celephais. Until that day Celephais remains behind its own force-screen, safe for now from the CCD, dreaming more wondrously than any other city in all dreamland."

The king laughed wryly before continuing. "Strange, I was hardly a warlike man in the waking world, but I shall command armies in dreamland! Mind you, it will not be the first time I have commanded the legions of dream, but those were strange dreams indeed." He paused again. "However—I would like you two to assist me, to be my generals. Certainly you know more of such matters than I, as your very presence here testifies. To have fought so long and hard against Cthulhu's hideous brethren—and to survive the unending battle! I fear, though, that new phases of that eternal conflict are in the offing."

"Sir," said Crow, "we would gladly join you, but there are many things we should like to know. Neither one of us is a great dreamer, and—"

"I understand," King Carter nodded, "but do not underestimate your ability to dream, my friends. Dreams are all things to all men, and men must shape their own dreams just as they shape their destinies in the waking world. Now, what is it you wish to know?"

"I want to know about my father," de Marigny immediately answered. "While we dined you mentioned his absence. If he is not here in Ilek-Vad, where is he?"

The king smiled. "Ah, Etienne. Where is he, you ask? Where indeed? He set out some years ago, before this latest trouble in dreamland began. His destination? Who can say? Let me explain that Etienne has become the greatest of all human dreamers. His dreamquests are unending; they have carried him beyond hitherto undreamed of regions—not only in Earth's dreamlands but in those of distant worlds and dimensions.

"He will return—of course he will—but I cannot say when. There was a period of peace in dreamland when he left, but it did not last. I would have gone with him . . ." he shrugged, "except that my adopted people are here in Ilek-Vad. So, at the moment I am both king and counselor. But make no mistake, Henri, your father will return. Someday . . .

"However, if you would be satisfied merely to see his *physical* form—why, that is simple! Come—"

The king led the way to one of the palace's inner sanctums where, upon a marble divan covered with rich silks and soft cushions, reclined the motionless form of Etienne-Laurent de Marigny. Wan and breathless, seemingly frozen in death, but undecayed, the spirit merely—absent—for the moment.

"He—" de Marigny broke the hush, "he is as I remember him. And this trancelike state of his: you and Tiania share this same type of sleep, Titus. You looked so much like this when I saw you in Elysia."

"Don't disturb yourself, Henri," Crow quietly said, sensing the depth of his friend's emotion. "It's simply a very deep form of dreaming. Worlds without end at his fingertips, my friend, and your father one of the greatest seekers of all time. Who knows what wonders he may be seeing even now? Would you really call him back?"

De Marigny made no attempt to answer.

For a long while the three men stood looking at the silent figure on the divan.

III

The Curse of Cthulhu

The next morning after breakfast King Carter of Ilek-Vad set out to tell his visitors of the shadow over Earth's dreamland, the curse of Cthulhu. Since Crow and de Marigny were aware of the general threat, the king confined himself to specific areas of the peril. He explained the defenses which he and Kuranes and several others had set up before it, detailing the forces they intended to throw against it.

The threat itself was of course the insidious encroachment of

Cthulhu's minions into dreamland, bringing His Word with them and spreading horror and evil wherever they were permitted to infiltrate men's dreams. If they were not stopped, eventually dreamland would be simply a barren place of nightmare and abomination, and the dreams of men would belong to Cthulhu to do with them as he desired. Following that, of course, the Lord of R'lyeh's next step would be an invasion of the waking world itself, the control of the conscious as well as the subconscious minds of men.

Against this threat—which King Carter himself had warned of long ago while yet an inexperienced wanderer in dreamland, though even he had not realized how far the cancer might spread—certain barriers had already been raised, behind which preparations had forged ahead to thwart, even repel the creeping invasion. Of these barriers two were believed to be completely impassable to anything tainted by the curse of Cthulhu: the force-screens about Celephais and Ilek-Vad. But even so, the inhabitants of those cities took no chances, for they were sworn to defy this persecution by Cthulhu's alien dreams. Hence the ray-projectors with which the Ilek-Vadians had bombarded the time-clock.

And behind the force-screens the armies of dreamland were being trained and its armadas built, strange weapons devised and plans for great battles laid. The King of Ilek-Vad had five thousand soldiers who would fight for him to the death, and in cloud-floating Cerannian Kuranes had built fifty great sky-yachts and was presently building fifty more.

Even before the arrival of Crow and de Marigny plans had been laid for an assault on Dylath-Leen. The intention was to rid the city forever of the horned ones of Leng, then to hold and protect its boundaries. Eventually the place might once more support the honest folk of dreamland, who would then patrol and protect the city's boundaries themselves.

Thus would Dylath-Leen become an outpost against the horned invaders, who would receive short shrift if ever they dared sail their abhorrent vessels into its harbors again. With the glad news that Carter's visitors brought, however,—that the power of the horned ones in Dylath-Leen was destroyed, however temporarily, and that in all likelihood they had already fled the city in their great black galleys—now it would be only a matter of days before the first of Kuranes' anti-gravity boats with its complement of Ilek-Vadian soldier-crewmen departed for Dylath-Leen.

Nor would the reclamation of dreamland's cities, those fallen into evil ways, end with Dylath-Leen. There were other suspect places lying far to the west, along the coast of the great Southern Sea. Zak, for instance, with its terraced temples wherein forgotten dreams fade and slowly vanish, seldom to be resurrected, would be an ideal haunt for Cthulhu's emissaries: there they might experience all the dreams of Man's youth, and thereby perhaps determine the course of dreams yet to come.

Then there was infamous Thalarion, the Demon City of a Thousand Dark Wonders, reigned over by the eidolon Lathi whose fleshly avatar was rumored to be of the Cthulhu Cycle Deities themselves! Surely, in a place where images of the CCD had been openly, immemorially worshipped, there would be many unwholesome things to root out and destroy. And what of the Charnel Gardens of Zura, land of pleasures unattained; and Sona-Nyl, a region of fancy where, legend had it, future dreams were shaped and implanted like seeds in the receptive minds of certain waking men, there to blossom and grow into full-fledged dreams in their own right? What a marvelous coup *that* would be for Cthulhu's minions!

As to how the friends and enemies of dreamland might be recognized one from the other, King Carter said that the true men of dreamland were dreamland's true friends, of whom only a handful were under Cthulhu's evil spell. The horned ones of Leng were not true men—indeed, they could hardly be said to be men at all—but were of the dreamland of a dark dimension paralleling Yuggoth on the Rim, whence the CCD had brought them when the dreams of men were very young.

And apart from true men and pseudo-men there were also the utterly inhuman creatures of dream, some sentient and others barely so. The loyalty of these beings was more often than not highly suspect. The "G" creatures, for instance, were especially suspicious—the gugs, ghasts and ghouls—and only slightly less sinister were the others: the shantaks, dholes and zoogs.

King Carter had had much to do with all such creatures in his youth, and in some of them he had found very strange allies indeed. The cats of Ulthar all knew and loved him; the zoogs of the Enchanted

Wood were not disinclined toward him. He had even befriended the ghouls of dreamland's nether-pits, whose leader was a special acquaintance of his.

As to the ghasts and gugs, mercifully they were usually content to remain in their own realms. The ghasts were least bothersome in that real light destroyed them. They were rarely to be found outside the lightless Vaults of Zin, where they were hunted by and in turn hunted the gigantic gugs.

Night-gaunts, however, were not to be dealt with so lightly. Though faceless, they were nevertheless believed to be the secret eyes of Cthulhu's minions in dreamland. Moreover, many of dream's people still believed that the night-gaunts held great power over all of dream's lesser creatures. And certainly the vast and hippocephalic shantak-birds were mortally afraid of them. Chiefly to be found near the summit of Ngranek on the Isle of Oriab, night-gaunts also guarded the grim gray peaks dividing Leng and Inquanok, where they spent the drab daylight hours in caves that scarred the topmost pinnacles. In the night, though, gaunts flew far and wide throughout dreamland, and their secretive nature was such that indeed they would make ideal spies for the CCD.

One of the first tasks for Kuranes' sky-yachts, once Dylath-Leen was secured, would be to destroy the nightgaunt stronghold atop Ngranek, then to block all of those entrances leading down into the black and reeking abyss beneath. In this manner that area of the underworld and all its terrors would be shut off forever from saner, upper regions of dream.

And so the armies of dream would go from strength to strength. Eventually there would be great battle-fleets upon the Southern Sea, barring access to the black galleys of the horned ones; vast stone fortresses would be built and manned along the border of Inquanok and Leng, ensuring that the horrors of the latter tableland might forever remain remote. Finally, a way would be sought to destroy those black places in dreamland—the evil foci of CCD influence—where Cthulhu's engines of nightmare pounded detestably, poisoning the healthy dreams of Earth's mortals.

Such places were known to exist in the Enchanted Wood, in certain green deeps of the Southern Sea, even in the perfumed and often beautiful jungles of fabled Kled; others were rumored to lie in subterranean vaults beneath Zura's elusive temples, and in the hinterland of ruined, primordial Sarkomand. There were many, many places to be freed or cleansed of the curse of Cthulhu; great battles to be fought and won; temples of evil to be razed and healthy frontier cities founded. And all to free Man's subconscious mind from the canker of CCD-inspired nightmares.

For unless Cthulhu's creeping incursion into dreams could be put an end to, neither the waking world of men nor the universe itself would ever be truly safe from the horror inherent in His aeon-devised design for the utter destruction of all sanity and order.

Such were the grim and doom-fraught subjects covered by King Carter through all of that long day; but in the evening a banquet was prepared in honor of the visitors from the waking world, and as they sipped the clean red wine of Ilek-Vad so their apprehension for dreamland's future eased a little. Later, reclining in silk-cushioned couches that swung gently to and fro beneath the crystal-clear dome of the city's highest tower, gazing out across the placid twilight sea where all the stars of night gleamed in a darkly fluid firmament, Crow and de Marigny talked a while and then fell silent. Both of them were thinking the same thing: they knew now all they had wanted to know of Ilek-Vad. It was time to move on.

The next morning King Carter wrote a letter of introduction for his visitors, a warrant authorizing their new ranks as Generals of the Armies of Dream, telling briefly of their origins and their present importance to all dreamland. They were to take this letter with them to Kuranes in cloud-floating Serannian, the pink marble city of the clouds; for the pair had intimated their desire to be once more on their way, and Serannian was to be their next stop.

Thus, at noon of that same day, the dreamers said their farewells to the king and flew up in the time-clock over the city. And as the powers that sustained the great invisible dome of hyperdimensional energy were momentarily revoked by Ilek-Vad's wizards, they sped away over the twilight sea in the direction of Serannian.

"Titus," said de Marigny as they gained speed, "things seem to be working out very well."

"At the moment, yes. Does it bother you?"

"Something bothers me. But it's difficult to pin it down. I mean, everything seems so easy now—the obstacles are behind us."

"Perhaps they are."

"And yet I somehow feel an urgency, a need for greater haste."

Crow nodded. "I feel it too. My instinct tells me that all is not as well as it might be."

"And there are still many questions," de Marigny went on. "For instance, the weapons we've seen so far. Are they magical or mechanical?"

"A bit of both, I suspect. But that takes us back to an old argument, Henri: just what *is* magic? This is Earth's dreamland, remember? If you had been to Elysia with me, then you might finally be able to put that word magic behind you. In Elysia there are islands that float a mile in the air, just like Serannian. Surely the science that holds such islands aloft is little short of magical? What you must remember is this: whether in the waking world or the world of dream, if a man wants something badly enough to be, he will *make it be!* Is a sky-yacht any more fantastic than an airplane? Are King Carter's ray-projectors any stranger than lasers? Dreamland and the waking world are two different spheres, Henri, certainly—but both were shaped in the minds of men, sleeping and waking alike!"

De Marigny frowned, then suddenly burst out: "Star-stones! That's something else that's been bothering me—are there no star-stones in dreamland? I had one hanging from a chain around my neck when I set out from Earth, but I'm damned if it's there now."

"Ah!" Crow smiled. "But the star-stones came to Earth from an alien universe, Henri, an alien dimension. Dreamland guards her boundaries well; she does not gladly suffer that which is not of Earth and Man's own dreaming."

"But what of Cthulhu and the CCD?" de Marigny argued. "What could possibly be more alien? And yet their emissaries are here."

"Sentience!" Crow answered. "They are here because Cthulhu wills it, just as we are here because we will it." He shrugged. "Quite apart from which, of course, Cthulhu is a master of dreams. And it could be argued, too, that we are the aliens on Earth and not the CCD. After all, they were here first—millions of years before man. Perhaps Cthulhu himself has put this stricture on the star-stones of ancient Mnar, that they may not exist in dreams. It has certainly taken us long enough to remember them and question their absence."

"Humph!" de Marigny grunted. "It's very odd: one minute everything seems so easy, the next—impossible!"

"That's the way of it, Henri," Crow agreed. "Often things are far simpler in dreams—but then again they can be a damned sight more difficult, too."

IV

Serannian

At first sight, even knowing he was dreaming, de Marigny found Serannian almost unbelievable. He had seen it before, certainly, in those telepathic visions showed to him by Kthanid in hyperdimensional Elysia, but the reality was a far greater thing. A cloud-washed coast of pink marble that seemed to stretch away to its own horizons; and built upon the shore, a splendid city that looked out over an ethereal sea of glowing cirrus and cirrocumulus.

Far below, glimpsed through roseate mists and pink-hued clouds, the Cerenarian Sea's white-tipped billows washed toward a distance-hazed land where Mount Aran was only just visible. That mountain, the dreamers knew, formed one of the valley-walls of Ooth-Nargai, where timeless Celephais reared her splendid domes, towers, and minarets beneath a dome of energy like that which protected Ilek-Vad. But because Celephais and Serannian both came under Kuranes' wise rule, trade went on as of old between the Timeless City and the Sky Island; except that now the force-screen about the former must periodically be relaxed, allowing the sky-galleys that brought the latter's supplies free passage out onto the Cerenarian Sea.

Indeed, the galleys they saw riding to the horizon, where they sailed skyward on rose-tinted mists, had recently put out from Celephais. Awed by the beauty of all they saw—marveling that the subconscious mind of man could dream such wonders—the travelers in the time-clock followed one of the galleys into the harbor of Serannian; and when Crow set the clock down on the walls of the pink-marble docks, they marveled again that Serannian had ever been built here, on this ethereal coast where the west wind flowed into the sky.

Moored in the harbor, floating impossibly on pink cloud-crests, the dreamers spied twenty-five of Kuranes' fleet of fifty war vessels;

along their decks, port and starboard, were single rows of mirror-bright devices that reflected sharp shafts of sunlight as the ships bobbed up and down. These were ray-projectors, like those they had seen in Ilek-Vad. In the distant sky, riding out on the west wind, the other half of the fleet was under sail.

Standing beside the time-clock on the dockside—which was deserted now, for sailors and dockers alike had quietly melted away into the wharfside taverns as soon as the time-clock had landed—Crow and de Marigny watched the receding sails of the ships until a voice informed: "They go out to practice the arts of war, arts which will soon be put to good use in Dylath-Leen and other places."

Turning, they came face to face with Kuranes, a man once of the waking world, now Lord of Ooth-Nargai, Celephais, and the Sky around Serannian. They knew him immediately from a description furnished by King Carter. Slightly built but regally robed, gray-bearded but sprightly and bright-eyed—and wary—Kuranes had with him a retinue of pike-armed guardsmen. He gazed briefly upon his visitors before continuing.

"Rumors have been reaching me for days now of a strange flying machine come into Earth's dreamland." He made a motion with his hand and the guardsmen clustered closer, moving between the two dreamers and their machine. Crow and de Marigny found themselves inside a circle of sharp pikeheads.

"I have wondered," Kuranes went on, "whether this device, this flying machine, was benign toward dreamland or—malignant." Again he beckoned, and his guardsmen laid restraining hands on the two strangers.

At last Crow spoke. "Lord Kuranes, we understand your apprehension perfectly, but you may put your mind at ease simply by reading this letter." He produced the carefully folded document. "It is from Randolph Carter in Ilek-Vad."

"A letter from Randolph Carter?" Kuranes' eyebrows went up and he seemed surprised. "Randolph, you say? Are you so familiar, then, with the King of Ilek-Vad?"

"My father was King Carter's counselor," de Marigny quickly answered, "before he took to exploring in undreamed of places. I am Henri-Laurent de Marigny, and this is Titus Crow."

As Kuranes read King Carter's letter, so the attitude of alert wariness fell from him. Finally he smiled and waved his guardsmen aside, clasping first de Marigny's hand, then Titus Crow's.

"Gentlemen," he said, "I am at your service."

A few minutes later, on their way to Kuranes' "palace"—which, astonishingly, they saw at a distance to be nothing less than a great Gothic manorhouse with a gray stone tower, typical of lordly English dwellings Kuranes had known in the Cornwall of his youth in the waking world—a servant of the Lord of Serannian approached in great haste. This man, a whiskered butler attired in typically English livery, though patently he was a denizen of dreamland, probably born and bred in Celephais or Ulthar, handed Kuranes a tiny metal tube.

Kuranes took square-framed spectacles from his robe and put them on, then unscrewed one end of the metal tube and carefully extracted a tightly rolled strip of extremely thin paper. "James," he asked of his butler, "what color was the bird that delivered this?"

"Pink as Serannian's clouds, my Lord," the butler answered, in an accent which was not quite Cornish.

"Hmm . . . Then it came from Atal in Ulthar. I wonder what he wants."

On hearing Atal's name spoken, the two dreamers exchanged quick, speculative glances. Then de Marigny's suddenly taut features relaxed and he shrugged, murmuring: "It can have nothing to do with us, Titus. No one knows we're here."

"Oh?" exclaimed Kuranes, his sharp ears catching de Marigny's remark. "But you are wrong, my young friend! It does concern you— both of you. And as to how Atal knew you would be here—none in dreamland is wise as Atal. Did he know you were going to Ilek-Vad?"

The two nodded in unison.

"Then it would not be hard to guess your next port of call." His eyes went back to the paper. "It says that you should return to Ulthar at once, that many of Leng's horned ones are in the city disguised as foreign traders, and that a man called Grant Enderby is worried about strange figures seen lurking near his house in the dead of night."

"Anything else?" Crow's voice was tense.

"Yes. Atal says that although there are no true soldiers in Ulthar— that is, no real force for the protection of the public—he has sent several young priests from the Temple of the Elder Ones to keep a discreet watch over Enderby's house. Hmm! And that's all there is. It seems to have been penned in some haste."

He handed the letter to Crow. "Take it, by all means, but you'll have to take my word for what's in it. It's written in an obscure glyph with which only a few in dreamland are familiar. Atal knows that I am one of the few."

"Lord Kuranes," said de Marigny, his voice urgent, "you must understand, we have loved ones in Ulthar. It's more than possible that our mutual enemies intend them harm."

"Yes," Crow continued when de Marigny paused. "It seems we must take our leave of you sooner than we expected. Immediately."

Kuranes nodded. "I understand. It's a pity, for I was looking forward to a long talk. It's rare now that I have distinguished visitors from the waking world. You will go in your flying machine, of course?"

"Yes," Crow answered, "but as soon as we get another chance we'll be back to try your hospitality, Kuranes."

"You won't find it wanting," the Lord of Serannian promised. "But listen, I have an idea. This could be my chance to exercise my armada a bit more realistically. It's known that the horned ones have a number of sky-galleys of their own. In fact, they once kidnapped King Carter to dreamland's moon—which is not like the moon of the waking world—in just such a galley. This could be how they plan to make their getaway from Ulthar once their dirty work, whatever it is, is done there. It's not unlikely that they've hidden one of their foul galleys somewhere on the coast, to which they'll flee when they're ready. How would it be if I sent a dozen of my sky-yachts, with full complement of trained crewmen, to follow you to Ulthar?"

"It's a very kind offer," Crow answered, "but the time-clock travels at an incredible pace. We'd leave your ships far behind. Still, I think it would be a good idea to send some of your vessels to Ulthar, perhaps to station them there permanently. There have always been a few horned ones in the city, or so I'm led to believe, and we can never tell what nests they may have built for themselves. Why not let a handful of your best ships and their crews form the city's first soldiery, a police force to guard against the subversion of the horned ones?"

"I'll do it!" Kuranes cried. "Even if my ships can be of no assistance to you two, still they can perform a useful service for the peoples of Ulthar. In any case, I can only send a handful of ships, for I'm short of crews. I'm to draw upon Ilek-Vad for most of my crewmen.

Now then, I can see that you're eager to be off, so I won't hold you. Off you go—and the very best of British luck to you!" He waved after them as they turned and hurriedly retraced their steps in the direction of the harbor.

To the young priest who anxiously scanned the skies from the roof of the temple's ivied tower, the coming of the clock into Ulthar was an awe-inspiring experience. Having seen many marvels as an initiate and acolyte at the Temple of the Elder Ones, he was used to wonders, but this was somehow different. There was no clap of thunder, no darkening over of the skies, none of the phenomena with which he was used to associating the onset of occult or paranormal occurrences. And yet surely this flying clock was a magick of the first water.

Out of an early afternoon sky touched with fleece the time-clock raced—at first a dot spied among the distant clouds, then a dark oblong shape that flew upright, finally a coffin shape that slowed and fell out of the sky—down past the tower so that the young priest could see the four hands that moved irregularly and in exotic sequences about the great dial. His warning shout had barely echoed down to the square in front of the temple's entrance, where three of his fellows awaited the clock's coming in their robes of priesthood, before the space-time vehicle alighted and its passengers stepped forth.

They were immediately ushered into the temple, along a maze of corridors, until finally they came to that inner sanctum where Atal the Elder reclined upon his bed of silks. Extreme in age and fragile as he was, warm recognition still showed in the patriarch's faded, almost colorless eyes as he welcomed the two dreamers into his presence. His trembling, whispery voice was urgent as he gave them the grim news:

"My young friends . . . it is terrible . . . terrible!" he quavered. "Sinister creatures in the city in greater numbers than ever before. Three of the temple's young priests bloodily slain—the lady Tiania of Elysia and the girl Litha Enderby of Ulthar kidnapped and carried off—and an almost tangible oppression settling like a shroud over the minds of all Ulthar's decent citizens. I sent a dozen of my pigeons to seek you out—to Nir, Serannian, Hatheg, Sona-Nyl, and Baharna; even to Ilek-Vad, though I was not sure the bird would be able to fly into the city—and I am only sorry that you . . . were not found . . . soon . . . enough . . ." He came to a faltering, panting halt.

"In your own time." Titus Crow calmed him, quickly seating himself beside the centuried high priest, cradling his head and shoulders against his own strong arm. "Now, from the beginning—"

And so, slowly and with many a pause, Atal told them how on the previous morning it had been noticed that there was an inordinate number of the strangely turbaned traders in the city, those squat beings of ill-legended Leng. Ulthar had never found it necessary to totally ban such creatures—only the trading of their blasphemous rubies was forbidden, and usually the horned ones were merely passing through the city on their way to less discerning places—but nevertheless Atal found this sudden increase in their numbers greatly disturbing.

He made discreet inquiries, discovered that furtive groups of the horned ones had been seen in that district where Tiania of Elysia was staying, and immediately his concern trebled—particularly when Grant Enderby himself later complained that he had seen suspicious evening shadows where none had been before, shadows that melted quickly away when he attempted to approach them.

Enderby had been sure that the horned ones were watching his house, and certainly his wide experience of these beings was such as must make him something of an expert on them. Thus he conveyed his concern for his exotic house guest to Atal, who in turn sent three priests from the Temple of the Elder Ones to watch over Enderby's house through the night. At the same time Atal gave orders that a dozen carrier pigeons were to be prepared for release to distant lands and cities, and with his own trembling hand he wrote the cryptograms to be tied to the legs of those blood-hued birds. All to no avail.

The straight, short ceremonial swords of the temple—with which the three young priests were not familiar in any other than esoteric connections—had been useless against the viciously curving blades of the horned ones, as the headless corpses of those priests had all too mutely testified the next morning. Enderby himself was lucky; he had been knocked unconscious from behind as he patrolled the walls around his house and garden. Mercifully his wife and sons had been away, visiting an ailing relative in a nearby hamlet.

At dawn, when the quarrier had achingly regained consciousness, he had found the decapitated priests lying in his garden where they had been dragged by their killers. Tiania of Elysia and Enderby's daughter Litha were nowhere to be found.

"And that," Atal brought his tale to an end at last, "was the way of it. Who can say what the rest of it will be?"

V

The Legions of Nightmare

As Atal finished speaking, Crow laid the patriarch's head gently back on the pillows and stood up. A wild rage shone in the dreamer's eyes and his whole attitude was that of a lion crouching before springing to the attack.

"De Marigny," he grated, "if ever I've felt sorry for my enemies before—if ever I've been guilty of feelings of sympathy for the CCD in their eternal banishment, or their dupes and minions caught up in the foul schemes of their prisoned masters—then may my soul *rot* before I ever shall again!"

And Henri-Laurent de Marigny, white and trembling with fury and horror, made his own vow. "Atal, we leave the Temple of the Elder Ones now—and we shall not return until these great wrongs are righted and their authors punished in full . . ." He paused, then turned despairingly to Titus Crow. "But where can we even begin to look for them—and for Litha and Tiania?"

Before Crow could answer, Atal spoke. "Wait, wait! I have sent out birds, dozens of them, the temple's pigeons, to all towns and hamlets in the vicinity of Ulthar. If the horned ones have passed by any one of fifty places, we shall soon know of it. Indeed, some of the birds have already returned, but as yet they have brought no word. You will fly off in your time-clock, I suppose, but if you have no success before evening, call back this way. By then we may know something. The priest at the top of the tower . . . will be kept . . . fully informed . . ." And once more exhausted, he again lay back on his pillows.

Without another word, the two grim-faced dreamers turned and left Atal's room, passing into the maze of corridors and making their way quickly out of the temple.

They split up, Crow taking the time-clock and de Marigny his anti-gravity cloak, flying outward from Ulthar in opposite directions to begin their aerial search of the surrounding regions. Crow headed for the coast, thinking that perhaps Kuranes had been right about a hidden sky-galley in which the horned ones would attempt an escape; and de Marigny followed the Skai down to distant Dylath-Leen, deserted now and strangely drab in the mid-afternoon sunlight.

Both dreamers were to find only bitter disappointment . . .

Titus Crow sought the sails of ships as he flew out over the sea—particularly ships headed for the horizon, where they might suddenly lift into the sky, bound perhaps for Kadath, Leng, or even dreamland's moon itself—and, sure enough, after searching for over an hour he spied sails, but these were already airborne. And they were not the ominous black galleys of the horned ones but the colorful battle-yachts of Serannian, on their way to Ulthar as Kuranes had promised.

Briefly Crow landed on the deck of the lead ship to inquire of the captain if perhaps anything had been seen of black galleys sailing the seas below. He was told that nothing had been seen at all to arouse any suspicion, neither on the Cerenarian nor on the Southern Sea. Crow quickly related what he knew of the recent trouble in Ulthar and took off again.

De Marigny, making ever widening, concentric sweeps about Dylath-Leen and eventually winging out over the great deserts, spied a caravan in an unseemly hurry and approached with some caution until he flew directly above it, unseen by its masters. But no, these were only honest merchants of dream about their business, and their haste was probably due to the close proximity of Dylath-Leen, whose gray towers reared in sinister fashion not too many miles distant. It would be a long time before that empty city lost its unenviable reputation in dreamland.

As the hours passed and afternoon began to grow toward evening, Titus Crow and Henri-Laurent de Marigny turned back for Ulthar. Over the City of Cats they spied one another across a league of sky, and winging down toward the tower of the temple both were attracted by the frantic waving of a priest behind the high, ivied parapet. They landed together on the roof, and as Crow stepped out of the time-clock de Marigny began to question the young, breathlessly excited priest.

Yes, at last there was news! A dozen of the horned ones, more furtive than ever, had been sighted in mid-morning on the outskirts of Nir. They had been making their way across the plain toward the Enchanted Wood, bearing two bundles like rolled carpets with open ends. And strange sounds had seemed to emanate from those bundles, like muffled cries for help. Later, a shepherd had found traces of the party in a cave, where they had doubtless rested out the night. Their journey must be very tiring; horned ones were not ideally structured for the carrying of heavy bundles, and they had no beasts of burden with them.

This news had come via one of the temple's carrier pigeons, sent back by a holy man in Nir, and it arrived just as Kuranes' sky-yachts had appeared over the city. With his vessel anchored firmly to the temple's high tower, the senior captain had alighted to learn of the kidnapping and of the route taken by the kidnappers toward the Enchanted Wood. The airborne ships had at once sailed off in the same direction, picking up a vengeful Grant Enderby and his sons on the way. This had occurred well over an hour ago.

"Into the clock, Henri!" Titus Crow cried. "I believe I know what they're up to now, and if I'm right we haven't a moment to spare."

"The Enchanted Wood, of course!" de Marigny exclaimed as the clock's door closed on them and they lifted to the sky. "The Enchanted Wood—and that great slab with its massive ring and runic inscriptions!"

"Right," Crow grimly affirmed, sending the clock racing across dreamland like a coffin-shaped blur in the sky. "One of those places King Randolph Carter told us about—where Cthulhu's engines of nightmare pound away down in the black, reeking underworld, manufacturing madness with which to disease the subconscious minds of men and subvert them to his cause. It's a place like the one we destroyed beyond the Peaks of Throk, whose guardian was the vast and leprous Keeper. I only hope we're in time, that's all."

Far down below, the grassy fields of the plain rushed by breathtakingly; then, ahead and to the left, Nir appeared, drew level, vanished behind in a twinkling; the singing Skai flashed for an instant like a narrow silver ribbon in the last rays of evening; Hatheg with its domed dwellings came and went. In the twilight they overtook the battle-yachts of Serannian and at last flew over the edge of the gloomy Enchanted Wood.

Then Crow reluctantly reduced the speed of their craft and brought it down to the level of the treetops in the rapidly fading light, and as the rush of the great trees beneath them slowed they covered another mile or so until they came to that shocking region of diseased oaks which was in fact almost a clearing of crumbling stumps, quaggy earth, and luminescent, bloated fungi. There Crow set the clock down and they alighted from its cleanly pulsating radiance into the rotten glow of putrefying foliage.

They carefully approached the center of that scabrous clearing, where lay the massive slab with its Titan ring. Eagerly their eyes searched the mold and mush-slimed edges of the great slab for signs that it had recently been moved.

"Thank all that's merciful!" cried de Marigny, his voice shattering the miasmal silence. "It hasn't been moved. We're in time, Titus!"

Crow nodded in the semidarkness. "Yes, if this is indeed their destination—" He suddenly cocked his head on one side and held up a cautionary finger. "Listen! Do you hear it? What do you make of that, Henri?"

All was gloom, fetor, and uneasy, misted silence. De Marigny held his breath and listened for a moment. He could hear nothing. "What is it, Titus?"

"Here, put your hand on the slab. Now do you hear it?"

"Yes . . . It's a pounding, deep down in the bowels of the earth."

"Well, we were right about that at least." Crow nodded in grim satisfaction. "This is certainly the portal to one of Cthulhu's factories of nightmare. And—"

"*Shh!*" de Marigny suddenly whispered. "Someone's coming!"

A moment later came definite sounds of disturbed underbrush not too far distant—immediately followed by an outraged cry from a female throat!

"Litha!" de Marigny choked, instinctively making to rush in the direction of the cry.

"Hold on, Henri," Crow restrained him. "Believe me I'm as eager to be at them as you are, but let's get the time-clock out of the way first and lie in wait for them. Let's see if we can discover just exactly what's going on here."

No sooner had they flown the time-clock into a deep, dense patch of bramble at the edge of the clearing, closing its panel behind them so that the clock's weird light would not give away their presence, than from the opposite side of the clearing appeared the fugitive group of horned ones. Between them—hands bound, shivering, and with their clothes in tatters—staggered the two fiercely protesting girls, Tiania and Litha. Crow and de Marigny saw all of this very clearly, for two of the horned ones had lanterns that cast a yellow, penetrating light all about as they moved forward, dragging the women toward the great slab.

"Titus," whispered de Marigny, his hand trembling violently on the other's arm, "I can't—"

"*Shh!*" Crow cut him off. "The girls are all right, Henri, just a bit roughed up, that's all. Let's learn what we can before we make a move."

In the center of the clearing one of the horned ones moved forward, held up his lantern before him, and commenced to read from the runes graven into the top of the slab. Such sounds as he made could never be echoed by the vocal chords of man, but the horned one was totally fluent in this unearthly tongue. And in response to the chanted rune, suddenly, with a harsh grating and shuddering, the great slab began to tilt upon some hidden spindle. As the horned one continued his weird chanting, so the girls were bundled forward.

"All right, Henri," Crow snapped, urgently gripping his friend's shoulder. "Now see what you can do to slow things down a bit while I bring the time-clock into play!"

De Marigny needed no more urging. He bounded aloft in his cloak, swooped down from on high, and crashed headlong into three of the squat creatures from Leng. One of these flew with a shrill shriek straight into the reeking gap where the edge of the slab had now lifted to reveal an inky hole beneath; a second was dashed to the mushy earth where he lay still; the third jumped to his feet—only to be grabbed about his fat neck and hoisted aloft as de Marigny flew his cloak up into darkness. A moment later and this third horned one's gurgling cry was cut off short as his squat body fell with a snapping of bones against the steadily tilting slab.

A few seconds more and de Marigny flashed out of the sky again—but this time they were ready for him. Four of them were still awkwardly struggling with the girls, doing their best to push them into the hole showing beneath the slab while keeping a nervous watch out for de Marigny. The other five slashed with their scimitars at the dreamer's hurtling form as he swerved over their heads.

Then Titus Crow took a hand in the matter. The time-clock crashed forward out of the brambles at the clearing's edge; and even as the horned ones saw that strange vehicle of the Elder Gods, so Crow triggered the clock's awesome weapon.

A beam of purest, dazzling light flashed forth from the four-handed dial, slicing first into those five horned ones whose blades were drawn against de Marigny, scything them down in an instant. The four who held the girls let go of them at once and turned to flee. Crow cut three down with another slashing beam of light, then, with that same beam, tracked the fourth—who immediately darted behind the now almost vertical slab!

Crow's beam struck the great slab . . . and the next instant the whole clearing shook with an ear-splitting roar as that monstrous door to the underworld shattered and flew asunder. It was sheer luck that the two girls, stumbling away toward the edge of the clearing, were not hit by the boulder-sized chunks of rock that hurtled in all directions; but they were not, and when the smoke cleared they stood clinging together, half-swooning, until de Marigny alighted beside them and hugged them to him.

Only then, when it appeared that the immediate danger was past, did the true horror of the situation become apparent.

For as de Marigny stood with his arms protectively about the two girls—and as Crow in the time-clock surveyed the scene in the clearing, ill-lit now that the lanterns of the horned ones were extinguished—so there came a subterranean rumbling and a geyser of slime and foul gases from the yawning pit. Hurriedly, half-carrying the girls with him, de Marigny backed away from that awful orifice; but Titus Crow, protected by the almost totally impervious shell of the time-clock, eased his vessel forward until it poised on the very lip of the pit.

Using the clock's scanners he gazed down into the dim and reeking abyss . . . *from which, suddenly and without warning, there burst a noisome stream of horrors straight out of a madman's blackest nightmares!*

Ethereal the things might well have been, but still they seemed solid enough to cause Crow to back his clock hastily away from the pit's edge. Dozens, hundreds of them, out they poured like pus from a ruptured abscess, an endless tide of monsters created by Cthulhu's machineries of madness, released now to plague the subconscious minds of mortal dreamers. And they were, quite literally—*nightmares!*

Misty, wraithlike, utterly malignant and malevolent, they swirled and billowed about the poisoned clearing while their shapes seemed to take on more form, more substance. Here were vampires, ghouls, werewolves and witches, monsters of every sort imaginable and others quite unimaginable. Burnt-out eye-sockets leered from melting faces; mad fangs gnashed hideously in mouths that drooled and chomped vacuously; eyestalks twined and twisted while leprous claws and stumps of fingers scrabbled spastically. The stenches of a thousand open tombs issued up from that hellish pit, and its gibbering depths reverberated with a throbbing cacophony of completely lunatic, utterly inhuman laughter.

And the worst was still to come, for de Marigny and the girls had no protection at all against these nightmares from the pit, which now swarmed about them in ever thickening, ever more threatening hordes. Illumined in the rotten glow of phosphorescent corruption, Crow saw the faces of the three convulse in ultimate horror, watched them quite literally going mad in the face of unthinkable, unbearable nightmare.

Again and again, frantically he triggered the clock's weapon, lighting up the clearing in blinding flashes of white light, shredding the monsters from the pit in their hundreds. But as quickly as they steamed off in vile evaporation others rushed from the hole to replace them. Then the unimaginable happened: suddenly Titus Crow himself was on the defensive!

At last he recognized his peril and cursed himself that he hadn't seen it sooner. These things were *nightmares,* and even in the dreamlands they were not "physical" but "psychical" phenomena. As such they were not subject to mundane laws of time and space. He could no more keep them out of the time-clock than he could keep from dreaming. Dreams come and go ignoring all walls and barriers—and so do nightmares!

Again he triggered the clock's mighty weapon, again, and yet again . . . until at last he felt his brain gripped and wrenched and squeezed by incredible terror, and knew that finally they had breached the time-clock's polydimensional walls! Then everything seemed to dissolve in one vast cataclysmic bombburst of flame and light . . .

VI

Nyarlathotep

For a single moment only—which Titus Crow reasonably believed might be his last—the blinding glare filled the clearing with its light, leaving a cascade of illusory fireworks dripping white fire on his retinae . . . and leaving his mind completely free from nightmare!

Instinctively, in complete astonishment, he had time enough to merely glance into the clock's scanners before turning from them to avoid suffering the glare again. For in the night sky above the Enchanted Wood he had seen a glad, fantastic sight; six battle-yachts in line, their ray-projectors aimed threateningly down into the heart of the nightmare-ridden clearing. The clearing itself had looked much as before, except that now the mist was that much denser through absorbing the ectoplasmic stuff of which a thousand defunct nightmares had recently been composed.

De Marigny, Tiania, and Litha had been stumbling to and fro, their hands to their heads, still suffering the mental aftermath of that concerted attack of blackest nightmares; and even as Crow had snapped shut his scanners to avoid the blaze of a second salvo from the ray-projectors, he had seen that the gaping, steaming pit still issued a vile stream of threatening, abyss-spawned horrors.

Flying blind but using all the skill with which his long experience of the time-clock had endowed him, he flew across the clearing, skirting the pit to fetch a halt close to the stricken trio. As he made to leave his exotic, hybrid machine—even within its hyperdimensional shell— still Crow felt again that blast of awesome illumination as the aerial gunners opened up on the nightmares from the pit a second time; then he quickly stepped out of the clock, snatched up Tiania, and pulled her to safety. He did the same for Litha and finally de Marigny, and no sooner was the clock's door shut than yet again there came a concerted blast of purifying light from the sky.

Only then did Titus Crow use the scanners again, and as he lifted the clock up out of the clearing he saw that the rush of nightmares from the subterranean abyss was greatly reduced. A few seconds later

he landed his vessel beneath the mainmast of the lead ship and assisted his rapidly recovering passengers out onto the deck.

"Titus," de Marigny caught his elbow as he turned back to the
clock. "What are you doing?"

"I intend to finish this job once and for all, Henri. Don't worry, I'm
not going down into the pit. I just intend to close it up forever—if I
can! These shipboard ray-projectors are fine used en masse, and their
powers must be very similar to the clock's own, but I think you'll find
they're only good for short bursts. This job will require more than
that."

Without another word he entered the clock and flew it back down
to the clearing, hovering directly above the pit. Only a thin trickle of
nightmares was issuing from that ghastly hole now, and keen-sighted
gunners on the battle-yachts were picking them off as fast as they appeared. Crow tilted the clock slightly, lining up its four-handed dial
with the mouth of the pit, then triggered his weapon in a long, continuous burst.

And Titus Crow was right, for while in unison the ray-projectors
were indeed a force to be reckoned with, as individual weapons they
simply could not be compared with the marvelous power of the Elder
Gods. Directly into the mouth of the pit he played that unbearably
pure beam, illuminating incredible depths that seemed to go down
forever, perhaps to the vaults at dreamland's core. For thirty seconds
or more that stream of concentrated purity—the very Essence of
Benevolence, the evil-destroying Light of the Elder Gods themselves—played into the pit, and slowly but surely the desired metamorphosis was brought about.

First the mushy ground in the immediate vicinity of the pit began
to glow with a radiance of its own, a light that throbbed like the beating of a great luminous heart. And this radiance spread outward until
it encompassed the entire clearing, pulsing ever faster, almost hypnotically, in a strange strobic splendor.

At the height of this activity—from which at its onset, as from a
suddenly erupting volcano, the six sky-yachts had sailed off to a safe
distance—without warning the ground in the clearing began to bubble and boil, flowing like molten lava and streaming into the pit. On
the heels of this phenomenon came others as the entire clearing and
the diseased oaks around it suddenly trembled, then heaved and

bucked in a seismic convulsion as muffled explosions sounded from deep down in the underworld. Then, blowing outward from the spot where the pit had been, there came a howling, madly rushing ghost-wind that hurled the six sky-yachts back across the sky like so many autumn leaves, a torrent of winds that continued long after Crow released the trigger of his awesome weapon. The ground in the clearing still steamed and bubbled, and it retained a little of its luminosity—in which eerie light Crow now witnessed the beginning of this strange drama's final act.

Slowly at first, then rapidly widening, a crack appeared in the glowing earth where the pit had been sealed off, and emerging from this ominous fissure came a rotten, greenish glow that seemed to ooze upward into the clearing. At first Crow was tempted to use the time-clock's weapon yet again, without waiting to see what this new threat might be, but his human curiosity got the better of him. Despite his recent experience with the nightmares from the pit, his faith in the clock's imperviousness remained all but unshaken; whatever this green glow was he did not believe it could harm him. In any case, it would be the work of the merest moment to bring his weapon to bear upon this unknown thing, for its "trigger" was in his own mind. He flew the time-clock down to a spot which he reckoned was at a safe distance from the as yet unidentified phenomenon.

The glowing sphere of green light slowly lost its opaque quality until Crow could make out a figure standing at its center—a human figure! And as the green glow grew dimmer yet and the winds ceased their frantic outward rush, so he made out the physical details of this unexpected apparition.

Tall and slim, clad in bright robes and crowned with a luminous yellow pshent, the figure seemed to become more solid as its heralding green glow died away. It was a man with the young, proud face of a Pharaoh of ancient Khem—but whose eyes were those of a dark God, where lurked a languid, sardonic humor.

"So you are the man Titus Crow," the figure finally spoke in rippling mellow tones. "A mere man—and yet much *more* than a man . . ."

On hearing that languorous voice—despite detecting a trace of malice in the emphasized word, which ought to have alerted, galvanized him—a creeping numbness fell over Crow's brain. Too late, he started to reach out a mental finger, intending to activate the time-clock's weapon, only to discover that halfway to the trigger his hand was stayed, his will frozen solid. An iciness like the chill of the deeps between the stars pervaded his whole being, robbing him of all volition. And at last Titus Crow recognized the newcomer, knew also that he was face to face with Doom, that he could not possibly survive the encounter. For this handsome young Pharaoh was none other than Nyarlathotep, the Crawling Chaos!

"Ah, yes!" The voice came inside Crow's head now. "You know me, Titus Crow, for we've had dealings before, you and I, when you've seen me in some of my thousand other forms. And you are one who knows me for what I really am, and you know the nature of my masters . . .

"Well, dreamer, it is at an end. Only a very few men have caused my masters so much concern, and doubtless you would go on to cause more trouble if you were not curbed. For you are impetuous and wild and do not understand my masters, who are great and glorious beyond all greatness and glory. So I have sought you out in dreams, and have brought about this meeting which will set your feet on the road to a greater destiny: to be one with my masters out among the stars and in the hidden places of the waking world!

"For they would like to know you, Titus Crow, more intimately. They would like to watch your reactions to terrors greater than any yet conceived by your race, and would taste of the entire range of your passions when, at the end, they scatter the shreds of your subconscious being to the very corners of existence. But never fear, Titus Crow, for they would not destroy you immediately. No, for there are punishments far worse than those imposed upon my masters by the so-called Elder Gods, and surely a suitable one will be found for you . . .

"Now come, dreamer, out of your time-clock and embrace me. Come, for we have far to go and must leave at once . . ." And Nyarlathotep beckoned, smiling sardonically and opening his arms wide as if welcoming an old friend.

Like a doll on the strings of a master puppeteer, Crow opened the clock and stepped out of its purple-glowing interior. He approached Nyarlathotep wide-eyed, moving like an automaton, and as the distance closed between them so the green glow began to return, springing up and deepening around the slim Pharaoh-like figure.

Behind the dreamer as he moved inexorably forward, the weird purple light from the open door of the time-clock grew deeper as its pulsing slowed; the glow itself expanded until it completely encompassed the clock and a wide area around it, finally matching in size and intensity the green and rotten luminescence about the form of Nyarlathotep. Abruptly in Crow's frozen mind a second commanding voice now resounded:

"Man of Earth, you, Titus Crow, *stop!* Turn about!"

Falteringly, zombie-like in his movements, the dreamer turned. A vast nebulous face was growing out of the purple glow about the clock, a face in which huge golden octopus eyes glared out in a terrible rage. Face-tentacles lashed and the entire visage of the Elder God shook and trembled in the spasms of a towering passion.

For this was of course the image of Kthanid, Tiania's guardian and Titus Crow's patron in Elysia—Kthanid, who now used the time-clock more truly as a gateway between dimensions to intrude on Crow's behalf in this his moment of direst peril.

"Titus Crow, come to me!" ordered Nyarlathotep, his mental voice slightly less mellow, less certain now. Obediently, the dreamer began to turn away from the clock.

"No!" came Kthanid's urgent denial. "Get out of the way if you can, Titus, so that I may strike him. I have a power here greater even than the time-clock's own. But it will destroy you, too if you stand before it!"

"He can't disobey me, fool!" Nyarlathotep laughed, his voice quickly deteriorating to a bass croaking in Crow's mind. "Come to me, Earthman—NOW!"

At that precise moment, down from the sky a batcloaked figure flew, hurling the stumbling, hypnotized dreamer from between the two beings in the clearing. Immediately the spell was broken; Crow shuddered as he clung to de Marigny and they lifted up above the treetops of the Enchanted Wood. Then, rising rapidly toward the sky-yachts, the two dreamers stared down at a fantastic scene.

A tremendous booming voice came up to them, a mental voice that reverberated in their minds as Kthanid addressed his Enemy: "You have threatened those in my protection—even Tiania who is flesh of my flesh—*and now you must pay!*"

Simultaneous with the last word, twin beams of pulsating golden light flashed from Kthanid's great eyes to penetrate the green glow of corruption and strike the figure of Nyarlathotep with their full force.

He staggered, that Great Messenger of the CCD, then swelled up huge and bloated. "Damn you, Kthanid! Let me . . . *go!*"

"Not until you have suffered . . . and would that I could make you suffer a thousand times more!" Again the twin beams leapt from his eyes to the grotesquely bloated figure of the Pharaoh—which instantly reformed itself into . . . *something else!*

A vast, monstrous congeries of iridescent globes and bubbles shifted and frothed where the bloated human figure had stood, and Kthanid's cry was glad and triumphant as he hurled his beams directly into this seething mass. Those sizzling golden beams struck home—and for a moment the two dreamers floating high above were afforded a glimpse of the *Thing* that lurked behind those globes and bubbles: a Titan primal jelly of wriggling ropes, bulging eyes, and tossing, convulsing pseudopods and mouths—an ultraevil, supersentient anemone from deepest oceans of horror!

"Ah, Yog-Sothoth! So, you have helped Him in this, have you? A joint effort, was it? And who else hides behind the lying mask of Nyarlathotep, how many more of the thousand forms?" Again the searing golden beams lashed out, and another metamorphosis immediately took place. Gone now the liquescent, purplish-blue loathsomeness of Yog-Sothoth, and in his place a towering black anthropomorphic outline that stood on great webbed feet and gazed with carmine stars for eyes!

"Ithaqua, too!" boomed Kthanid. "The Thing that Walks on the Wind. Well, begone, Ithaqua, and let us see what others there are . . ."

Then, in rapid succession, using his twin golden beams like great knives, Kthanid peeled away the outer layers of telepathic consciousness that shielded the innermost, ultimate blasphemy. Many members of the CCD there were that Crow and de Marigny recognized, and many they did not know at all. Shuddle-M'ell was there, the dreaded burrower beneath; yes, and fiery Cthugha and tentacled Hastur, too. A single, shocking glimpse of slimy Yibb-Tstll; and one of Yig, Father of Serpents; and Zhar, Chaugnar Faugn, and many others. And finally—Cthulhu!

Cthulhu, the dread Lord of R'lyeh, dreaming but not dead, sending his dreams from drowned R'lyeh to infest and desecrate the sacred lands of Earth's human dreamers. He was almost the twin of Kthanid, but where Kthanid was golden Cthulhu was leaden, where the former was Good the latter was absolute Evil. Evil writhed and twisted in twining face-tentacles, leered out of kraken eyes, and twitched convulsively in vastly arched wings. Evil glowered hideously, unblinkingly at the shining image of Kthanid—until once again, for the last time, twin beams of pulsating yellow fire reached out to strike the monster dead center.

"Get you gone from here, Cthulhu," boomed the Elder God, "back to R'lyeh where you belong. Will you never learn to keep your mad dreams to yourself? Begone!"

Then there echoed up from the clearing a tremendous, rumbling explosion like a great clap of thunder, and when the dazed dreamers flying high above next dared to look down Cthulhu was indeed gone. Gone, too, was Kthanid, and the time-clock stood alone and issued its softly pulsing glow in a clearing that lay blasted and barren and silent, where, in the morning, birds might safely sing as they never had since time immemorial . . .

Epilogue

Ah, yes, the Inn of a Thousand Sleeping Cats, in Ulthar!

Of course, I didn't hear all of the tale that one evening, merely snatches of it that reached me from the fabled group at the head of the massive banquet table. The Enderbys were there—with dark-eyed Litha seated blushingly alongside Henri-Laurent de Marigny—and Tiania of Elysia, side by side with her Earthman, Titus Crow; and all around the table were dignitaries from all of dreamland's districts and counties and cities. Yes, even Atal of Hatheg-Kla. And all of them come to applaud the exploits of the adventurers from the waking world.

As to the tale's total veracity: well, I for one would swear to it. Have I not myself visited the Enchanted Wood and chatted with the Zoogs, all of them telling me of that night when the wood was bright with strange lights, following which the birds returned to nest in the great oaks about the place where once had rested a monstrous slab of stone graven with strange runes?

Aye, and there are other proofs. I have already booked passage on a galley out of Theelys bound for Dylath-Leen, and who would once have braved that place? And what captain dared to sail his ship there? Too, bright sky-yachts float above dreamland's cities and patrol her farthest borders, reporting their findings back to ever-watchful Kuranes in Serannian and King Carter in Ilek-Vad. And I'm told that so far they've had precious little to report, for which I'm glad.

But it must not be believed that the Forces of Evil are finished in dreamland. No, for beyond the frontiers of sanity there still lie lands of ill-legend and temples of terror. Leng breeds her horrors as of old on the borders of dream, and Kadath broods gray and gaunt in the Cold Waste. Aye, and man is an infant in dreams compared with great Cthulhu, who slumbers on eternally in R'lyeh, waiting . . . waiting.

And what of the heroes of the story now? Well, I have it on good authority that de Marigny is dreaming a white-walled villa in timeless Celephais, to which he'll return one day when at last he's traveled the road to Elysia. And Tiania and Titus Crow?

Strange visions wake. Fearsome starlanes and the gulfs between dimensions beckon. How long before even the marvels and wonders of dreamland pall and the lure of the Unknown calls Crow and his love away again? Who can say?

Worlds without end.

SPAWN OF THE
WINDS

◆

"For Gail"

Introduction

by Professor Wingate Peaslee of Miskatonic University,
Director of the Wilmarth Foundation

In 1966 the Wilmarth Foundation recruited a telepath of exceptional talent, a man who could tune his mind to the aberrant sendings of the CCD, the Cthulhu Cycle Deities, and make a sort of sense out of what he "heard." Hank Silberhutte was the man: a tall, tow-headed Texan of daring and adventurous, albeit hasty and often hot-headed, inclinations.

Several years prior to his joining the Foundation, Silberhutte had lost a cousin in the cold wastes of Canada. The circumstances had been mysterious; following an unexpected cold snap of especial ferocity the party of six, engaged on government survey work, was suddenly missing, "lost from all contact with the civilized world." He joined in the Foundation. Having learned something of the CCD, it dawned on Silberhutte that his cousin's disappearance had coincided with strange undercurrents of unrest in the Canadian trail towns and logging camps, and with the peculiarly feverish culmination of a five-year cycle of esoteric religious festivities as practiced by certain local Indians and, farther north, Eskimos.

In short, he became interested in Ithaqua, that fearful airelemental of the CCD. It was this fascination of Silberhutte's—one might almost say obsession—which, following the very successful part he had played in a major Foundation project, prompted me to offer him the job of researching, compiling and correlating a working file or dossier on this mythical being of the Arctic snows; further, of carrying out his own survey work in Canada on the periphery of the WindWalker's domain, and over the line of the Arctic Circle into the interior of that frozen territory itself.

Silberhutte immediately jumped at the chance I offered and in very short order produced an almost Fortean file of related incidents and occurrences, all of them showing definite connections with that monstrous manifestation known as Ithaqua, "the Thing that walks on the wind." I was amazed that any single man could have accumulated so vast an amount of lore in such a short time—much of which had previously been overlooked, had gone unnoticed, or was quite frankly unknown to the Foundation archives—until I recalled that the Wind-Walker had a very special attraction for him.

Genial and affable though Hank Silberhutte invariably was, at the merest mention of elementals of the air, Eskimo legend, or cycles of morbid CCD influence, his face would harden and his eyes narrow. He was a Texan and was as proud of that fact as any man of his race, and his cousin had died in the white wastes of Ithaqua's Arctic domain. Enough said.

Perhaps in retrospect, knowing what I knew of him, I should have thought twice about giving Silberhutte the job of tracking down the Snow Thing. One needs a cool head when dealing with such horrors, and the Texan could fly off the handle in as little time as it takes to tell. But the man's physical strength and keen intelligence, his dedication and great telepathic talent, more than balanced the odds and qualified him for the tasks he might need to perform. Or so I thought.

It came about that at a time when I myself was in Denizli, directing the commencement of certain operations in Turkey, Silberhutte was making preparations for an aerial reconnaissance of the Arctic Circle, or rather of its rim, from the Bering Strait to Baffin Island. His reason for this survey, in his own words, was to allow him "to get the feel of it; to look down on the ice-wastes from on high and see them as a great bird might see them—or as a Thing that Walks on the Wind!"

But of course there was more to his planned survey than that. There would be a strenuous series of treks to follow it, commencing before the thaws set in, for which he intended to prepare detailed routes from the air. Of these treks, one would be across the Brooks Range northwest of Fort Yukon on the Arctic Circle; another would cover a large area north of the Great Bear Lake; yet another should prove to be particularly grueling and would take the Texan's team along the Mackenzie Mountains Trail to Aklavik.

Tough groundwork of this nature was to be a period of acclimatization for the team rather than an actual frontal attack on the Snow Thing. Those regions where Ithaqua had made his awesome presence known in the past—and where doubtless he would make it known again in the future—were to receive the team's attention at a later date, when its members had been made more able to survive by these "toughening-up" exercises of Silberhutte's.

Finally, the third and possibly most important of all reasons for this aerial survey: he intended to put his telepathic talents to the test in a series of attempts to search out from the air the massed mental seedings of local religious cults and sects. Strangers of many lands with no easily discernible purposes were massing northward; rumours of a "Great Coming" were legion among the barely civilized inhabitants of the whole vast region, and whispers were already filtering back to Miskatonic through strategically placed Foundation agents.

This, in the main, formed the core of my knowledge of Hank Silberhutte's initial plan of campaign against Ithaqua. Busy as I was in Denizli, he was now completely in charge of Project Wind-Walker, free to get on with it in his own way. All that I asked of him was that I be kept notified of the operation's progress.

And here I find I must insert something about Juanita Alvarez. Silberhutte was on vacation in Mexico prior to being offered Project Wind-Walker. He found Juanita in Monterrey working as an interpreter with an international firm. She was young and single, very well educated, extremely independent, and spoke four languages without a trace of accent in any of them—and she was telepathic! And here an exceedingly strange thing: Juanita's talent was in a way as unique as Silberhutte's, for she was only telepathic with him. In exhaustive tests later carried out at Miskatonic, this proved to be an enigma that baffled all the experts. Only Hank Silberhutte could receive her mind-sendings; she in turn could only receive his. It was as if, at their first accidental meeting in Monterrey, Hank had sparked off something in her mind, something that had found and formed a unique empathy with his own extraordinary talent. They had seen one another—and they had *known*. It was as simple as that.

And of course Hank had known that this would be a major break-through for the Foundation, because very few members of its telepathic fraternity were actually capable of communicating with one another; those who could were usually only able to receive very vague and ill-defined mental pictures. It was not their purpose to talk telepathically with *people,* but to use their talents to detect the machinations of the lurking, alien CCD and their minions; in Hank Silberhutte and Juanita Alvarez, however, the perfect link of mental communication had been forged.

So it was to the utter despair of the theorists and telepathic technicians at Miskatonic when Hank accepted his new job, and even more so when after some months he left Arkham to travel up to Edmonton with his team, there to form a Foundation detachment for the duration of the project. In his absence they would have to temporarily suspend their attempts to discover what made Hank and Juanita tick. As Hank himself pointed out, he would not be completely out of touch; they could contact him any time they so desired—through Juanita. Still, the professors would have preferred the telepathic "twins" together in the laboratory, in a controlled environment.

However they might have wanted it, the girl stayed on while her alter ego (that was how they had come to think of one another, even though there was absolutely nothing else between them; there was no romantic connection) was off to Canada at the start of the greatest adventure of his life. In the days that followed, try as they might, the Foundation's experts in mental telepathy could get nothing out of the girl. To all intents and purposes, except for her ability instantly to contact the Texan whenever she felt inclined or obliged to do so, she was telepathically deaf, dumb, and blind.

That was how things stood when, on January 22, I received word from Miskatonic that Hank's plane was missing somewhere over the Mackenzie Mountains. Had there been an accident? A long letter from Juanita Alvarez, doubling as a report and confirming the disaster, followed. The following excerpt is part of what Hank Silberhutte's devastated alter ego had to say of the matter:

> His call was like an alarm clock, waking me from nightmares that I could not quite remember—but the reality was worse than any dream. It was about 9:15 a.m. and I had slept late. Immediately I was wide awake, knowing that he had called out to me, feeling for him with my mind.
>
> "Hank," I answered him, speaking it out loud as well as with my mind, "what is it?"
>
> "Juanita!" he answered, "Get all of this—don't miss a thing!" And then he simply opened up all his senses to me and let me see it all, everything that was happening . . .
>
> . . . The plane was low, skimming the undersides of boiling black clouds as the pilot tried to keep his craft below the weather but above the white peaks of mountains that rushed madly by on both sides. Weaving and bucking, riding the wind wildly and

whirling in mad currents of air, the plane fought its pilot like a wild animal, and through all this Hank started to tell me the story:

"*We spotted him, Juanita—Ithaqua, the Wind-Walker—and our very first time out at that. It was no coincidence; we were looking for him, certainly, but he was just as surely looking for us. Or at least he was looking for me, and he certainly picked me up easily enough. We were at about N. 63°, W. 127° when we first felt it—that fantastic pull!*

"*. . . What a bloody fool I am, to go chasing the Snow Thing in the sky, his own element! We can forget whatever remains of that old fallacy about Ithaqua being restricted to the Arctic Circle. To the Far North, yes, but we have ample evidence that he's ventured as far south as North Manitoba, and so he could certainly—*"

Abruptly he stopped consciously sending to let me see more clearly through his eyes. Only a few miles ahead of the rushing plane the white peaks reached up to the turbulent clouds. The pilot was wrestling with the controls, trying to pull the plane's nose up into the swirling cauldron above, but the wind seemed actually to be blowing now from on high, blowing *down* on the wings of the straining plane and driving it toward the harsh ice-peaks of the mountains.

Hank could see what was going to happen—what *must* happen—and now his mental transmissions became a frenzied gabble as he tried to tell me all before—before—

"*We must have been somewhere between Dawson and Norman Wells when we saw him: a great blot in the sky like smoke solidifying, taking on a vaguely manlike but gigantic shape, a beast exactly as described in the Lawton Manuscript, but a description is one thing while actually to see him is—*

"*Then the skies darkened over in what seemed like only a few seconds and the black clouds boiled up out of nowhere and he walked up the wind on his great splayed feet and disappeared into the clouds. But before he went completely his awful face came out of the clouds to look at us through flickering carmine stars that were like the very pits of hell!*

"*Juanita—look!*"

And again Hank's mind opened up to show me the scene he himself saw at that exact moment of time, allowing me to participate visually in his experience. It was a favor I might well have done without; the Thing that Walks on the Wind had returned.

I had read something about Ithaqua, and Hank had told me a lot more. There is one part of the legend that warns of an unholy curse; to see the Snow Thing is to be doomed, for having seen him is to know that you must become his victim—sooner or later.

With me it is sooner. I can no longer close my eyes without that hideous vision of Ithaqua being there, lurking in my mind, behind my eyelids, etched on my memory's retina. Professor Peaslee, Ithaqua is a monster, indeed a "Prime Evil," a being that never was spawned on this world and could never be accepted in any sane universe.

He—*it*—was there, perched atop that mountain peak directly ahead of the crazily lurching plane, a black bulk against the white snow and blue ice, filling the space between frozen peak and tortured sky and radiating his alienness more tangibly than the sun radiates light. To look at the sun for too long would burn one's eyes out, but to gaze into those carmine pits that Ithaqua wears for eyes—that is to scar one's very mind!

Oh, I can well believe that Ithaqua's curse might work. Out there in the snowy wastes, it must be a very strange and lonely world. A weak person, perhaps even a strong one, having seen the Wind-Walker, might easily be drawn to go in search of him, simply to prove that the nightmare he had suffered was only a nightmare. Then again, perhaps it is the being's mind that draws its victims back again, as in post-hypnotic commands.

It could be so, Professor, I know it. Why, I can almost hear his command in my own mind at this very moment! But I am strong and I understand what this hellish attraction is. I can fight it.

There he was, that monster, stretching out his great arms to snatch with massive hands at the plane before it could crash into the peak, drawing it to him until the metallic gray of its wings and fuselage glowed a flickering pink and red in the reflection from the twin stars that burned in his face.

I had seen all this with Hank's own eyes, until the last moment when he deliberately shut the vision out. But even so I could still read what was in his mind. I saw the cold despair and bleak but useless anger and hatred there. So powerfully was he transmitting that I could actually feel the machine gun in my own hands as Hank put a flaming stream of tracers across the snarling dark visage of the Wind-Walker, tracers that seemed to pass right through the horror's face and into the furious clouds above.

Then Hank sought out an eye, and his shells found its center to pour into it like a swarm of angry bees—only to burst from the back of the darkly massive head as a shower of drifting sparks! And that monstrous being threw back his head and laughed, shaking with hellish glee; but his shaking turned instantly into the hideously aberrant, spastic twitchings of indescribable madness, and this in turn gave way just as abruptly to anger and then to megalomaniac rage as finally . . . I *heard* him!

For until that last moment of time the Wind-Walker had been

a creature of silence; indeed, I believe he is vocally dumb, inarticulate—but mentally . . . ?

I have been told, Professor, that telepathy is telepathy and thought is thought, and there are theories and theories of which the majority agree that one telepathic being sends thoughts which must be at least partially understandable to any other. It is not so. The minority which has it that truly alien thoughts would be incomprehensible are right. *Nothing* is more alien than the Wind-Walker, despite his anthropomorphism—nothing that I can imagine anyway—and his thoughts are . . . they are terrible things.

I *think* that it was an alien mixture of glee and murderous rage I heard, an obscene flux reflecting telepathically from Hank's mind like images from a cracked mirror, but the thoughts of Hank himself came to me clear as crystal in the final moment. He knew what must happen, you see, and I anticipated his shutting me out.

And I fought him because I wanted to be there, to help if I could. Oh, Hank won, but even as he drove me from his thoughts and back to my bedroom at Miskatonic, still I received impressions of the terrific acceleration he felt as Ithaqua lifted the plane high, high in his hands, even reaching up through the clouds—as a child lifts up a stone to skim across the water, or a ball to bounce.

And at the very end Hank said, "*Juanita, tell them—*"

And that was all, he was gone. There was nothing in my mind at all; it was a vacuum into which the Miskatonic morning flooded as if all the doors and windows had been opened together. And though I screamed for Hank to come back, to talk to me, all the while searching desperately for even the faintest echo of his telepathic voice, I knew that it was over.

There is one other thing, Professor. I believe that Hank's sister, Tracy Silberhutte, was on board the plane. I do not know why; she was not part of his team (in fact I do not think that she knew anything of his work with the Wilmarth Foundation), but she was certainly on board. His mind was full of her, worrying about her . . .

And Juanita was right; Tracy Silberhutte was on board Hank's plane. Later we were to discover how she came to be there, but not for a period of some four months. In the meantime Juanita, no longer of any telepathic value and having no desire to become an agent of the Wilmarth Foundation, went back to Monterrey. Search parties, both aerial and on foot, scoured the area north of Hank's last known position but found nothing; it was as if the plane had been lifted from the face of the Earth.

Then, late in May, when I was busy organizing my expedition to the Great Sandy Desert of Western Australia, Juanita returned to Miskatonic. Her arrival was as unexpected as her personal appearance was changed. She looked as though she had not had a wink of sleep in a week. She was distraught, haggard; when she saw me she threw herself into my arms and began babbling hysterically and incoherently. Plainly she had received a terrific shock.

I immediately ordered that a sedative be administered and that she be put to bed. Even under sedation, however, she rambled on about Hank, about his being alive somewhere, and about the terrible winds that blow between the worlds and the thing that walks those winds, often carrying its victims with it out of this place and time into alien voids.

When the effects of the sedative wore off, experts at the University verified that she was indeed in contact with someone; but while they were able to detect the phenomenon of telepathic communication, they were completely at a loss as to whom *exactly* she was talking to. There was only one thing to do and that was to accept what she said as truth.

It was at this point, too, that one of my "hunchmen"—a member of a team of psychically aware specialists, the scientifically enlightened counterparts of medieval mediums and spiritualists—asked me a rather strange question. Quite casually, he stopped me to ask if Hank Silberhutte had ever been an astronaut.

I might normally have laughed but was in no mood. Instead I told him curtly that no, Silberhutte had never been an astronaut—what was this, some sort of macabre riddle? He answered in these words, which I will always remember:

"No riddle, Professor, and no offense intended—but after all I am a hunchman. And I'll tell you something; I'd bet a month's salary that it *is* Hank Silberhutte who's trying to contact Miss Alvarez. And one other thing—wherever he's transmitting from, it's no part of this Earth!"

On the morning of June 3 Juanita began picking up a very clear telepathic transmission. The following narrative, relayed through her mind from incredible and unknown voids of space and time, was recorded exactly as she received it.

Part One

◆

I

Winds of the Void

(Recorded through the Medium of Juanita Alvarez)

I'm sorry about that, Juanita, I realize now that it must have given you a terrific jolt to receive what must have seemed like messages from a dead man. But I've been trying to reach you ever since we got here three months ago, and—

You say it's been *four* months? Well, that tells me something; it took us a month to get here. And during that month we were all dead to the world except for Tracy, who had the stone, and of course poor Dick Selway, the pilot. He was just . . . dead. I'm not being callous, Juanita, but it's been three pretty hellish months for us, one way or another, and we've seen enough of death in that time to—

We? Yes, Tracy, Jimmy Franklin, Paul White and myself. All right, I'll go right back to square one for you, Juanita—back to where I cut you off when I thought that Ithaqua was going to flatten the plane against that mountain. . . .

Oh, I knew we were done for, no doubt about it. And that damned . . . *Thing!* He was massive enough when we first spotted him—shapeless, writhing like disturbed smoke, big as a building—but when he has a mind to he can simply, well, *expand.* He was just starting to puff himself up when be caught hold of the plane with a hand black as night, five-fingered but like a bird's claw, with talons instead of fingers, and his strength was unbelievable.

I thought he intended to crush us; I actually saw the inner wall of the fuselage starting to buckle as he tightened his grip. But then he lifted us up into the sky, way up above those clouds, and for an instant he paused in that position. Juanita, I admit that when he did that I just closed my eyes, gritted my teeth and prayed. And I'm not a man that prays too often.

That was when Tracy grabbed me. Scared to death, all tears and snuffles, just like when she was a little kid sister. She threw her arms around my neck, and I felt the star-stone pressed between us.

I hadn't realized it but the thing outside the plane must have been listening and watching inside my head. He pounced on the picture of that star-stone right there in my mind, stared for a split second—then threw it straight back, withdrawing his mind from mine completely. Only after he had gone was I sure he'd ever been there.

Now, I suppose you caught his thoughts when he was—laughing?—just before he grabbed the plane? Well, I've since learned that his mind-talk can only be picked up when he's really angry or, yes, frightened. Even then, though, his thoughts can't positively be interpreted. But still I somehow knew that when the great beast saw the star-stone in my mind it had shocked him rigid, frightened him. And it had made him angry!

He was snarling and mewling in a frenzy of frustration and rage. I guessed right away then that he couldn't hurt us, not directly at any rate, and for the first time since I joined the Foundation I really appreciated the power of the five-pointed stars. Think of it—a thing that can walk on the wind, an alien monster from God only knows what infinities of space and time—and a little star-shaped stone from Miskatonic's kilns rendered him powerless to harm us. Almost.

No, he couldn't directly hurt us any worse than he had already, but he certainly didn't intend to let us off lightly.

By then I think Dick Selway was already dead. He'd cracked his head against the control panel and there was blood everywhere; he just hung limp, trapped in the pilot's seat. Still, even with Dick gone, if Ithaqua had let go of the plane right then—which I thought he was going to for a second—I think that perhaps I could have landed her. And I believe the horror outside picked *that* little fact right out of my head, too. Only he had worked it out differently.

After being hoisted up to the sky, I had fallen back away from the gun in the nose; now Paul White, hunchman and photographer, made it up there hand over hand and checked Dick Selway's pulse. Whitey cursed softly and pushed Dick's body over to one side, then wedged himself against the gun. He had taken all the pictures he wanted; now he wanted something else.

Jimmy Franklin was still on the radio but getting nowhere; the aerial must have been ripped away. And so Whitey started hammering away with the tracers, hitting the Wind-Walker almost point-blank right in those eyes of his. And all he got for his pains was a shower of harmless sparks from somewhere at the back of Ithaqua's head.

Then the creature was off with us, loping across the Arctic skies in lengthening strides that took us even farther north and farther—*up!* The ice-wastes fell away beneath the plane as we rose into the sky ever faster; the acceleration was tremendous and I was slammed against the buckled wall of the fuselage with Tracy still in my arms.

Whitey, shaken loose from the gun, whirled by us and fell down into the tail section as the whole plane suddenly tilted. Before I blacked out I managed to clear the frost from one of the windows. Looking out I saw a black sky, and away and below I could plainly make out the curve of the Earth.

Yes, frost on the windows, Juanita. That started the moment Ithaqua grabbed us; ice formed on the inside as well as the outside of the plane, but without making us feel any normal sort of chill. Oh, yes, it was a strange cold. Not merely the subzero temperatures of Arctic climes but an iciness unique in Ithaqua and the weird ways he treads. It was the bitter chill of the winds that blow between the worlds.

From then on until we touched down on the littered plains of Borea—beneath vast, pitted triplet moons that hung low over the plateau on the horizon, eternally frozen in a starless sky—Whitey, Jimmy and I were unconscious. Yes, for a whole month, it seems. Some sort of deep-frozen suspended animation, I suppose. But not Tracy.

Oh, she passed out initially, but later she regained consciousness while we were still en route. She didn't know that right off, though, for there was no sensation of movement or acceleration. She believed that we were down somewhere in the mountains; coming from outside was an eerie whine or hum, like the thin winds of high peaks. The inside of the plane was all white with frost; the windows were completely iced over and opaque; she could detect no sign of life in any of us and our bodies were heavily rimed with frost. Poor kid, she could hardly be blamed for thinking that we were all dead.

Yet in a way she was lucky, too, because the door of the plane was frozen shut, and though she put everything she could into getting it open it simply wouldn't budge. God knows what might have happened if she *had* opened that door!

It was when she realized that she couldn't get out of the plane that Tracy panicked and tried to smash one of the windows in the nose. Well, she could make no impression on the window either, but she did manage to clear the frost and ice away from an area of the glass. And so she looked out.

Picture it for yourself, Juanita: to be in a plane full of icy corpses, like the interior of some weirdo outsize freezer, listening to a strange rushing hum, like a distant wind blowing through a thousand telegraph wires. To know the nightmare of being lost and alone, trapped in an ice-tomb high in mountain fastnesses. And then to peep out and discover that as bad as your plight might have seemed a moment ago, its terrors could never have equalled the horror facing you now. For staring right back at her, with the plane held at arm's length in front of him as he flew through the star-voids, was Ithaqua, the Thing that Walks on the Wind!

Strange starlanes—a hyperspace dimension where inconceivable currents rush and roar in interstellar spaces—and a being of utterly alien energies who knows the ways between the spheres as an eel knows the derelict and weed-strewn deeps of the dark Sargasso. But it wasn't only this sudden inundating flood of revelation that caused Tracy to faint away on the frosted floor of the plane. Neither that nor the sight of strange stars shooting dizzyingly by—like summer showers of meteorites magnified a thousand times—as Ithaqua hurtled through the void. No, it was the *look* on the Wind-Walker's face. It was those eyes, seeming to peel away the metal hull of the plane like tinsel to stare into Tracy's very soul. For she knew that those eyes saw her even as they narrowed in that inhuman face—and she knew, too, that they had filled suddenly with all the lusts of hell.

Thinking back to what Tracy told me when I came out of the freeze on Borea, I'm inclined to believe that time must be different for Ithaqua when he glides along the star winds, and for anything he carries with him. Not slowed down, as might be expected, but accelerated somehow. According to our calculations we've been on Borea for three months, and we left Earth four months ago, but Tracy reckons she slept only three or four times during the whole trip. As for myself, I wouldn't know one way or the other. I do remember dreams—of Tracy's head on my cold chest and her hands on my face, and her voice, crying out to me about the horror outside the plane.

But that's jumping things a bit. I'll tell it as Tracy told it to me.

When she came to after her faint it was dark; she'd accidentally knocked off the cabin lights when she slipped down the wall. The control-panel lights were still on though, and she could see well enough in their glow. Deciding to leave the main lights off to conserve the batteries, she set about making herself a sandwich and some coffee.

That was when she first noticed that despite the ice and frost everywhere she herself was not unbearably cold. And the star-stone about her neck was warm.

She felt a lot better after a bite to eat and a cup of hot coffee; but she kept well away from the windows and refused even to think about what was outside. And through all this there was no sensation of free-falling, none of the physiological phenomena of spaceflight at all; which leads me to believe that in fact Ithaqua was moving *between* dimensions.

Then Tracy noticed another queer thing. She had moved over to sit beside me on the cabin floor, and as she sipped the last of her coffee she saw that my right arm had moved; it had left a clear space in the frost on the rubberized surface of the deck. She caught her breath. I couldn't be alive, could I? No, not possibly. There I was, white as a snowflake and looking stiff as mutton in a freezer. But putting her ear to my chest Tracy listened breathlessly until she heard a heartbeat. Just one, and then several seconds later, another.

From then on, except during those periods when she was sleeping, Tracy spent her time frantically trying to rouse me from my strange, frozen sleep; not only me but Whitey and Jimmy, too. Jimmy Franklin lost the skin off his lower lip through Tracy's ministrations with hot coffee! But for all this she was out of luck and had to be satisfied with the knowledge that at least we were alive when by rights we ought to have been dead.

The answer, of course, lay in the star-stones of ancient Mnar, but she didn't know that. Besides the stone she wore about her neck there was one other aboard the plane—in the first-aid cabinet, of all places. That was Paul White's stone. If it weren't for those stones we really would have been dead by then, all of us. Only their presence in the plane had forced the Wind-Walker to exercise restraint. The ancient magic of the Elder Gods was still at work.

Like myself, this was for Whitey his first really active stint with the Wilmarth Foundation, and he had made the same mistake as I had. I had always sort of scorned the star-stones, in the way a greenhorn soldier might scorn a bulletproof vest before he's seen the terrible mess a bullet can make of a man's chest—or in my case, before I really knew the kind of horror a Thing that Walks on the Wind might wreak. Whitey, a do-it-by-the-book man, had brought his stone along all right but felt stupid wearing it, so he'd placed it in the plane's first-aid cabinet out of the way. Dick Selway and Jimmy Franklin, greener in the ways of the CCD even than Whitey and I, hadn't bothered with their stones at all! And all Tracy knew of these things, of the star-stones, was that the one she wore about her neck, which by then she'd forgotten was there at all, had been my good luck charm, my rabbit's foot.

In fact that star-stone was Tracy's reason for being on the plane in the first place. It was pure coincidence that she had been staying with friends in Edmonton for a few days while I was starting out on Project Wind-Walker. The night before we started the flying program I attended a party at the home of her friends. I had a few drinks and must have mentioned something of my preparatory work at the airfield. The next morning when Paul White picked me up, I forgot my star-stone and left it in the room where I had bunked down. Tracy found it. Since she intended to start the long trip back down to our home in Texas that same morning, she decided to go via the airfield and return the stone to me. Driving out to the field, she worked out a little prank to play on me.

For some time Tracy and my father had been speculating on my work with "The Government," and now finally her curiosity had gotten the better of her. She saw this situation as a chance to find out what it was all about.

The Foundation had secured for my team an outlying area of the airport; a fenced-off, run-down, dusty area with its own rather worse-for-wear landing strip. But it was good enough for us and anyway, our plane was no luxury airliner. We had also been supplied with a full-time guard for the gated entrance, though I have to admit that I didn't brief him well. I was hardly expecting trouble, certainly not Tracy's sort. She arrived at the gates, told the guard who she was and showed

him my star-stone. She said I had forgotten it and she knew I wouldn't
want to go off without it.

Well, Tracy's a damned good-looking girl. She probably turned on
the charm. And since the guard could have no idea just what she intended to do, I don't suppose he could really be blamed for letting her
in. . . .

Delighted with herself that her plan was working out, Tracy
parked her car behind a hangar and sneaked over to our plane. She
couldn't mistake it. It was the only one, standing out on the runway
close to the hangar. The door was open; she climbed in and tucked
herself away in the tail, and that was that.

Some time later, together with the three legitimate members of
my team, I left our headquarters shack at the other side of the field
and slung my gear into our jeep. We drove to the plane and boarded.
Tracy didn't show herself until we were airborne and well to the
north. And like a fool, after first blowing my stack, I decided to let her
stay. To head back then would have been to slow the work down for a
whole day, and the team was anxious to get on with the job. In any
case, there wouldn't be a great deal for Tracy to see, would there?

So that was how she came to be on board, and looking back now I
suppose it's just as well for the rest of us that she was. God only knows
what our fate might have been without her. But I've been straying a
bit, I think.

After her third or fourth period of sleep, Tracy woke to an unset-
tling, irritable and unaccustomed feeling quite different from any
emotional disturbance she might have expected to suffer in her present circumstances. She felt drawn somehow to the frosted windows,
and even began to clear a large area of one of them before she realized what she was doing, but not before the huge form of the horror
hurtling through the void outside began to take on an ominous shape
through the glass.

Then Tracy knew that the compulsion she felt and the inner voice
she heard in her head insistently demanding that she warm the glass
of the window until it cleared to its normal transparency, was not her
own but the hypnotically telepathic voice of the being who now
rushed with the plane on an unguessable course. And recognizing the
fact that she knew him, Ithaqua grew angry. He doubled, then redoubled his mental effort to control her.

She saw his alien lust clearly in her mind even as she stepped

closer to the window, reaching out her warm, trembling zombie hands
to the task imposed by the Wind-Walker's will. And she knew, too, his
purpose; to bend her mind, body and soul, completely and everlast-
ingly to his will through those evilly flaring eyes of his, which loomed
dully behind an all-too-thin layer of frosted glass.

And instinctively, impelled by horror alone, Tracy's hands flew to
her breast, finding my star-shaped talisman there and unconsciously
pressing that sigil of the Elder Gods to her heart. Instantly the Wind-
Walker withdrew from her mind, recoiling and shrivelling before that
abhorred symbol of the power of Good as a feather before a candle's
flame. And Tracy did not know why, suddenly, the magnet pull on her
mind was at an end, leaving her stumbling, numb, almost completely
drained of strength. She only knew that beyond the semi-opaque window those eyes blazed more hideously yet, and that the plane now
shook like a toy in the fist of a demented giant as Ithaqua's rage
brought on a massive trembling.

She moved away from the window on unsteady legs and gradually
the shaking of the plane subsided. For a spell she moved dazedly
about the aircraft, listening to the maddeningly slow beatings of our
hearts and doing what she could to improve our comfort until, feeling
hunger stir, she turned herself again to making coffee and preparing
something to eat. And as she was about that task, the temperature began to drop in the aircraft, plunging in the space of only a minute or
so from its previously frozen chill into sub-zero temperatures. A sheet
of deep white stretched itself over the windows of the nose and fuselage, completely obscuring once more the horror sailing on the winds
of the void outside. Icy fingers spread over the metal walls, rubber
floor coverings, equipment and motionless men.

It was no natural cold, but an awful condition brought about
through the will of Ithaqua. As such it could not affect Tracy, un-
knowingly protected as she was by the star-shaped symbol of Eld that
she wore about her neck, instead it speeded her to the task of throwing extra blankets over our all but inanimate forms where they lay
about the floor, to insulate us as much as possible from the incredible
cold.

Having done what she could for us and astonished and frightened
that she herself should feel nothing of the effects of the plummeting
temperature, Tracy turned once more to her coffee, only to discover
that though the electricity still freely flowed, nevertheless the water

had frozen solid in the kettle. Only then, briefly, did she think of giving in, bursting into tears and crying unashamedly as she tried once more, futilely, to shake me awake.

The depth of frost thickened in the interior of the plane, blanketing it in white crystals that glittered in the glow from colored panel lights. Finally, completely exhausted of physical strength and drained of emotion, Tracy lay down beside me and crept under the parka that covered me, hugging my cold form to her. And one by one the glass instruments of the pilot's control panel cracked and splintered as the temperature fell still lower.

II

World of the Winds

(Recorded through the Medium of Juanita Alvarez)

When Tracy next awakened it was to find her body a mass of bruises and aching bones. The interior of the plane was in complete disorder but—miracle of miracles!—her three "corpses" were all stirring, and we were groaning almost with one voice. I can vouch for that last. I most certainly was groaning! My entire body felt swollen and inflamed.

We had obviously been tossed down hard. The door was hanging open on snapped safety bolts; one of the windows had been shattered outward, I guessed by a box of ammunition flying against it; the broken box and a number of ammunition belts were strewn across the narrow deck. Snow was hissing softly in through the open door and broken window, settling in small drifts on the tilted floor. The nose of the plane was down, tail up, at an angle of between fifteen and twenty degrees. I remember thinking as I climbed stiffly, painfully to my feet that I ought to feel terribly cold, so high up in the mountains of the far North. . . .

Then it was a matter of fighting Tracy off. She was hysterical with relief, going from me to Whitey, then to Jimmy, finally back to me, crying and kissing us and babbling out her story, which I gradually began to take in. It took me a few moments to get oriented. I seemed to be more or less whole—nothing broken at any rate, despite the multiple aches and pains—and Whitey seemed fine, too, just a little shaken up. But Jimmy had a nasty bump on his head and he hadn't quite managed to get to his feet yet.

Since it was plain we weren't about to die or stiffen up on her again, Tracy soon calmed down enough to make coffee. She was shivering like a leaf in a gale, which I believed was probably just as much the result of shaken nerves as physical coldness. I managed to get the door shut and fixed up a blanket over the broken window. That would keep some of the cold out, at least. Even though I didn't feel any real discomfort myself, there was no telling what shock might do to the others. One glance out of the door as I closed it had been sufficient to confirm at least part of Tracy's story; we certainly weren't down in any mountains. Outside, under lowering clouds, a vast white plain stretched away, with strangely shaped hummocks of snow dotting it at intervals. In the distance I could just make out what looked like—but then the snow blew up like an opaque white curtain. It was a relief, though, to note that if Tracy's story should prove to be one hundred percent fact and not fifty percent fancy, fever or nightmare, then at least there was no sign of the Wind-Walker for the moment. Wherever he had gone, I hoped he would stay there.

But why wasn't I cold? Already the blanket at the open window had frozen stiff as a board, and Tracy was still shivering as if she would shake herself to pieces. I noticed that like myself, Whitey and Jimmy didn't seem uncomfortable, and immediately something began tugging at the back of my memory, something I had read of Ithaqua. The Wind-Walker was able to bring about alterations in the body temperatures of those he contaminated. Were we then contaminated? I suspected that my sister was not.

Breaking into my thoughts, Tracy passed me a steaming cup of coffee. Her hands were white and they shook. I looked at the cup for a moment, then passed it right back. "You drink it, Tracy. I think you need it more than I do."

I shrugged out of my outsize parka and wrapped it around her shoulders over the one she wore already, zipping it up the front. Then I moved past Jimmy, on his feet now, and opened up the first-aid cabinet. The kit inside was all tumbled about but I found a clinical thermometer and put it under my tongue. I also found Whitey's starstone.

I lifted the thing out of the debris of bandages and bottles, turning to the other three. "Who does this belong—" I started to mumble around the thermometer—then dropped the star-stone. It was hot as hell! A tiny puff of steam or smoke rose up from my stinging fingers; the skin of my palm was cracked where I had held the five-pointed star.

"That's mine," Whitey said, sipping his coffee and starting to look a lot more human. He was frowning, plainly wondering why I had dropped the star-stone. "What's up?"

Tracy hurried over and took hold of my damaged hand, staring in astonishment at the redly blistering flesh, then at me, finally stooping to pick up the star-stone. I started to stop her until I saw that she plainly couldn't feel the thing's heat. But was it really hot?

I took the thermometer out of my mouth and squinted at it. The scale started at 35° Centigrade, its lowest point—useful if someone were suffering from extreme hypothermia or exposure—but the mercury wasn't showing at that level. It had shrunk back into a silver blob at the frozen end of the scale. I was dead, or should be!

I knew then that Whitey and Jimmy would be the same. Wherever we were, well, it could get as cold as it damn well wanted to; *we* weren't going to freeze to death. But Tracy was something else again.

Obviously the star-stone she wore had saved her from this effect of close proximity to the Wind-Walker, but it had also left her as vulnerable to normal low temperatures as she had been before, as any normal person always is. Now I could see why Ithaqua had placed this weird stricture upon us, why Whitey, Jimmy and I had suffered this incredible change. This way Ithaqua wouldn't have to worry about our threatening him with our star-stones. We wouldn't be able to touch the damned things.

I looked at the others and saw a little of the panic hidden in their eyes, the grim fears hiding behind the white masks of their faces. The telepathic impressions I was getting were nervous, disorganized, bordering on the hysterical. Things needed sorting out right now, before matters got worse.

"Tracy," I said, "you'd better put that second stone around your neck along with the other. We can hardly afford to lose them, and you're the only one who can handle them." I brought out my metal security box from where it was stowed beneath a seat and unlocked it, taking out a duplicate copy of my complete file on Project Wind-Walker.

"You'd better read this, too," I said, passing her the heavy file of papers and documents. "Then you'll know what you've gotten yourself into."

While I was busy dealing with Tracy's education, Whitey took a small electric heater from among the items in his personal kit, a tiny Japanese model with its own adapter. He plugged it into a battery-fed outlet. In a matter of only a minute or so warm air began to pour from the grill, driven by a hidden fan. Whitey directed the stream of warmth at Tracy where she sat turning the pages of my file and sipping her coffee.

"All right," I said to the two men, inclining my head toward the back of the fuselage. We moved into a rather cramped huddle.

"Boys," I started, "I think we're in a pretty bad mess, and I admit that I'm mainly to blame. Things happened a lot too fast for me; but that's no excuse, or at best a lame one. Up to now this has been a pretty messed-up job. And again, well, I suppose the fault is mine; I *know* it's mine. So if you're starting to feel that it's high time we voted in a new chief, then—"

"You're joking, Hank!" Whitey's naturally mournful voice cut me off in mid-sentence, his eyebrows seeming to droop from the center where they met over his nose as he frowned.

"No way," Jimmy agreed with Whitey, shaking his head, dark eyes bright in his bronze face. "You got us into this, you get us out."

They were both smiling now, albeit lopsidedly. Whitey continued, "I'm a hunchman, Hank, and it's my bet that you'll boss this show no matter what anyone else decides. Anyway, we're all equally to blame for what's happened."

"All right," I told them, relieved that they were still with me, "but that's something else we need to decide; just exactly what *has* happened. I don't know if you were listening to Tracy while she was going on about all she saw, her experiences since the Big Fellow grabbed us?"

"I was listening," Whitey answered, his eyebrows drooping again.

Jimmy nodded grimly. "Sounded to me like Tracy believes we're no longer on Earth."

"Yes, that's what it sounded like," I agreed. "But we'll talk about that in a minute. First I want to clear up this thing with the star-stones."

"Confession," Jimmy sheepishly offered. "I forgot to bring mine."

"I wouldn't feel too bad about it," I told him. "I forgot mine, too. If it weren't for Tracy we'd only have the one—Whitey's. And I have a feeling that we didn't simply 'forget' them, either. No, it wasn't bravado but something else. The Wind-Walker is telepathic; if anyone knows that I do. If I'm right, then it's an even bet he's known about us all along, probably right from the moment Peaslee decided we should have a go at him. I think he's been applying subtle telepathic pressures that have gone completely undetected. I can show you evidence for what I say. Here's Whitey, a strong-willed man. He brings along his stone but then doesn't wear it. Then I conveniently 'forget' my stone. You, Jimmy, and poor Dick—you don't bother with your stones at all! Oh, yes, I guess we can be truly thankful for Tracy. She's thrown one hell of a monkeywrench right in Ithaqua's works."

"And my star-stone really burned you?" Whitey asked, confirming more than questioning the fact.

"Would you like to go and ask Tracy to let you have it back?" I said. "Perhaps wear it round your neck?" I showed him my blistered hand.

"I'll take your word for it. But how?"

Here Jimmy cut in. "I think I know. When Ithaqua grabbed the plane we were unprotected, all of us except Tracy. I must have read everything you ever put together, Hank, on Ithaqua. Don't know of a single case where he was involved when there wasn't some mention of this tremendous drop in body temperature. He—he *changes* people!"

"Right," I put in. "He brings them under his influence, subtly alters them, imbues them, I believe, with something of his own aura, which he radiates as intense cold."

Jimmy chewed his lip. "Isn't that a whole lot of guesswork, Hank?"

"Not really," I answered. "The star-stone burned me, didn't it? Just like I was Ithaqua myself, or one of his minions."

"Are you saying that we are—his?"

"Not necessarily. You've read the case histories. There was that woman, Lucille Bridgeman. She certainly didn't knuckle under to him, and she suffered the same fate. In fact I think we may soon be glad we're immune to the cold. Wherever we are, it seems a pretty grim place. *We* should be all right, but we'll have to look after Tracy. She's more than just my sister; she's the only one who can handle the star-stones. As long as she can do that we're 'untouchable'—I hope."

"Maybe," Whitey interrupted, "maybe we *have* to be immune to the cold simply to live here."

"I know what you mean. You think that Ithaqua has acclimatized us, right?"

"Something like that, yes," he answered.

"Which brings us back to an earlier question," Jimmy put in. "Just where *is* this place? Where the hell are we?"

"That's something that will have to wait, for now," I told him. "There are other things we have to do. We ought to take inventory, see what we've got that we can use, decide what should be done immediately, and work out plans to cover as many eventualities as we can think of. That last should be a good one for you, Whitey, although at the moment it's the least important of the lot. Survival is the main thing, but we won't know until the snow clears just exactly what our position is. Or how to improve it."

"Obviously we can't stay in the plane," Jimmy said. "Not for any great length of time. But if we are going to move on, we'll need to take as much of our kit with us as we can carry."

"The door will lift right off its hinges," Whitey said. "It ought to make a good sledge."

"And of course we have our guns," Jimmy butted in. "There's a rifle in Dick's kit, and a couple of pistols. He was looking after the weapons side of it, but now—" He let it tail off, his eyes straying to the nose of the plane where a frozen shape lay wrapped in blankets.

"Yes," I nodded, "and we'll need to take care of Dick, too."

Whitey added, "If we're going to leave the plane anyway, I think perhaps Dick would be just as happy if he stayed right here. Captain of his ship, so to speak."

I nodded. "Maybe you're right. Right now I suggest we see what we can pack away. We'll carry the weapons openly, of course. Jimmy, you can start—"

"Hank!" Tracy suddenly shouted, her voice somehow managing to rise hysterically in the space of that single exclamation.

I half-leaped, half-skidded down the frosted floor of the tilted fuselage to where she stood at a window. She had cleared the frost from one corner of the glass. Outside the snow had stopped. The great plain with its strange snow hummocks stood out stark against a dull gray sky. In the distance a pyramidal structure stood up from the snow. At its apex—a shape. And that shape was unmistakable.

"Ithaqua!" I heard myself say, the name hissing off my tongue.

The two men joined me as Tracy moved shakily away from the window, her hand to her throat. Clearing the frost from a larger area of the glass, I asked, "How far, do you think?"

"Mile and a half, two miles," Jimmy answered, producing a pair of binoculars. He put them to his eyes. "God, look at that—*horror!*"

I took the binoculars from him, put them to my eyes, and the distant scene sprang up large as life. Indeed, the Wind-Walker was larger than life; a fantastic, towering shape, black as a starless night, with gaping eyes that glowered and burned in his awful face. He straddled the apex of the pyramid on massive legs, gesticulating with his threatening arms.

Gesticulating, threatening what? Whom?

I increased the magnification of the binoculars and followed the outline of the pyramid down to its base. People, a crowd of them, on their knees, heads down in supplication—worshippers.

Their faces were indistinct, blurred, but I could see that they were a squat, dark people, most of them. Of Eskimo or Mongol origins, perhaps.

At the front of this prone assembly stood two men, whites, long-haired and dressed in black robes. Priests or spokesmen. Managing to get the magnification just right at last, I focused upon the nearer of the two. European, at a guess; his gaunt face seemed full of fanatic fervor. I turned my attention to the pyramid, Ithaqua's "altar." I judged the thing to be all of eighty, maybe ninety feet in height.

"That pyramid is like a damned junk-pile!" I gasped. "A heap of scrap sheathed in ice. Near the base there's what looks like a small airplane. Yes, I can see the cockpit clearly, and part of one wing. Halfway up there's some sort of tracked vehicle, and a bit higher something that looks like the gondola of a balloon. And, by God, I believe there's a heavy-duty truck in there as well! Other stuff, too, things I can't quite identify. All encased in ice, frozen solid."

I went on to describe the worshippers at the base of the conglomerate cone, then did a slow sweep of the plain in its immediate vicinity. "There are totems. Huge carved totems circling the pyramid; Eskimo, I'm sure of it, and crowned with effigies of Ithaqua. These are his worshippers, all right, and this is their place of worship."

I looked again at the thing standing splay-footed atop its altar, with one great misshapen foot resting upon what looked like the jutting bonnet of an automobile, the other gripping a second projection on the opposite side of the ice pyramid. As I did so I saw him fling out an arm in my direction, the hand pointing.

His black face with its alien contours and flaring eyes convulsed briefly, then turned to stare in the direction of the pointing hand, towards the plane. His other hand lifted high to the leaden sky and the great fist clenched. He struck himself in the chest with a downward-sweeping, imperious blow.

By that time Whitey had found a second pair of binoculars. He too had seen these last actions of the Wind-Walker. "He's giving orders," Whitey said. "Can you get to him telepathically, Hank?"

"I daren't," I answered. "Not right now. For the moment he holds all the aces. Later, if the situation improves—then, maybe—"

"In that case I'll voice a hunch; a pretty safe one, too, I think."

"Let me take a guess at it," I said, thinking about what I had just seen. "You think we've been sent for—that Ithaqua has told his boys to come and get us, right?"

Whitey frowned, his eyebrows drooping ominously. He handed his binoculars to Jimmy, then looked around to make sure Tracy was out of the way. She had moved up close to the tiny heater and had her nose stuck deep in my file again, seemingly absorbed in it. "Not necessarily *us*," Whitey quietly corrected me. "I don't think Ithaqua gives a hoot for us." He grimaced. "Except perhaps for our entertainment value. But," he nodded in Tracy's direction, "your sister—"

At that same moment she looked up, meeting our gaze. She had been listening in on us after all. "I've just been reading all about him," she said, her face ashen. "About his appetites. You don't need to whisper."

"Forget it, Tracy," I told her, anger roughening my voice. "No harm will come to you. I'll see to that, no matter what."

She tried to smile, failed to make it all the way and settled for a tragicomic pose with her hands held up before her against an unseen menace. "A fate worse than death!" she shrilled, much too shrilly.

"You just hang onto those star-stones, Tracy," Jimmy Franklin told her from the nose of the plane. He had taken the gun off its mountings and now dragged it into position in front of the closed door. "Old Windy will hardly dare to bother you while you have those hanging round your neck." He sat behind the gun and traversed it left to right and back again on its swivel, squinting down the sights. "Just let us worry about the rest of it, all right?"

III

Children of the Winds

(Recorded through the Medium of Juanita Alvarez)

From that time on our salvage work went ahead full speed, with one brief break when Tracy called us over to look out of a window she had cleared of frost on that side of the plane away from the altar of the Snow-Thing. And if we had needed convincing that indeed we were stranded on a world other than our own Earth, now we were convinced.

Tracy had started on the job of clearing the windows when she saw how quickly the steady increase in temperature in the plane was breaking up the ice and frost. Obviously we were now subject to a "natural" cold as opposed to the preternatural iciness generated by the Wind-Walker. The plane's batteries were quickly failing, true, but Whitey's heater had sent the temperature in the plane soaring, however temporarily. That the frost inside the aircraft and the ice on its wings and fuselage were formed initially through the presence of Ithaqua seemed undeniable, but obviously in the Wind-Walker's absence the frozen inorganic residuum of his passing became subject once more to mundane laws and conditions.

Unfortunately the same was not true for my crew. Tracy appreciated the warmth, of course. That was obvious from the way she had thrown off her parkas. We three men, however, remained in that same cold condition to which we had awakened. Not that we *felt* physically cold in ourselves; no, though our body temperatures were such as would not normally support human life, we suffered no abnormal discomfort whatever. To further complicate matters our circulatory and respiratory systems, in fact almost the entire scale of our physiological functions, seemed somehow contracted, slowed down. But not, mercifully, the speed of our mental and physical reactions and responses.

A very ironic situation to say the least: Tracy was affected quite normally by low temperatures of natural sources, but protected from the monstrous machineries of the Wind-Walker while the rest of us were impervious to subzero temperatures but incapable of handling the only real weapons we had against our awesome enemy.

But there I go, straying from the point again.

Let me show you the scene as we viewed it once the windows of our aircraft were back to their normal state of transparency. To one side of us, sloping almost imperceptibly down and away from our crippled machine, stretched a great white expanse that reached to a distant and gray horizon, an expanse dotted here and there with strange piles of snow whose often fascinatingly familiar shapes kept drawing my eyes to them more and more frequently as time passed.

To the other side, topping a very gradually rising slope, a vast, sheer-sided hump of rock sat at a distance of some four to five miles. This solitary feature in the otherwise featureless white expanse was a relief to the eyes, though I admit we speculated rather morbidly about the black tunnel entrances that could be seen in the base of the massive, plateau-like formation. There was life there too, showing especially in an increasing amount of activity about the mouths of the tunnels and behind turrets cut into the icy roof of the ominous stone face, but our binoculars were not strong enough to show just who or what was responsible for this activity, or to what end it was directed.

And how did all of this tell us that we were no longer on Mother Earth? Couldn't we have been somewhere in Canada, in Greenland or Baffin Island, or maybe even Siberia? Well, perhaps we could have been—but not with those three great moons hanging in the sky behind the plateau!

All gray and green, those moons, completely awe-inspiring in the grandeur they lent the otherwise desolate scene. These were the Moons of Borea, though we were not to know what this place was called until later; and those moons moved across the heavens not at all but hung immobile and unchanging always over the horizon. Even the most distant of the three orbs, its disc three-quarters hidden by that of the second, was bigger than the moon of Earth as we had known it.

And it was as I stood there in awe of this scene that Tracy, whose fearful interest was firmly and not surprisingly centered in Ithaqua rather than in this alien planet and its moons, called out to me from the other side of the plane. Two short strides took me to her side; Jimmy and Whitey crowded a second window.

For the better part of an hour while we had worked in the plane the Wind-Walker had simply stood, arms folded across his chest, atop the distant pyramid. His worshippers had remained kneeling during that period, while their lord and master stared out through partly lidded eyes over their heads and across the white plains. Now, however, he was expanding, raising his arms up to the skies, growing upward and outward faster and faster until, billowing skyward like some djinn from an Arabian bottle, he bent his legs and thrust himself up.

Then his great webbed feet spread wide and he walked the wind that suddenly came rushing out of nowhere. Rising up and up, he turned, headed toward the Moons of Borea and, passing high over our plane in an instant, finally seemed to dwindle to a dot and vanish over the distant horizon. Only once did he pause; that was when he passed over the plateau. Then his gravity-defying steps seemed to falter momentarily and his great head inclined toward the world below. His eyes turned almost sulphurous as he gazed intently down; his great arms seemed to reach toward the plateau, about which no single sign of life could now be seen. But then he checked himself and was off again, striding into the heavens. From the time he left his position atop the pyramid, he passed completely out of sight in less than twenty seconds.

That strange wind the Snow-Thing had called up carried now to the plane, flurrying the loose snow in white wind-devils and bringing with it the cries and ululations of Ithaqua's worshippers as they voiced their songs of praise. Eerily they reached out to us on the lessening squalls that shook the frozen blanket where I had fastened it up, filling the plane with an ominous foreboding.

"Batteries are nearly dead," Whitey said, cocking an ear at the dying whir of the heater.

"Yes, I think it's pretty near time we were leaving," I told him. "Tracy, you'd better get back into your parka. Wrap yourself up as much as you can."

Standing at the window as before, with a pair of binoculars lifted to her eyes, she answered, "His worshippers are leaving the altar. They—they seem to be—disappearing!"

Again I moved to her side, taking the binoculars from her. For half a minute I gazed. "They're leaving, yes, but not disappearing. They have white cloaks or pelts; when they use them to cover their bodies they seem to vanish against the snow." Then I repeated my words of a few seconds earlier, this time with more urgency. "I think we'd better be getting on our way."

"All right," Jimmy Franklin said, standing up as he finished securing his load of packs and equipment. "I'm all ready."

"Me too," Whitey agreed, heading for the door. "I'll get down outside. You two can lift the door off its hinges and pass it down to me, or simply let it fall. Then you can toss down the extra supplies and I'll stow them on our sledge. With three of us to do the hauling, Tracy might like to ride."

"Oh, no!" she cried. "I'm not going to be an extra weight for you three. Besides, I would probably freeze to death sitting still. I'll walk. And I'll do my share of the carrying. Which way are we going?"

Before I could answer her Whitey said, "Toward the plateau." He managed a grin and his eyebrows lifted momentarily from their accustomed droop. "Sorry to anticipate you Hank, but we are heading for the plateau, aren't we?"

I nodded. "Yes, there's something there that Ithaqua doesn't like, and what's bad for him is good enough for me!"

Whitey unbolted and threw open the damaged door of the aircraft, making as if to jump down—then froze as he stared out at our immediate surroundings. An instant later he stepped back and slammed the door shut behind him. I, too, had seen what waited for us outside, and suddenly the flesh crawled on my back with a life of its own. Obviously not all of Ithaqua's followers had stayed to see the end of his ceremonies, to watch him take his departure. They were waiting on the frozen snows of the plain outside even now, encircling the aircraft in a single row, having approached unnoticed in their white robes.

It was as I had suspected when I saw them through the binoculars; they were of an ancient Eskimo breed, the majority of them, although here and there in the surrounding circle I had seen white faces, too. But it was not the sight of these squat, flat-featured men that filled me with dread and set my flesh to creeping—they were, after all, only men. No, it was their mounts.

Wolves! Great white wolves as big as ponies, fanged and fire-eyed, pawed the snow with heavy pads, tongues lolling redly and hot breath condensing as it left flaring nostrils. And their silent riders sat these lupine mounts surely and with authority, arrogantly. Well, we would see about their arrogance; despite the initial dread that had filled me, we were not without weapons.

"Whitey, get the gun set up again in front of the door here," I snapped. "Jimmy, you're a good shot. Get into the nose with the rifle. Pull down that blanket so you can see what you're doing. Tracy, you'd better keep out of sight in the tail of the plane."

I carefully shot out a window in the wall opposite the door, then knocked the remaining fragments of laminated glass loose from the frame. For a minute or so there was frantic activity in the confines of the plane, then an unnerving quiet. Our breathing began to form plumes, especially Tracy's, and of course she was the only one to actually suffer from the falling temperature. We waited, not wanting to precipitate matters.

From the door, which he had opened just a fraction, Whitey suddenly called out to me, "Hank, one of the white men is making his way to the plane on foot. He's holding his hands up in the air. Doesn't appear to be armed. I think he wants to talk."

"Let him in," I answered. "But watch him closely."

Whitey swung the door open, pivoting his gun in an arc that covered a quarter of the surrounding circle. In the center of his arc a thin-featured white man stepped forward. He was dressed in a snowy pelt that covered him head to toe. He was tall. He moved right up to the door and his head and shoulders came level with the lower sill. I kept him covered while Whitey stood up to slide the metal steps into position.

The stranger climbed the steps, lowering his head to enter, then threw back the hood of his robe and shook loose his hair. It was long and white, complimenting the glacial paleness of his face in which, in complete contrast, huge dark eyes blazed with mad fervor. This was that priest I had seen at the foot of Ithaqua's altar.

As Whitey slid the steps back into their recess, closing the door again to its previous crack of an opening, I asked the stranger, "Do you speak English?"

"I speak it," he answered, in what I recognized as a Russian accent. "I used to teach it, at the College of Cultural Sciences at Kiev. I also speak the languages of the Canadian Indians and the Eskimos. I am versed, too, in the tongues of Greenland, Sweden, Finland, Norway, and Iceland—in all of the tongues of the lands that encroach upon the Wind-Walker's domain on Earth. Besides all these, I speak Ithaqua's tongue, which is not a tongue at all. The Snow-Thing knew this when he called me to Igarka. There I went, ostensibly to ski in the mountains, and there Ithaqua found me. Now I am the most powerful of all his priests!"

"You're a telepath, then," I said, making it more a statement of fact than a question.

He turned to face me more fully and raised one white eyebrow. "What would you know of telepathy?" he asked, in a voice which told me that my own talents were less than important. "What I am—who I am—is of no consequence." He looked round the interior of the plane. In profile, the hook of his nose gave him the look of some strange white bird of prey. His eyes became slits staring at Tracy where she huddled down in the narrow tail section. "What I have been sent to do, however," he continued, "is all important!"

He pointed imperiously at Tracy: "You, girl. You are to come with me—now!"

Before I could deny him, before I could even recover from the shock of his words, which had choked me with astonishment and rage, he turned again to me. "You are the leader here, yes? I see that it is so. The rest of your party—the three of you—all are invited to join the Brotherhood of Ithaqua."

His black eyes seemed to burn into mine as he scrutinized me intently; then they narrowed. "The Wind-Walker is particularly interested in your welfare. We are his people here on Borea, the Children of the Winds, and I am his messenger. You will have a short time to think about his offer. Consider it carefully; the alternative is terrible. Now I will take the girl, whom Ithaqua has found fair, and then I will return for your answer. You have three hours."

He turned back to Tracy, a devilish smile twisting the line of his cold mouth. "Come, girl. We go to prepare you for Ithaqua!"

Moving closer to him, I jammed my pistol into the hollow under his chin. "What's your name, you dog?" I choked, no longer fully able to control my voice.

He drew himself up to his full height, an inch or two greater even than my own, and his eyes were like dark marbles as he answered: "My name *was* Boris Zchakow, which is meaningless. Now I am High Priest of Ithaqua, who is not to be denied. Do you refuse to let the girl accompany me?"

"Listen, Boris Zchakow," I answered, my mind seething with murderous thoughts. "This girl is my sister. Neither you nor any other man—or monster—may take her where she will not go. Not while I live. You came here unarmed, so I won't kill you, not now. But if we ever meet again—"

"Then the pleasure will be mine!" he cut me off.

For a moment longer we stood face to face, then with a contemptuous gesture he turned once more to Tracy. "Well, girl, do you want to see your brother and his friends dead, and perhaps yourself with them? Or would you not prefer to be one with Ithaqua, bride of the Snow-Thing, and live in wonder and glory forever?" His black eyes blazed insanely.

Tracy had come forward. Before I could make a move to stop her she reached out a trembling hand to the Russian, a peculiar, half-amazed, bemused expression on her face. He took her hand in his own pale claw—then threw back his head and screamed as though pierced through with a whitehot spike!

For a long moment his outstretched arm seemed to vibrate, as if he had taken hold of a naked high-tension cable; then he snatched back his hand and, cradling it, fell to his knees. His eyes were no longer imperious and huge but sunken black holes in a dead white face. As Tracy stepped nearer still he held up his hands before him, cringing away from her like a whipped dog. And then I understood, for the hand with which he had taken hold on her was black as pitch; the flesh curled crisply from the little finger, exposing white bone!

Tracy's face, too, had changed. Gone the bemused, hypnotized look that had fooled me, her own brother, no less than it had fooled the Russian. She again held out her hand, this time palm up, to show him one of the star-stones. Then she dangled it at the end of its chain, swinging it before Zchakow's contorted face.

"You tell Ithaqua that if he wants Tracy Silberhutte, he'll have to take these, too!" she said.

Gasping, sobbing in his pain, terror and rage, with the madness in his eyes beginning to shine out as blackly as before, the Russian slowly climbed to his feet. He held his roasted hand close to him, averting his mad eyes from the star-stone, seeking only Tracy's face as he backed toward the door.

"You—" he choked out the word. "You *will* be Ithaqua's, I promise you!" His voice rose, bubbling with insane rage. "And when he's done with you, if I have to wait a lifetime, then—"

"Out!" I told him. "Now—before I kill you out of hand!"

I motioned to Whitey. He opened the door—then threw his

weight against the Russian's back. With a gurgled cry of astonishment Zchakow hurtled out and down. Moments later he staggered into view on the snow and without looking back made his way to a wolf mount. He was helped onto its back and took a fistful of white mane, yanking the animal about face. He kicked the wolf's flanks, driving it in the direction of the pyramid.

Hunched over his mount's back like some nightmare hag, Zchakow threw up his head to utter a weird, ululant cry that rang loud in frozen air. As its echoes died away there came the sharp crack of Jimmy's rifle from the nose of the plane.

"Here they come!" Whitey yelled, crouching down quickly behind his machine gun. I moved to my window. And then all hell broke loose.

IV

Battle on Borea

(Recorded through the Medium of Juanita Alvarez)

Out there on the plains of snow behind the advancing single rank of wolf-warriors, six white-robed priests threw up their arms to the skies and repeated the departing Russian's eerie cry. We heard that concerted wail even as we opened fire on the charging warriors—heard it and saw its result.

As the first of the advancing riders went down beneath our bullets, the gray skies of Borea began to darken over. Black clouds piled up out of nowhere and a rushing wind filled the air with loose snow. Through this whirling white screen the wolf-warriors reached the plane, dividing into two main groups, one battering at the windows of the nose while the other gathered about the door. Whitey's target was a mass of snarling wolf-masks and inscrutable, flat leathery faces. Riders stood up on the backs of their mounts, ready to leap in at us through the open door, only to find a deadly hail of lead spraying out at them from that opening. The snow of the plain in a wide area about the door began to turn red with spouting blood, animal and human alike, spilling out like scarlet pearls on a vast white feather bed. On and on the machine gun chattered its mad message of death, hot barrel swinging in a wide arc.

In the nose of the aircraft Jimmy constantly changed his position, now firing to the left, now right, and the sharp crack of his rifle was accompanied by a steady piling up of white-robed bodies and huge carcasses. In my own position, I was able to lean out of the window and pick off riders as they circled the plane trying to find vulnerable spots in our defenses. But seeing that the fuselage windows were too small to admit our attackers, I quickly moved down into the plane's nose to put a shot through a window on that side away from Jimmy. Then we sat back to back. He blazed away with his rifle; I rested my pistol across my forearm as I carefully picked off my targets one by one.

It was a sickening, bloody massacre—there could be no thrill in this wholesale taking of life. And no sooner had this thought occurred to me than the wolf-warriors broke off their attack, drawing back to their previous positions away from the plane and becoming lost in the madly blowing snow. Many riderless wolves trotted after the surviving party of mounted animals.

"Hold your fire!" I cried. "No point in wasting ammunition." I looked around the interior of the aircraft. "Anyone hurt?"

Grim faces turned in my direction. Thumbs up from Whitey; a cheerless grin from Jimmy. Tracy came to me and took hold of my arm. It suddenly dawned on me how cold the plane must be now— how cold Tracy must be.

"Tracy, I—"

"It's all right, Hank," she hushed me. "I'm fine."

"You're sure?"

She nodded. "I was frightened at first—of the Russian, of those wolf-things—but now I'm fine. Just a bit cold." She blew on her hands and thrust them deep into parka pockets. "Didn't Jimmy say that there were two pistols?"

Before I could answer her, Whitey called to me from the door. "Hank, they're up to something. Come and have a look."

I went to the door and peered over his shoulder. The wind still moaned like a thousand demons in pain, like all the ghosts of the spaces between the spheres, rushing here and there and flinging up the snow in our faces. Between flurries I saw that Whitey was right; the Children of the Winds were definitely up to something. Having lost about twenty percent of their number, several of the remaining riders had now dismounted. I saw one of them call over a pair of riderless animals and pull their great heads close—and in the next instant I understood.

"They're going to send in the wolves alone!" I yelled.

The words were barely out of my mouth when a great white shape came leaping up out of the flurrying snow to slam head and forelegs in through the open door. The huge wolf hung there for a moment, yellow eyes wild above snarling gnashing fangs, scrabbling at the rubber of the floor with massive paws before falling back outside. The sight of the thing had so petrified me that I hadn't managed to get off a shot. Now I pulled myself together.

Whitey had been thrown back from his position, the machine gun too, and as he struggled to get his weapon back into place a second wolf flew at the door. I almost had the door shut when the beast landed; its wild rush and weight jammed the door wide open on bent hinges, throwing me back.

Yet another wolf leaped, sending the gun flying for a second time. The beast found a purchase with three of its great paws before I could start forward, ram my pistol in its ear and pull the trigger. The convulsing body fell back outside.

Now Jimmy had come out of the nose to help Whitey with the big gun, at the same time firing his rifle with one hand, as if it were a pistol. A snarling mask with yellow eyes appeared, framed momentarily in the opening as forepaws gripped the lower sill—then one of the eyes turned red as I fired point-blank into that grinning wolf-face. Again the door was clear, and now there came a brief lull in which I quickly reloaded my spare magazines.

But the lull was far too brief, for as Whitey finally got the machine gun back into position yet another wolf crashed into the opening of the door, scrabbling and snarling hideously as it fought to get inside. Both Jimmy and I fired simultaneously, and again a great white body toppled out of sight.

Tracy suddenly yelled and Jimmy dived past me to pump off three rapid shots at a massive white head that was tearing with slavering jaws at the frame of the broken window in the nose. As the wolf howled and jerked back its bloodied head, so the machine gun coughed back into life. With a wild glad cry Whitey traversed left and right, hurling a deadly stream of lead out into the teeth of the wind.

For several moments he fired until, realizing that this second attack had stopped as quickly as it had begun, I yelled, "Save your shots!"

The lunatic chatter of the machine gun died away, and with it the howling of the wind seemed also to retreat, crying with a distant voice as the whirling snowflakes fell once more to the frozen plain.

"Save it," I said yet again, unnecessarily. "I think we've won the first round. Let's keep something for later."

Within the space of only a few more minutes the frozen plain outside our aircraft was as still as a winter scene on a postcard. The remainder of the wolf-warriors and their mounts, and a fair number, too, of riderless wolves, stood well back and out of effective range.

And it was then, when even the smallest of the swirling snowdevils had subsided, that I saw for the first time the true composition of those previously noted anomalous humps out on the great white plain. Unwilling at first to credit the evidence of my own eyes, I focused on the nearest mass with a pair of binoculars. That unnatural wind called up by Ithaqua's priests had blown much of the surface snow from the queer shape, revealing much more of its basic outline. Half of it, at least, was completely clear of the shrouding snow.

It was a ship. As a boy ships had always fascinated me. British by the style of her, there she lay on the snow, keeled over on one side like some vast, stranded whale. A vessel of heavy steel plates with powerful propellers and a reinforced steering system. At a guess, an icebreaker of the late '20s, fashioned perhaps in the shipyards of the Weir or the Tyne and long since paid for by Lloyds of London; "lost with all hands, somewhere inside the Arctic Circle." Little they knew of it . . .

Again I swept the plain with my binoculars until I found another shape I recognized. And again it was the shape of a ship—a Viking dragonship!

Proudly that ancient sea-serpentprow lifted yet from the sea— albeit a sea of snow—and still a number of round, painted shields adorned the sweeping line of the hull. A *big* dragon, this ship, like Fafnir risen from deeps of frozen ocean, but the great mast was broken and the decks were awash in ice. It seemed to me as I gazed that the songs of old Norse ghosts came whispering to me across the bitter wastes, and a voice that called on Odin and screamed for red revenge.

When Jimmy Franklin's hand fell on my shoulder I started violently. "What the—?"

"Easy, Hank," he calmed me. "It's just me, Jimmy. I've been using the glasses too, and I too have felt it, the aching and the loneliness. The Snow-Thing has a lot to pay for."

I nodded. "Yes, he has."

"See over there," Jimmy pointed across the gleaming plain at what looked like a large outcrop of rock jutting up through the snow and ice. "Part of Earth's heritage, stolen by Ithaqua like a magpie might steal a bright button. What do you make of it?"

I turned my binoculars in that direction, focusing on the monolith. The view I got was not as distinct as I would have liked, but nevertheless the outlines of that tremendous *menhir* showed up clear enough to suggest the origins of the primitive but colossal artists whose work it was. Eskimo, very probably, though of no really definite ethnic lineage that I could pinpoint—that mansion-sized block of carved black basalt reeked of age.

Vague images stirred behind my mind's eye—of the gauntly gigantic carvings of Easter Island and the Temple of Ramses the Great at Abu Simbel, which would be dwarfed beside this monumental work—but I guessed, I *knew*, that it was older by far than these. Lost Mu and legendary Lomar might have raised vaguely similar colossi in those ages when the forebears of Khem and Babylon were wandering desert tribes, but this vast sculpture predated even such lost or drowned monuments as these.

Cut into many of the monolith's flat facets were larger-than-life pictures of mighty mammoths, shown mainly in attitudes of frenzied fear, flight, stampede! And beside the carved pachyderms ran men, squat aborigines carrying axes and spears, and also sabertooth tigers, massive reindeer and bison, wolves, bears and foxes. A primitive, Paleolithic panorama, wherein all the characters fled in terror of one universal enemy. And that enemy stood out suddenly in the upper areas of the massive block as finally I corrected the magnification of the binoculars until the hitherto blurred pictures came up fine and sharply etched.

Ithaqua! A crude representation, true, but no less obscene for that, the Thing that Walks on the Wind, a being known and dreaded and worshipped by the very earliest of man's forebears. Alien the Snow-Thing most certainly was, but his *conceit* was almost human. The primitives of Earth had sculpted a vast monument to his might, and he had brought it here with him to this world of snow and winds.

"I think I can understand why he wanted to bring *that* here," Jimmy said, perhaps reading what was in my mind. "But why the ships, why *people?* What sort of creature is Ithaqua really, and why does he, well, *migrate* between worlds, between dimensions? I've read just about all you ever collected on the Wind-Walker, Hank, but sometimes I really think that we all must be missing something somewhere."

"I don't think we've missed much, Jimmy," I told him. "But there are certain things that haven't been written down yet—ideas Peaslee has been toying with, odd bits and pieces of information that the Wilmarth Foundation hasn't yet categorized, probabilities that the hunchmen have come up with—stuff like that. And since I've had to coordinate all this, well, I have ideas of my own."

I put down the binoculars and looked to see how the others were making out. Whitey had made himself comfortable behind the machine gun. A cigarette drooped from his mouth and he appeared to be completely relaxed. His finger lay alongside his weapon's trigger-guard, however, and his partly hooded eyes were sharply alert as they moved slowly over the thinned ranks of the seemingly impassive wolf-warriors. Tracy was merely a green and brown bulk in her camouflaged parka, calmly watchful where she half-reclined in a leather bucket-seat in the nose of the plane. I couldn't see her face for she had the hood of the inner parka up over her head, but her breathing made small regular plumes in the icy air.

Jimmy looked at me expectantly. "Go on, I'm still listening," he reminded me.

I paused for a moment to sort out my thoughts, then began to talk. "All right, let's see if I can tell you something you don't already know." It seemed a good idea at that, to chat about it, pass a little time until—until whatever was going to happen, happened.

"Ithaqua," I began, "is a horror come down the ages from the very mists of myth. He was known to the Ptetholites and his image may be found on Auderic cromlechs. The ancient peoples of all the lands adjacent to the Arctic Circle have left evidence of his being, and as recently as the early 19th Century certain North American and Canadian Indian tribes have fashioned likenesses of him on their totems. Just such as we've seen on the totems of his worshippers here on Borea."

"Speak up, big brother," Tracy's voice interrupted, coming to me from the front of the plane. She inclined her head slightly in my direction. "I'm not quite in on all of this yet, so if there's anything else I should know I'll gladly listen in."

I nodded, pleased with her plucky acceptance of everything, and raised my voice. "Among many other names, Ithaqua has been called 'God of the Great White Silence,' 'the Snow-Thing,' 'God of the Winds,' 'the Death-Walker,' 'the Thing that Walks on the Wind,' 'the Strider in Strange Spaces,' 'the Wind-Walker' and 'Lord of the Winds.' Such is his fascination, his morbid attraction for various popular writers that they have created remarkably good fictions based upon the ancient legends. Algernon Blackwood, a British author of world-wide repute, no doubt fashioned his 'Wendigo' on Ithaqua; and August Derleth, whose home was in Wisconsin and not so very far removed from the far northern territories, was the author of a number of extremely original and remarkably accurate stories about Ithaqua's incursions.

"He is the original air-elemental, in which every other Earthly myth and legend having regard to beings of the air has its source. The prototype of Gaoh, Chastri-Shahl, Quetzalcoatl, Negafok, Hotura, Tha'thka and Enlil, Ithaqua is given mention in the most ancient and most forbidden works known to man; and his winged totem-symbol is carved upon Geph's broken columns and crumbling stelae along with the insignia of the rest of the loathsome Cthulhu Cycle Deities. For of course Ithaqua is of the CCD, a prime elemental whose true origin is as dim and conjectural as that of the Universe itself.

"The Wilmarth Foundation believes that in forgotten prehistoric times, in ages predating Earthly life as we know and recognize it in its mundane forms, there was a battle. Earth and the Solar System formed the battleground. Beings of whom little is now known—super scientists named in those same forbidden books I have already mentioned as 'the Elder Gods'—won the interplanetary war. The CCD, defeated but still threatening, were banished to prison environments. Mental and genetic blocks were planted upon them, imprinted *within* them, just as modern criminals are made to wear handcuffs or shackles. These blocks were designed to repeat through heredity, so that any offspring of the CCD would be imprisoned by those same restrictions no less than their forebears.

"Ithaqua was perhaps the least penalized of all the Cthulhu Cycle

Deities in that he was banished to the alien star-winds which he still walks and, on Earth, to the windswept icewastes of the Arctic Circle and lands adjacent. In this he is the fulcrum upon which the futures of all his alien 'cousins' of the cycle balance. Comparatively free of the restrictions of the Elder Gods, he is the hope of the CCD; he is the one to whom all of the others look for eventual release from their immemorial imprisonment. And that is not his only ambition.

"Ithaqua is miscegenetic, with a taste for strong, beautiful white women. In this respect as in all others he is completely unscrupulous, sating his lusts whenever the mood takes him and with whatever woman is unfortunate enough to be to hand. He has already foisted children upon mankind—mated with 'the daughters of Adam'—but of his progeny there are no known survivors. Three children there were that we know of, all of them born to white women; and all of them, mercifully, too alien to live. There may have been others that we don't know of, but that seems unlikely.

"Certainly, though, there have been other women out in the snows; women who have known Ithaqua's attentions without being strong enough, either physically or mentally, to suffer them and live knowing what they knew. Why, there's evidence to show that the Wind-Walker has had whole communities of worshippers in Canada, and that human sacrifices are still periodically made to him. Nearly always young, attractive women. As to why he desires children—"

"It's a terribly lonely existence," Whitey cut in, "walking the spaces between the spheres."

I nodded. "Yes, that's probably it in a nutshell."

"That—*thing*—lonely?" Jimmy Franklin frowned. "But loneliness is a human emotion, surely?"

"What about a swan that loses its mate?" Tracy argued. "Or a dog when his master dies? Surely that is loneliness?"

Whitey half nodded his head, half shook it in a curiously self-denying gesture. "He *is* lonely," he said, "but it's a loneliness that's different from anything we could ever conceive of. And it's more than just loneliness, too. He has a definite purpose."

"Whitey's right," I agreed, "I'm sure of it. It all goes back to the monster's ultimate purpose, that of freeing his hellish kith and kin. Think about it; there's only one Ithaqua, one Wind-Walker, and his ambition is to turn all of his alien, hideous cousins loose from their many prisons. Cthulhu from sunken R'lyeh, Hastur from the Lake of Hali, Yog-Sothoth from some dark dimension—oh, all of them.

"But if there were *two* such as Ithaqua, two 'Things that Walk on the Winds,' why, then the task would be that much easier. And if there were three—four?

"The mercy is that he is not invincible. There are weapons which work against him. We have such weapons in the star-stones from forgotten Mnar." I looked at my hand, at the large blisters that covered my palm, and I laughed ruefully. "True, only Tracy can handle the things, but that's a lot better than—"

"Hank!" Whitey called. I looked at him in time to see his eyebrows shoot up, then lower again quickly as he squinted down the sights of his machine gun. "Reinforcements," he grunted.

I jerked the binoculars up to my eyes and scanned the white plain in the direction of the pyramid altar.

Reinforcements, yes! Led by the Russian priest they came, gathering out of the ice-shrouded bases of the plain's weird hummocks. For those relics of Ithaqua's visits to Earth over eon-embracing ages were nothing less than the artificial wigwams and igloos of these Children of the Winds, provided for them by their Lord and Master, Ithaqua of the Snows. Wolf-warriors in their hundreds, and in their midst a large sledge, and upon that sledge—

"What do you make of that, Jimmy?" I asked.

"I would say it was a totem," he answered. "A heavy pole, lashed to the sledge and carved with faces and figures."

"Yes," Whitey snorted derisively, "it would need to be a heavy pole. It *has* to be." He looked at me and his eyebrows drooped ominously. "It's a battering-ram!"

V

Ships of the Snow

(Recorded through the Medium of Juanita Alvarez)

As the great sledge bearing the battering-ram totem drew closer, the wolf-warriors formed a circle round our crippled airplane as before, only now they were three and four ranks deep. There must have been twelve hundred men and beasts surrounding us, and I doubted that we had enough ammunition to fire more than one shot at each of them. Even then, if every single round we fired found its target, we would still be swamped, inundated by sheer numbers.

The battering-ram was all of fifty feet long. Drawn by a dozen massive wolves in harness, with the leading pair bearing riders, it bumped roughly over the snow, jerking at the lashings that held it to the straining sledge. Cut from some giant pine the thing must have been, though as yet I had seen no tree growing on Borea, carved in designs of gods and devils, its head shaped into a blunt likeness of Ithaqua. That heavy head now pointed toward the plane, and as the wolf-warriors gave way to let the totem through their ranks its purpose suddenly became obvious. The nose of our craft was mainly of laminated glass and comparatively thin metal frames; the ram was directed straight at that fragile bubble.

"Whitey," I said, knowing that the battle must break at any moment, "whatever else you do, try to bring down those wolves pulling the totem. Same goes for you, Jimmy. Tracy, you give Jimmy cover; I'll cover Whitey from the door. Make all your shots count."

Now, as the circle of wolf-warriors tightened and beasts and riders drew closer to the plane, a contingent of them gathered around the totem-bearing sledge, making the animals that pulled it much more difficult targets. Closer the sea of faces came—flat faces and copper faces, slant-eyed and straight, Eskimo, Indian and white—faces and pointed muzzles.

"If we don't cut loose soon," Whitey breathed, "we'll never thin them down."

Even as he spoke the closing ranks began to move faster, human heels digging into animal flanks in a concerted spurring. From behind the wolf-warriors an eerie cry rang out in the frozen air: the wailing of the Priests of Ithaqua, begging the Wind-Walker to look favorably upon his warriors in battle.

"Here they come," I yelled. "Now . . . *let them have it!*"

The words were hardly out of my mouth before they were drowned by the stuttering rattle of the machine gun and the rapidly repeating crack of the rifle. Down went a dozen of the warriors escorting the battering-ram, one of them vanishing with a scream beneath the runners of the great sledge, and Whitey's roaring battle cry rang out triumphant—only to turn to a yelp of surprise as the first of the mounted Eskimos and Indians reached the plane.

A mass of white fur flashed by the jammed door; simultaneously a squat figure hurtled into the plane over the top of Whitey's deadly arc of fire. My single shot, striking the Eskimo in the chest, threw him sideways, dead before he hit the floor. Down he crashed, his fur-clad feet flopping across the barrel of the machine gun. The gun's chattering stilled at once and shapes swiftly gathered at the door. I fired point-blank into dark and light faces and slavering, snarling muzzles alike until my pistol was empty—but by that time Whitey had freed the gun.

Now he traversed the weapon, triggering it back into deadly life. But though the gun was alive its harshly uttered message was death. Death flew out through the open door in an arc, slicing into the wolf-warriors milling on the bloody snow. Whitey's attention, however, had been successfully drawn from the battering-ram; in the next instant we knew that the first stroke of that wolf-drawn totem was a telling one.

Still firing rapidly, Jimmy Franklin gave a sudden yell of warning as there came a tremendous crash from the nose of the plane. In the same second, caught unawares and in the act of reloading, I was thrown off my feet as the entire aircraft jerked violently. Whitey, firing the machine gun with one hand, somehow managed to hang on until the rocking of the plane subsided. Then the firing-pin of the machine gun fell on an empty chamber; the ammunition belt was exhausted.

I grabbed up another belt and threw it toward Whitey, kicking as I did so at a flat, oval-eyed face that appeared suddenly over the lower sill of the door. Then I was sent hurtling backward, knocked off my feet by a huge furry shape that shot in through the door with outstretched paws and bared fangs. Sprawling on my back I threw up my pistol against the pony-sized wolf crouching over me. I looked straight into the eyes of death as the beast's hideous muzzle descended. Then my bullet went in through his dripping jaws to blow out the back of his skull, lifting him from me with the shock of its impact. I rolled out of the way as the toppling, shuddering carcass collapsed with a crash where I had lain.

Through all of this it dawned on me that I had not heard the crack of Jimmy Franklin's rifle since the jarring crash when the totem struck the plane. Similarly the spitting sounds of Tracy's pistol had been absent. Now, as I leaped to my feet, the machine gun began to snarl once more to the accompaniment of Whitey's whooping. Mercifully, when the great wolf had leaped at me, it had done little more than pass over Whitey's head, causing him to duck down and momentarily lose control of his weapon.

I saw this and barely had time to breathe a sigh of relief before a gasp from Tracy swung me in her direction. She was spreadeagled against the curving wall of the plane, moving slowly away from the shattered nose section, staring back hypnotized at a squat white figure that moved after her with outstretched arms. She pointed her empty pistol at the Eskimo warrior, repeatedly, uselessly pulling at the trigger. Over and over she gasped my name.

At Tracy's stumbling feet, stretched on his back with a great bruise shining on his forehead, Jimmy Franklin lay, his rifle inches from hands that were limp and motionless. Faster the Eskimo moved after Tracy, black eyes glittering as he grabbed at her. In that same moment the head and shoulders of a second wolf-warrior appeared at the gaping hole where half the plane's nose had been caved in.

I aimed my pistol as carefully as my shaking hand would allow, pulled the trigger, aimed and fired again. My first shot went high, but was nonetheless effective for that. It seemed that the face of Tracy's attacker had barely flown apart, his corpse slamming backward into the nose section like a felled tree, before the second Eskimo was flying out through the gaping hole in the nose of the plane. As he went his arms flapped loosely, nervelessly, while the white furs on his upper body turned red in a sudden spouting.

I dropped to one knee beside Jimmy, snatched up his rifle and pumped off one quick shot into the wreckage of the nose section where I thought I saw a movement beyond the shattered windows. Then I slapped the downed man's face until he opened his eyes. Groggily he lifted his head from the floor and tried to get up; he was not seriously hurt.

"What happened?" he asked.

"You got a knock on the head," I told him. "Here, take your rifle."

As I began to busy myself, swiftly reloading magazines for Tracy's and my own weapon, suddenly the lunatic chatter of the machine gun died. There came an abrupt, unbelievable silence; then, filling that silence, springing up all around the aircraft, came the moaning of vast winds.

Listening to that wind I felt the hair of my neck rise. I knew that it was unnatural, this wind, but I was equally sure that its source was *not*

Ithaqua. This wind was—different. I felt no chill in my heart, my soul, listening to the blowing of this wind—only a sense of awe, of wonder.

"Whitey, what is it?" I cried. "Why have you stopped firing?"

"Gun jammed," he hoarsely answered, his hands tearing ineffectually at the breech-block mechanism of his weapon. "Can't be fixed this side of—of Earth!"

"But what's happening?" Jimmy Franklin asked, staggering to a window.

Whitey's eyes went wide and his black eyebrows lifted. He peered out through the door and across the white wastes. The moaning of the wind grew louder, intermingled now with strange low cries of—fear?—from the horde outside. Snow blew into the shattered nose section, whirling along the inside of the plane and settling on our parkas. The wind howled more mournfully yet.

I went to the door, stood there beside Whitey and gazed out onto the plains of Borea. The wolf-warriors were lining up, reforming their ranks parallel to our battered aircraft, but their faces were turned away from the plane and they gazed as one toward the enigmatic plateau. Though the bodies of hundreds of their erstwhile fellows littered the snow, they had momentarily forgotten us and their attention was centered upon something else.

Then, from the direction of the pyramid altar, two more sledges rushed forward toward the lines of warriors. They were hauled by howling wolves that answered to the crack of Eskimo whips, and they were laden with weapons; large, tomahawk-like axes, harpoons and spears.

"I wondered where all their weaponry was," Jimmy Franklin said. "It looked for a while as though we were supposed to be taken alive. But now—now it looks like we're really in for it!"

Whitey studied the scene out on the snows a moment longer and his eyebrows knitted as his frown deepened. "No, no. Those weapons are not intended for use on us."

"What do you mean?" I questioned.

He grinned in answer, then pulled me over to the opposite window. Louder and louder howled the eerie wind, blowing now quite perceptibly from the direction of the plateau, bringing with it the sound of—*slapping sails and creaking rigging!*

"It's my hunch we're about to be rescued," Whitey grinned again. "Look, here comes the cavalry!"

I looked, and at first could not believe my eyes.

Down the gradual slope from the plateau they sailed, majestic and awesome on huge skis, with billowing triangular sails reaching high into whistling air—platforms with shallow hulls, upon whose decks crouched half-naked warriors amid what at first appeared to be great heaps of furs—ships, a dozen of them, sailing the snows! I snatched my binoculars up to my eyes incredulously, cursed the flurries of snow blown up by the phantom wind to obscure my vision, then finally managed to focus on one of the snow-ships.

Triple skis each perhaps forty feet long and six wide, one fore and two aft, supported the structure of the snow-ship's deck; the high mast was secured fore and aft, port and starboard with heavy lines. Crouching behind narrow gunwales were the warriors, wiry white bodies and squat brown ones together, gleaming with oils, eyes eager and staring straight ahead. And those piles of furs I had seen—now I could make them out more clearly. Piles of fur they were indeed, but more fearsome furs a man never saw.

Suddenly one of them *stood up*, a great white mass that pawed the air and stretched itself, dwarfing its human master. Then the warrior jumped up to throw an arm about the animal's neck and push it down again to the deck. But I had seen it, and could only gape in amazement.

A bear! They were all bears, those vast furry heaps, huge white Polar bears almost twice as big as any I ever saw in the zoos of Earth.

"The—the cavalry." I lamely echoed Whitey's words.

"Right," he nodded, turning to step back to the door, "and just look at those so-called 'priests' run!"

The two sledges were flying back across the snows now, back toward the pyramid altar. Emptied of their weapon loads, now they carried the priests of Ithaqua three to a sledge. Like rats from a sinking ship. "No fighters, those priests," Whitey muttered.

"Jimmy," I swung about, an idea forming in my mind. "How do you feel?"

"I think I'm all right," he answered, gingerly fingering his bruise. "An almighty headache, that's all."

"And you, Tracy?"

"Fine, Hank," her voice began to tremble, then steadied. "But what's on your mind?"

"Whitey reckons that these ships and their crews are here to dig us out of this mess we're in. I say let's make their job a bit easier. We can perhaps leave the plane and fight our way over to the men of the ships. If they are here to pull us out of the fire, they'll be able to disengage that much earlier and take us back to the plateau. Who's for it?"

All three nodded as one person; then Whitey reminded, "We have only three guns among us."

"We'll keep Tracy in the middle," I answered. "Form a triangle around her. Jimmy keeps his rifle; you and I, Whitey, have the pistols."

"And all these supplies of ours, that we planned to take with us?" Jimmy asked.

"They may still come in handy," I told him. "We'll take them."

The three of us tugged and wrestled at the door while Tracy urged us on. Finally we forced it from bent hinges, letting it fall onto the reddened snow outside. We quickly threw down our belongings and equipment, then jumped down ourselves. Tracy came last, dropping into Jimmy's arms.

Now we could clearly hear the swish of the great skis and the crack of snapping sails. Hurrying around under the tail of our crippled aircraft, loaded down with equipment and hauling a sledge heaped high with bundles, we caught our first glimpse of the two factions as they faced up to one another.

The snow-ships were still now, twelve of them in a line, sails already half-furled and decks half-cleared; and the gleaming warriors who had crowded those decks were mounting massive bears on the plain and moving their mounts into a tight formation. Men and bears; a fearful army, a fantastic sight!

In their right hands the fighting men of the ships carried lances, and swinging from their leather waist-belts were picklike weapons, polished bright. The bears, of course, required neither arms nor armor; their furs were thick and their hides tough, and their terrible claws were the most lethal weapons for hand-to-hand fighting that I had ever seen. The two armies of warriors, both double-ranked now, moved toward each other. Fur-clad Eskimo, Indian and white man, spurring on their huge wolves; face to face with men of similar origins but different ideals and creeds, mounted on massive Polar bears. The armies moved closer, seemed to poise for an instant of time on the white plains of Borea, then rushed together in the clash and roar of terrible battle!

In a moment the double line of wolf-warriors broke and the bears surged through the gap, tearing all apart that stood in their way. But for all their giant strength and determined ferocity, not all of them won through. I saw one bear go down, hamstrung by the slashing claws of a great wolf; but even as the Eskimo rider of the bear fell, so he hurled his weapon at a mounted, copper-colored wolf-warrior. Such was the force of the Eskimo's hurled lance that even striking its target a glancing blow it lifted the Indian from his wolf's back. In another second the two unseated men were hand-to-hand, and in the next the squat man of the snow-ships had driven his bright picklike weapon through the proud hawk face of the redskin wolf-warrior. Then the battle surged over that gory, heroic scene and it was lost to me.

We ran as best we could toward the break in the ranks of the Children of the Winds, hauling our sledge behind us, keeping close together and forming a knot around Tracy. As we went we fired our weapons at the closest of the wolf-warriors and their mounts. We had been spotted as we left the plane and this closest group of our previous attackers was already fighting its way desperately toward us; the wolf-warriors did not intend to let us go so easily. Then additional orders were given by someone behind us, from the direction of the distant pyramid.

A strange, drawn-out ululation sounded, and it caused a greater contingent of the fighting wolf-warriors to wheel about face and come racing back toward us!

Cursing the utterer of that cry out loud, glancing back as I urged the other three on to the spitting song of the pistols and the cracking tune of Jimmy Franklin's rifle, I saw a sleek sledge knifing over the plain. The crusty snow flew in a white sleeting as bright runners cut through it, crushed it, hurled it aside. Six massive wolves hauled the sledge at a loping run, laboring under the whip of an Eskimo driver, and holding to the skimming vehicle's chariotlike prow crouched a half-dozen of the fiercest, largest men I have ever seen. Giants all, only three of these prime warriors were Eskimo; two others were copper-skinned Indians, the last a white man.

Ah, yes. And behind them crouched the utterer of that ululant alarm; Boris Zchakow, the fanatic, wind-maddened Russian, Ithaqua's number one priest. Behind Zchakow's sledge sped two others recently fled, returning again with their complement of lesser priests; and bringing up the very rear, at a distance of about a mile, as many wolf-warriors again as I had yet seen.

Twelve, no fifteen hundred of them. All armed and hurtling pell-mell in a strong, wedge-shaped formation, harpoons and spears tilted forward—and then, even as we threw ourselves to one side to sprawl on the frozen snow, the runners of the leading sledge hurled ice in our faces as it careened past. The six great warriors leaped from it to rush upon us. Now I could see that they carried metal shields—and huge metal tomahawks!

Crouching low, advancing with their weapons held high, they closed in a circle backed by a dozen wolves and their riders. From my prone position I could see the Russian priest's face. His eyes were triumphantly ablaze as, behind the advancing warriors, he peered over the prow of the now stationary sledge.

"Zchakow, you dog!" I yelled, firing one quick shot in his direction. I saw splinters fly from the sledge's woodwork near his face, then was forced to turn my weapon to more immediate work. Almost upon us, at point-blank range, was a fur-clad giant, then a second. My first shot clanged harmlessly off metal, the second took its target full in the throat above the giant's shield. This was the white man, towering at least seventy-eight inches and broad-bodied, screaming bubblingly and clawing at his scarlet throat as he went down in a welter of blood. Far from deterring the remaining five warriors, my shots seemed to spur them on. They leaped forward—

Jimmy Franklin's weapon had more penetrating power than the two pistols; crouching, he now slammed round after round into whichever target presented itself. Two of the huge Eskimos and an Indian fell, gaping holes showing in both shields and bodies. A pair of the wolf-warriors, too, reeling bloodily from their mounts. My own and Whitey's weapon both were taking their toll in support of the rifle, but they were simply not enough. Spears flew; the warriors rushed in; tomahawks flashed—

Knocked down, I rolled, and hearing a shrill scream from Tracy bounded back to my feet. Whitey was down, struggling with the shaft of a spear where it pinned his thigh to the snow. A great arm had snatched my sister aloft to throw her across a broad, fur-draped shoulder. I fired a bullet straight into the heart of the hawkfaced redskin who held her struggling form, heard his scream as he toppled.

Tracy fell beside me, winded and sobbing. Whitey had passed out flat on the snow. Jimmy Franklin's hoarse cry rang out, bringing me whirling about in a crouch to seek a new target. None was near. Some way off stood the single remaining giant Eskimo. I aimed at him carefully and pulled the trigger. The hammer fell on an empty chamber.

Now I saw that Jimmy deliberately held his fire, noticed that the special force of wolf-warriors had fallen back along with the sole surviving giant. And yet still the Russian priest roared with rage from the safety of the sledge. Without understanding a single word of the language he spoke I knew that he goaded them on, calling them cowards and heaping all kinds of insults upon them. But they were not listening to him, and though they were suddenly fearful I knew that it was neither fear of my pitifully small party nor of our marvelous weapons that stayed them.

They stared at something behind us, *above* us—stared openmouthed, wide-eyed—fearfully! They lowered their weapons and backed still farther away from us, a lone footsoldier springing into the saddle of a riderless wolf; and all the time they stared, yes, and they *listened*.

In another second the mad Russian's roaring stopped abruptly as he, too, looked beyond and above us, stared and listened. Now there was an amazing hush as the armies froze in the midst of bloody battle. Slowly we turned our heads, Tracy, Jimmy and I. We looked in the direction of the plateau.

Part Two

◆

I

Woman of the Winds

(Recorded through the Medium of Juanita Alvarez)

Staring at the sky above the low, ominous outcropping of the plateau, I thought: *One of two things; either these people have especially sensitive hearing, or they are accustomed to listening for things that I would not normally expect to hear.*

But then I did hear it; a whirling of high winds, a great tumult in the heavens of Borea whose physical effects could not for the moment be felt on the plain where I stood. Then, slowly but surely, the whirling became a rushing, a roaring as of a swollen river.

Since the battle on the plain first began the skies had been piling up with cloud. Over the plateau the air was dark and writhing, pulsating as if alive; and now, in the center of this chaos, there formed a circle of madly spinning black cloud like a slice cut through the upper stem of a tornado.

Weirdly that disc of frenzied vapour tilted toward us and with quickening pace, independent of all other atmospheric formations, sped across the lowering skies. Such was its independence that all other clouds, large and small, fled to clear a gray path for it that led straight across the heavens! Strangely, seeing that clearing of the sky-path, the stricken wolf-warriors were mortally afraid, while I personally felt great awe but no fear. Neither did the men of the snow-ships nor my own small team, although judging by the gasps of amazement from the latter they were as much in awe of this fantastic sight as I was.

Tilting my head up higher, I followed the flight of the disc of whirling cloud along the sky-path until it slowed and stopped almost immediately overhead. And now a vast and gasping sigh, composed of a mass moaning from the wolf-warriors and a concerted, ecstatic exhalation from the rest, went up from the hypnotized tableau on the plain. In the next moment, as if a spell had been lifted by that sighing murmur of the armies, the battle resumed.

But now there was a difference, for from the instant of resumption the battle progressed clearly in favor of the men of the snow-ships. The wolf-warriors fought as they retreated, true, but their lines were bending like grass before a breeze as they milled back from the swaggering bears and their jubilant riders, and to a man they seemed to keep one eye on the sky overhead—on the sky, and on the ominous black disc that whirled and roared above us.

Seeing that the battle was rejoined and having clipped a fresh magazine into my pistol, I prepared to defend myself once more. I crouched beside Tracy where she huddled over Whitey's still form, trying to free the spear that pinned his leg to the frozen surface. Whitey's pistol, flown from his hand when he fell, was nowhere to be seen.

Jimmy Franklin, out of ammunition, had reversed his rifle and now gripped the barrel with both hands like a club. For a moment we stared at each other, Jimmy and I, and then he said, "Hank, it looks to me like these people here are scared to death—almost as scared as I am. This could be our chance to make a break for the snow-ships."

He was right. The circling wolf-warriors had pulled farther back from us; much closer were the advancing lines of fighting bears, cutting off our attackers from the rest of the wolf-warrior pack. I handed Tracy my pistol, put both hands to the shaft of the spear (mercifully a true spear and not a barbed harpoon) that fastened Whitey down, and pulled it free as smoothly and gently as I could.

Whitey moaned and trembled on the frozen ground. Tracy handed the pistol back to me and sat down to cradle Whitey's head, wiping his brow with snow.

Jimmy Franklin threw down his useless rifle and reached for the bloodied spear. "All right," I told him, "we'll make a break for it. I'll carry Whitey; Tracy will have to stay between us."

Then, before we could make our move—even above the crazed rushing and roaring of the whirling black disc hanging above us, over the clash of battle and the screams of dying men and beasts—again the mad Russian priest's scornful voice rang out, lashing our ring of attackers into activity.

But no, despite the fact that they obviously feared this wild-eyed white man, the warriors would have none of it. True, they made a half-hearted show of rushing upon us, but as soon as my pistol resumed its vicious spitting they spurred their wolves to a hurried retreat. And now they were gathering into a group, no longer ringing us, backing away in the direction of the distant pyramid altar and prepared at any moment to turn and flee.

It could have been that their reluctance was due to the fact that the men of the snow-ships were now breaking through the disordered wolf-warrior lines in a dozen different places, but I was sure that it was much more than this, that it still had a lot to do with the whirling disc in the maddened sky. But now, however hesitantly, indecisively, massive wolf-warrior reinforcements were arriving to bolster the faltering morale of their battered brothers. Well over a thousand of them, these were the men of that wedge-shaped formation I had seen bringing up the rear behind the three sledges of the priests. They paused momentarily before entering the battle.

It was at that moment that the insane Russian, wearied now of trying to goad his men to the attack, grabbed the Eskimo driver of his sledge by the arm and screamed a harsh command into his ear. Immediately the squat driver leaned forward to crack his whip across the backs of the six harnessed wolves.

Round in a semicircle the heavy sledge skidded, while Zchakow clung like a great white leech to its prow. Now, as the team of wolves hurtled straight toward us, I saw that it was the Russian's intention simply to run us down. I yanked Tracy to her feet and thrust her away, slipping and stumbling over the snow.

The sledge of the high priest hissed down upon us, and again he screamed a harsh command. In answer to that urgent cry, spurring his wolf forward out of a milling, snarling crush of human and animal bodies, rode that massive Eskimo survivor of the six warriors Zchakow had sent against us. Straight for Tracy the giant guided his massive mount, leaning out to reach for her with avid, grasping hands.

"Tracy!" I yelled. "Tracy—*look out!*"

And at that precise instant of time, simultaneous with my cry, came a fantastic intervention. Twin, deafening reports sounded from the sky, a double-barreled blast like that of some cosmic shotgun.

High in the heavens, emanating from the center of the whirling disc of cloud, two great dazzling bands of fire reached out, curling over and down, swaying above the plain like twin serpent heads before leaping earthward to flash unerringly to their targets. Magnificent, awesome, fearfully *sentient* they were—thunderbolts that crashed down with pin-point accuracy on those who would destroy us!

When they were almost upon us, suddenly the wolves that hauled Zchakow's sledge were enveloped in crackling white flame that reached from the sky. One second they were there, caught in that awful holocaust of electrical energies, and the next second that pillar of fire was gone and they were ashes through which the sledge, its prow blazing, careened to spill onto its side.

Two figures were thrown like rag dolls onto the snow: the Russian and his Eskimo driver. The latter got to his knees—just in time to catch a stray spear full in the back. The shaft ran him through, knocking him face down and stone dead upon the frozen ground. It was just as well for him that he died that way. He had been screaming hideously even before the spear hit him, and I had seen that his arms ended in steaming, redly dripping stumps at the elbows. Reaching over the prow of the sledge, those arms of his must have been caught in that same pillar of flame that incinerated the wolves.

But what of Zchakow? Where was he now? Then I saw him, mounting a riderless wolf, in a hurry to make good his escape. I lifted my weapon and had him fairly in my sights when a stumbling figure fell against me, deflecting my aim. It was Tracy, weakly calling my name, half-fainting with shock and terror.

"Oh, Hank, Hank—it was *terrible!*" she cried. I tried to clasp her to me but she pulled free to point shudderingly at a pile of smoldering fur and gray ashes on the snow: the remains of the giant Eskimo warrior and his mount. "That fire—that awful fire from the sky!"

"Come on!" Jimmy Franklin suddenly cried. "Now we can make it!"

I saw that he was right; the tide of battle had washed by us. Apart from a narrow strip of frozen plain littered with dead and dying men and animals, nothing now stood between us and the line of motionless snow-ships.

I threw Whitey across my shoulders and Jimmy picked up Tracy. As we stumbled toward the snow-ships a quartet of massive bears lumbered forward, their riders holding out brawny arms to us. Tracy was taken from Jimmy by a black-haired, hawkfaced man who could only be of pure Indian stock, possibly Tlingit or Chinook. She clung to him grimly as his huge mount turned about. Ten or eleven feet tall, a second bear approached me. At the command of its Eskimo rider, this moving mountain of fur lifted Whitey from my back to tuck him under a massive limb. Yet another rider reached down a hand to me, and as I swung up beside him I saw the fourth pick up Jimmy. Then we were off at a lumbering run for the nearest ship of the snow.

As we reached the ship, willing hands reached down to lift us aboard from the backs of the bears. The deck was of rough planking, along which we were hurried to the upward-sweeping prow. Whitey was borne away to the rear of the ship; I assumed that his wound was to be given immediate attention.

Tracy was on her own feet again by then, and as we gathered at the rail of the bird-beaked prow to watch the battle from this point of higher elevation, so Jimmy Franklin struck up a conversation with the stern-faced brave whose arms had lifted my sister from him. They spoke slowly at first, Jimmy finding his way with the Koluscha-Tlingit tongue, but soon the conversation became an excited babble. Shortly Jimmy held up his hand to still the tongue of his new friend; he turned to me.

"He says that we showed great courage in defying Ithaqua, and that we have done the people of the Plateau a great service in ridding Borea of so many of Ithaqua's people. He welcomes us aboard the ship of Northan the Warlord, where we await the coming of Armandra, the Woman of the Winds."

"Hold on, Jimmy," I told him. "Let's take it slowly. Is your friend here this, er, Northan the Warlord? And who is Armandra?"

Again they engaged in the obscure Indian dialect, then, "No, this is not Northan; his name is Kota'na, and he is the Keeper of the Bears. Northan is a man like you—and yet not like you. He has your height and your blue eyes, but he is darker skinned and his hair is jet."

"And Armandra?" Tracy asked him.

Jimmy lifted his eyes to stare out over the battle that still raged on the white plain, then turned them skyward to that enigmatic disc of madly spinning darkness. "He says that Armandra is Priestess of the

Plateau, the Woman of the Winds." He paused, then lifted an unsteady hand to point at the whirling disc. "And he says that Armandra is—*there!*"

"Look!" Tracy cried. "Hank, what's happening?"

Decimated, the ranks of wolf-warriors had drawn back to form triple lines of perhaps four hundred and fifty men mounted, and another two hundred or so riderless wolves. Behind them, spaced out along the line they formed, Ithaqua's six lesser priests leaped and cavorted on the snow, their cries reaching us on the wings of a wind that suddenly rose up to blow from the distant altar into the faces of the warriors of the snow-ships. Behind the six priests, raised high atop a human pyramid of white-robed warriors, Boris Zchakow held up his arms to the skies and offered up a cry the like of which I was sure civilized man never heard before from the throat of man.

Close about us pressed a dozen or so of the half-naked men of the ships, murmuring excitedly, expectantly, staring out across the plain. Jimmy Franklin asked a further guttural question of Kota'na and on receipt of the answer again turned to me.

"He says that Ithaqua's priests are fools; that while their master is undisputed 'First Lord of the Winds,' Armandra's powers are second only to his, and that any forces the priests can call up will be child's play for the Woman of the Winds. And such tomfoolery, he says, will only anger her. Look!"

As he spoke he flung out an arm to point across the battlefield. About two hundred yards of death-littered plain separated the two armies. Now, between them and growing up out of the frozen ground in front of the ranks of wolf-warriors, six towering tornadoes reached skyward. Thin spirals at their bases, thickening at their tops to about one hundred feet in diameter, they whirled like spinning tops, gathering up all of the loose surface rime of the plain and rapidly becoming almost solid cones of snow and ice.

Then, with almost military precision, these evocations of an alien science began to move forward toward the opposing army. As they crossed the open space the bodies of fallen men and beasts—Eskimo, Indian, Mongol and European, and the carcasses of wolves and bears alike—were swept up into their funnels to whirl madly in the tumult of frozen debris.

Now those six priests also moved forward, advancing between the wolf-warriors, urging their fantastic, inhuman charges on with cries and crazed cavortings. All of this I saw through the binoculars which I still wore round my neck, but soon I could no longer hear the cries of those priests for they were utterly drowned out in the torrent of sound that washed outward from the awesome scene on the plain.

Staunchly stood the men and bears of the ships, unfaltering in a whipping wind that threatened to blow them all away like leaves in a gale, facing the whirligigs of doom that rushed upon them. And then a gasp went up from the figures that crowded me in the prow of the snow-ship. In the sky above the armies, something was happening.

Dead center in the whirling disc of black cloud an opening had appeared, and down through this opening a shape now lowered—a human shape. No, perhaps not human, for how could any person of flesh and blood be up there, walking down the wind beneath that enormous aerial Catherine-wheel? And yet, unless my own eyes played games with me, that figure was indeed human—the gorgeous shape of a woman whose flesh was as white as the snow of the plain—a woman garbed in white fur boots and a short fur smock, who fell in a swift but *controlled* motion down through the air with her arms held wide and parallel to the ground, forming a living cross. Her hair was billowing above her, long and flaming red, rippling as she fell like the tail of some fiery meteorite of flesh.

Down she came, slowing to a gradual halt, still as a hawk on the wind, level with and facing the flat caps of the viciously spinning tornadoes. She stood in thin air, surveying the scene before and beneath her with lowered head. Her back was toward us and her face hidden, but nevertheless I knew she must be beautiful. Beautiful and regal—and powerful.

Now she moved her arms out toward the six white titans that threatened her with their spinning, nodding heads, palms flat against them, denying them—and they paused in their forward motion as if suddenly come up against an invisible wall. Trembling and swaying wildly, fighting to move forward against the will of that Woman of the Winds, the great spinning tops strove to obey the ecstasies of the priests behind them. But her will was stronger than theirs, stronger than the combined wills of all the priests of Ithaqua together.

Faster the tornadoes whirled, frenziedly battering themselves against the invisible wall of Armandra's will, gyrating erratically and losing all of that precision with which they had marched across the plain. Their end was quick; unable to move forward they began to sway from side to side, falling one against the next like dominoes tumbling in a row, and since they could not tumble forward they fell back the way they had come.

And that was a sight to remember, the tumbling and crashing of those nearly solid inverted cones of snow and ice. An avalanche from the sky, the collapsing columns smashed down to raise a thick haze of ice-dust that momentarily obscured the panic gripping the wolf-warrior army. How the Priests of Ithaqua escaped with their lives in that shattering deluge I could never say, but escape they did, for when the white haze began to settle they were already aboard their sledges, and Boris Zchakow with them, rushing back across the white waste toward the distantly towering pyramid altar.

With my binoculars I found the mad Russian, saw him turn to glare, eyes bulging, at the figure of the woman in the sky, mouthing some unheard obscenity and shaking a fist at her in lunatic fury.

Ah, the fool—for Armandra saw him too!

The flaming hair of that fantastic figure billowed up on her head and seemed to glow with an unnatural light, turning her whole body and the simple garment she wore a peculiar copper color, like frozen gold. Slowly, deliberately, she reached up, one slender arm above her head and the chill copper glow extended from her pointing hand to spiral upward to the great disc of black cloud that yet whirled and roared above her, a primal watchdog guarding its mistress.

She began to rotate her arm, the circle rapidly growing wider as if she twirled the rope of some enormous lasso. And the cloud-disc, the loop of that lasso, spun with her arm, speeding up until its edges became a wispy blur laced with flickering traceries of electrical fire.

Now the wolf-warrior army was in full flight, hurtling away down the slight slope toward the distant circle of totems and its central altar. Totally disarrayed, chaotic, theirs was a panic flight which, like a stampede, would not be checked until men and beasts had run themselves out. They were done with fighting for this day, hurrying home to lick their wounds and count their dead; and riding with them in their midst went Boris Zchakow, head and shoulders taller than the three men who rode his sledge with him.

From this fleeing rabble back to the Woman of the Winds my binoculars flew, and now I could almost feel the anger radiating from her where she stood in coppery splendor atop the very air. *"Zchakow,"* I told the distant madman under my breath, *"Russian—if you think*

you have an enemy in me, you don't know the half of it. Human ene-
mies you can possibly afford, but not such as this Woman of the
Winds!"

And oh, I was right.

Now the figure in the sky seemed to swell outward, burning
bronze to match the billowing tresses that crowned her—and for a
moment I thought I knew where I had seen a similar *expansion* before. But then, in another moment, the shape was human again, only
human.

Human? I laughed at myself derisively. There must be that in this
being which was human, yes, but there was more, much more than
that to her. There was this power of hers over the elements—and
there was her anger.

Now she lowered that slender arm of hers to a horizontal position,
and the great disc above her head tilted forward, dipped, slid down
the wind, rushed like some gigantic discus thrown by a god in the
Games of Heaven—or a demon in hell's chaos. Leveling out over the
white waste, it rushed after the fleeing army of wolf-warriors.

Tracy clutched my arm, her breath pluming faster as she watched
that incredible scene. "Oh, Hank—how *could* she?"

It was one thing to be engaged in a fight for one's life with fallible,
mortal enemies, but another thing entirely to see this Woman of the
Winds, this being who fought with weapons fashioned of the forces of
nature, ruthlessly, cold-bloodedly destroy a small army.

And surely that army, or what was left of it, would be destroyed if
the whirling juggernaut Armandra had unleashed upon it were allowed to run amuck through its scattered, fleeing ranks.

"I—I don't know," finally I answered Tracy's question, surprised to
find that my throat was dry and my voice cracked.

"They are terrible people," Tracy continued, "but they *are* people!" Then she closed her eyes and turned her face to me as the great
disc caught up with the hindmost of the fleeing wolf-warriors.

Unable to tear my eyes away from the scene, I felt my lips draw
back in a gasp of horror as the disc struck, tearing into and ripping
through men and beasts as the blade of a circular saw rips wood, flinging the debris of its passing hundreds of feet into the icy air and across
the white waste. And then, even as I watched, the disc paused, hesi-
tated.

With shaking hands I focused yet again upon the Woman of the

Winds. Now she had thrown up an arm before her eyes, her other hand thrust out before her as if to ward off some unseen horror—the horror of her own inhuman anger unleashed. In the next instant she shook her head, sending her magnificent red tresses billowing, then waved her arms outward in a sharp, clear sign of dismissal.

And suddenly there was a tremendous roaring from the plain, such as a tidal wave might make breaking on some unsuspecting promontory. The weapon she had hurled at the fleeing army flew apart, disintegrated, returned in the space of a few seconds to its elemental form, lay inert over the plain as a gray cloud! A cloud that settled to a ground haze, revealing at last the hundred or so remaining wolf-warriors racing frenziedly on beyond its drifting, curling tendrils.

Faintly, breaking the sudden silence, reaching us on a mournful wind that sprang up in the wake of all that had passed, came a distant rumbling and hysterical screaming from the spared, fleeing wolf-warriors. For certainly Armandra had spared them, and I knew now that there was more of the human in her than I had suspected.

"She let them go!" breathed Tracy.

"Let them go!" Jimmy Franklin gasped, echoing her, his voice clearly displaying relief.

"Yes she did," said another well know voice, edged now with pain, from behind us.

It was Whitey, hobbling on one leg, his arm around the fat neck of a grinning Eskimo. "She did, so there's hope for her yet," he finished.

"Whitey, what do you mean?" I asked.

He nodded grimly in answer, eyebrows lowering, staring at the figure of the woman in the sky. "See for yourself," he said.

As a tremendous accolade of cheering, whooping, and the rattling of hundreds of weapons on shields went up from the victorious army of the snow-ships, I looked up and saw—and understood. I understood this woman's power over the elements of the air, her ability to walk on the wind, her inhuman anger and her all-too-human anguish.

For now she had turned to face her people, and hearing their wildly clamorous applause she held out her slender arms to them. Her marvelous hair swirled above her and her eyes shone momentarily as a great queen's to the ringing cheers of her subjects.

Her eyes shone, then for the space of a single instant blazed bright carmine, twin stars in her regal face!

Whitey nodded again, then said, "The safest hunch I ever had in my life, Hank. That woman is without doubt a child of Ithaqua, and we must thank our lucky stars that she appears to have broken away from her monstrous father!"

II

On the Ship of Northan

(Recorded through the Medium of Juanita Alvarez)

Half an hour later, during which time the ski-borne ships were brought about and the great bears paraded up onto their decks to be chained to individual rings, the last few wounded men and animals were being brought aboard when Armandra herself took her place at the prow of this ship of her warlord.

During that interval we had also met Northan the Warlord, if it could be called a meeting. A big man, tall as myself and muscled about his arms and shoulders like one of the bears, he had paused momentarily in the issuing of multilingual commands to stride to the prow of the ship and look us over. He literally did that; looked us over, and the frown of disdain that grew on his darkly handsome face told me that he hardly considered us worth the effort.

I immediately, irrationally, took a dislike to him. Blue-eyed with light brown skin and long dark hair, his face and form seemed to me to hold elements of many races, a powerful lineage.

My dislike increased by leaps and bounds when he casually chucked Tracy under the chin, lifted her head and grunted grudgingly. Before I could say or do anything he had strode away again, but from then on I watched him more closely; not because I believed that Tracy needed a watchdog, but simply because I don't like being held in any sort of contempt. The man who does that to me or mine must then live up to it.

I was still thinking dark and as yet unjustified thoughts when finally Armandra came aboard. Her arrival at the prow of the snow-ship was as awe-inspiring as anything we had seen of her yet, for of course she walked down the wind to step aboard the vessel from an invisible platform of air that buoyed her up as if she were a bubble.

Watching Northan as he strode the deck issuing his orders and pointing here and there with the stock of a short whip, I turned only in time to see her take the last step that brought her aboard—from a position some fifteen to twenty feet above the frozen surface of the plain—and I would have missed even that last step but for the sudden gasp that went up from the vessel's crew. That and the fact that all around me men were falling to their knees, heads bowed in absolute reverence. Kota'na went down instantly, dragging Jimmy Franklin with him unprotesting; even Whitey knelt, though it brought a moan of pain to his lips to have to bend his wounded leg. I couldn't see Tracy for she stood slightly to my rear, but I later learned that even she had humbly lowered her head; Tracy, as proud a girl as ever walked.

Without any shadow of doubt this Woman of the Winds had magic; a magic which, while my body must ever stay rooted to earth, was nevertheless powerful enough to send my soul walking on air. Oh, yes, she was beautiful, this Armandra.

Draped as she was in a white fur smock, still her long full body was a wonder of half-real, half-imagined curves that grew out of the perfect pillars of her white thighs. Her neck, framed now in the red silk of her tresses, was long and slender, adorned with a large golden medallion.

I have never been much of a poet, and no less could do justice to her face. It was the face of an angel; oval and beautifully molded, white as snow. In it great green eyes—mercifully green where once I had seen them glow red—stared out from beneath fine golden eyebrows that lay straight and horizontal beneath a high brow. Her nose was straight, too, but delicate and rounded at its tip, while her mouth was curved in a perfect, if a fraction too ample, cupid's bow.

Hair red as fire and eyes green as the deep northern seas of Earth, and a skin as white and smooth as the snowy marble of quarries of dream; this was Armandra's face. And as I gazed at that face I saw one eyebrow lift a little, wonderingly, and the smallest of smiles beginning to—

—And then I was knocked from my feet by a charging blow to my shoulder that would have brought down an ox! I went flying, to crash jarringly against the rail of the prow where I fell to my knees. The next moment Northan appeared over me, legs spread wide and eyes blazing.

I knew immediately that the warlord's anger sprang from my apparently irreverent attitude toward the Woman of the Winds, in which he could not in fact be more mistaken. Indeed, I already revered this woman, but not as any religious worshiper. Snarling and blustering the bully raised his whip, and as I came to my feet he snapped the thing to send its single metal-tipped thong flying in my face. How easily he might have caught my eye, but instead the metal cut me high on the cheek—and higher still on my pride. Pride goes before a fall they say, but be that as it may this time it would be Northan's fall. On that I was determined.

I reached up a hand to my face to feel a thin trickle of blood, and I felt my eyes widen and the skin about my mouth tighten involuntarily. Northan's arm went back again—and immediately a chiming voice rang out. Too late that golden voice of imperial command, for already the whip was snapping, and I was moving forward inside its wicked radius.

As the metal-tipped thong flew harmlessly over my shoulder I turned slightly to one side and drove my elbow deep into Northan's body below his ribcage. He bent over, almost double, and as he expelled air in a great gasp of surprise, so my cupped hands, clenched into a hard knot, rose up to strike his descending brow.

Most men would have died there and then, of a fractured skull or broken neck, but not Northan the Warlord. His neck was like that of a bull. The shock of the blow I had delivered nearly broke my arms as my opponent's body lifted clean from the planking, flew across the narrow prow and smashed through the opposite rail. He spun out of sight and fell to earth. The fact that I had not killed him was all too obvious from the cry of disbelieving rage that swelled up a moment later from below, and in the outraged bellow that followed as the warlord came limping up the wide gangplank amidships, his dark face working and a picklike weapon gleaming in his fist.

But again Armandra's bell-like tones rang out, and this time she spoke in English. "Stop this now, Northan! You should be ashamed of yourself, thus to treat a man who has fought so well against Ithaqua's wolf-warriors. And you—" she turned her now wrathful eyes on me, "to attack the man whose army has saved all of your lives!"

"I only returned his blows," I answered, neither liking this chastisement nor yet quite knowing how to answer it.

"My brother allows no man to strike him." Tracy's sweet, angry voice came from beside me as Northan swung himself up onto the raised platform. "The warlord must consider himself lucky to be alive!"

I had to grin at my sister's pluck and her faith in me; and I saw now that Armandra also smiled at Tracy, that her smile widened noticeably as she said, "Your brother? I had thought perhaps that—"

"You, man, stand and fight!" came Northan's rage-filled, guttural voice. He crouched before me on the raised deck eyes red with fury, picklike weapon grasped tightly in a massive, bloodless hand.

"Northan!" the Woman of the Winds gasped. "I have told you that—"

"But Armandra, he refused to kneel before you, and struck me with his naked hands when I would have punished him! The dog must—"

"He struck fair blows when you should have expected them, and they were telling blows," she taunted him. "And where you used a weapon, he did not, though his weapon," she indicated the pistol at my waist, "could have killed you instantly."

For a moment longer we stood there, the three of us, in some sort of confrontation. Then, "Enough," the Woman of the Winds cried. "It is done now, finished. We are wasting time and no one knows when Ithaqua might return to Borea." She fingered the medallion she wore about her neck, seeming suddenly nervous. "It is time we were away. I will call a wind to blow us home to the plateau."

The dark frown stayed on Northan's face, but as Armandra spoke he lifted his head and sniffed the air. "It's much too quiet," he finally rumbled in agreement. "Can you not see, Armandra, what Ithaqua's devils are up to?"

"No, not now," she shook her head. "I need my strength to call the wind. Today's work was hard."

So saying, she stepped into the very point of the prow, lifting up her arms until she resembled some perfectly carved figurehead. As she assumed that posture her red tresses eerily floated up over her head, while tiny gusts of wind sprang up from nowhere to play with the fur collar of her smock. A moment later the great, loosely hanging sails began to fill out. Behind us, far back across the death-strewn white waste, a hundred snow-devils grew up from the frozen ground to race toward us, lifting into the air and swirling themselves into nothingness.

And then the wind came, moaning in tune to the sudden groaning of the rigging and the creaking of straining timbers, and we were off with a lurch and a slither and a hissing of huge skis, riding the snow-ship of Northan the Warlord back to its berth in the base of the plateau. Gracefully the great ships slid into an arrowhead formation, and the wind Armandra had called blew us steadily away from the scene of the recent battle.

Oh, there were sights to be seen and thrills to be experienced during that short, strange voyage, no doubt about that; but for me—I could not take my eyes off the figure of the not-quite-human woman-creature who stood so proudly in the prow with her hair floating weirdly over her head and her slender arms held up to feel the loving caress of currents of air. And I envied those gentle currents whose soft fingers caressed her. The others—Tracy, Whitey, and Jimmy—they could watch the sailors of the snow-ship about their tasks, speculate on the origins of the many tongues they heard, thrill to the sway of the deck and the strange odors of men and beasts. For my eyes there was only Armandra.

After a while she must have felt my eyes upon her for she turned her head slightly in my direction. Can snow blush? I believe I saw the slightest tinge of red blossoming on her cheeks, or was it only the reflection of that red halo of hair she wore? Whichever it was, she immediately lifted her head higher and looked straight ahead, but I saw that now her great green eyes twinkled with something that had not been there before.

I was just wondering if I dared attempt to touch her telepathically, if that were at all possible, when suddenly, without looking at me, she said, "Why do you stare at me so?"

I was taken unawares. "Why—because—because you are a fascinating woman. You have strange powers," I lamely answered.

"And is that all?" Still she stared straight ahead, but I sensed disappointment in her tone.

Encouraged, I told her, "No, that's not all. You are very beautiful. In my world women are seldom so beautiful."

"In your world," she dreamily answered. "In the Motherworld. And are they also fascinating, these women of the Motherworld?"

"Not like you."

"Northan would whip you for your boldness. He would have Ko-ta'na set his bears on you." Her warning was offered in grave tones, but there was color in her cheeks.

"Is the fervor of Northan's loyalty really so great, or does he lay claim to you as a woman, Armandra?" Having uttered these words I could have bitten my tongue clean through. Her eyebrows lifted and her smile disappeared in a twinkling. She half-lowered her arms and tossed her head angrily, setting her red tresses in motion. Most of her humanity was gone in as much time as it takes to tell. She was now the Woman of the Winds again, a chill priestess of powers unknown.

"Am I a spear or axe or piece of fine fur that a man shall *claim* me?" her voice cracked as sharply as had Northan's whip. "Northan? He has hopes, the warlord, and he is a strong man and a brave warrior. But a claim? No man has any claim over Armandra—no man! What mere man could ever hope to hold me, when the winds themselves want me for their bride?"

Finally she turned to me, anger and frustration bubbling up from oceanic depths of eyes, flaming tresses alive upon her head. "I have promised my people that soon I will take a man, and it will be so. But no man claims Armandra. I will have a mate, yes; and bear his children as my duty to the plateau. But he will not be my lover on his terms, nor my 'husband' on any terms. His task may give him pleasure but it will only give me children. Children to walk the winds like their mother, and do mortal battle with their unutterable grandfather!"

Now she leaped up—or did she float?—nimbly to the rail of the prow, poising for a moment before diving headlong to breast the air, to spiral up, up to the skies, borne aloft in a cauldron of rushing wind that almost bowled me from my position. She disappeared over the rim of the now looming plateau.

As suddenly as she was gone Northan was at my side. He had plainly been close at hand, had seen the anger in Armandra's face. His own face was not so dark now; blue eyes glittered slyly as he said, "Perhaps I should have warned you, man of the Motherworld. Men do not speak to Armandra as they do to other women. She is no pretty toy but a princess of the gods."

He turned as if to leave me, then looked back. "One other thing: when Armandra takes a mate it will be Northan the Warlord. Others want her, true, and they may challenge my right if they dare. Make sure that *you* do not challenge it. You have yet to pay for shaming me today, in which you were exceedingly lucky, and though Armandra has forbidden it I would dearly love to crush you like a snowflake. Do not give me the opportunity."

"If I loved a woman enough, then I might fight for her, Northan," I told him. "But Armandra? She is like the great glacier whose chill wears away even the mountain. Can you warm her, Northan? I doubt it. And take heed; Armandra is no snowflake to be crushed in your hand, and neither am I."

Now the wind that filled our sails quickly fell away and the twelve ships turned to run parallel with the base of the plateau in single file, gradually slowing upon their polished skis until they were all brought to a halt by use of a system of spiked brakes. Then the great bears were paraded down the gangplanks and chained up in teams fifty strong to haul the snow-ships to anchorage in entrances at the base of the plateau.

As the men and bears finished their various tasks and went off along tunnels that pointed directly into the heart of the vast, flat-topped outcropping, my small party and I began to feel more and more out of things. Ignored and feeling inconsequential, not knowing what else to do, we simply stood idle aboard the snow-ship watching as the members of her crew and their mounts gradually dispersed. Jimmy Franklin tried to catch Kota'na's eye, but the Indian was busy organizing the bears into groups to be led away. Northan had long since gone off with a party of his men.

When it seemed that we were to be left to our own devices, as we descended the steep gangplank to the frozen floor of this rock-walled harbor, a young girl ran out from one of the cavelike entrances to approach us, bowing and curtsying as she came. She was an Indian, and spoke a very broken, pleasantly quaint English.

"She is a Blackfoot!" Jimmy excitedly, laughingly exclaimed. "A pureblood Blackfoot, not diluted like me through contact with you palefaces." Then he delighted the girl by speaking in her native tongue. As they conversed, the rest of us kept a polite silence, taking note of how pretty the girl was and the pride of her bearing. She was dressed as richly as an Indian princess, the daughter of a chief, and this opulence was finally explained as Jimmy told us:

"Oontawa is handmaiden and companion to the Woman of the Winds. She has been sent to look after us until we go before the

Council of Elders, the 'government' of the People of the Plateau. First, though, we are to be shown our quarters. Oontawa will stay with us while we eat. After sleeping, we will see the Council of Elders. They will decide what's to be done with us. Also, there's to be a guided tour of this place. Apparently the plateau is honeycombed with caves and corridors, a multi-level labyrinth like some super beehive!"

"Well, then," Tracy answered him, "you'd better tell Oontawa to lead on. I don't know about you boys, but I could do with a bite to eat."

As we trooped along behind Jimmy Franklin and the Indian girl, with Whitey hobbling along with one arm about Tracy's shoulders and the other around my neck, my sister added, "Oh, and Jimmy, if I'm going for an interview," she sniffed disdainfully at the heavy parkas that wrapped her slim girl's figure, "perhaps Oontawa has a spare fur or two for me? Do be a sweetheart and ask her for me, will you?"

III

In the Hall of the Elders

(Recorded through the Medium of Juanita Alvarez)

After a distance of some forty yards or so, the tunnel we followed into the basalt bowels of the plateau opened into a gallery from which many more tunnels led off. Each of these shafts had its own symbol carved into the rock above it, and Oontawa pointed out the symbol we were to follow to our quarters, a long, inverted heart or arrowhead shape. Once these many symbols were memorized it would not be difficult to find one's way about the cave-system.

The shafts were lighted by flambeaux formed of stone bowls of oil supported upon wooden brackets fixed to the walls at intervals of about fifty feet. The smell of their burning was like a pungent but not overly unpleasant incense. As we went I dipped a finger into one of the bowls, sniffed at the greasy fuel and gingerly tasted it. Mineral oil, with some sweet, sticky additive. I was surprised. Animal fats would have been far more likely. Where would the plateau's people get oil?

On our way we saw single members and groups of the plateau's inhabitants going about their various businesses. They all paid us what passed for compliments as they met us in the corridors. Though they were mainly of Eskimo and Indian extraction, many other elements were also present, including Mongol, white European and white American. Whenever we met up with a group of them they would politely stand aside for us. Oontawa explained that news of my run-in with Northan had already spread and that it had been greeted in many quarters with no uncertain delight. Plainly the warlord's bullying ways were not generally appreciated.

Passing through at least three more galleries and crossing as many major tunnel systems, we finally arrived at a gallery larger than any we had seen so far. Here, cut into the walls between tunnel mouths, rock-hewn steps ascended to higher levels. Climbing a wide stairway and entering a shaft two levels higher, I noted that we seemed to have turned at right angles to our original course, that now we were moving back toward the outer wall of the plateau, which fronted on the white wastes of the frozen plain and the distant scene of the recent battle.

When I mentioned this to Jimmy Franklin, he replied, "Yes, our apartments are right on the outer wall. Oontawa tells me that we are particularly fortunate; our rooms are comfortable, light and airy, and they command a view overlooking the entire front of the plateau. She says that Tracy's room is really something; all furs and fancy carvings. It seems that Armandra is quite taken with you, Tracy."

"How much farther are these rooms of ours?" Whitey painfully asked. "This leg's giving me hell."

"Almost there," Jimmy answered.

As he spoke there came the smell of good, hot food from somewhere ahead. Suddenly I was very hungry. "Jimmy," I said, "ask Oontawa what kind of food her people eat, will you? It strikes me that they're bound to be short on vegetables. In fact from what we've seen of this world so far I'd say they only eat meat. But surely they couldn't make out on a diet of meat alone?"

"Sure they could," he answered. "The Eskimos of good old Mother Earth have always been meat eaters—*just* meat—and raw at that! In fact that's what the word Eskimo means; 'eater of raw meat.' And all of the northern Indian tribes lived mainly on meat. They had their berries and fruits, yes, but their diet was ninety percent flesh, and they did pretty well on it, too."

Whitey sniffed the air. "You've convinced me, Jimmy, at least," he said. "If that's our meal I can smell—well, I only hope it tastes as good, that's all."

We rounded a slight bend in the tunnel and natural light suddenly flooded the shaft, showing curtained entranceways to caves on both sides. Here, too, the tunnel ended, and we saw that the light came in through square windows cut into the shaft's terminal wall. Oontawa beckoned us forward to these windows, indicating that we should look out.

We were at a height of some seventy feet above the white waste that gently, almost unnoticeably sloped away down to the distant, ominous pyramid whose hazy outline, even at this distance, marred the view. The very sight of the evil altar filled me with the same shuddery feeling I might get from the sight of a black, triangular fin cutting the surface of inviting blue waters . . .

"Rooms with a view," said Tracy. "But where's this meal?"

Oontawa led us in through one of the curtained entrances to a large cave beyond. Since this cave stood away from the outer wall, here the light was from candles in stone holders that stood upon a large ornamental stone table. The weak light of these candles was supplemented by a flickering of flames that leaped up from a metal grill, set in the floor of the farthest corner, to disappear with a quiet, controlled murmur through a similar grill in the ceiling.

While I could feel no change in the temperature (my own flesh remained as chill as Ithaqua's influence had left it), Tracy was obviously delighted with the cave's warmth; she immediately threw off her parkas and stretched herself luxuriously. "Hey," she asked Jimmy, "do all of these people live like this?"

For in this cave the austerity of the tunnels and passageways ended. Here the walls were hung with sumptuous drapes of an American Indian weave; the floors were thick with soft furs; wherever naked rock might have shown unadorned it was carved with ethnic designs so intermingled that their ancient origins were no longer easily discernible.

Oontawa was plainly pleased that we were impressed. She sat down to eat with us. The still steaming meats, of appetizing cuts, were in stone bowls; and I was surprised to note that there were also two types of vegetable preparations upon the table, not counting the mushrooms that decorated the central dish, a splendid joint of meat not unlike a leg of pork. Each place of the five at the table was set with a large, slightly hollowed slab of agate and a goblet of the same exotic material.

Jimmy and Oontawa conversed while we ate, but I had little time for talking. I have never enjoyed food so much in my entire life. When at last we were done we washed down the meal with cool sweet water from the goblets. Then Jimmy told us of his conversation with Oontawa.

"I asked her about the fire in the corner there," he nodded at the flickering column of flame. "Told her I saw no point in warming the plateau when no one seems to appreciate or need heat. Apparently all of the plateau's outer caves are heated, not for the comfort of their dwellers but simply to stop them from freezing over and filling with ice! Apparently the weather is quite mild at the moment.

"She also tells me that the interiors of all the dwelling-caves are done up in pretty much the same way as this one. She'll show us our personal caves in a moment. I asked her how many people there are in the plateau. She says there are some twenty thousand, and—"

"Twenty thousand!" I cut him off. "But where did they all come from? They can't be indigenous to Borea?"

Jimmy cocked his head at me. "They are *now*, I suppose, but certainly their forebears came from Earth, the Motherworld. They were brought here by Ithaqua, just like us. Their history goes back thousands of years, before the races of Earth had writing, but their numbers have been kept down through warring with the Children of the Winds, Ithaqua's own people. It is only recently, since Armandra grew to womanhood, that the People of the Plateau have started to win out over the Wind-Walker's worshippers.

"Now there are twenty thousand of them in the plateau, and room for ten times that number. It is a spare-time task of each family unit or military group to prepare dwelling-caves, barrack halls and stables for future families and armies, future generations. In this way the plateau's many natural tunnel systems have been supplemented over the centuries, or extended and improved. The entire outer wall of the plateau, its face, is a fortress, with hundreds of observation posts and hidden exits from which the warriors and their bears can go out to battle in times of siege."

"Times of siege?" Whitey repeated him. "You mean when Ithaqua and his lads are about?"

Oontawa nodded, speaking now for herself. "Yes, when Ithaqua leads Children of Winds against us, then we must stay within walls of plateau or die. Only bravest of our warriors go out to defend outer tunnels and snow-ship harbors."

"And Armandra?" I asked. "Does she fight with the warriors, as we saw her fighting today?"

The girl's almond eyes widened and her hand flew to her breast. "No, lord, not when Ithaqua rides wind, for it is only to trap her and take her back that he wages war against plateau's people. She is his daughter, but she rebels against her father's tyranny, defying him."

As she finished speaking I saw that my question had disturbed her deeply; the thought of losing Armandra to Ithaqua and the Children of the Winds was too dreadful to contemplate. Now Oontawa stood up.

"Come, I show you your rooms and bathing place. And you—" she turned to Whitey, "I tend to your leg. Then you all sleep before going to Council of Elders."

And sleep we did, but not before bathing.

I bathed quickly, along with the other two men, in the hot waters of a cave with a scooped out rock floor. Tracy had a smaller, private bath, a hypocaust affair, in the quite large and sumptuous cave that was her apartment. The water of these baths was constantly changing itself; melting and dripping down from higher, outer ramparts of the plateau, heated by the oil-fire systems of the outer caves and channeled to the baths, finally overflowing to spill away down stone sluices into the plateau's heart, there to turn the wheels of the workshops.

My own small room was as richly appointed as the others and had a deep square window that looked out over the white wastes. There, stretched out on my back on a pile of furs a foot thick, I quickly fell into a deep, dreamless sleep, one of complete exhaustion and oblivion.

And I came even more quickly awake at the urgent touch of Oontawa's hand. I felt refreshed, reborn, a new man from the moment she shook me awake, and I knew that my sleep must have been a long one.

"Up, up," Oontawa was saying. "You are summoned to Council of

Elders. Armandra is there. She prepares to see—to see—" She stumbled over her words, searching for an expression. "She looks over long distances. I do not know, in your tongue, how—"

"Tell me, Oontawa," said Jimmy Franklin from the door. "Tell me in your own tongue."

They conversed rapidly while I put on fur boots, then Jimmy said: "It appears that Armandra is, well, a seer, I suppose you could call her. She can see things at a distance, with her mind, things that are happening here on Borea. But she can only do this when—when her father himself is personally concerned."

Snapping shut the heavy buckle of my fur belt, I turned to Oontawa "You mean Ithaqua is back on Borea?"

She nodded. "He is at his temple. Armandra desires that you should know your enemy better. When she is finished with her seeing, then you speak with Council of Elders. But hurry, they are waiting."

We went out into the tunnel where Tracy soon joined us. She was dressed in fur trousers, fur boots and a splendid fur jacket with a high collar. She seemed to glow. Whitey appeared last, and it amazed me that his limp was barely noticeable. Whatever ointments these people used, they were certainly effective.

Then, with Oontawa leading, this time following a rock-carved symbol we all recognized well, a five-pointed star!—we proceeded to the Hall of the Elders. The way must have been half a mile, on a course that saw us climbing massive flights of stone stairs and passing through at least a dozen of the great galleries. Finally we approached the end of a wide tunnel that terminated in a smooth stone face of rock through which a great doorway had been cut. Above this entrance a huge five-pointed star was deeply carved in the rock. The Hall of the Elders.

Some fifty feet ahead of us, passing through the entrance in something of a hurry, went three Indians dressed in what looked to me like full ceremonial regalia. Jimmy stared after them and gasped. "Blackfoot, Chinook and Nootka, chiefs of the most northerly of the Northwest Tribes, just as they were two hundred years ago! Ithaqua doesn't seem to have strayed off limits very far south of the Canadian border."

"Come," Oontawa whispered, leading the way through the door. "We are last to enter, but not too late."

We followed her into a vast cave or chamber lit by huge, brightly flaring flambeaux. The first thing that caught my eye was a carved

throne in the dead center of the chamber. Decked in furs and standing upon a raised section of the floor with stone steps leading up to it,
the thing was massively ornate. Seated upon it with her white hands
curved over its stone arms, her head upright and her eyes closed, was
Armandra. Her breast moved slowly beneath the beautiful jacket of
fox fur that she wore.

She was in a deep trancelike state; before her face, hanging motionless from a golden chain suspended from the top of the high
throne's back where it curved forward over her head, was the medallion she had previously worn about her neck. Motionless? Perhaps
not. The medallion was not distinct to my eyes; its disc seemed
blurred. Slowly, very slowly, it turned on its golden chain.

The second most noticeable thing in the Hall of the Elders was
the silence. Though the descending tiers of stone benches that circled
the amphitheater-like chamber were filled almost to capacity, not a
single whisper stirred the assembly. Or was I mistaken in this also?
Mistaken I was, for now I heard a distinct sound, a humming as of
winds blowing far away, and it issued from that slowly turning, *vibrat-
ing* medallion!

The medallion hummed and vibrated, echoing however faintly the
hum and roar of weird winds blowing out beyond the rim of the universe. It hung before Armandra's face and she heard it, and I knew instinctively that its voice formed pictures for her—sounds transmuted
into visions—so that what she heard she also saw.

But now Oontawa was standing on tiptoe, whispering something
urgently into my ear and tugging at my hand, indicating that my party
should take seats. A space had been cleared for us; the occupants of
the lowest tiers of seats had moved silently along to make room. I
blinked my eyes and shook my head. I had been very nearly hypnotized by the sight of Armandra in her trance.

As I followed Tracy and my friends to our places, every eye in the
Hall of the Elders was upon me. At a guess some four thousand eyes
frowned at me, the latecomer. While we sat down Oontawa moved
quickly to the raised dais, climbing its steps to stand at the left hand of
Armandra. For a moment she leaned forward to peer anxiously into
Armandra's white face, at the closed eyes and drawn, regal features.
Then she knelt and bowed her head, this handmaiden to a goddess.

The silence in the Hall of the Elders seemed to deepen, or perhaps it was simply that the humming and roaring of the suspended

medallion increased. Whichever, soon it was as though a torrent of whispering ghost-winds rushed through the chamber. And ghost-winds they must have been, for despite the fact that the distant tumult rapidly increased, not a single breath of disturbed air touched us and the fires of the flambeaux burned as steadily as before. And now I sensed that the rushing of air was only an illusion, like the crash of waves heard in a shell, an illusion magnified by the absolute silence of the assembly.

So the shock of Armanda's voice, clear, golden and belllike, breaking that ghost-ridden whisper of weird winds, was electric! I felt the hair of my neck prickle as she spoke, and instantly all heads turned once more in the direction of my party. The Woman of the Winds was speaking in English, plainly for our benefit, and in the eyes of all present our importance had immediately trebled.

"Ithaqua stands atop his altar," Armandra intoned in a voice which, except for its singular golden ring, was so void of modulation or emotion that it might have been the voice of Death himself. "He is returned from dark meditations in the moons of Borea and now awaits his tribute—of which there is none, for we have snatched the girl he lusted after and the men whose souls he wanted from the very jaws of his wolf-warriors!

"There he stands." Her hand, alabaster in motion, trembling slightly, pointed eerily across the hall at nothing. Her eyes remained closed; her hair, living fire, stirred strangely and began to rise up over her head. "There he stands atop his pedestal of ice, my *father!*" The last word fell like a golden icicle from her lips, seeming to splinter into shards of ice in the air of the great cave.

Her hand fell back to rest upon the carved arm of her throne while her hair continued its coppery swirling above her head. "They gather, his priests, cowering about the foot of his altar: whipped wolf puppies that snarl at each other, eager to give the blame, grovelling within the circle of totems. Outside the totem ring the Children of the Winds wait. Ithaqua has called them forth from far across the white wastes to see his justice. And he *is* just, for he commanded and his commands went unanswered, his hunger unappeased. And how shall a god correct such deliberate contempt?

"But see, there are only six of them within the totem ring. The High Priest is not there . . .

"Ah, *now* I see him!" She leaned forward slightly, her fingers tightening upon the arms of her throne. "I see the dog, fighting and screaming, dragged from his hiding place and thrown before the altar of his master. He grovels, begs, pleads—this so-called priest who dared to threaten, to curse me—and Ithaqua stands over him, dark atop the pyramid of ice. Now the groveller rages at the lesser priests and they cower, fearing the Wind-Walker's wrath. But the Wind-Walker is cold and still.

"Now the High Priest bows himself down, kneels and cries out his innocence to Ithaqua, giving the six lesser priests the blame. Ah, but they stand united now, those six, ringing him about and pointing their accusation.

"See! The game is up! He tries to run! . . . They bring him down! . . . And now—*now Ithaqua takes a hand!*"

It became obvious to me then that the entire audience understood at least the rudiments of the English language; almost every head in that great cave, my own included, must have moved forward in unison as Armandra spoke those words. I sensed the concerted movement all about me; the rapt attention of every one of us was full upon Armandra. And we all saw and gasped together at the change that stole swiftly over her face.

A ruddy light seemed to burn upon her cheeks, upon her high brow and closed eyes, subtly complementing the flaming copper of her hair. The medallion upon its chain glittered brightly as its gyrations grew more visibly erratic, its humming and roaring forming a definite presence in the great chamber.

Armandra leaned forward further yet until her face almost touched the spinning disc. Her fingers gripped the arms of her throne like claws. Gone now was the calm, deathlike mask she had worn. In its place a feral skull snarled beneath wildly swaying masses of burning hair.

This was the moment I had waited for, my chance to attempt a penetration of Armandra's mind. Oh, I entertained no real doubt that her trance was genuine—nor did I doubt that she was indeed the daughter of Ithaqua—but if the latter were true then she was only half human, spawn of a demon or god of the Cthulhu Cycle of Myth, in which event I should at least be able to gauge the power and direction of her mental emissions.

As to *why* I wanted to do this thing: I found in this woman-creature a vast enigma, a great challenge. Not once did I think of myself as an intruder. If her concentration was as great as it appeared to be, then she would not even notice my presence. When I think now of my audacity . . .

Tentatively I reached out my mind to her, and instantly I was *enveloped!*

She was a whirlpool of concentrated mental energy that sucked me in like a spider flushed down a drain. I could neither fight nor withdraw. I became part of her, hearing what she heard, seeing what she saw. And so superior was her power that my own puny energies were not even perceptible in the mental vortex.

Physically I sat there on that stone bench between Tracy and Jimmy Franklin, but mentally I was a mote in the cosmos of Armandra's psyche. I whirled away with her on the wings of strange winds and stared down with her upon a distant scene . . .

IV

"Bring this Man to Me!"

(Recorded through the Medium of Juanita Alvarez)

"Now Ithaqua takes a hand!"

The words seemed to repeat over and over, receding into vast distances and returning to reverberate in my mind. Then, abruptly, there was only the wind; a wind that blew mournfully across the white wastes, bringing with it the distant howling of frightened wolves. And perhaps those wolves sensed that which would frighten any living creature: Ithaqua, the Thing that Walks on the Wind!

For now I saw him, bloated with anger where he stood at the apex of his pyramid altar, and I saw the six priests scatter like cockroaches as the monster stepped down onto the frozen surface within the totem ring. Ah, but those were no human feet with which the Wind-Walker strode the crushed snow. They were huge and webbed, out of all proportion even to the towering size he had attained, which now lifted him head and shoulders above his own altar.

Doomed, Zchakow the Russian fled, feet flying, arms reaching, eyes bulging and fear foaming from between his champing jaws. He fled before the tread of his monstrous master.

With a thrill of pure horror I suddenly found myself lusting for the Russian's blood, eager to see him struck down and destroyed! It dawned on me that this was not Hank Silberhutte but Armandra. I was now part of Armandra, influenced by her emotions, her desires, which were stronger than mine. And yet, paradoxically, human compassion was not absent in her; indeed it was strong. I could feel it like the pulse of a powerful heart. Ah, but that compassion was fighting a losing battle with her inhuman side, the incalculably alien and abhorrent cruelty inherited from her father. And Zchakow was her enemy.

Now I moved closer to the terrible drama being enacted down on the frozen plain. Out between the carved totems raced Boris Zchakow, his face twisted with hideous fear. He was, or had been, Ithaqua's High Priest, with power of life and death over the Children of the Winds. He *knew* his master; he recognized his fate. And perhaps it was this knowledge of that ultimate fate of all of Ithaqua's followers that robbed the Russian of his senses. When I saw what that fate was, I thought that I too might easily go mad confronted with it.

But even transfixed with horror, feeling empathy with the madman with every psychic nerve I possessed, nevertheless I also thrilled to the chase. For Armandra was Hank Silberhutte, and he was only a tiny part of Armandra, and both were lost now to a raging vortex of bloodlust!

I remembered her face as I had last seen it: a skull-like mask surmounted by living, flaming hair; lips drawn back from gleaming white teeth; the whole burning with hell's own fires. And now I saw that face again, only her eyes were no longer closed.

Carmine pits blazed where only depths of submarine green had opened before, eyes that burned with the energies of alien suns, and somewhere, like subdued background music to a conversation, I heard again a concerted gasping from two thousand throats.

The Hall of the Elders! Struggling still to free myself from Armandra's magnet mind, I had almost made it back to that great cave deep in the bowels of the plateau, only to be snatched back again to my mental vantage point above the Temple of Ithaqua.

In that same instant, as if my mind were not already more than sufficiently whirling, I sensed that something was different, wrong—

terribly wrong! I was no longer merely a part of the Woman of the Winds but of something far greater, something utterly alien.

Ithaqua-Armandra-I brushed aside massive totems, smashing them like matchsticks, reached to snatch the gibbering lunatic from the frozen ground and hold him high aloft. He-we tossed him into the sky, limbs thrashing like a crippled bird, catching him before he could crash to earth.

Then we laughed, Ithaqua-Armandra and I—laughed in a maelstrom of mirth that I knew could only be subdued, could only end in an act of the cruelest horror.

I fought against the unholy glee that filled me, fought to be free of its hold as it moved toward livid, lunatic rage. But I might as well have tried to beat down the winds with my bare fists. And Armandra fought too, bravely, but uselessly, as the human side of her nature strove harder than ever to turn her back from her monstrous sire's dread attraction.

Physically I was Hank Silberhutte, a man sitting between his sister and a friend in the Hall of the Elders; mentally I was a telepathic observer, an unseen intruder, a part of Armandra's psyche. But since she in turn had been drawn into the Ithaqua id, then I was also part of Him. Part of the ultimate horror He had planned for Boris Zchakow.

The Wind-Walker, Armandra and I stared through avid carmine orbs, shrinking ocean depths of green, flinching blue slits, as he-she-we lifted Zchakow up to his-her-my face, where he screamed and frothed as Ithaqua-Armandra-I scrutinized him minutely.

Then, in another instant, it was over. We threw back our hideous head and lifted the shrieking figure of the mad, wildly kicking Russian up, up into the air. A sudden moan of horror, rising to rival the mournfully moaning wind, came up from the assembled thousands of Ithaqua's people, held captive audience. But no, they could not watch, they had seen this before. To a man they turned and fled, even those six lesser priests whose accusations had brought Zchakow to this—to the very gates of hell! Yes, the gates of hell, in the shape of Ithaqua's eyes—*into one of which he-she-I now dropped the wriggling form of the mad Russian!*

A bubbling scream, shrill and rising, cut off in a shower of carmine sparks that burst upwards from the flickering rim of that seething crater eye like lava bombs from a volcano—and Zchakow was gone.

And I had felt something. Something which I cannot, must not attempt to describe in detail, except to say that perhaps it was an over-flow of Ithaqua's hideous *satisfaction* . . .

Now for a moment the Wind-Walker grimly surveyed the fleeing hordes of his people, then turned to stride up a staircase of air back to his position at the summit of the pyramid altar. There he stood, arms akimbo, great feet gripping the sides of the ice mountain, and as his rage subsided I found myself freed of the tremendous attraction of his id. I began to withdraw, to retreat along with Armandra from the mental maw of the Wind-Walker.

—And at that very moment he saw us!

No, he saw *her*, only Armandra, for my own feeble essence was insignificant. I call it essence because I realize now that it was no simple mind-web that had enmeshed me, and therefore that I had not been trapped telepathically. After all, I had looked into Ithaqua's mind before without any of this. But the power Armandra had which enabled her to visit and observe scenes afar was more than merely telepathic; it was more truly psychic, the essential power of the id itself. Her *Ka* had been part of her awesome father for a few brief moments of time, hers and mine too; and now, when we had almost managed to break free—

Quickly the scene of the monster atop his pyramid of ice shrank as I fled with Armandra back toward the plateau, and quickly Ithaqua turned his head to stare after us, realization growing in the flickering of his flaring eyes. He reached out bestial psychic arms after Armandra, again casting that net whose meshes she had managed to escape before he even knew she was there. Ah, but now he *did* know she was there, and again she was caught.

Armandra was caught and so was I, and it seemed as good a time as any to make my presence known, this time telepathically, as I had intended in the first place.

"*Armandra!*" I cried with my mind. "*Fight him. You have to fight him. I'm here to help you. Together we can beat him!*"

"*What?*" Armandra's mind reached out unbelievingly to mine. "*Who is it that offers aid, and how did—*" but that was all.

At last Ithaqua had seen me too, but too late. Something that seethed like acid touched my mind, touched Armandra too, then burned through to the Being of Ithaqua himself. He staggered atop his pyramid. He snatched back those greedily reaching mental and physical arms of his and slammed down the shutters of his alien id, his psyche, his mind, cutting us free of him. No, cutting *himself* free of us! We fled back to our bodies in the Hall of the Elders.

I was stretched out full length on the stone floor. Tracy and Jimmy were trying to get me to my feet. I shook my head and stood up, noting that the chamber was now empty of all but a group of magnificently robed old men, my own party, Oontawa, and—

I started forward when I saw Armandra being helped down the dais steps by Oontawa. The Indian girl's eyes flashed a warning, saying that this was not the time to approach the Woman of the Winds. But perhaps she was wrong.

Armandra's beautiful face was drawn, strained. As she passed close to me she held up a trembling hand and turned my way. "What is your name, man of the Motherworld?"

"Hank," I told her. "Hank Silberhutte."

"And it was you that—?"

I nodded. "Yes."

She leaned toward me, searching my face. "At the end there— what was it that came to sting my mind, burning Ithaqua and making him release me?"

"Was it this?" Tracy asked, holding up one of the five-pointed star-stones from her neck, where the fur of her jacket had kept it and its twin hidden. "When you cried out, Hank, when you shouted to Armandra that she must fight her father, I sort of instinctively held the stone up before your eyes. Then you leaped up and fell to the floor, and Armandra almost toppled from her throne."

Tracy stopped talking, gazed nervously about as the elders all around her stepped quickly back, away from the star-stone sigil, and I stepped back with them. Armandra's eyes grew huge and round. She pointed a trembling hand at the powerful symbol of old gods spinning at the end of the chain Tracy held. Then she fell back weakly, leaning on Oontawa.

The group of elders, ten of them, now clustered closer, and one of them stretched out a finger before I could offer a warning. Briefly he touched the star-stone—and instantly snatched his finger back, the skin of its tip scorched and blackened. For a moment anguish showed on his face, then he turned to his colleagues.

"The stone is genuine—and yet," he stared fascinated at Tracy, "the girl is unhurt!"

"Elders, I go now," Armandra broke in, stronger now, commanding everyone's attention. "But there are things I would know. See to the strangers and ask what questions you will, but do not keep these people here too long. They are to be our special guests until I decide on the best way to employ their talents." She turned to move on, paused.

"This man," she barely looked at me, "Oontawa will return for him. She will bring him to me." With that she turned and walked with her handmaiden from the hall.

When the two had gone, the oldest of the ten elders invited us to talk. He was an Eskimo of very ancient lineage, a tough old ivory chief of tribes forgotten except in Arctic legend. Explaining that his English was very, very bad, he spoke through Jimmy Franklin, turning his attention immediately to Tracy.

I had noticed that the elders seated themselves carefully out of her way for an obvious reason. How to explain her immunity to the star-stones whose shape was the greatest symbol of benign power known to the People of the Plateau? Despite their perfectly natural dread of the real item, it was necessary that we tell our entire story right from the beginning. This we did, using Jimmy as our interpreter whenever we were in difficulties.

The elders were fascinated with our story, astounded that we had deliberately set out to track Ithaqua down, and when our tale was done they stood up to give us their applause. Then their youngest member, a man until now silent, finally said, "Permit me to introduce myself. I am Charlie Tacomah, a Shawnee late of the Motherworld."

"A Shawnee who speaks perfect English," Jimmy answered him, eyeing the tall, bronzed figure whose features, though fine, were plainly American Indian. "But Nashville and Chattanooga are a long way from the Arctic Circle, and you are a much younger man than the others here."

"I think he's a man pretty much like yourself, Jimmy," Whitey said. "A man of the reservations, who figured that there might be better things in life. I guess his ambitions led him astray, though."

The elder nodded, glancing at Whitey appreciatively. "Yes, it was twenty-eight years ago. After the war when I got back home to Memphis, I found the same old prejudices. I wanted to do something about it, decided to write a book on all the Indian tribes, ancient and modern. I eventually, travelled north, seeking out the little-known Eskimo tribes, and—"

"We can guess," I broke in on him sympathetically. "You fell afoul of Ithaqua. He brought you to Borea."

Charlie Tacomah nodded. "I lived for a few days with the Children of the Winds, then ran off and came here. The elders found out that I was something of a military strategist—I had been a major in the infantry—and I became adviser to the old warlords. Five years ago Northan took over as warlord, controlling all of the plateau's army, and I was granted a seat in the Council of Elders.

"Of all the People of the Plateau, I reckon that about sixty of them have arrived here on Borea within the last twenty or thirty years. They learn to fit in pretty quickly. Of course, the great majority of folks that Ithaqua brings stay out on the plains, too frightened to try to escape. If an escapee is recaptured," he shrugged, "Ithaqua has his own ways of punishing deserters."

"And now?" Tracy prompted him after a moment's silence. "What's to become of us?"

"Well, you heard what Armandra said. There's not a great deal we can do with you just yet. Right now, though, it is my pleasure to show you all around the plateau; a fascinating place, as you'll see. Eventually my colleagues' proposals will be put before Armandra for her approval. It is not anticipated that you will be required to contribute in any mundane fashion to the plateau's welfare. Of course, you are far different from run-of-the-mill newcomers."

As he finished speaking Oontawa returned. Tracy cocked her head to one side and smiled wickedly at me. She whispered: "Here comes the handmaiden, Hank. Before she takes you to Armandra, you'd better promise me you'll be a good boy. I've noticed the way you look at the Woman of the Winds."

"Star-stones or not," I told her, grinning, "another crack like that, little sister, and you go over my knee—and I'll do a bit of wind-raising myself!"

And so I started out with Oontawa for Armandra's apartments, and it immediately became apparent that the Priestess of the Plateau dwelt in the topmost levels of her realm. Staircase after stone staircase we climbed, ever spiralling upward through basalt caverns and tunnels until I was sure we must soon reach the battlements of the roof; and we could not have been far short of that roof when finally we came to the first corridor I had seen with its own selected guardsmen.

During our long climb the symbols above tunnel entrances or at the feet of the staircases had been gradually narrowing down to a handful, but already I had guessed which symbol led to Armandra: that of a flash of lightning. Sure enough, above that last, guarded corridor entrance, the lightning flash was the sole remaining symbol, and I saw that beyond it even the tunnel walls themselves were draped with priceless furs.

Two huge squat Eskimo guards, each attended by a towering white bear that swayed and yawned in a rock-cut niche to his rear, stood up straight and saluted with their viciously barbed, ceremonial harpoons as we passed. Flambeaux were now absent where natural light flooded in through windows lining the vast curve of the outer wall. By "windows" I may give the wrong impression; I paused to look out through one of them and found myself staring into a shaft, for the window was cut through a wall of rock all of fifteen feet thick!

Closer to our destination the light flooded in more brightly, and here I saw that the thickness of the outer wall was much diminished. We came to a huge, iron-barred balcony with a stone ceiling; the balcony reached out from the face of the plateau into open air. Now I saw indeed that we were at a great height above the white waste. Fighting the wind that howled in from outside, I put my head out between the bars and looked down. More than two hundred and fifty feet beneath me, the rocky base of the plateau froze into the surface of the surrounding ground. Craning my neck I looked upward and saw that the topmost ramparts were still some twenty to thirty feet higher than this level, that the solid rock above my head must form the ceiling of Armandra's rooms.

I turned to Oontawa, saying; "A dangerous place. A careless person could be sucked out by the wind, or fall through the bars."

She nodded. "Yes, Armandra sometimes—walks out—from here. When she seeks solitude."

With those innocent words; so naively spoken, the Indian girl brought back to me all that I had tried to forget of the woman who was about to give me audience. Here was I, going to Armandra's apartments almost like some fancy courtier on his way to the boudoir of a precocious princess, and yet it was not like that at all. Armandra was more goddess than woman, as much an alien creature as a human being, and I was merely a man of the Motherworld.

Oontawa chattered away as we walked the perimeter corridor, practicing her English and doubtlessly trying to be very informative, but I scarcely heard a word she said; my mind was now fully on her mistress. Perhaps fifty yards beyond the great balcony we came to a curtained entrance where the lightning flash symbol was inlaid in gold; the door to Armandra's quarters. Oontawa passed through the curtains ahead of me, murmuring something as she went, but again my mind was not on what the Indian girl was saying. I followed directly behind her through the curtains.

The room beyond was gorgeously appointed, rich as an eastern sultan's wildest dreams of opulence. Delicately carved, curtained archways led off into adjoining rooms; soft furs of a texture and coloring guaranteed to delight any furrier of the Motherworld overlapped across the floor; the white walls were carved with pillars and arches and intricate arabesques; gold and silver ornaments stood in arched niches in the walls, and fretted agate and marble furniture was cushioned with white furs as soft as freshly fallen snow. But in the very center of the room stood the greatest wonder of all—Armandra, rising naked from a crystal pool!

We saw each other and froze, and simultaneously Oontawa realized that I had followed her into the chamber of her mistress without waiting. She turned with a sharp cry of consternation, her almond eyes wide and flashing.

"Calm yourself, Oontawa," Armandra said. "I am sure that my guest has seen naked women before. The Motherworld is full of 'fascinating' women!"

Stepping from the pool she folded herself in a white fur wrap that covered her body completely. Before her feet vanished in the robe's folds, I thought for a moment that I saw something odd about them. What it was I could not have said exactly, just that they seemed to be—scarred? It had been only a glimpse.

"Well," she continued, shaking her red hair and sprinkling crystal droplets all about; "you might as well sit, Hank Silberhutte, or do all men of the Motherworld stand like statues with their mouths open?"

At that I offered an awkward, embarrassed grin, in answer to which I saw mischievous lights dancing momentarily in the depths of her fjord eyes. "Oontawa, leave us," she told the girl. "I will call you when I want you. Oh!—" she called out in an afterthought as, with a look of disbelief stamped upon her face, the girl turned to go. "Though I trust you above all others, Oontawa, make sure you say nothing of this man's unfortunate eagerness to attend me; there are those it would surely enrage. You may see to it that the elders, too, remain silent about this interview. Particularly those with whom the warlord has influence."

Oontawa bowed and went out through the curtains. I sat at a delicately carved table, hardly daring to rest the weight of my arms upon it in case it fell apart. Armandra seated herself upon the fur cushions of a settee carved of a single gigantic agate, hugging her robe about her and gazing at me curiously.

She said: "Are your hands gentle, Hank Silberhutte?"

Again she had me tongue-tied. "My hands?"

"Are they *gentle*," she frowned impatiently, "for the drying of my hair?"

"They can be gentle," I answered, "when they need to be."

"Good. Come and dry my hair."

I went to her and took the square of woven material that she handed me. She continued: "I know that your hands can be hard, for you knocked down that strutting bear, Northan. But I expect that they are soft, too; how else would you handle all of those 'fascinating' women of the Motherworld?"

I caught up her damp tresses and began to dry them, pausing to turn her head away so that I could make a decent job of it.

"Your hands *are* gentle," she told me, laughing at me out of sea green eyes. "Perhaps I'll find a place for you as a handmaiden, and—"

At that point I stopped her. To say what she had said to any man, which most ordinary women of Earth would know better than to do, would surely be folly. To say it to a Texan . . .

I turned her head back and kissed her fiercely, feeling her fingers fly to the back of my neck and head to tear at my hair, ignoring the shock and anger obvious in her suddenly squirming, furiously fighting body, until she no longer fought but sank her nails into my neck and drank as deeply as I.

For a moment only!

Then, as I relaxed my hold upon her, she snatched herself back from me and slapped me so hard that my ears rang.

"You beautiful *witch!*" I said through clenched teeth.

But now she tilted her head warningly and I thought her eyes were suddenly flecked with pink. Those great eyes widened and,

seemingly of its own accord, the still damp hair of her head lifted
eerily to float free of her shoulders. For a moment she was a goddess
again, utterly inhuman. But then, amazingly, she burst into tears and
buried her face in her hands!

V

Armandra Chooses a Mate

(Recorded through the Medium of Juanita Alvarez)

Her tears were the perfectly normal tears of a woman face to face
with utter mental and physical frustration. The tears of a *woman*, not
a being of supermundane powers. Telepathically probing the edge of
her emotions, gently, so as to remain undiscovered, I found a stark island of bitter frustration afloat in a sea of loneliness.

Whitey's words came back to me, about Ithaqua's need for a companion: *It's a terribly lonely existence,* he had said, *walking the spaces
between the spheres.* How much more true for a human or half-
human child of the Snow Thing with alien powers trapped in a human
psyche, framed by human emotions?

Carefully, concentrating on what I was doing, I allowed sympathy
to flow along the line of one-way communication I had established,
and instantly the bleak hopelessness in Armandra's mind began to
soften. She lifted her head and leaned toward me, searching my face
with eyes as round as saucers. Her tears were already drying.

"Was it really you, Hank, that came to me when my father held me
fast?"

I nodded, answering her in a manner guaranteed to satisfy her curiosity and quell any last doubt she might have. *"Yes."* I said. *"It really
was. It's a power I have."*

And she could see that it was so, that I was speaking in her mind.
Proof of my success showed in her frown, then in the widening of eyes
already huge. "A very dangerous power," she said, forming her words
carefully. "How can any woman trust a man who listens to her
thoughts?"

"She must first learn to believe that he would not listen uninvited," I answered. Then I launched into an explanation of my telepathic power, briefly telling her what I had already made known to the

Council of Elders. "So you see," I finished, "that among my colleagues of the Motherworld it is considered outrageous for one telepath to 'listen' to another without his permission. But in any case, my own power is rather special."

And there I paused, for how could I say that I was limited to intercourse with alien thoughts, the hideous mental gibberings of monsters, when Armandra herself was now a vehicle for my talent? I groped for words. "I can only detect the thoughts of—of very special Beings."

"Other people?"

"There is one other woman I can talk to in this fashion," I hedged, "and she is like a sister, the same as Tracy."

"But you have listened to my mind. Is it not so?"

"No, not really. When you spied upon your father out over the frozen wastes, it was not telepathy that trapped me there when you were trapped. It was your own power, yours and your father's, a power in no way like mine. It is far greater, different."

She nodded, warming to the empathy growing between us. "I believe you. I know it is true. The power I have, which came to me from my father, is not like yours. But have you not listened to my mind within the last few moments, here in this very room?"

"No," I again denied it. "I merely felt your hurt, your loneliness, and tried to comfort you. I have not stolen a single thought out of your lovely head, though any man might easily be tempted to try. Particularly if he thought you were thinking about him." I stared at her pointedly.

"One day, Hank Silberhutte, I might invite you into my head," she said, quite seriously. "Would you come to me if I called you? If I needed you?"

"That I promise."

"But wait," she said. "I have heard *your* voice talking to *my* mind, yes, but how do we know if—"

"Would you like to try an experiment?"

She nodded eagerly.

"Then think something at me, anything. See if I can read it in your mind."

She opened her eyes wide and stared straight at me. It was very strange, that sensation, like the chiming of golden bells at the bottom of some mental well, rising slowly to the surface, forming pictures. I looked, then chuckled as the mischievous lights again lit in Arman-dra's eyes. "Yes," I nodded, "I think perhaps Northan would be angry if he knew I was here. But it does not worry me. Do you fear him, Ar-mandra?"

"Fear Northan? I fear only Ithaqua—but I know that many of my people, even a handful of the elders, do fear the warlord." Her eyes narrowed thoughtfully. "He is ambitious. And he does not like his am-bitions thwarted. You must watch out for him, Hank. Be very watch-ful of Northan."

"It surprises me," I said, "that he was not in the Hall of the Elders for your—seeing."

"No, he would be celebrating the victory of the ships over the wolf-warriors. Sometimes the celebrations last for days. Oh, they strut and boast, as their forefathers did before them. In many ways they are like children."

"Well," I answered, "the battle was well won, with your help. But without you Northan would have been hard put. And he lost a lot of face when I returned his blows. I can hardly see that he has much to celebrate!"

"Oh, he'll knock a few heads together, find excuses for your beat-ing him on his own ship and awe his cronies with feats of strength." Again her eyes narrowed. "I know Northan the Warlord. It will not take him long to regain whatever face he feels he has lost. He is am-bitious." Again that word.

"And what is his ambition, do you think?"

"Is it not obvious?" she lifted her eyebrows. "He desires to share these apartments with me. For while the People of the Plateau are satisfied with their princess, Northan would give them a king, a High Priest. And in a way the elders aid him, for they want me to have chil-dren."

"But you do not want him?"

"I could do worse," she tossed her hair, dry now, and began to comb it. "Does the thought annoy you?"

"No," I immediately answered, then bit my tongue and spoke in her mind. *"You damn well know it does!"*

She laughed. "Because I am fascinating, and beautiful?"

"Those are good reasons," I agreed.

"I am not all beautiful," she told me, her face becoming serious in an instant. "You saw my feet when I left the pool?"

"Your feet? Yes, they looked—"

She flicked the fur wrap so that it flew wide below her knees. "They are ugly!" she said.

For a moment she stared down in something like horror at her feet, then said; "My mother was stolen from your green Earth by Ithaqua. She was given into the care of the Children of the Winds until I was born. Later, in my father's absence, having learned that he had fathered a child upon a human woman, the plateau people stole me away in a raid and brought me here; my mother too, but she died from the wound of a harpoon hurled in the fighting. They say she was very beautiful.

The elders raised me. When I was ten a physician, specially trained for ten years to perform one work, cut my feet down from the great webbed pads they were to their present shape. He was supposed to leave them looking like normal human feet, so that I would forget my origins, but the operation was not very successful. For a long time I was in constant pain."

A moment longer I looked at her feet. They were the shape of human feet but with square looking, nailless toes and a covering of smooth scar tissue. Then she flicked her wrap back into place.

"When my feet had healed, about a year after the operation, I had a terrible dream of great angry winds and of the physician whose knives had scarred me. When I awakened the elders told me that there had been an accident; that same physician had fallen from a window of his room high in the outer wall of the plateau. A freak gust of wind, they said.

"When I told them that I had sent that wind to kill him—sent it in my sleep to settle a debt I hardly recognized in my waking hours— then they stood in awe of me and knew that they could never suppress that in me which was of Ithaqua. Thus I became what I am.

"But there," she looked at me and sighed. "Now you must go. Soon I meet with the elders again and I need a few hours sleep. The seeing drained me. Today was especially hard. I became too involved with my father's awful justice. He has never come so close to trapping me before. But, Hank Silberhutte, I am glad you are my friend. And I know that if I call you will come to me. Now go."

"There's a lot you could tell me, many questions you—"

"Your questions will be answered, in time." She stood up, holding her wrap about her. She held out her free hand and I took it, following her to the curtained exit. "Only promise me," she said, "that however tempted you may be, you will never look into my mind uninvited. When I want you to know my thoughts, you shall know them."

"I promise."

"Wait!" she cried as I was about to leave. "You gave me something I did not ask for. Now take it back." She leaned forward, brushed my lips with hers, and quickly withdrew. Seeing the mischief rising in her eyes I reached out my arms to her, and she drew the curtains in my face and was gone.

On returning to my room I felt suddenly exhausted. That experience I had shared with Armandra's psyche had severely sapped my strength, as much as the fight against her father's alien will had taxed hers. Since the others were not back yet from their sightseeing, I lay down and slept.

No sooner had I awakened than they returned. They were tired, but so full of what they had seen I decided that in the near future I most explore the plateau for myself.

"This place," said Whitey, "is a maze of marvels. We've seen the wells that supply half of the plateau's water, and the cavern where weeds and mushrooms grow at the edge of the geyser flats. We've seen cave pools chock-full of fish, and watched the Eskimos spearing them."

"From the other side of the plateau," Tracy cut in, "we've seen the rim of Borea's sun. Like the moons, it never moves; only its upper curve shows. There's a forest of pines on that side, too, and in the distance a great stretch of woodland that reaches to the horizon. It looks like a rather flat version of Canada."

Jimmy was less enthusiastic. "We saw the pool of oil where they draw their fuel in wooden buckets, and we saw the dark tunnel whose entrance has a skull carved above it as a warning: We felt the horror lurking there, emanating from forbidden nether-caves. No one knows what lies at the tunnel's lower level; its mysteries have never been explored. It reeks of—fear!"

When Tracy shivered I knew it was not because of any normal chill she might feel. "It's funny," she said. "Jimmy and Whitey felt this— this *thing*—and so did Charlie Tacomah. All of the People of the Plateau feel it when they are close to the tunnel. No one will enter it, not by a single step. And yet I felt nothing. Well, I felt something, but not fear. If anything, I felt safer there. But not really safe, if you know what I mean." Suddenly she clung to my arm: "Hank, when can we . . . I mean, do you think—"

"Tracy," Whitey cut her off. "Let's have it out in the open. We must all have thought of the same thing, and I've been trying my best to see what the outcome might be. You know, I've been looking for a hunch. But I haven't found one."

"You don't come over too well, Whitey," I told him. "You mean we're stuck here?"

He nodded. "I think so. It looks like we're here for good. If these people have been on Borea for thousands of years and haven't found a way back yet, what chance do we stand?"

Tracy looked miserable so I put my arm round her. "Not much of a chance," I agreed. Then I thought of Armandra and realized that the thought of staying on Borea hadn't really been bothering me too much.

"Still," I added, "never say die."

For me the next month passed slowly. I seemed always to be waiting for a call from Armandra, but I only saw her twice, at meetings of the council to which I was invited as a courtesy. On both occasions, though, I had caught her eyes on me when she thought I was looking elsewhere. Between times my dreams were full of her.

Once I dreamed we walked together on the wind between the worlds. We moved where stars were frosted to the firmament and Borea was far away. And yet, though I saw Armandra mostly in my dreams, there was always this peculiar feeling that she was with me in the waking world also. I began to suspect that she was "peeking" into my mind. If so, then she knew well enough by now my feelings for her.

I say the time passed slowly, and yet there were diversions. The plateau's weapon-masters took me in hand and I was trained for three hours daily in a variety of weapons. I soon discovered that what skill could not achieve in a tight spot might often be realized by use of my considerable size and strength. And my strength never failed to amaze my instructors.

During one such session Northan entered the exercise cave. I was throwing a harpoon at a painted target of woven hide when the warlord came in. I saw him and his presence put me off; my throw went a few inches wide of the bull.

Northan grinned and picked up a harpoon. "Not nearly good

enough," he said. "If that target was a wolf, he'd be tearing you in half by now."

He turned, casually hurled his weapon and it slammed home dead center of the target, burying its barbs. We moved to the target together. "Now that was a cast," Northan chuckled.

He tugged at the shaft of his harpoon but it was stuck fast. Lifting a foot to the target, he strained. Still the harpoon would not come. He grunted, shrugged, stepped back. I caught hold of both weapons, one in each hand, placed a knee against the target and pulled the harpoons free in a snapping of leather thongs. Northan's face went gray, then darkened over. Before he could speak I said, "That wolf you mentioned might not find me such easy meat, Northan. Perhaps, seeing you weaponless, he'd turn on you instead."

It was just a small incident, but word of this second encounter spread as rapidly as the story of our confrontation on the snow-ship. Whitey had warned me on more than one occasion that the warlord would bring me down if he could, and having seen Northan's face as he strode angrily from the exercise cave I could only agree.

Still, I had things other than the strutting warlord to worry about.

As the weeks passed I grew almost to envy Tracy. She was with Armandra almost every day, learning the royal routine and speedily becoming the Woman of the Wind's constant companion along with Oontawa. When she was not with Armandra, Tracy spent most of her time with Jimmy. I noticed the strong bond developing between them and was pleased.

And if any member of my team was in his element, surely it was Jimmy Franklin. Apart from Tracy's attentions, he was now in a position to study the old tribes as they had really been. The Nootka and Micmac, Chimakua and Algonquin, Huron and Ojibwa, Onondaga, Chilkat, Mohawk and Tlingit; all of the northern tribes of old were represented, and Jimmy must surely have felt that he was now among the ancestors of his race.

I had asked him about the plateau's Indians, about their weapons. Why had I seen no single trace of the traditional bow and arrow? It all had to do with the nature of Borea and its people, he told me. In a world where alien, elemental powers were used as super-weapons, mere bows could easily be made useless. Temperatures could be sent down to a point where bowstrings, and even the wooden bows themselves, would break at the slightest pressure. Arrows could simply be blown aside. On the other hand, spears, harpoons and handaxes were less susceptible to such forces.

And it was Jimmy, too, who first learned the legends of the plateau, myths that went back for something like five thousand years and maybe more. These tales had it that at a time forgotten in the dim mists of immemorial lore, Ithaqua had been prisoned in the bowels of the plateau. This had followed an act of defiance against the Elder Gods, when he had waged war on the early civilized races of Earth, striding the skies across all the dawn world and ravaging far and wide. The Wind-Walker was imprisoned thus for thousands of years before finally being released (or escaping, the legends were confused on that point) but ever since then he had been leery of the plateau, his one-time prison.

When I heard of this legend I couldn't help but tie certain facts up together. Strangely enough, Tracy featured strongly in these reckonings of mine. The fact, for instance, that my sister was the only one of all the plateau's people who possessed a positive defense against the Snow Thing; and likewise that she knew no fear when confronted with that forbidden tunnel deep in the bowels of the plateau, the tunnel whose almost physical emanations held all others back.

What lay at the other end of that dark shaft, and was it necessarily dangerous to the People of the Plateau? Tracy's star-stones, after all, were only injurious to us because we had been touched with the contamination of Ithaqua. And while we were naturally wary of the things, still they were far more dangerous—indeed lethal—to the Wind-Walker himself and his minions. Was it possible that the secret of the tunnel was that which Ithaqua also feared, the thing that held him back from destroying the plateau itself and all of its people?

Once, with Whitey, I stood at the entrance to that dark shaft, and both of us felt the thrust of forces that bade us go away or face an indefinite but very real doom. It was not only fear but a wall, a barrier real as any wall of bricks and mortar.

When I asked Whitey what he made of it, he said, "I don't really know, Hank. I feel much the same as Tracy, I guess. On the one hand this place gives me the creeps—I don't know what's going to jump out at me, you know?—but on the other hand I feel, well, that the whole future of, oh, of *everything* is tied up at the far end of this tunnel."

"Is that a hunch?"

"Yes, a strong one, but don't ask me to explain it. You couldn't get me down this shaft anyhow, not even for a ticket back to Earth!"

By the end of the second month I was more or less sure that Armandra had been spying on me mentally. Whether or not she was getting any clear mental pictures I did not really know; I had made no effort to project any thoughts in her telepathic direction. Nevertheless, and despite my suspicions, I stuck to my own promise not to look into her mind, though I admit that I was tempted.

Toward the end of the month, however, her prying had become so intense that I could feel her with me at almost any time in any given twenty-four hour period. At the same time I was being teased by Tracy whenever she saw me. She swore that Armandra's interest in me knew no bounds, that the Woman of the Winds had sucked her dry of all facts concerning me and my life before Borea! And I believed Tracy, for she made me promise not to repeat anything she told me; Armandra did not want me to know of her interest in me. She was no common woman to throw herself at a man.

Still, Armandra's constant presence on the borders of my mind bothered me considerably (there are things a man might want to keep secret; emotions, fears and ambitions he might not want to disclose), and so I determined to teach her a lesson if her peeking continued. It was when I had awakened from the middle of a nightmare in which I had fought to free Armandra from her father's swollen fingers, discovering her presence there at the edge of my surfacing awareness, that I found my opportunity.

"*Very well,*" I spoke to her deliberately with my mind. "*I don't know what you seek in my thoughts, Armandra, but if it is this—*" and here I projected a vivid and exceptionally erotic scene concerning the two of us, a perfectly natural fantasy which until then I had forced myself to keep out of my mind, "*—then now you know!*"

For a moment longer she was with me and I sensed sudden, explosive outrage, and something else, before she was gone. I waited a minute or two longer but the ether was completely free of telepathic influences. Later I awakened again to find strange, gentle little winds caressing my body and ruffling my hair where I lay upon my bed of furs. And I knew where they came from, for beyond my stone window the gray and white Boreal scene was calm and quiet.

And so things stood for perhaps a further week, so that it was a few days into the third month when Oontawa came to bring me Armandra's invitation to the Choosing of a Champion, when a suitable mate would be found from among all the men of the plateau. I say Oontawa came with an invitation, and yet I was ready to go before she and the others of my small party brought me the news. Armandra had already uttered these words in my mind: *"Now you can come to me, Hank Silberhutte, if you want me!"*

Simply those few words and yet every nerve in my body was suddenly energized and fires I had only guessed to exist raced in my blood, however unnaturally cold that blood might be. She had called to me, and I would go to her, yes. But on my terms.

We made our way quickly to the Hall of the Elders, and as we went Oontawa told me things I would need to know. I knew of the ritual Choosing of a Champion, but did not know the finer details of the rite. It appeared that since women were slightly in the minority, most of them were sought after as prizes by the unmarried men. Therefore a girl would usually make known to her favorite that she intended to choose a champion, and he in turn would pick a close male friend who he could trust to accept his challenge. When the girl offered herself publicly, her lover would then have to put himself forward for acceptance or rejection, and offer a challenge to anyone else who fancied the girl. His friend would then step forward and a short fight would ensue in which the "usurper" would be "beaten." That was the way the ritual usually went. Usually.

This time it would be different. For one thing it was Armandra choosing a champion. For another she had made no approaches—no physical approaches, at least—to any of the plateau's males. Finally, Northan had long made known his ambition to take Armandra to wife. If any man challenged his right to the Woman of the Winds, the warlord would be merciless.

We entered the Hall of the Elders to find its amphitheater tiers of seats already filled to capacity. Young men of all the tribes jostled each other nervously just within the door, elbow to elbow with Eskimo warriors, pure whites, and mixtures of varied background and lineage. We pushed through to a clear space where I saw that a tight circle had been chalked round the base of the dais.

At the head of the dais Armandra stood, head bowed as the ritual demanded, for she must make no sign to any man in the assembly that she favored him. She was absolutely beautiful—white as the fine furs that concealed little of the perfection of her body, the fur boots that hid the imperfection of her feet—a gorgeously carved candle of flesh crowned with the living fire of her hair.

Across the hall, in a ring of his own admirers and cohorts stood Northan, powerfully armored in the manner of a warlord. Yet forbidding as his armor was, the black scowl he directed all round him would surely be even more of a deterrent to anyone foolish enough to cross him in this matter.

For the moment no one in Northan's party had seen me, and from the oily smiles on the faces of his companions I could tell that they expected no interference. Well, let them expect what they would. My chill blood had been fired; Armandra meant so much to me now that death itself would be almost preferable to the thought of her in the warlord's arms.

No sooner had the thought crossed my mind than I felt Armandra's mental fingers probing. They brushed me, lingered as if to make certain of my identity, then withdrew. She trembled where she stood, then, without looking up, she spoke.

"This woman now offers herself as wife and seeks a champion. Who will fight for me, for the glory of the plateau and its people?"

Her words were hardly out before Northan stepped forward, climbed the dais steps and took Armandra's arm. Immediately the blood raced faster in my veins. Now Northan saw me; his hot eyes lingered on me for a second, then contemptuously flicked by me to sweep the hall. There was complete silence. It seemed as if the entire assembly held its breath, waiting for the warlord to speak. And he did.

"I, Northan, her champion, claim this woman, to fight for her, for the glory of the plateau and its people. Is there a man to challenge my right?" His voice itself was a threat, a promise of violent, certain death to anyone who challenged him. I felt a movement beside me in the crush of people and held back, waiting to see what this disturbance could be.

A young brave was moving forward, hawk-featured and proud, flushed with reckless excitement. Before he could reach the forward edge of the crowd a friend caught hold of him, whispering urgently, fearfully into his ear. Their eyes went to Northan where he stood watching them, an ugly grin twisting his face. Suddenly the grin dropped away and his lips hardened. His eyes bored into those of the young brave and their message was perfectly clear. So as to make it even clearer, the warlord spoke again.

"Let any challenger come forward now, and let him know that Northan fights to the death!"

Suddenly white, the young brave stepped back and quickly disappeared in the crowd, his nerve broken. Northan's grin returned and again his fierce eyes, swept the hall. And still I waited, for I knew that the ritual demanded that a challenge be made. In threatening a fight to the death, surely the warlord had put paid to any plans he might previously have made for one of his own men to take up the challenge.

Then that which I had waited for happened; Armandra's thoughts rushed in upon me. I stared at her and slowly her head lifted. She gazed straight into my eyes.

"If you hold back much longer, Hank Silberhutte, the council might declare me Northan's woman without the ritual being fully completed. They are eager to have me wed."

"I hold back for one reason only, Armandra, and you know that reason. I would be no mate to crawl to you when you fancied me, to father your children and then be pensioned off with a seat on the Council of Elders. If I'm to be a husband then I will be a husband, not some sort of privileged lapdog!"

Now the elders of the council had moved forward to stand at the foot of the dais. They turned outward, facing the crowd. Armandra's anger flooded into my mind for an instant before she cried out; "Oh, you fool! Do you not know why I dared not let you look into my thoughts? I am a woman, Hank Silberhutte, but a woman can have thoughts as lustful as any man!"

And now Northan had finally seen the two of us staring intently at each other. His lips drew back in warning and his eyes slitted with fury. I felt the hate radiating from him. The spokesman of the elders stepped up beside the warlord and Armandra. He raised his arm, opened his mouth to speak——

"I challenge you, Northan," I shouted, moving forward. "I challenge your right to this woman and will fight you, with any weapons you choose, for the glory of the plateau and its people!"

From behind me, completely dry and without banter, I heard

Whitey whisper, "If we ever get back to Earth, that's fifty dollars you owe me, Jimmy. Never bet against a hunchman!"

Tracy breathlessly added, "And a hundred to me. I guess you just don't know Hank, Jimmy." Then their whispers were drowned out in the wild and amazed clamor that roared up from the thronging audience.

Part Three

◆

I

Northan—Traitor!

(Recorded through the Medium of Juanita Alvarez)

At first I thought that Northan would explode. His mouth fell open and his eyes bulged in outrage and disbelief. He let go of Armandra's arm and began to descend the dais steps; then, noticing the way I was dressed—my sandals, soft leather trunks and fur-collared jacket—his eyes narrowed craftily. For a split second he paused, seeming to ponder something, and then his astonishment and rage appeared to increase twofold.

The spokesman of the elders had now left the dais but Northan's shout stopped him in his tracks as he hurried out of the chalked combat area. "You there, elder! Do you see how this man mocks the Woman of the Winds, how he ridicules this ancient ceremony? He is recently come to us, and yet his attitude is not nearly what it should be. He even dares resent my authority as Warlord of the Plateau! Look at him. He is not dressed for combat, and if he were I could hardly lower myself to accept his challenge. He should not be in a position to lay claim to the lowliest, most miserable whore from the barracks areas, and yet here he is, offering himself as a mate for the Woman of the Winds! This is more than mere mockery," his voice lifted to a bellow of artificial outrage. "It is insolence—defilement!"

Now I knew what the warlord was up to, and as he finished speaking I saw a nodding of heads among his cronies. Even one or two of the elders seemed to be in agreement with him, much to the obvious disgust of others, particularly Charlie Tacomah. Well, Northan had

had his say, now it was my turn. Before the elder he had addressed could answer him, I spoke up.

"Elder," I began, speaking to the same old man, "in the Mother-world I was a leader of men, not given to accepting insults from puffed up dogs. I do not intend to lower my standards here on Borea. While it disgusts me to soil myself in combat with such as your present warlord, if that is the only way to elevate my position to one of acceptable status, I am prepared to do so." I allowed a moment for that to sink in, then continued. "Over and above the question of mere position, however, there is the fact that I believe I am in love with the Woman of the Winds. Because of this, I cannot stand and watch Northan take her unchallenged. If she is the prize of this contest, then I can imagine no more desirable prize. It is one which I will treasure always." Again I briefly paused.

"I have been given to understand it is desirable that Armandra has children, that the Council of Elders has long been pressing her to wed. In the interest of the plateau I ask you this question: are your future princes to be strutting peacocks and boasters, or great men with powers as great as, and perhaps greater than their mother's own? That is the difference between Northan taking Armandra to wife, and—"

"I have heard of your so-called 'powers,' you dollop of—" Northan bellowed in genuine fury, until I stilled his tongue by turning my back on him. I addressed the thronging People of the Plateau now, letting them see that plainly the warlord was beneath my contempt.

"But if you, the people, or if Armandra herself has any objection to my challenging Northan, then I will withdraw my challenge, however reluctantly."

Now this was what Northan himself had tried to do with his blustered insults; place Armandra in a position to refuse me as a prospective champion, on the grounds that I was unsuitable and beneath her contempt, without breaking any of the ceremonial rules of conduct. He had suspected something and wanted to see how the land lay between us, to see if she really did find my challenge objectionable.

She had not risen to Northan's bait; she had held her tongue. Well, I too had wanted the warlord to know the lay of the land, and so I had answered him myself, trying to force Armandra's hand. Now we both looked to her for an answer, and finally she said, "You are both strong, able men. I have no preference, for I am the Woman of the Winds and above such things. There is no objection to either one of you, or to any man who would fight to be my champion."

"*Liar!*" I told her with a sharp thought.

"*I cannot completely alienate the warlord,*" she answered.

"*Alienate him? He might kill me!*"

"*You must not let him—and you must not kill him! For all his strutting he leads the warriors well and is no coward in battle.*"

Meanwhile Northan had stepped slowly, menacingly down, approaching until we were face to face. I could almost see the dark thoughts revolving in his head. While he had insulted me, I had doubly insulted him; Armandra's little speech had told him nothing, had been completely unsatisfactory, merely explaining her acceptance of the ancient code. Things were not the way he would have them; his anger was now very real, and his face black as thunder. He clenched and unclenched his great hands.

"Will you not dress yourself for battle before I kill you, Earthman?" he ground the words out.

"I came into the Motherworld naked, Northan," I told him evenly. "These few rags should not hinder my exit from Borea, even if I were ready to make one. I choose to fight as I stand, unless your choice of weapon is the cutting whip, in which case I will dress as you are dressed."

"Then let's get it over with quickly," he snarled, hurriedly stripping himself of his armor and hurling each piece away. "If you're afraid of the whip—"

"I don't fear the whip," I cut him off, "but whips are for dogs, not men."

"Then let it be the handaxe," he snarled. "Either way, you die!"

Handaxes! I would rather have had unarmed combat, in which I had trained on Earth for eleven years, but if it had to be with weapons then the handaxe suited me as well as any other.

From somewhere close at hand two young Indian boys brought a golden tray bearing a pair of matched, highly decorated but nevertheless deadly, picklike handaxes. The head of each was burnished until it shone, displaying a fine cutting edge on the wide blade, and a needle tip at the end of the rearward spine. I saw that this slender, piercing spine was barbed and cut with runners to keep blood from flowing down the shafts of the weapons to the hands of their users. I looked at the things for a long moment, and as Northan noticed the expression on my face he grinned, regaining a little of his composure.

The tray was placed on the floor between us and two more youths brought an iron chain with a manacle at each end. These clasps were secured to our left wrists. Now we were tied together, with seven or eight feet of chain between us. I waited uneasily for someone to explain the rules but apparently there were none, or I should already be in possession of them.

"Are you ready?" Armandra's voice came from the dais, trembling a little. Northan went into a crouch above the golden tray, resting the wrist of his free right hand lightly on his right knee. I followed suit. This was it then. Obviously no rules were necessary; they would be self-explanatory.

The warlord's eyes flicked sideways as he watched Armandra. I watched her too. She stood with a square of some fine weave in her hand, held high. *"When I drop the cloth, Hank Silberhutte, take up your weapon—swiftly!"*

It was an effort to stop myself nodding. I flicked my gaze from Armandra to Northan and saw the muscles standing out along his shoulders and arms; his right hand trembled over his knee in tension. Sweat suddenly burst out upon his brow. I could feel cold sweat pouring down my own face and arms.

"Now!" came Armandra's mental warning—and yet it was no real warning for she dropped the square simultaneously with her thought.

As if in slow motion I saw Northan's hand reaching down for his weapon, the glint of a razor-honed edge as the handaxe rose up and back as if with a life of its own. At the same time I took up my own weapon, feeling the shaped grip in my hand like something alive.

Then Northan jerked on the chain and I shot forward, already off balance. I saw his eyes burning fiercely as his weapon began to descend, instinctively threw myself into a dive. I passed straight between his spread legs, dragging his chained arm down and deflecting the blow he aimed at my back.

Sprawling behind him I yanked on the chain, but Northan had played this game before. He instantly tucked his head between his legs and flipped over onto his back, rolling as I directed a swift blow at the wrist of his weapon hand. My handaxe brought sparks from the floor as he jerked his wrist out of harm's way. We got to our feet together, the warlord immediately stepping forward to swing his weapon horizontally, hauling on the chain at the same time to bring me within reach.

I arched my back, felt the sharp leading edge of Northan's weapon slice a shallow groove along my belly, yanked down with my left hand to bring the warlord forward and block any backhand blow he might have planned, then leaned into a sideways swipe at his legs below the knees. He sprang high, grunting as my weapon swished through empty air.

The silence of the crowd was broken now by a succession of concerted sighings and moanings, the hissing of sharply indrawn breath. I took what little pleasure I could in the fact that what concern was being shown was mainly for me; the warlord's popularity was nothing to envy. His enemies, usually silent, were more vociferous now in the passion and excitement of the spectacle.

As we circled each other with the chain stretched between us, I noted the warlord's attitude of merciless, murderous intent. There was absolutely no doubt in Northan's mind that he would win this contest. My physical strength was greater than his, true—and he doubtless recognized that fact, however grudgingly—but his skill and experience were making me look amateurish.

So far I had been lucky: Northan had only cut me once, not seriously. Could it be that he was playing with me? Well, one way or the other, the thing must be gotten over with quickly. While the Borean warlord's skill would not diminish, my strength certainly would. In any event, brute strength can rarely compete for very long against experienced dexterity.

And as that last thought entered my head I stumbled sideways into the bottom step of the dais and went sprawling headlong. Northan had waltzed me right into it, had planned it this way, knowing I would trip myself up. All right, then let him believe that his plan had worked even better than he expected, that things were worse for me than they really were.

I forced myself to go limp on the steps. Sprawling there, I put on a look of uncomprehending, dazed bafflement. This was the work of only a second, and I never once took my eyes off the warlord.

He laughed wildly, leaping to the attack, his arm lifting to deliver the final stroke. At the last moment I threw up my own weapon to ward off the descending blow, and at the same time I threw a loop of the chain about Northan's neck. Twisting the chain, I hugged him to me.

Now I could use my strength. Gripping the chain tighter where it circled Northan's neck, I flipped him over onto his back. I locked his right arm with my own weapon and quickly trapped his right wrist in a second, smaller loop of chain. Then I applied pressure with both arms, throttling my victim while dragging him backward up the dais steps.

Choking out curses and obscenities, the warlord flopped up the steps after me, still attempting to impale me on the spine of his weapon with repeated flicks of his trapped wrist. Near the top of the steps I put an end to that by wrapping my legs about his arm. Now his left hand stretched blindly up between my legs, reaching for me with hooked fingers. I freed my handaxe, transferred both loops of chain to my left hand and struck at Northan's left elbow with the flat of my weapon. He howled as his arm vibrated violently for a second, then flopped uselessly.

Squeezing hard and twisting the chain, I watched the warlord's face begin to go blue, purple. Slowly his right fist opened and he dropped his weapon. The handaxe went clattering down the steps. I relaxed my grip a fraction, sitting upright until I looked down into my enemy's bulging eyes. Hatred still glared out of them unconcealed.

Releasing my grip a little more, I raised my handaxe almost to arm's length and said, "Do you admit defeat, Northan?"

For an instant indecision showed in his blood-dark features, then slyness. From his answer it was plain that he did not think I would kill him. "It's your play, Earthman," he gasped. "Get it over with!"

Gritting my teeth I lifted my weapon higher yet.

The crowd gasped; Northan fainted; Armandra's voice screamed in my head: *"No!"*

I slammed the handaxe down, cutting through the knot of chain above Northan's head and sending a shower of sparks from the stone steps. Then, as a great sigh went up from the assembly, I lifted him up by his hair and put both feet to his back. Kicking him forward, I sent his unconscious body somersaulting down the steps.

"There," I told the breathless hall as Northan landed jarringly, face down on the stone floor. "Keep your warlord!"

I got to my feet and stepped up beside Armandra, folding my arms and taking as dramatic a stance as I knew how. "Keep him," I repeated. "Perhaps now, with his strutting stilled, he'll learn to be as good a citizen as he is a soldier."

Then, as a delighted uproar burst out all about the hall, I said to Armandra, "And what, princess, if Northan had killed me? It seems to me a shallow sort of affection that risks a life for a barbaric code of existence!"

She leaned on me, her beautiful face pale and drawn as death. "Have I more faith in your friend Whitey than you?" she asked.

"Whitey? You mean you—" I sought Whitey's face in the crush of people at the foot of the dais. He was grinning cheerfully, heavy eyebrows arched happily. "But why didn't he—why didn't *you*—tell me?"

"We did not want you to relax your vigilance for a moment."

"Good old Whitey," I grinned.

"He has earned my eternal respect," she agreed. "But if you had died, I might well have had him thrown from the roof of the plateau!"

If I had thought that now the door would be open to Armandra's chambers, then I had thought wrong. I was her champion, certainly, with the right to attend her at any time during her waking hours and counsel her, and be counseled in return, but as for anything else—forget it. We could not be together; there would not be, could not be, anything other than a sort of courting between us until I had proved myself yet again, in battle against those true enemies of the plateau, the Children of the Wind. And to be absolutely sure that the opportunity would not come for us to be alone together (perhaps she did not trust herself to adhere to the plateau's ancient rules), Armandra kept either Tracy or Oontawa with her constantly.

Not only was this extremely frustrating for me but it soon began to get on Jimmy Franklin's nerves, too. Because of this, and the fact that by now Tracy was as much taken with Jimmy as he was with her, Armandra allowed the two to be together fairly regularly for short periods, but she never failed to ensure that Oontawa was there to give her moral support in Tracy's absence.

It wasn't very long before I became so unhappy with this situation that I would take myself off for long periods to the exercise cave to work off my frustrations in mock but nevertheless furious combat. Indeed, as the weeks stretched out, I began to believe—almost to fear—

that all serious battling was over and done with between the People of the Plateau and the wolf-warriors of Ithaqua, that I would never again be given the chance to fight for Armandra's favors.

Certainly I did not give much thought to the possibility of any real sort of crisis developing within the plateau itself. And yet, looking back on it, I recall that there were warnings enough. Whitey was nervous and jumpy, and kept going on at me to look out for the warlord and his friends.

It was during a session in the exercise cave that Jimmy Franklin brought me word of the trouble, of Northan's treachery. Since his humiliation the warlord had slowly but surely been losing his authority with the chiefs and headmen, and now only a few of his closest friends and lieutenants remained faithful to him.

I knew of this and had already put it to Armandra that perhaps I should formally replace Northan as head of the plateau's warrior army; should become warlord in his stead. She would not hear of it. She pointed out that if Northan were deposed, stripped of rank and military power completely, this would only make him hate me more, if that were possible. Also, it would leave him free to create a variety of mischiefs on the plateau's political side. There were still those among his few cronies who, having been elevated to positions of power by the warlord, would assist him in fresh ambitions rather than risk falling into obscurity along with him. He could also compromise certain of the elders, who feared for their own positions. Even in this alien world, politics were by no means free of corruption; though from what I knew of it, Northan was at the root of everything that was bad. Well, Armandra had stressed the fact that he was ambitious . . .

I had just landed two spears in the bull from a distance of about twenty-five yards when Jimmy Franklin ran into the vast, high-ceilinged exercise cave. There was blood on the right shoulder of his fur jacket; blood dripped from a deep gash in his left thigh.

"Hank—Tracy's hurt!" he gasped it out.

"Hurt? How badly?" I grabbed him by his good shoulder, searching his face anxiously. "What do you mean, she's hurt? Who hurt her? *How* is she hurt?"

"Northan," Jimmy panted, "he's defecting! He sent three of his men after Tracy. They tried to take her while she was sleeping but she woke up in time to avoid whatever they had planned. She got one of them with a star-stone. Hit him in the ear with it. Damn near burned half his head away! One of the others clubbed her unconscious. Then they split up, one heading one way to lead off any pursuit, the other making for the harbor area, where Northan's ship is tied up. He tried to take Tracy with him but it didn't work out. Her star-stones are gone, though."

"You're not making sense," I spoke urgently, firing questions at him. "What do you mean, he tried to take Tracy with him? Where is she now?"

"She's all right, Hank. As luck would have it I was on my way to see her. I saw this Eskimo with her across his shoulder. That was in the perimeter tunnel leading away from our rooms. When I challenged the Eskimo he had to put her down to deal with me. We had a bit of a fight and I got a few cuts," he indicated his shoulder and leg wounds, "but the noise attracted a couple of Indian friends of ours. One of them was Charlie Tacomah. His room is somewhere above ours. Well, the Eskimo told Charlie that he was only carrying out Armandra's orders, but I said he must be lying. He made a run for it and Charlie brought him down with a spear. Apparently Charlie and his friend were on their way here to work out with you."

"Right. I had arranged to meet them here. But where is Tracy now? And what about the third member of the group? And where's that dog Northan?" My voice trembled with fury.

"Charlie and his friend are taking her to Armandra. They're raising the alarm along the way. Your other questions—" he spread his arms and shrugged. "You know as much as I do now."

Then he swayed and half fell against me. I steadied him and noticed for the first time how much blood he was losing.

I caught him as he fell and carried him to a rest couch, telling the two astonished weapon masters, "Look after him, get him attended to immediately. I'm going to Armandra."

On my way out I turned to Jimmy. "Thanks for everything, Jimmy," I said. "Are you going to be all right?"

"I think so."

"I reckon that Tracy's just about got to accept you as her champion now, eh?"

He managed a grin. "She was going to anyway," he said.

Racing through the plateau's labyrinthine ways, I could see that Charlie Tacomah had been busy alerting the entire place. Indians wearing the insignia of guardsmen were hurrying to positions at the base of the outer wall; powerfully built, squat Eskimo warriors were padding along the corridors leading to the snow-ship harbors; the entire plateau was alive to emergency measures that had been in force for hundreds of years. There was no aimless milling about; these men were moving in military precision, reacting to whatever dangers the plateau now faced, hurrying to their battle stations.

"*Hank!*" Armandra's urgent thought came to me. "*Tracy is with me now and she has just regained consciousness. Charlie Tacomah has told me what he knows. Are you coming to us? Do you know what has happened?*"

"*I'm almost with you now,*" I told her, "*and I know what happened. That dog Northan; has he really defected?*"

"*Yes, with two dozen of his officers and men. His snow-ship is no longer at its mooring. They are fleeing now across the white waste, heading for Ithaqua's altar.*"

I let my disgust at the thought of the traitor flare in my mind. "*He tried to take my sister with him, as an offering to Ithaqua, no doubt. Can we get after him? I want to be aboard the first snow-ship out of the plateau.*"

"*You cannot, Hank,*" she answered as I raced by her Eskimo guardsmen and their bears. "*We are making no pursuit. My father, Ithaqua, is back on Borea; Northan was waiting for him to return. He chose the hour of his treachery well.*"

"*Then the dog gets clean away?*"

"*Not so,*" ominous undertones showed in her thought patterns. "*I am sending a wind after him even now!*"

I ducked through the curtains and entered Armandra's chambers. Oontawa was tending to Tracy who lay propped up on a couch. My sister had a bump like a hen's egg on the side of her head. Armandra, eyes closed and face grim, head tilted back, held out her arms before her while her hands described forward, stirring motions.

"Armandra," I began, stepping forward. But at that precise moment her entire face started to glow bloodred while the hair of her head rose up to undulate above her as in an updraft of air. A wind blew out from her, thrusting me aside as it raced across the room to set the curtains flapping violently. A moment more this phenomenon continued, then Armandra's hair settled down again, the flush left her face, the wind ceased. She lowered her hands and opened her eyes.

"Come," she said. "We will see what games my familiars can play with Northan's snow-ship."

"Wait," I answered, hurrying through into a second room, Armandra's resting chamber, to fetch my binoculars. Then we went out, back along the corridor to the viewing balcony with its widely spaced bars. Tracy and Oontawa followed us. I put an arm around my sister and asked her if she was all right.

"Yes. A bit dizzy, that's all. That was quite a bump I took."

"Not nearly as painful as the bump I'll deal the ex-warlord when next we meet!" I promised her.

"*If* you meet him again Hank," Armandra grimly put in. We had arrived at the balcony and now she pointed out through the bars. "See . . ."

Through the binoculars I saw the snow-ship fleeing, already two-thirds of the way to the circle of totems with its central altar. Atop that altar I could see the Snow Thing, and he too was watching the snow-ship's progress. At that distance the monster's outline was indistinct, but the flaring of his eyes was clearly discernible. I turned my binoculars back to the snow-ship, seeing that the vessel fairly leaped across the snow.

"See," Armandra said again, "the winds are answering my father's call and Northan's ship flies on their wings. But I, too, have sent a wind, one to vex the warlord's flight!"

Now, building up behind the snow-ship, growing out of the frozen white surface of the plain, the gray funnel of a tornado raised itself up, twisting and bending furiously as it rushed down upon the fleeing vessel. Closer to the ship the pursuing tornado roared, the howling of its passage coming back to us like the mad wail of some vengeful god.

Then Armandra cried out in anger and frustration, "Ah! My father is curious . . . he joins the play . . . Ithaqua displays his power!"

And sure enough the figure atop the pyramid altar had held up a massive hand to the onrushing tornado, and with a sweeping contemptuous gesture he *brushed it aside!*

The tornado, towering high and threateningly over the snow-ship, suddenly swerved aside and teetered crazily, blindly in the wrong direction. The snow-ship sped on. Armandra began to close her eyes, set her jaw stubbornly and raised her arms—then shook her head and let her arms fall.

"What is the use?" she asked. "He is not to be denied his mastery of the winds."

Out over the white waste the tornado came to an abrupt halt. Ithaqua, from atop his pyramid altar, dismissed it with a wave of his hand. It collapsed in upon itself and spilled to the ground as a fine haze of snow and ice particles.

"But won't Ithaqua kill Northan and his crew?" I asked.

"No, Hank," Armandra turned to me. "Northan was the plateau's warlord; he knows all of the secret ways, the many tunnels that lead from the base of the plateau to its halls, barracks, recreation caves and dwellings. He will be a mine of information to Ithaqua's priests and soldiers. When they are ready, he will lead them against the plateau, have no doubt of it."

"Will he try to come back for you?"

She shook her head grimly. "No, my father would never allow it. He would destroy everyone on Borea first. Ithaqua is a lonely creature, Hank. He desires a friend to walk the winds between the worlds with him." For a moment her face glowed with a strange passion. "And sometimes," her voice was suddenly far away, "sometimes—"

Without knowing why I felt a strange chill grip me. Instinctively I focused upon the horror atop the distant altar. His eyes were burning brightly, staring directly at the plateau. I knew then that he saw us, if not physically, certainly with his mind.

"Stop that!" I cried, taking the Woman of the Winds into my arms and kissing her tenderly. "Stop it. You're not his, Armandra, you're mine!"

She clung to me gratefully, drank of my strength, and an anger blew up in me that led almost to disaster. Without thinking I put her behind me, gripped the wide bars of the balcony with both hands and stared straight out at Ithaqua.

I screamed at him with my mind. *You great, loathsome, alien blasphemy! When the day of reckoning comes, may the Elder Gods burn out your black heart and float your soul on a sea of fire, to fry until the end of time! Until then, know this. Your daughter is mine, mine! and neither man nor monster can ever take her from me!*

The defiant gesture of a spoiled child! But not satisfied with that, I also conjured up a mental picture of a star-stone of ancient Mnar and, hurling that at him too, added intended injury to the insult.

Immediately, violently, the thing at the apex of the ice altar reacted. First I sensed his mental derision at the star-stone symbol, as if he already knew that we were no longer in possession of the stones; then came his anger as he lifted his arms up to the gray skies and expanded, bulging upward and outward until he towered fully a hundred feet into the air; and finally he stepped aloft to walk up the wind, reaching into the suddenly boiling sky to draw down weirdly flickering lightnings that played in his hands. For a moment longer he held that inferno of electrical energies in his hands.

"*Back!*" came Armandra's warning cry. "Back from the bars!" She tugged at my arm until I followed her at a run, pushing Tracy and Oontawa in front of me. We had covered only a few paces when a weird, hissing blue light filled the balcony and corridor. Then the hissing became a deafening crackling as a large hand picked me up and hurled me headlong. The two girls flew with me—but not Armandra.

From where I dazedly lay I looked back at the Woman of the Winds, and at the balcony beyond her. Her hands were held up against the blue light that flickered angrily about her but did her no harm. Lightning played about the bars of the balcony, heating them a glowing white and running in rivers of sparks all about the floor, ceiling and walls. Tongues of flickering fire reached hungrily after us, but were held back by Armandra's power. For a moment longer the scene seared itself upon my mind, then the blaze of electrical fire died away.

In my mind's eyes I pictured a horrific figure striding in icy air over Borea, throwing back his head to roar with glee; then that vision too was gone and I was left knowing that Ithaqua had sent it.

Armandra came to me as I got to my feet. Chidingly she said, "That was no way to talk to the Wind-Walker." Then she hugged and kissed me, glad that no harm had come to me. Obviously she had heard what I said to her monstrous father, and it seemed she was no longer so vehemently opposed to someone's laying claim to her, provided I was that someone.

She kissed me again and with her kisses came a great yearning inside me. She sensed it and held me away at arm's length, turning her head confusedly to where the women had now regained their feet. She disengaged herself, asking them if they were hurt in any way. They were not.

Then watching me out of the corner of her eye, in a very low tone she said, "You must be very careful, Hank, how you taunt or tempt a being with the power to hurl the very lightning of the storm against you. Be it Ithaqua or Ithaqua's daughter!"

The yearning in me doubled as I saw again the mischief floating to the surface of her ocean eyes. She quickly sobered. "Come," she said. "We will return to my rooms and wait for news."

II

How Many Tomorrows?

(Recorded through the Medium of Juanita Alvarez)

News was not long in coming. An Eskimo guard soon arrived and, with much bowing and scraping, was let into Armandra's chambers. "Good, good," she said, drawing him upright and cutting short the formalities. "What news?"

She listened intently to his rather slow, guttural speech—words meaningless to me, for where she had spoken in English he answered in *Eskimo*—until he was done, then dismissed him. In all of his short report I had caught only one phrase, a phrase repeated in something akin to awe and horror: "The Madness!"

As the guardsman bowed himself out Armandra turned to me. "They have caught the third traitor, the one who took Tracy's star-stones. He was hiding in the forbidden tunnel."

"In the tunnel?" I repeated. "Hiding there?" I frowned, shaking my head. "But how could any man of the plateau ever manage to steal Tracy's star-stones in the first place? And I thought no man could ever venture into the forbidden tunnel, that its emanations were impenetrable. Now you tell me this man was hiding there!"

"Perhaps not *hiding* then," she looked at me pointedly. "No, he was—trapped—there. I do not care to think about it. They had him cornered and he had only one way to go. They caught him when he came out. As for the star-stones, that was simple. He caught them up at the end of his spear, lifted them by their chains, kept them away from him so they could not harm him."

"Even so," I said, "he must be a very brave man. Brave and misguided."

"A frightened man," she answered. "Frightened of Northan."

"I want to see him, question him," I told her. "I want to discover Northan's intentions, what he's up to."

She shook her head. "You'll get no sense out of him, Hank. The history of the plateau tells that once, hundreds of years ago, offenders against the common good, thieves and the like, were driven into the forbidden tunnel as punishment for their crimes. The records all show the same end result. It will be the same now; this underling of Northan's, he will not be coherent."

The way she said the last word found me looking at her inquiringly, but she avoided my eyes. She did not like to talk about that enigmatic tunnel in the bowels of the plateau, or of its effect upon men.

Tracy spoke up. "And have they got the star-stones back?"

Armandra shook her head; "No, he must have left them behind him, in that place. If so, they will remain there forever."

At that point there came again the sound of padding feet from the corridor. Oontawa went out and returned after a few seconds. "The man is being held in the council hall," she told her mistress. "The elders have tried to question him, in vain. Now they ask what you want done with him."

Armandra began to answer, then checked herself. She turned to me. For a long moment she looked at me. Finally she said to Oontawa: "That is not a matter for me. Better you speak to the warlord."

For a moment Oontawa looked puzzled, but then understanding dawned in her eyes. Of course. Now there was a new warlord! Speaking to me, the girl repeated, "The elders are holding the man; has the warlord any instructions?"

"I'll come to see him," I told her, "and I'll talk to the elders, too. Send word that I'll be there shortly."

Oontawa left immediately and Tracy went with her. My sister knew that Jimmy Franklin had been hurt and wanted to go to him. Finally I was alone with Armandra. Now she relaxed a little, became a woman again and not a goddess.

"Big trouble is coming, Armandra," I said. "We don't need a hunchman to tell us that much."

"I know," she answered. "And I think—I think that I am frightened, Hank. Things are all coming to a head too soon, too quickly. Troubles pile up all about us. The plateau's problems seem about to engulf us all. And now you have accepted a task that might daunt any man. You are the plateau's new warlord, and at a time such as this!"

"This was the way it had to happen," I answered. "In a way I'm glad. It's my chance to prove myself once and for all—to the People of the Plateau and to you. You know what that means to me." I forced myself to grin, making light of things, kissing her forehead while she clung to me.

Her voice was molten gold when she said, "We may not have much time, Hank. That is what frightens me most."

"We've wasted a lot of time," I answered, fires melting my iced blood. She pushed me away, her face suddenly flushed.

"When you have spoken to the elders, return to me," she hurriedly said. "Make what arrangements you must—do what must be done— then come back." She opened her mind to me: *visions of lurking, half-formed fears and fierce, tumultuous passions!*

"I am your warrior, Armandra, your champion, but not yet truly your husband. What of the plateau's rules? The ancient codes?"

The flush left her face and disbelief replaced it. Thunderheads darkened her brows and lightning flashed in her eyes. *"Dare* you make excuses when I have offered—?"

"But the ancient codes!" I protested, unable now to contain my laughter.

"Codes! Rules!" she started to flare up, then burst out laughing with me when she realized I was playing. Suddenly we both sobered, and I saw that her eyes were now wantonly seductive, Icelandic pools beneath which volcanic fires roared. "We will have to forget the rules, Hank."

"Armandra—"

"No!" she broke away from me. "Go to the elders now, then come back to me."

On my way to the Hall of the Elders I found myself shadowed by two lean, powerful Indians who took up a steady, loping walk at my heels. I began to feel alarmed when it dawned on me that these could be two more of Northan's men, left behind to take care of me.

After they had followed me for at least half the distance to my destination, when it seemed that they were stealthily closing the gap between us, I turned on them. I drove my elbow deep into the stomach of the one on my right, snatching his handaxe from his belt as he doubled over, retching. Dropping to a crouch and twisting into a good position to deliver a low, killing kick at the second of the two, I was stopped dead in my tracks by the sight of the man prostrate upon the tunnel floor!

I took away his handaxe and hauled him to his feet, demanding to know what was going on. He had a fair grasp of English, speaking to me rapidly, babbling while his companion slowly managed to compose himself. They were my personal bodyguards and messengers, sent by Oontawa to attend me.

I offered my apologies and clumsily attempted to brush the winded Indian down. He assured me that he considered himself the recipient of a great honor; he could now claim to have seen and experienced the lightning ferocity of "Sil-ber-hut-te" at first hand. His children's children would talk about me, and he, Kasna'chi, would be a part of my legend. He would doubtless have gone on had I not stopped him. It is disconcerting to say the least to find oneself growing into a living legend!

And so, with Kasna'chi and Gosan-ha close at my heels, I eventually arrived at the Hall of the Elders. The Indians waited outside while I went in to see the elders and their prisoner.

Other than the ten elders, two Eskimo guardsmen were also present in the great cave, The latter pair held between them a man who had plainly been of French-Canadian extraction. They were not so much detaining him as holding him up. I mention him in the past tense because quite simply he was no longer—anything; whatever he had been, he was no longer.

Though his body showed few of the normal signs of age, his face was deeply lined, his hair visibly graying. His eyes bulged and stared blankly and a slack grin or grimace made his lower lip seem to droop. Saliva ran down his chin. He babbled quietly, incoherently to himself. Armandra was quite right. No one would ever again get any sense out of this man.

I had him taken sway. His guards were to give him into the hands of those who would do what could be done for him. Useless to punish a man who could not remember his crime, could remember nothing at all.

Then I spoke to the elders, placing emphasis on the plateau's near invulnerability, making light of Northan's defection and stating that we were all now better off without him. I told them I doubted the ex-warlord's immediate ability to attack us, that for the moment we had nothing to fear from him. While I was delivering my pep-talk, Charlie Tacomah caught my eye. When I had done he drew me to one side.

"I see what you are doing," he told me, "and it is good, but I hope you are not fooling yourself. Northan knows all of the plateau's intricacies, its strong defensive positions and its weak spots. Until now we have been fortunate; the great majority of the Wind-Walker's people have been weak-willed and ignorant. Northan is neither of these things. At last Ithaqua has an ally he can use."

"And I have allies, too, Charlie," I answered. "You are one of them. The elders will have to do without you from now on. Tactician you once were, tactician you will be again. You are more use to me right now than to the elders."

"What do you want me to do?"

"I want you to start by having a good look at the plateau's defenses. Find me all the weak spots and devise ways to protect them. And I want to know our vantage points and cave entrances which can be made impregnable, but from which special forces might make telling forays. I need to know these things in order to prepare a plan of defense. In fact I want you to prepare such a plan, and the sooner you get started the better."

His eyes had taken on a keen glint as I talked; a new fire now shone out of them. "Do you think that the attack will come soon?"

"As soon as Northan can turn Ithaqua's rabble into an army, yes. They have their rough edges, the wolf-warriors, but those can soon be hammered out. I've seen them in battle and I was impressed. Led by Northan, backed up by the Wind-Walker's hellish powers—oh, yes, it's certainly coming, Charlie. I want us to be ready, that's all. If only there was a way we could get those star-stones back."

He shook his head at that. "If they have been left in the forbidden tunnel as we fear, then they cannot be recovered. They must—simply—remain—" He checked himself in midsentence, brightening. "But wait! Haven't I heard your sister say that—"

"Forget it!" I snapped. "She may not be afraid of the tunnel but I certainly am, for myself and for Tracy. If there's something down there that can do what we've seen done to a man—something that turns my bones to jelly just standing at the entrance to its lair—then I'm not asking my sister to face it!"

"Of course not," he quickly replied. "It was a stupid thing to suggest." After a pause he added, "I have a lot to do now, and you will be even more occupied. If you will excuse me—"

"Yes, Charlie. And let me have the answers as soon as you know them."

After Charlie left the Hall of the Elders I had a few more words with the council before setting out to look for Whitey. It dawned on me that I had not laid eyes on him for four or five days. I wondered what he was up to, and I wanted his advice. He was my hunchman, and if anyone ever needed a few decent hunches it was me.

I found myself wondering: what kind of a hunchman was Whitey anyway? Oh, he'd warned me often enough about Northan, certainly, but there had been nothing specific, nothing definite. Whitey must be losing his touch. Soon enough I was to find out just how right I was.

Then, realizing that I need not look for Whitey myself, I sent Kasna'chi to find him, keeping Gosan-ha with me when I went to the roof of the plateau for a breath of fresh air.

All around the great flat roof, massive battlements had been cut from the solid rock. Behind them, spaced at intervals of about one hundred yards, keen-eyed watchers observed the white waste from this supreme vantage point. The scene to the front of the plateau was one which, despite its monochrome sterility, perhaps because of it, seemed starkly beautiful to me. Only one thing marred it: the obscene fingers of the distant totems pointing at a leaden sky, circling the pyramid altar like dancers frozen in some evil ritual.

And the being atop the pyramid seemed frozen too, as he motionlessly surveyed the strangely littered terrain of his territory, the white waste. A rage quickly built up in me and I had to force myself to carefully put down the binoculars, clipping them to my belt. It wouldn't do to drive the Wind-Walker into another frenzy, not while I was up here.

My mind was a muddle of conflicting thoughts, all of them having to do with the plateau's safety and future. Finally I left the roof. I walked with my thoughts, measuring the rock corridors until, almost without realizing it, I found myself on the penultimate level. There, at that entrance where Eskimo guardsmen stood in rich ceremonial robes with their bears shuffling behind them, I awoke to my surroundings. Deep in thought though I had been, busy with mad flights of heroic fancy as well as very real plans for the protection of the plateau, my feet had led me back to Armandra.

I dismissed Gosan-ha there, leaving orders with the guardsmen that I was not to be disturbed unless it was a matter of the gravest urgency, and then I went on along the richly furnished corridor.

The next morning, Oontawa awakened us. She was shocked and it showed on her face. Armandra took charge of the situation at once, saying, "Oontawa, do you disapprove? This is my husband that fought for me in the Choosing of a Champion. Yes, and I love him."

"Yes, Armandra," the Indian girl began, "but—"

"There may be very little time left for us," Armandra interrupted. "In the battle that must soon come we may be the losers. It is not a thought I want spread among my people but the possibility exists. You are just a maiden, a girl who has been friend and companion to me and who loves me. I love you too, for your innocence. Though not too many years separate us, our minds are centuries apart. I am old in strange wisdom and you are innocent. In your innocence I have seen you smile favorably upon a certain brave. Is it not so?"

"It is so," Oontawa bowed her head and flushed.

"And is he not the handsome brave that keeps the bears for our warlord? His name is—"

"Kota'na, my princess."

"Just so. Then I repeat that time is very precious, Oontawa. I suggest we arrange a Choosing of Champions for you. As of this moment you are dismissed from my service, but I know you will remain my friend. Go, girl, and find your happiness, as I have found mine."

Oontawa bowed again and when she lifted her head there were glad tears in her eyes. She turned to me. "Lord Sil-ber-hut-te, your friend Whitey waits to see you. He is with Gosan-ha and Kasna'chi. They wait where the guardsmen stand with their bears."

I smiled and nodded. "I will come."

Oontawa waited on the far side of the curtained doorway that closed off Armandra's rooms, and when I was ready we walked together to the guarded end of the corridor where Whitey and my bodyguards waited. She left me there to go in search of Kota'na, taking him the news that Armandra had ended her service so that the Keeper of the Bears could take her to wife.

I walked with Whitey, slowly pacing the fantastic labyrinths of the plateau and talking to him while my bodyguards kept a discreet distance to the rear. Whitey was up-to-date on everything, had heard of my new office, was pleased that Armandra had placed the might of the plateau in my hands. He said as much, and yet I sensed that something was bothering him.

"I feel I've kind of let you down this time, Hank," he finally said after a long period of silence. "Something—I don't know what—isn't right."

"How do you mean, Whitey?"

"It's hard to explain, a funny thing. And yet not so funny, if you follow me. All my life, even before I was fully aware of this power of mine to, well, to gauge the mood of the future, so to speak, before I was a hunchman proper, I could kind of *sense the existence* of tomorrow. I was as much aware of the reality of the future as other people were of the past. Tomorrow was as certain to me as yesterday." He paused for a moment, then continued, "I suppose it must be a difficult concept for anyone who's not a hunchman. Anyway, as I've grown older the impressions of tomorrow have occasionally been clearer. Such flashes have been my hunches, of course, the end results of the special talent that made me valuable to the Wilmarth Foundation. Until recently . . ."

"Oh." I frowned. "Well, go on, Whitey. What's the problem?"

He shrugged resignedly. "It's a worrying thing, Hank. I feel like I just lost a leg or something. You know what I mean?"

"No more hunches, eh?"

"Right the first time. Sorry, Hank."

"But how could it happen? Have you any ideas?"

"Yeah, I have an idea," he grimly answered. "My idea is, how can I see tomorrows that aren't going to be?"

"Not going to be? There'll always be tomorrows, Whitey."

"Sure!" he said. "But will we be here to enjoy them?"

III

The Lull Before the Storm

(Recorded through the Medium of Juanita Alvarez)

The next fortnight was one of frantic activity. Working to Charlie Tacomah's suggestions I garrisoned soldiers close to the plateau's outer walls, in temporary cavern-barracks from which they could rapidly deploy to defensive positions. The plateau's weak spots—several large and easily accessible entrances opening straight into the guts of the plateau from the plain—were specially strengthened and fortified to my orders. Quarriers worked nonstop to cut and lever massive blocks of stone into place. We did a similar job with the snowship keeps, those fjordlike, frozen reentries where the great ski-borne battlecraft were harbored. These tasks, wherever possible, I personally supervised. If I was not available, Charlie was there in my stead. With each and every person in the plateau realizing the urgency of the situation, the work went ahead with very few complications; the plateau's peoples were all right there behind their princess—yes, and behind their new warlord, too.

Heartening as all this was, over that same period of time there were worrying things happening out on the white waste in the vicinity of the Wind-Walker's temple. The watchers on the roof of the plateau had reported the activity; I myself had seen it enlarged in my binoculars. The Children of the Winds had gathered from far and wide, were exercising in orderly military maneuvers across the frozen terrain of their territory. Northan was flexing his new and savagely powerful muscles, making a vast and disciplined fighting body out of the entire nation of Ithaqua's worshippers. And always the Snow-Thing watched over the ex-warlord's progress, and always the tension heightened.

Then, during the third week, there were two new developments. Ithaqua departed yet again, walking away across the winds and disappearing over Borea's rim, and Jimmy Franklin brought me news of that which I could only consider an act of sheerest lunacy. The latter concerned Tracy.

It was midweek and I was with Armandra, who was trying to explain to me her alien father's eternal wanderlust, his apparent inability to remain in any specific sphere for any appreciable length of time, which she explained as being simply one of the conditions of the limited freedom allowed him by the Elder Gods, when Jimmy came to us. He breathlessly told us his story.

He and my sister had been walking together through the complexes of the plateau when their wanderings had taken them to the forbidden tunnel. They had stood together at that dark entrance, and suddenly he had noticed a new light in Tracy's eyes. She was aware, of course, that her star-stones were believed to be somewhere in that sinister burrow, left there by Northan's now incurably crazed underling.

Realizing what she intended to do, Franklin had tried to stop her but discovered he was neither physically nor mentally strong enough to do so. His wounds had healed, true, but his strength was not yet back to normal. When she broke loose from him and ran off down the tunnel, bearing with her a torch snatched from the nearest flambeau, he had tried to follow her but was held back by the dreadful *power* emanating from that hideous shaft. It had been as if he threw himself against the solid wall of some castle of evil, while a brain-eating acid was dripped upon his head from the unseen battlements.

Finally, reeling and clutching at his sanity where the *power* had brought him to a halt just a few paces inside the nightmare entrance—knowing that to remain would certainly mean succumbing to madness—he realized that he could do nothing at all to help Tracy. She would not return until she either found the star-stones or satisfied herself that they were not there. Then Franklin crawled from the place on all fours, and as soon as he had recovered he hurried to me.

We returned to the forbidden tunnel immediately, Armandra and my bodyguards with us, and on our way I obtained a slender spear. Seeing that I had armed myself, Armandra clung desperately to my arm and I felt her mental fingers worriedly probing the edges of my telepathic consciousness. I closed my mind to her, though already she must have known what I intended to do—what I would at least attempt.

I expected objections but at the tunnel mouth no one tried to stop me; it would have been futile to do so. I simply ran into the tunnel, a burning brand in one hand, my spear in the other, shouting Tracy's name. And immediately the *power* was there pushing against me, trying to hold me back with fingers of fear that worked in my brain, so that with every step I felt I was leaping from a precipice, or hurling myself down the living throat of some primordial reptile. And the echoes of my cries came back to me: "Tracy! . . . Tracy! . . . *Tracy!*"

And then I was on my knees, pushing forward, spear and torch before me, with shadows leaping on the walls and ceiling like mad demons while fear tore at my insides. And I knew I was going to go mad with fear. I knew it.

And I would have gone mad if I had forced myself on—but I didn't have to. From around a bend in the tunnel It came, waves of fear beating out from It, the horror that the plateau dreaded, hitherto unseen, unknown. Manlike It was, an inky anthropomorphic blot that dripped namelessly; but small as I could never have expected It to be, this Thing that radiated such *fear!*

As It came closer I backed away on all fours, dropping my torch from nerveless fingers, feeling the fear eating my brain. And then I remembered Tracy.

"Monster!" I screamed. I got to my feet, drew back my arm and balanced the slender spear, which the instinct for self-preservation had made me hold on to, aiming at the thing's heart—

And the monster spoke!

"Hank? Is that you? Are you all right?"

Tracy! But if this was my sister, why should I feel the *fear* radiating from her? Why should my stomach twist and writhe with every step she took toward me?

I backed away, noting through waves of terror how the inky figure kept well away from the sputtering flame as it edged around the still burning torch where it flared upon the floor. With every step the figure advanced I had to retreat, pushed back by the *fear.*

"Tracy." I somehow managed to force words from my parched throat. "Is it really you? What's happened to you?"

"Of course it's me, Hank," the figure replied, and certainly it spoke with Tracy's voice. "Yes, it's me. I'm covered in oil, that's all."

"But Tracy," I pressed her, still backing away, "why—why am I *afraid* of you?"

"What?" she stopped moving toward me and I detected the growing concern and disbelief in her voice. A moment later she laughed and I knew at last that it really was Tracy. "Oh, it must be the star-stones!" she said in sudden relief. "I came down here to look for two of them—and I found hundreds! Down at the other end of the tunnel there's a huge cavern, with star-shaped symbols on the walls and all over the ceiling, and the floor is literally covered with the stones. I'm carrying dozens of them with me right now, and they're heavy! It must be the stones you can sense; you're frightened of *them*, not me."

She was right, of course she was. "And this cavern," I questioned, still retreating before her. "Is it—empty?"

"Yes, apart from the star-stones and the oil. At one place the cavern wall is cracked and oil is seeping in, I guess from the place where the plateau's people draw off their fuel. I left my torch stuck in the floor while I was gathering up some of the stones. Then I slipped and fell in the oil. That's why I had to leave the torch behind and come back in the dark. Are you all right, Hank?"

Now it was my turn to laugh, weakly, almost hysterically.

"Oh, yes, I'm all right—but you'd better let me warn the others or they're likely to make a pincushion of you as you come out."

"Yes, yes do!" she cried. "Oh, go on, Hank, get out of here. You sound dreadful. Please hurry on ahead. And don't worry. There's absolutely nothing down here to hurt you. Oh, except the star-stones, of course."

Of course. Nothing but the star-stones!

I turned then and ran, or rather I staggered, back along the way I had come. And all the way the *fear* snapped at my heels, right behind me. Only now I knew exactly what I was afraid of—what everyone in the plateau had feared—and though the knowledge made no difference and I was still desperately afraid, I was also jubilant!

"Let them come," my spirit cried inside me, "and Ithaqua with them. At least the odds are balanced a lot more in our favor now!"

And that brings us up to five days ago, Juanita. I've probably missed things, I know, but nothing that I think is of any real importance. Let's see now, how long have we been in touch? With time off for a few breaks and a couple of hours sleep, I reckon it must have been all of thirty-six hours. Is that a record for telepathic contact between worlds—or rather, between "spheres?" I suppose it must be. You say Peaslee has given you a team of stenographers, typists, tape recorders? Methodical as ever. He doesn't miss a trick.

With you right now? Yes, I see in your mind that he is. He says to quit the casual chatter and get on with it, does he? Well, you can tell him from me that the Wilmarth Foundation doesn't carry much weight way out here on Borea! He's right, though, so I suppose we'd better get on with it. Not that there's a lot left to tell.

We're simply waiting now, there's nothing else to do. Armandra has been resting for two days, seeing no one, not even me. She says she'll need all her strength for the coming fight, and try as I might I can't convince her that she won't have any part of it. The trouble is, I know that if she wanted to join in there's not much I could do to stop her; she would only be fighting for her people after all. And for her freedom.

It can't be far off now, the fight, for Northan has quit exercising his army and holds it in readiness. And Ithaqua is back. The Wind-Walker perches atop his pyramid as always, except that he no longer stares out and away over the white wastes. Now he faces squarely in the direction of the plateau.

Tracy has been busier than anyone else since she found the star-stones in the cave at the end of the forbidden tunnel, those same star-stones that once held the Wind-Walker imprisoned deep in the guts of the plateau. That's why the horror has always held the plateau in great respect, why he himself has not yet seen fit directly to attack the place.

But to get back to Tracy: she must have walked miles, poor kid, before she let Kota'na talk her into riding one of his bears. Since then she's been getting about much faster. And her work is probably the most important of all, for Tracy has been putting the finishing touches to the plateau's defenses.

I suppose I could say that the idea was a group effort of Charlie Tacomah, Tracy and myself—but the truth is that Tracy's had the lion's share of the work. I had a rough idea how I wanted the star-stones used; Charlie worked out the mechanical details; Tracy is still working to finish it off, but it's just about done now.

Roughly the idea was this: that the stones be used as a secondary defense behind the new tunnel barriers, to deny entry into the plateau should the barriers be breached. Charlie designed heavy wooden frames, had them built and suspended from the ceilings of the outer tunnels. Fixed to the fronts of these frames are spears set in two rows. The bottom row consists of conventional spears fixed about two feet apart, and these are meant to impale the giant wolves. The upper rows are less conventional; in fact they're not spears at all but simply stout poles, like slender battering rams. Only nailed to the end of each pole is a star-stone—and these are not meant for wolves . . .

Tracy's hands are a mass of blisters. Because she's the only one able to handle the star-stones, by now she must have nailed up almost two hundred of the things.

Anyway, Charlie's devices work like this: swinging from the ceilings of the tunnels and operated by teams of men hauling on ropes from the rear, they should form impassable barriers. The spears are not barbed; that is, they will impale men and wolves alike, but their victims will not pile up on the shafts. By the time a wall of bodies has built up in front of one of these fearsome devices, well, the passage will be impassable by then anyway. And when they are not in use the spear-frames can be hauled up to the tunnel ceilings to allow my warriors passage beneath them.

There have been one or two minor accidents when Tracy's assistants have come into momentary contact with her stones, but once burned means twice shy. Those who suffer make sure they don't get burned a second time! I imagine that when these terrible weapons are in action, nothing Ithaqua can send against them will stand a chance.

And that is only one of the uses to which the star-stones have been put. They've also been fixed on the massive gates that guard the snowship keeps, and they form a five-pointed design in the battlements of the plateau's roof. All in all, I believe we've used them to their best advantage. Time alone will tell, and I think there's precious little time left.

Speaking for myself, I would prefer to hold back when the battle starts, let the Children of the Winds come to me and make them fight on my terms, but my generals tell me that to do so would be to severely demoralize the warriors of the plateau. To many of the young braves this seems their golden opportunity to distinguish themselves in bloody battle. I daren't deny them that which is their right according to the plateau's ancient codes and customs. That's why, before Ithaqua returned, I had the snow-ships out exercising and maneuvering all about the foot of the plateau, while Armandra sent fair winds to fill their sails.

Thus, when the time comes, they will go out to attack the wolf-warriors and their battle-sledges. At the same time, foot soldiers and mounted bears will protect the tunnel entrances and keeps, while the fortified positions will be manned by strong but older men who are past their prime. Then, if things go badly, survivors of the fighting will fall back with the wounded and take over the plateau's defensive positions. They will be replaced in the field of battle by reserves, while the wounded will be passed back along the tunnels to first-aid and hospital centers. The crews of the snow-ships will simply have to fend for themselves if their vessels are wrecked, getting back to the safety of the plateau as best they can.

But I need not go on. All of this is prearranged. The plan in its entirety is complicated and would be meaningless to you, Juanita, unless you knew the plateau as I now know it; which is why I have only given you the basic outline. Now we wait.

Jimmy has just been to see me, excited about a device he's had built and positioned in the mouth of a small cave fifty feet above ground level. It's a powerful catapult on a swiveling base. He and Tracy have been practicing with pebbles and they can now accurately land a stone—a *star*-stone when the time comes—almost anywhere inside a two hundred-and-fifty-yard radius. Jimmy will aim and release the "shells," Tracy will load for him. Now she's gone off yet again to the forbidden tunnel to replenish her stock of stones.

Meanwhile, I've managed to convince Armandra that she must stay out of the fight. She promises not to join the battle unless Ithaqua himself takes a strong hand. I can't really picture him trying to do that once he sees what we have waiting for his wolf-warriors. Of course, there was a condition to Armandra's agreement to stay out of things; I have to keep out of it too, despite the fact that I've a personal score to settle with Northan. It was the only way I could make Armandra see sense.

So here I am right now where I've positioned myself in an observation cave a third of the way up the face of the plateau, surrounded by a gang of runners who will take my commands below to the fighting men once the battle begins. It's a pretty basic system of communication, but the best I can do.

And that's our present position. Jimmy and his catapult, along with a couple of runners and assistants of his own, are below me on the face of the plateau and about one hundred yards to my right, where Tracy should soon be joining them. Whitey should be up on the roof, still desperately trying to get a peek into the future and keeping a keen eye on the now very much increased activity out across the white waste. Armandra is high above in her rooms, no doubt still nervously fretting. The warriors and their bears are resting up in temporary quarters and barracks down below, and the crews of the snow-ships are ready to man their vessels at a moment's notice, though I can't see them doing a great deal if Ithaqua decides to blow in the wrong direction. That's the trouble with this situation; nothing is certain, everything is a big *if*—everything except the one really definite fact that Ithaqua *will* send the Children of the Winds against us.

Now I'm going to stop sending, Juanita. There are a few last details I have to see to. I'll contact you again when I can, or when there's something to report.

NOTE: Following this last telepathic transmission from Hank Silber-hutte, which ended at 10 a.m., June 5, nothing further was heard from him until 2 p.m. the next day. Then, from across unknown gulfs of space and time, Juanita Alvarez again began to receive his thoughts. The following, final recordings, forming as they do the last part of this document, were commenced at that time.

Part Four

◆

I

The Assault Begins

(Recorded through the Medium of Juanita Alvarez)

Whitey is dead, crushed and destroyed as if he had never been, *removed* as he gave all he had, his very life, to save Armandra from her dreadful father and the alien star-voids he eternally wanders. Armandra is hurt, perhaps crippled, I don't know yet. The physicians are with her now.

Tracy and Jimmy are safe, and I'm thankful for that, but Paul White . . . poor Whitey. No wonder he could see no more tomorrows, no futures; for him there was no future.

This last day has been completely hideous! Even now that it's all over, my nerves jump and my scalp prickles at the very thought of it. I can still hear the screams of dying men and beasts, the shrill whistling of Ithaqua's man-carrying kites as they soared down upon the plateau out of raging skies, the blasts of the thunderbolts that turned the plateau's roof to an incredible inferno; and I can still smell the ozone reek of alien energies, the stench of living fear, the sordid stink of death. But let me tell you Ithaqua did not have it all his own way. And for all the plateau's losses the Wind-Walker strides by no means triumphant in Borea's skies this day. He licks an awful wound, and his warriors are scattered far and wide.

But I can't get Whitey out of my mind, poor Whitey, who will have no grave for there is nothing to bury. But, by God!—we shall raise to him a memorial where he died, a tower of stone on the very roof of the plateau, to overlook this whole demon-damned world forever.

And I'm sorry, Juanita; as yet you know nothing of all this, and here I rave like a man demented. Well, perhaps you will understand when I am finished.

It started within an hour of my last contact with you . . .

One minute the strangely hummocked white expanse, with all its frozen loot of the Motherworld of men, seemed empty of life, except about the totem ring and its central altar, where tents and shelters had been set up to house the army that Northan had gathered and disciplined for the Wind-Walker. The next moment the whole plain turned black! Shedding the white furs which until then had kept them hidden, the massed might of the Children of the Winds was revealed.

To think that a few moments earlier I had been wondering where all of Ithaqua's warriors had gone! Having watched them gathering for days, from far and wide, I had noticed that paradoxically there never seemed to be more than a few thousand of them visible at any one time. Now at last they showed themselves. Ten ranks deep, only a shoulder's width between them, forming a straight line that stretched for at least five miles across the wastes, I calculated that they numbered close to two hundred thousand. And these were only the foot soldiers!

Behind them, three deep and stretching in a line all of two miles long, in the next moment appeared the wolf-warriors. They too threw down their robes to reveal their great numbers, a move calculated to unnerve us. And certainly Ithaqua's army was an unnerving sight. Oh, the Wind-Walker was not playing games this time, neither him nor his new warlord, Northan.

Northan! My lips drew back from my teeth involuntarily as I thought of the treacherous hound, and almost as if I had once more thrown a challenge in his face, so the sails of the plateau's once-flagship filled out as it slipped anchor near the pyramid altar. My nails bit into the metal of my binoculars as I focused them on the ship of Northan, though at that distance the figures crowding her decks were tinier than ants and I could never have said for certain which one was he.

The ship rode out to the forefront of the army, gathering speed as it took up a central position, and now the army itself began to move, forming an arrowhead behind the ship. I could see the wolf-warriors spurring their huge mounts to advance through the ranks of the foot soldiers. As the wolves came, so the men on foot jumped up to cling to their great sides and be carried forward.

Bringing up the rear came great battle-sledges hauled by teams of lesser wolves, and these picked up the remaining foot soldiers. I kept my binoculars upon these battle-sledges and after a few seconds managed to obtain a better view of them. They were mounted with stout, pointed battering-rams.

Finally, behind all the others, Ithaqua's priests rode in their own sledges. Forming a backdrop to that awesome army of men and beasts, the Wind-Walker himself stood atop his frozen altar with massive arms folded and terrible eyes hooded as in deep, dark thoughts.

I put down my binoculars. The V-shaped formation could mean only one thing: a direct assault upon the plateau, concentrated upon a narrow front. And the battering-rams told me that the attack must come at the gates of the snowship keeps, which were all positioned along an uneven half-mile of the plateau's front.

Once through those heavy gates the wolf-warriors might well manage to breach one or more of the larger tunnels that led directly into the plateau's bowels, doubly fortified as they now were. I was sure that this was what Northan intended to do, and so issued my first orders. All of the runners were fluent in English, and no sooner had the first of my messengers darted away down the steep flights of stone steps with my instructions than the next was there, eager to receive my next command. I told all of them to sit down and try to relax; orders would be issued as they were required.

That was when Charlie Tacomah entered from one of the two horizontal shafts that led back into the plateau. I appreciated his company and repeated for his benefit the orders I had given a few seconds earlier. He borrowed my binoculars, studied the advancing army and nodded.

"I think I would have done the same thing," he said. "It's a pity we had no time to build sufficient of our swinging weapons to completely block off the larger tunnels that enter from the keeps. They form our weakest points. Yes, I too would have sent more men there." He paused, and at length added, "And what of our elite corps?"

"The snow-ships? I want to hold them back until Northan and his army are closer, then release them all at once. As I see it, Ithaqua is filling the sails of Northan's ship with just sufficient wind to blow him to the plateau along with the rest of the army. From here we are looking at them down a very slight slope, and in that we have an advantage. If we keep the snow-ships back until the last moment, then get

Armandra to give them a push, they ought at least to be able to punch a couple of holes through that V-formation. After that—" I shook my head, frowning. "If I had my way I wouldn't let them sail at all. Not only does it mean bringing Armandra into it, albeit indirectly, and not in any real sort of confrontation with the Wind-Walker—but I'm sure that it will be certain death for many of the lads who man the snow-ships."

"They would not thank you for holding them back, Hank."

"And will I thank myself for sending them out to die?"

"That has always been the lot of generals, and of warlords."

I nodded grimly, then took the binoculars back and put them to my eyes once more. Now Northan's army was a quarter of the way to the plateau, and already one or two stragglers could be seen stretching out to the rear. Northan's ship still rode slightly to the fore, and that must be the traitor himself in the prow, surrounded by his lieutenants. There were wolves aboard that ship too, massive white beasts that strained at their chains. An idea—a suspicion—came to me.

"Do you think it's possible," I asked, "that Northan intends to crash one of the gates with his ship, then release those great wolves to ravage along the tunnels? There are about three dozen of the beasts aboard, but I can see damn few handlers."

"Wolves? Without handlers?" He took back the binoculars and a moment later said, "You could well be right. They will be lean and hungry animals, those wolves."

I turned to one of my runners. "Go tell the crews of the snow-ships to be ready. The keep gates are to be opened. All are then to wait for new orders."

As the runner hurried off I turned again to Charlie. "It seems we'll have to deal with the ship of Northan first," I said. "But just in case he should manage to break into one of the keeps with those wolves of his—" I clapped the next boy in line on the shoulder. "Go to Kota'na. I want twenty of his biggest, most powerful bears positioned in each of the keeps. The rest of them he is to use to their best advantage as soon as the fighting starts."

Now Ithaqua's army had covered more than half the distance to the plateau and the tension was rapidly heightening. I began to pace the floor, then forced myself to sit down when I noticed the eyes of my runners upon me. Charlie opened his mouth to say something, and at that precise moment there came a swelling cry from the central snow-ship keep somewhere below and to the left of my position, a cry that was echoed almost immediately from the flanking keeps.

"Sil-ber-*hut-te!* Sil-ber-*hut-te!*"

Obviously the runner had passed on my message to the men of the snow-ships, and now they signaled their whole-hearted approval. Something swelled up inside me as once more, in unison, the men of the snow-ships roared out their new battle cry. "Sil-ber-*hut-te!* Sil-ber-*hut-te!*"

The swelling thing inside me burst in a flood of resolution. I stood up and said to my Indian friend, "You keep the binoculars, Charlie. You'll need them if you're to command the battle. Those men out there are calling my name. They're not going to fight without me."

"*No!*" came Armandra's almost hysterical, mental denial in my head. "*You shall not, for if you do—then I swear I will walk out now on the winds to fight my father. Aye, even knowing that he will snatch me up and take me away with him to alien worlds. Without you, man of the Motherworld, there would be nothing for me here on Borea. Do you hear me, Hank? You shall not give your life away!*"

"But they call my name, and—"

"*They draw upon your name for its strength. They invoke your passions, your power. Why should you go out to fight, Hank, when every man of the plateau will fight with your great strength and fervor? They know you are worthy of them, now let them prove that they are worthy of you. And remember, husband, we made a bargain. If you fight, then so do I.*"

"They are closer, Hank." Charlie's voice snatched me back to the task at hand. "What are you going to do?"

Still torn two ways but realizing there was nothing I could do about it, I said, "Armandra leaves me no choice. I can't let her do battle with her father, so I must stay here and command from this position of safety. You stay with me, Charlie. Two heads are better than one."

Out on the plain, less than two miles now from the foot of the plateau, the wolf-warrior army swept toward us, its arrowhead formation slightly less pronounced. Northan had lined up his vessel on the central snow-ship keep. I slapped my next runner on his back. "Go tell the crews of the snowships to move out and position their craft along the front of the plateau." I took up my pistol. There was one bullet left in its magazine. "When they hear a loud report from this cave, they'll go straight out and cut through the advancing wolf-warriors. The two central ships will engage Northan's vessel and try to wreck it."

"*Armandra*," I continued telepathically, "*we will need a wind . . .*"

"*You shall have one. With luck it will take my father by surprise.*"

"This is it, Hank." Charlie said breathlessly. "Only a few seconds now."

He had the binoculars to his eyes. "You were right about those wolves on Northan's ship. They are huge, lean, ferocious animals. They look half-wild, barely trained and certainly starved."

I spoke to yet another runner. "Every man of the plateau should now be in position. I want the swinging weapons set in motion and the keep gates closed as soon as the ships are out. More of our bears are to be stationed just within the gates."

As he raced away down one of the steep shafts I stepped over to the lip of the cave and looked down to where the snow-ships would soon be lining up. After only a minute or so they began to appear from the keeps, dragged by teams of men and bears. There were eleven of them, and as they lined up the eyes of all crew members turned up to me.

Now Northan's army was little more than a half-mile away and gaining speed. The sails of the traitor's ship belled out in front, drawing the vessel straight for the gates of the central keep. The rumble of that army swept up to me as I turned to look at Charlie Tacomah. I nodded my head and he grimly nodded back. Then I pointed my weapon out over the white wastes and pulled the trigger for the last time. I said to the Woman of the Winds, "*Now we need that wind, Armandra.*"

"*You have it,*" she answered.

Flurries of ice particles swirled up all around the snowships and their great sails filled. They lurched forward, masts straining as the force of the wind Armandra had sent rapidly increased. And once more that massed cry came up to me as if from one vast throat: "Sil-ber-*hut-te!* Sil-ber-*hut-te!*"

Down the shallow decline the ships sailed, their skis throwing up a silver spray, and now the wolf-warrior army also felt the wind sent by Armandra. Northan's ship visibly slowed and its sails seemed to slacken as the plateau's two central vessels bore down upon it. I had ordered that those ships engage Northan's craft; now I saw that they intended to ram him!

But if that fact was plain to me, it was equally obvious to the wolf-warriors. A battle sledge was hurriedly thrown into the path of the starboard vessel, and as its skis cut great swaths through wolves and men, so they ran into the bulky obstacle. A snapping of timbers as two of the skis were ripped away; then the screams of men and animals as the snow-ship toppled, crushing down upon the milling ranks of those around it, flinging its crew to the frozen ground where, miraculously unhurt, they quickly formed themselves and their bears into a savage fighting unit.

The other ship fared somewhat better. Its bird's-beak prow struck Northan's vessel a glancing blow that threw both ships a little starboard. As their decks passed each other, scraping together, men of the plateau leaped the gunwales to engage hand-to-hand with Northan's crew. Then I saw that indeed Charlie had been right about those wolves on Northan's ship; these were not wolves bred to be ridden as mounts, nor were they bulky for the hauling of heavy loads. They were lean and rangy killers!

And three or four of them had hurdled the rails between the passing ships and were now ravaging among the crew of the plateau's vessel, while their snarling brothers tore to pieces that brave raiding party aboard the ship of Northan. Ah, but in a few moments more the bears of the plateau's ship had turned on the attacking wolves to throw their mangled bodies from the swaying deck. The ship sailed on, leaving in its wake a crushed and bloody swath.

There were ten such swaths, red on the white plain as those heroic vessels ploughed through the wolf-warrior ranks; ten one instant, but in the next only seven as three more of the great ships were wrecked upon battle-sledge reefs. And as I watched, two more, steering wildly from their courses to pick up survivors, were flung onto their sides; in a moment only five ships remained and the plain was a tumult of fighting men and animals.

But no! Those brave men of the surviving snow-ships could not see their brothers go down alone against such odds. As their vessels slowed and stopped, brought to a halt by the sheer weight of shattered flesh-and-bone that clogged their massive skis, so their crews lowered the gangplanks and rushed down them onto the plain.

At last the snow-ships stood empty, while on the plain about them the Children of the Winds turned inwards on the now desperately battling, stranded crews. I turned my eyes away as that wolf-warrior tide washed over them, drowned them as a wave covers pebbles on a beach, then seethed forward again in triumph.

Gone, all those brave men gone. They had sailed out to their deaths with my name on their lips. But their lives were not wasted, for the snow was red beneath that surging tide of wolf-warriors, red with the blood of hundreds of men and wolves crushed beneath the skis, and certainly in the hand-to-hand fighting the plateau's braves had not given their lives cheaply.

Meanwhile Northan's ship, thrown off course by the glancing collision, had come about in a tight circle. Now, heedless of the scrambling men and beasts too slow to clear a path for him, the traitor returned his vessel to its previous course. Straight for the central keep gates its beaked prow was aimed, the breath of Ithaqua in its sails, and the sea of men and wolves before it parted in frantic haste as it sped to its target.

Would Northan see the star-stone where Tracy had nailed it to the center of the great gate? Would it deter him? I had had concentric red circles painted around all such protective stars, to draw the eyes of the attacking army and fill them with dread. Surely Northan would see the star-stone. I took my binoculars back from Charlie and, with hands I could scarcely control, refocused upon Northan's ship.

There stood the ex-warlord upon the raised deck of the prow, eyes slitted and staring straight ahead, lips drawn back in a snarl. He would breach that gate if it was the last act he ever performed, and to hell with whatever awaited him on the other side!

Below me where I stood at the very lip of the cave, the forward part of the central keep and its gates were just visible. In that moment I looked down at a steep angle upon the ship of Northan. And at the same time, with something less than twice the length of his ship between him and the gates, finally Northan spotted the star-stone within its painted circles. He saw it and knew it to be genuine. I still had him in my binoculars when that happened, and the effect upon him was dramatic!

The snarl slid like butter from his face. He gabbled frenzied orders, motioned wildly with spastic arms, then hung on tight to the rail of the prow. Two of his lieutenants standing with him threw up their arms before their faces as they, too, spotted the star-stones. Then the ship slewed crazily as its crew finally interpreted and acted upon Northan's orders. Chunks of ice flew up from the skis of his ship as they bit into the frozen surface.

Broadside, the traitor's vessel slammed splinteringly into the gate.

II

Battle for the Plateau

(Recorded through the Medium of Juanita Alvarez)

As Northan's snow-ship came to a shuddering halt at the splintered gates of the central keep, a clattering and shouting reached me from the almost vertical shafts. From closer at hand there came a savage howl as, turning, I barely found time to throw myself to one side. A hurled spear flashed past me and out through the open mouth of the cave.

Intent upon Northan's activities, I had given little thought to what was happening with the rest of the plateau. I had seen the wolf-warrior tide surging about the foot of our massive refuge; now it was made perfectly plain to me that one or more of the lesser tunnels had been breached. An Eskimo warrior, wearing on his back, shoulders and head the pelt and snarling visage of a wolf, stood astride the broken body of a youthful runner at the head of one of the steep shafts. Pulling out a long knife from his belt he stepped menacingly into the cave.

Just inside the cave, hidden from the Eskimo by a wall-like bulge of rock, Charlie Tacomah had seen the flight of the spear. He remained silent and as the Eskimo came forward swung his handaxe full in the intruder's face. The spine of that hideous weapon drove to its hilt in the fatally surprised Eskimo's forehead, splitting his skull open like a ripe melon and sending him toppling back and out of sight down the vertiginous steps. He gave a single gurgling shriek as he went.

Before I could thank Charlie, a guardsman wearing Armandra's royal insignia appeared from that same shaft. How he had avoided being knocked from the steps by the Eskimo's falling body I was unable to think. Covered with blood—which clearly was not his own—the man bowed as he pantingly entered. Quickly he addressed me in his own tongue, which Charlie roughly translated:

"Three of the tunnels have been entered and a number of men and wolves are loose within the plateau. The rear parties and guardsmen are tracking them down. One of them has already surrendered himself and has volunteered important information. He was one of Northan's men originally and fled the plateau only under extreme pressure from the warlord. Northan's intention is to wreck the plateau and carry off both Tracy and Armandra. Even if he cannot take the plateau, he must not return without the women. Ithaqua will not allow Northan to fail him."

A terrible foreboding suddenly gripped me. "Charlie, take over." I tossed him the binoculars as I ran past the bloodied guardsman and swerved into a shaft that led into the plateau's labyrinths. "I have to get to Tracy. She's with Jimmy Franklin, and if the wolf-warriors have managed to get men this far into the plateau so quickly I'm taking no chances!"

I need not have worried. As I arrived at the head of a flight of stairs that reached down to the lower levels and the open cave where Jimmy had set up his catapult, he and my sister were just appearing from below. They were accompanied by four massive Eskimo guardsmen. Tracy was dishevelled and Jimmy had bruises and a few cuts, but aside from a superficial roughing-up neither of them seemed seriously hurt.

Relief flooded my being at the sight of Tracy's shaky but reassuring smile. "I must be crazy," I told Jimmy, "to let you set up that sling of yours so close to the foot of the plateau. What happened?"

"No one's fault, Hank," he answered. "I guess we just underestimated the enemy's penetration power. A pair of wolf-warriors made it up to our cave." He looked grim as he added, "They weren't so hard, though—not after they saw Tracy's pile of star-stones. And I know just how they felt. I was pretty terrified of those stones myself."

Excitement suddenly filled his voice. "You should have seen it, Hank. When we started hurling the stones at Ithaqua's army—what a frenzy and a scattering! Anyway, during the scrabble the catapult was wrecked, then I got one of the intruders with his own spear. But by God—spears and tomahawks are no match for star-stones! While I was occupied with my man the other one tried to get behind me. Tracy managed to hit him with a stone. It seemed to stick in him and burn there. His side seemed to roast away!"

"Oh, Jimmy, don't!" Tracy cried, the tremulous smile dropping instantly from her face. She looked suddenly very small, pale and frightened. Only her tremendous courage was keeping her going.

"A couple of seconds after that," Jimmy finished off, "these fellows arrived—just too late to give us a hand. They told us it wouldn't be safe for a while in the lower levels. There are about a hundred enemy warriors loose down there, not to mention some two dozen wolves."

"That many!" I gasped. "Look, you'd better follow me to Armandra. Two of the guardsmen will stay with you, in case you come up against trouble along the way. The other two can go and help Charlie Tacomah. He's running the show now. I have to get a move on. And look after Tracy, Jimmy. I happen to know that Northan has plans to kidnap her. He's after Armandra, too. I'll see you both later."

No sooner had I left them, climbing in a spiral toward the uppermost levels, then I sensed Armandra's mental presence. I opened my mind and she said, *"Hank, what is happening?"*

"There are wolf-warriors in the plateau, I don't know how many. The guardsmen and rear parties are hunting them down but you may be in danger, Armandra. Northan means to take you back to Ithaqua, and Tracy with you. Tracy is safe enough for now, but what about you?"

"There are eight guardsmen within hailing distance, plus Kasna'chi and Gosan-ha. All are sworn to protect me with their lives."

"You should have ten," I told her.

She answered, *"I sent two of them away with their bears. I ordered them to the snow-ship keeps, to the side of Kota'na, Oontawa's man."*

"Good," I said. *"I'm sure there's a lot more of your mother's nature in you than you suspect, Armandra. Anyway, I'm on my way to you. I've left Charlie Tacomah in command; he will make a better job of it than I could. Right now I'm wondering what tricks Northan and Ithaqua have up their sleeves."*

With that thought another occurred to me; the plateau had a couple of tricks of its own. By now the wolf-warriors should be attacking in a frustrated crush all along the face of the plateau. I hoped the holes they had already found in our defenses had by now been blocked. All being well, Charlie Tacomah should have ordered the pouring of the burning oil down upon the heads of the invaders. The plateau's mineral oil reserves had provided a defensive device of hideous potency.

Armandra plucked the thought out of my head.

"*Yes, I have been to the balcony. The foot of the plateau is a sea of fire. The Children of the Winds are dying by the hundreds.*" No trace of pleasure showed in her thoughts. Alien though her anger might be, her compassion was warm and human.

"*Go back to the balcony,*" I told her. "*I'll meet you there. I want to see how things are going.*"

"*Things seem to be going well for us indeed. But war is—terrible. The only thing in it that gives me pleasure is the thought of my father at this very moment. He must be beside himself with rage! I will go now to the balcony. Hank?*"

"*Yes?*"

"*Take care.*"

Two thirds of the way to my destination the sounds of a chase reached me. I slowed to a halt and as I stood there trying to control my breathing and listening in the light of many flickering flambeaux, it soon became apparent that the sounds of flight and pursuit were coming closer. In a few seconds more three wolf-warriors, clinging to the sides of one great wolf, burst from the mouth of a horizontal tunnel.

They saw me. As they dropped from the wolf's sides like ticks from an infested dog, one of them spoke to the beast. It sprang at me, its massive muzzle thrusting forward. I had a spear but no time to throw it. I leaned back on the shaft of the weapon until its hilt found a purchase against the uneven floor, bracing it against the wolf's spring. The great beast impaled itself on the spear, knocking me aside and wrenching the weapon from my hands.

While the wolf howled out its life in agony on the floor, the three warriors came at me in a rush. Weaponless, I threw myself up a flight of steps, turning to kick the fastest of my pursuers full in the face. He fell from the steps with a scream and crashed to the stone floor head first.

I made to climb higher and one of the remaining warrior threw himself after me. He grabbed my foot, causing me to loose my balance and fall between him and his companion. On my back, I managed to catch the wrist of one of my attackers as he aimed his tomahawk at my face, and while I briefly wrestled with him on the steps I wondered why the other man made no attempt to help his colleague.

Then as finally I overcame my attacker and throttled him with the haft of his own weapon, I saw why his friend had not helped him. The last of the three invaders was tottering down the steps, uselessly tugging at a spear that transfixed him. A second flashing spear pierced him as I watched, hurling him from the steps.

Then two of the plateau's guardsmen hurried up to me while five more positioned themselves at the mouths of the gallery's tunnels. "Are you all right, Lord?" one of my rescuers, a strapping young Viking, asked as I climbed to my feet.

"My thanks for your timely intervention," I answered. "Yes, I'm unhurt. But how goes it now? How many more of Northan's warriors lurk in the plateau's caves and tunnels?"

"Perhaps a dozen of them," he answered, "but they, too, will soon be hunted down."

"And their wolves?"

"Few remain, Lord."

This man seemed well informed; he had obviously been in a position to follow the course of events closely. "What about the plateau's losses?"

"The snow-ships and their crews are lost."

"I know," I answered. "I saw it. They were brave men."

"Within the plateau, when the first wolf-warriors found a way in, we lost some men and bears. A man for a man, a bear for two wolves, perhaps. Now that they can no longer get in—"

"I have no time now for talk," I cut him off, "but you have made my mind easier. Do not stop, but keep on searching the wolf-warriors out. Tell any others of the plateau's men you may meet the same thing. Now I go to Armandra."

And as I continued on my way, as if invoked by my mentioning her name, Armandra's mental voice came to me again: *"I am at the balcony, Hank. Is anything wrong?"*

"A bit of a scuffle," I answered. *"Don't worry, nothing came of it."*

"The wolf-warrior hordes have pulled back from the foot of the plateau," she informed me, *"out of the way of the blazing oil. But it seems to me that Ithaqua's priests are up to some trickery."*

"I'll be with you in a minute or so," I said, entering the final gallery and crossing it to the tunnel with the lightning-flash symbol. And there I was brought up short in sheerest shock and terror. Terror not for myself, for Armandra. There, sprawled in attitudes of grisly death,

lay three of my woman's guardsmen—a bear, too, its spilled entrails still steaming—and the bodies of four wolf-warriors and a wolf.

Tired as I was from my race against gravity and time, my heels grew wings as I threw myself down the perimeter corridor and finally turned into the jutting balcony with its widely spaced bars. And there, his back to me, tomahawk raised to deliver a stunning blow, an Indian in the matted apparel of a wolf-warrior furtively crouched.

Beyond him, ignorant of his presence, Armandra stood at the bars, staring down at the plain where the Children of the Winds milled in confusion and frustration; but as I entered in a rush they both turned. She saw him even as he saw me, and as he leaped to meet me she cried out, *"No!"*

His reactions were quick and I was tired. His weapon caught me a glancing blow on the head that sent me dazed to my knees. Up went his tomahawk again and his wild cry was one of certain victory—cut short in strangled amazement!

He was whirled off his feet, thrust aloft and spreadeagled in midair by centrifugal force as his body spun ever faster in mad currents of air. The suddenly howling wind that filled the balcony snatched at my hair, hurled me aside, slammed the shrieking wolf-warrior time and again against the uneven surface of the ceiling, finally shot him headlong, with a snapping of bones, out through the bars and away into empty abysses of icy air.

And slowly the sentient hair fell back upon her head and her blazing crimson eyes dulled as Armandra ran to me sobbing, a woman once more, where only seconds earlier an elemental of the air had commanded familiar winds!

I held her tight and for the moment there was no war in progress, no shadow over Borea. Then I became angry.

"Where are the rest of your guardsmen? I saw only three of them, all dead, back along the perimeter tunnel—what of the rest?"

"Three of my men, dead?"

"They died to stop this man and his brothers reaching you—and they almost died in vain."

"I sent the others away," she admitted, leading me over to the bars of the balcony. "They wanted to join in the fighting and I felt capable of fending for my—"

"Oh, did you?" I cut her off. "And if I had not come along when I did?"

"But you *did* come, Hank. Now come, we have no time for quarreling. Look down there. What do you make of that?"

I took hold of the bars and looked out. The wolf-warrior army had pulled back to a distance of about one hundred and fifty yards from the foot of the plateau. There against the white of the plain they formed a deep dark band that stretched away and around the curving protective walls of rock to both sides. Between them and the fortified tunnels and keeps an ocean of fire, its warmth reaching up to me even at this height, blazed and roared. At first I could not see what was causing Armandra's concern, then I saw that the wolf-warriors were opening up to leave clear paths through their ranks from the rear to the front. They were making way for something. But what?

"My father's so-called 'priests,' see?" Armandra said, pointing. "There, at the rear of the army. And now I know what they are about."

"Yes, I've seen them cavorting like that before," I agreed. "Then they were calling up those tornadoes of theirs, working their devilish magic through your father."

"That is exactly what they are doing now," she said. "See? And once they have called up their snow-devils they will throw them into the fire and smother it. And then—"

"Then?"

She turned to look at me with wide, unflinching eyes. "Then they will hurl those whirligigs at the tunnel entrances, the keep gates. They will drive them deep into the plateau and the wolf-warriors will follow behind!"

"Armandra, I—"

"I have promised not to fight my father, Hank, but those—*creatures* of his, his 'priests'—they must be stopped!"

"If you interfere, it may draw Ithaqua into the battle."

"And if I don't, the plateau is lost anyway."

Down below six spinning tops had appeared, each with its own capering master behind it, urging it on. Six alien whirlwinds that grew up rapidly out of the frozen plain and moved threateningly forward, roaring along the paths cleared by the wolf-warriors, entering and obscuring in clouds of steam and smoke the field of blazing oil fires.

Armandra was right and I knew it. In another moment Ithaqua's priests would hurl those spinning pillars directly at the keeps and major tunnel entrances. They would wipe the tunnels clean of men and bears in seconds. The swinging engines that carried the star-stones might be safe enough, Ithaqua's familiar winds and powers were restricted by his own limitations. But not all of the tunnels were so well protected, and only the actual gates of the keeps carried those symbols of Eld. To simply allow these priests of the Wind-Walker to use their tools of an alien science as they desired would be suicidal.

"Armandra," I told her, "do whatever must be done."

From beside me, so close that I felt her breath fanning my cheek as she spoke, and in a tone that called up visions of unknown star-voids, she said, "It is already begun!"

I glanced at her and felt the hair of my neck prickle at the sight of that strange pink flush that spread outward from the closed eyes to fill her pale face. I stepped quickly back as her hair began to rise up in undulating coils above her head and the white fur smock she wore stirred with weird life.

Gone again was the woman I loved, gone in a matter of seconds to make way for this child of Ithaqua, whose arms now reached up to beckon to the suddenly agitated sky. High above, gray clouds turned black, then blue, boiling in an instant and flashing with trapped energies. A continuous rumbling filled the pregnant air.

The fine bones of Armandra's head and neck showed redly through luminous flesh, a grinning skull of death. Her eyes opened; beams of blinding ruby radiance shot forth to the pulsating sky; she made stabbing motions with her hands, which were curved downward now like the heads of swans.

And then I was sent staggering back from the bars, away from the vicious rain of red lightnings that lashed down in staccato precision from the sky to the plain below! I did not see those deadly white funnels destroyed—saw nothing of the carnage among the massed ranks of the wolf-warriors when, finished with the sundered tornadoes, Armandra simply rained her devastating energies down upon flesh and blood. I was told of it later, and then I was glad I had not seen it.

No, I saw nothing; nor, deafened from the first hellish salvo, did I hear anything, for which I am also grateful. And even when it was done, several minutes elapsed before I was able to perceive anything but the scarlet blaze burning on my retinas and the pounding of blood in my nearly ruptured eardrums.

Armandra lay huddled beside the bars, sobbing and momentarily spent. Again her terrific anger had vented itself uncontrollably, and again the human side of her nature was betrayed. I went dazedly forward to comfort her but then, as my eyes inadvertently looked down upon the plain, I froze in awed disbelief. Where an army had massed in premature triumph, a demoralized rabble now moved in blind, crippled agony.

Great black smoking craters littered the plain all along the front of the plateau, as if a squadron of bombers had unloaded their bomb bays there. Where the priests had capered to the rear, now a gutted trench lay straight as the furrow of a giant's plow in the icy ground. And in the wake of Armandra's inferno of lunatic lightnings, at last there sprang up a mournful wind that caught up the billowing smoke and steam to lay it like a veil across the whole scene, as if to hide the horror there.

Now, cradling the Woman of the Winds in my arms and rocking her, I heard drifting up to me a thousand amazed cries of utter disbelief and nameless horror from the survivors of that destroyed army. And rising above those cries came the lustful, reverberating battle cry of the plateau's fighting men:

"Sil-ber-*hut-te!* Sil-ber-*hut-te!*"

For a moment I cursed aloud, wildly and blasphemously. God, no! I would not have my name as a seal upon *that*—upon the carnage Armandra's blind fury had wrought. But then I was amazed to see that even now the remaining wolf-warriors, who still far outnumbered the men of the plateau, were rallying to the sort of battle they could understand.

And once more I felt my heart surge within me as out from the base of the plateau, from its tunnels and keeps, rushed the authors of that concerted battle cry, unleashed at last by Charlie Tacomah to earn their honor on a field of bloodied snow and ice!

III

War of the Winds

(Recorded through the Medium of Juanita Alvarez)

No sooner was the battle joined than my attention was distracted from it by footfalls sounding in the perimeter tunnel. One of the guardsmen I had left with Jimmy and Tracy hurried into view. He gave a cry of relief when he found us unharmed; he had passed the bodies of his colleagues at the entrance to the tunnel.

Now he composed himself, bowed first to Armandra and then turned to me. "Lord, your sister, and your friend have gone to the roof of the plateau to view the fighting. They bade me come and tell you."

I nodded. "And your partner—did he go with them?"

"Yes, Lord."

"Then you had better follow them. Stay with them until this is all over."

He bowed again to me and again to Armandra, then hurried back the way he had come.

"If they wish to view the fighting," Armandra said when he had gone, "there are few better places from which to do so than here."

"Perhaps they were seeking Whitey. The three of them have grown very close."

"Whitey," she mused, "whose powers have deserted him. Is it a dark omen, I wonder?"

"It's a disadvantage, certainly, but I wouldn't consider it a dark omen. On the contrary, things are going very well. See, despite the odds your people are fighting an inspired battle. They are making a shambles of Ithaqua's army."

"They are *our* people, Hank, yours and mine. And they will be victorious because my father's wolf-warriors are demoralized. I have crippled them." She stared for a few seconds at the milling scene below, then lifted her eyes to the distant pyramid altar of ice and heterogeneous "trophies." I followed her gaze as her eyes widened—and then we gasped in unison.

The Wind-Walker was raging, swelling out; his arms were lifted in a threatening attitude; his carmine eyes were blazing in his bloating face. In another moment he had stepped from his altar to stride aloft, and he was coming straight for the plateau!

"They have failed him," Armandra gasped. "The Children of the Winds have failed him yet again. Now he will seek vengeance upon the plateau—and upon his own men!"

"But how can he strike us?" I protested. "The plateau is safeguarded by the star-stones."

"Those star-stones of the Elder Gods!" she passionately cried. "I loathe and abhor the things and the gloom they cast over the plateau and its people."

"They are a symbol of benign power in the plateau," I argued, "and without them all would long ago have been lost."

"A benign symbol, yes," she answered, "like the crucifix in the Motherworld. Don't you see, Hank, that all great symbols of power are horrific in their way?"

At the time I didn't give it a lot of thought, but now that I've thought about it I can see what she meant. Certainly the star-stone is benign to anyone not contaminated by Ithaqua or his hideous brothers of the Cthulhu Cycle. Of course the crucifix is a symbol of goodness, despite the fact that it is a model of a most terrible torture machine. The swastika too was an emblem of life, luck and power long before it became the outline of horror. What more innocuous than the hammer and sickle; tools of everyday life and labor?

"But look," she said, "perhaps you are right that my father is helpless to harm us. See, he hesitates."

High above his totem temple the Wind-Walker hung motionless in the sky, his evil eyes glaring at the plateau. I knew that he saw—or felt—the power of the star-stones, those same stones which had held him so long impotent, and I knew that they repulsed him as surely as like magnetic poles repel each other.

"What is he doing?" I asked, as he commenced upward sweeping motions with monstrously bloated arms.

"He calls a wind," she answered, frowning. "But to what purpose, for surely no energies of his devising may strike us now?"

"Look!" I exclaimed. "Those dots on the plain, black dots rising into the air, what are they?"

Rapidly the things I referred to climbed into the sky and were blown forward ahead of the Wind-Walker as he recommenced his striding toward the plateau, and a moment later I believed I knew what they were.

"Kites!" Armandra cried, confirming my own opinion. "Kites shaped like bats that fly on my father's breath. And they carry men."

"Man-carrying kites," I gasped. "But that must mean that he intends to land them—"

"On the roof," she finished for me.

Then her eyes went very wide. "Hank, I think it would have been better if Tracy and Jimmy had come here to us instead of going to the roof!"

"Oh my God!" I whispered, instinctively turning from her, heading for the perimeter tunnel.

She called out after me, "Hank, wait!"

I came to a hesitant halt, half turned. "I have to get them off the roof, out of harm's way."

"If you go up there," she said breathlessly, "you will have to fight. See, already my father's man-kites approach. And if you fight. . . ." She shook her head wildly, as if shaking off the dark shapes of nightmare. "I must not lose you now, man of Earth."

"My sister and my friends, Armandra," I quickly answered. "I have no choice. I could never live with myself." Then, wasting no more time, I ran from the balcony.

In my mind, before I could shut her out, she cried after me: *"Hank! Hank! Our bargain!"*

I knew that from the gallery at the far end of the perimeter corridor a long flight of steps wound their way up to the roof; it should take me no more than two or three minutes to get up there. I raced along the corridor, started up the winding steps, taking them in threes, and as I went I gave credit to the evil intelligence that was Ithaqua.

He had known the weakest spot in the plateau's defenses all along; the roof, where only a handful of men, few of them warriors, kept wary watch over the white wastes. Well, I was sure of one thing at least. No matter how many of his kites Ithaqua hurled at the plateau, no matter how heavy the odds, those watchers on the roof would stand and fight to the end.

Only four passageways in all led up to the flat, ruggedly stark roof, four orifices opening into the gray light of Borea. All four were spaced out across the roof's surface, the only accesses. What if Tracy and the others had been cut off from them? These and similar thoughts ran circles in my mind as I flew up the last few steps. In fact I must have taken well under the three minutes I had allowed myself, but it seemed as though half an hour had elapsed before finally I stood panting out in the open air, where the wind rushed over the slippery stone in furious blasts.

I paused briefly to assess the situation and get my breath back. Apart from the presence of a number of kite-men, there was something very wrong with the sight that now met my eyes—something which was soon to become plain to me.

I picked out the figures of Tracy, Jimmy and Whitey almost immediately; they were fighting with those of Ithaqua's raiders who had already effected landings. With them were about a dozen watchmen, also caught unaware by the aerial attack.

They were not together in a group. Tracy was the most distant from me; about eighty yards separated us. She held up one of her star-stones before her, a threat to any of the Wind-Walker's men who might attempt to get too close. She had found this stone still on its chain where Northan's dupe had left it. The other one was lost, gone forever in some dark crevice in the forbidden tunnel. Tracy had not yet seen me. She appeared to be trying to make her way to Jimmy. I called out to her but my shout was lost in a frenzy of winds.

Jimmy was at the forward edge of the plateau, where waist-high battlements faced out across the white waste. As I saw him he was in the act of spearing one of the raiders who was just attempting a landing. Having killed his man with a single thrust, Jimmy toppled him from the roof along with his kite.

Whitey was the closest to me. Flanked by two of the watchmen, who fought equally furiously, he was battling like a madman to hold off a handful of the invaders. There were fifteen of us in all, against about the same number of kite-men, but more of the latter were landing all the time. One thing was heartening at least; for the moment Ithaqua stood away.

Dark and bloated against the gray skies, ten times taller than a tall man, the monster trod the air half a mile from the plateau's roof almost as a swimmer treads water. With his eyes blazing avidly and his arms half reaching forward, he formed the most fantastic part of the whole scene. I knew that he noted every detail of the situation, but that as eager as he was to destroy the plateau and steal back his daughter—and take Tracy, too, for his monstrous purposes—still the star-stones held him at bay.

The star-stones! Now I knew what had bothered me about the scene on the roof. Ithaqua's raiders were not trying to break into the plateau, they were there simply to clear the way for their master. He had sent them to destroy the great protective star that my sister had traced with star-stones on the plateau's roof! With that out of the way,

Ithaqua would be able to completely command the roof and land as many of his aerial warriors upon it as he could muster.

And now, out there on the wings of the wind, I could see that there were *hundreds* of the kites. The brilliance of the Wind-Walker's stratagem was obvious. Ninety-five percent of the plateau's soldiery were engaged in the battle down below, and the rest of the able-bodied men were at their posts deep down in the rocky labyrinths. Reinforcements would doubtless come, but would they be in time?

But no, my reasoning was way off—I must be wrong! The Children of the Winds couldn't possibly have been sent to get rid of the star-stones. They were as helpless against them as Ithaqua himself!

All of these things rushed through my mind as I surveyed the roof. Then I started to run toward Tracy, slowing for a second to snatch up a tomahawk from beside a dead kite man. As I went I called her name again, and this time she heard me. That was a wonder, for above the howling of the wind, at precisely the same time that I called her, there came a shrieking like none I had ever heard before. It was the sound of a soul in torment, a banshee howling that froze my unnaturally chilled blood even further, causing me to seek, wide-eyed for its source.

And when I found that source I knew that I had been right after all, and that the fear Ithaqua inspired in his "children" was absolute.

One of the kite-men was tearing at a star-stone where it was fastened to the battlements. The flesh was visibly blackening on his hands as he scrabbled frenziedly to tear the stone loose. His screams did not stop for a single moment but grew shriller still as his fingers began to fall off. Finally he tore the stone free and clutched it to his chest, then gave the most hideous scream of all as black smoke poured out from him. He tottered for a moment, then, as the stench of his burning reached me on the rushing wind, crumbled like rotting wood and fell from the battlements.

Suddenly the wind increased, blowing especially from that region of the roof now unprotected by the stone sigil of Eld, and at the same time I noted shrieks of mortal terror and horror springing up from four other distinct points all around the rim of the plateau. Heedless of their fatal torment—which must have been the ultimate in physical and psychic agony—Ithaqua's aerial suicide squadron was proceeding with its task of clearing the roof. And as the star-stones were removed one by one, the Wind-Walker himself came closer, suspended in the sky.

I had not quite reached Tracy when two kite-men, freshly free of the harnesses of their aircraft, sprang at her. Their weapons were still in their belts and it was plain that their task was to render her helpless and somehow bear her away. I threw my weapon just as one of them went to strike her with his clenched fist. As she ducked his blow and swung her star-stone on its chain full in his face, my tomahawk bit into his side. It is possible that he didn't even feel the bite of my weapon for the agony of Tracy's. His face caved in, black and ruined, and he went down as though a truck had hit him. The second man turned toward me but was thrown down by the force of my rush. As he started to rise I kicked him in the throat as hard as I could. Tracy freed her star-stone from the mess of the first man's face, and as I backed hastily away she began to be sick.

Looking about me I saw that almost all of the invaders had been dealt with, killed and swept from the roof as they had gone about their task of clearing its surface of star-stones. Nevertheless, they seemed to have successfully completed that task. There came a weird, shrill whistling, emanating from the hundreds of batlike shapes that still hung in the sky between the plateau's roof and the swollen figure of the Snow-Thing. The kites were soaring forward, the wind whistling its demon song in their frames of poles and stretched hides. Now Ithaqua could take possession of the roof, land the rest of his airborne forces and invade the plateau.

"Tracy!" I yelled in her ear. "Get below. I want everyone off the roof. We'll be outnumbered in no time at all and Ithaqua himself may even make a landing here." I pointed her in the direction of the tunnel I had used and gave her a gentle push. She started to slip and stumble away from me, barely keeping her feet as the wind's strength rapidly increased.

Having seen her on her way to safety, I signalled to Whitey, Jimmy and the remaining handful of watchmen that they, too, should get below where they could better defend the four entrances. Seeing that they understood my signals, I turned to follow Tracy and was greeted by a sight that shocked me rigid. She had fallen and was sliding in the wind across the icy surface of the roof. Ithaqua had seen her and was moving after her!

He came forward and poised himself above the rim of the plateau, his vast feet seeking purchase on the battlements. From side to side his great bloated head went, slitted star-eyes taking in every detail of what was happening. They found Tracy again and stayed upon her where she finally slid to a halt against a projection of rock. Then the Wind-Walker stepped down onto the roof and reached for her with a massive hand. Immediately she held up her star-stone against his approach . . .

Slits of burning evil opened huge and round as the horror stepped hastily back and lifted into the air. Rage filled every line of his nightmare form. He trembled with an inner fury that swelled him out more hugely yet, completely distorting his already grotesque proportions, then he abruptly thrust up a hand to the clouds that raced across the sky.

I knew instinctively what he was about. While his alien powers could not work *directly* against my sister as long as she held that star-stone, he could use them *indirectly* in a purely physical attack, and now he would simply kill her out of hand and be done with it. I tried to go after her, only to be blown off my feet and sent slithering helplessly across the roof. Fighting to find a hold on the slippery surface, I managed to keep my eyes on Ithaqua and saw him pluck a great ball of ice out of the clouds. I saw his face convulse insanely as he hurled his missile at the roof.

I thought then that Tracy was done for, but I had reckoned without Jimmy Franklin. Tracy was my sister, yes, and I loved her, but Jimmy's love was that of a man for his woman. He fought his way to where she crouched against the outcrop of rock, and dragged her behind it at the very instant that Ithaqua released his ice-bomb. Now that bomb burst like a massive grenade where she had crouched a second earlier, but in the protective lee of the great rock, she and Jimmy were unharmed.

Since she was no longer visible to Ithaqua after the flying shards of ice dispersed, perhaps the monster thought her dead. I think it must have been so, for apparently without another thought for her he turned his attention to me.

And if horror can grin, now this monster grinned; if evil can express delight, Ithaqua was delighted.

Sliding helplessly before the howling wind, flat on my back and scrabbling at the icy stone beneath me, I felt his mind probe mine. Before I could shut him out he said something to me, showed me alien pictures, made me understand. It was no sort of telepathic transmission that I could ever hope to explain, not even to another telepath, and yet I understood its meaning:

"*So. You are that man of Earth who dared set himself against me. That same one who hurls insults with his mind and threatens with powers of Eld. You are the one who would take the very seed of my being for your own, to make a mere mortal of her. You are nothing, man of Earth, and nothing you shall remain.*"

He reached one arm to the sky and pointed his other hand at me. I saw strange energies forming in the clouds, a flickering radiance that ran down his extended arm to his body and turned its barely manlike outline to an ever-changing display of crimson and golden traceries of light. In another instant that electrical nightmare would leap from his outstretched finger to me, and I would cease to be.

"*Father!*" There came a pure, bell-like resonance in my mind, a call which I heard even though it was not directed at me. "*Ithaqua— you will not take what is mine!*"

Unable to face the crackling holocaust that I knew was soon to come, I had closed my eyes. Now I opened them and lifted my head from the frozen stone surface. Of a number of things that were happening, the most important to me was that Ithaqua had partly turned away from me to face the forward rim of the plateau where now, floating slowly into view, the form of Armandra rose up. With her appearance the wind seemed abruptly to die away, to crouch down into itself and back off like a scolded dog.

"*Armandra,*" I said to her, reaching beyond the alien mask she wore to the sane and human side of her nature, "*I thank you for my life—but not at the expense of your own!*"

"*Do not distract me, Hank. All is not lost, not yet, but I need my concentration.*" To think that those mental tones of purest gold had come from the female horror that rode the wind above the rim of the plateau! Her hair was floating in fiery, undulating waves over her head; her face was a deathmask. In that skull-like face, carmine pits of hell blazed in supernatural fury to match her father's own. She was tiny, compared to him, but her hatred and anger were great.

As she rose higher above the battlements, streams of guardsmen and warriors began to rush from the four exits. Pouring out onto the roof, they looked much fiercer than I ever remembered seeing them before, and I believed I knew why. One way or the other this was to be the final scene, and they knew it. They were here to lay down their lives for their princess, their world. At last they had been given an opportunity to fight, these men who had formed the rear parties, and they had arrived barely in time. Now great hordes of Ithaqua's kitemen were landing all about the roof, freeing themselves from their harnesses, moving into battle positions.

While all this was happening, I was almost unable to believe that somehow I had been spared. I came back to life, and my heart began to beat a little more freely as I saw that those energies Ithaqua had almost hurled at me were dying away, that the traceries of fire no longer permeated his dark form. He had apparently forgotten all about me; now he held out his bloated arms to Armandra in an attitude which, despite his completely alien nature, was almost humanly imploring. In answer she raised one pale arm above her head and rotated her hand, as if to spin the sky upon her fingers. And indeed the clouds immediately above her began to turn with her hand.

Undaunted, Ithaqua stepped closer, his monstrous feet treading air as he narrowed the gap separating him from his daughter. But this was no gap of merely physical dimensions. It was unbridgeable in anything other than the crudest physical sense. She floated back away from him, glowing with a scarlet flush, and faster yet her arm twirled above her head. Then, without warning, she lowered her hand to a forward, horizontal position and jabbed it viciously in her hideous father's direction.

From the whirling clouds directly above her, lightning at once struck, branching into a blinding fork that speared at Ithaqua's eyes. He never moved, stood unblinking and still as a hawk on the wind. Only those hellish orbs of his changed; they momentarily flared brighter as twin tongues of lightning were quenched in them. He had not even bothered to ward off Armandra's initial attack; what is the blow of a child to a man full grown? Ah, but that first blow of hers had opened up floodgates of accumulated loathing.

Now she stabbed at her father again and again, her hand like the tongue of some venomous reptile, invoking powers I had once believed to belong to nature alone. Lightning flashed in an almost continuous stream from the clouds to Ithaqua's form, filling him with blue and white fire. Through all of this he stood unharmed, but if she did not hurt him, certainly she angered him.

The imploring attitude he had seemed to adopt fell away and his massive body began to tremble in rage. One of the hands he held out to Armandra clenched and rose up threateningly, swept across to strike his own shoulder in a strangely human gesture of pride. The game was over, the "offer" was withdrawn—now the Wind-Walker *demanded* obedience! He might as well have asked it of the wide seas of Earth or the desert's sands. She simply moved farther away and continued to rain down her lightnings, whose bolts became increasingly violent.

So much I saw before being drawn into the tide of renewed battle that washed across the roof. For with Armandra holding Ithaqua's attention so completely, his aerial invaders were on their own against the men of the plateau, and where the latter were concerned, no quarter would be asked and none given. Hearing my name on the lips of every man who fought for the plateau, I joined them, hurling myself headlong into the fighting.

It was then that Whitey found his way to me through the mass of struggling bodies. "Hank," he gasped, dragging me behind a natural wall of rock that protected one of the openings into the plateau. "Hank, I have an idea."

"A hunch?"

"No, just an idea. My hunch days are over."

"All right, what is it?"

"Tracy has a star-stone with her, right? Well, if she can somehow manage to fasten it to a spearhead—tie it firmly with a thong or something—do you suppose you could land it on Ithaqua's warty hide?"

"He makes a big enough target," I answered. "I suppose I should be able to do it. Come on, let's see if we can get to Tracy and Jimmy."

Making our way across the roof was not easy. Through gaps in the tumult we got occasional glimpses of the two of them, Jimmy fighting like a madman side by side with a massive Eskimo guardsman, and Tracy behind them, her back to the same rocky projection that had kept her safe from Ithaqua's ice-bomb, protecting their flanks with her star-stone. But halfway to them we got split up. The last I saw of Whitey for a while, he was tackling a lean Viking, while I myself was faced with a pair of hatchet-faced braves.

I was lucky, managing to kill both my men without being hurt. At the same time I discovered a strange thing; though there was more than one occasion when nearby guardsmen might have stepped in and made things easier, not one of them lifted a hand to help me. I had obviously reached new heights of legend; Sil-ber-hut-te could look after himself and wouldn't thank anyone for interfering!

But if I could look after myself, the same could no longer be said of Armandra. As I cleared a path for myself through the crush of fighting men, I saw that Armandra was almost spent. The energies she drew from the whirling clouds were less powerful, her stance less steady above the plateau's rim. And her father was beginning to enjoy his invulnerability. As the lightning rained about him, so he would use his great hands to deflect the bolts into the groups of furiously fighting men on the roof. It seemed of absolutely no concern to Ithaqua where these bolts fell or what mayhem they caused; the deaths of his own followers were of no consequence to him.

In any case, within the space of a few seconds more it could be seen that with or without Ithaqua's concern, his human allies were well and truly beaten. Though they fought a desperate, ragged retreat to the battlements, where at last the monstrous shadow of their lord and master fell upon them, still the men of the plateau followed them up, determined that not one of them would escape. The end came quickly even as I watched. Taking full advantage of their opportunity the plateau's soldiers made one last effort, forming an unbreakable wall and moving inexorably forward until the remaining kite-men were simply pushed off the roof into empty space. They fell in a screaming human rain from the rim.

Then I turned my eyes again to the sky, to the bloated figure of Ithaqua and the tiny shape of his daughter as their aerial confrontation continued. But that battle, too, if such an unequal contest could rightly be termed a battle, was almost done. Exhausted, Armandra seemed to waver in the sky, her eyes dulling and brightening spasmodically, while her father waxed ever more triumphant in his mockery of her efforts.

Now there was a complete absence of movement on the roof as every eye followed Armandra's struggle. I was on the point of reaching out to her with my mind to offer whatever mental assistance I could, when above the crazed howling of the wind and following immediately in the wake of yet another deflected bolt of lightning, I heard Whitey cry, "Hank—I've got it!"

He was making his way to me across the death-strewn roof with Jimmy and Tracy on his heels. In his hand he carried his secret weapon, its fatal head held well out in front of and away from his body.

And it was at that very moment that Ithaqua suddenly reached out and snatched Armandra out of the sky. Drained of all her strength, she made no effort to escape him but seemed simply to collapse, a doll in the fist of a giant.

"Armandra, hang on!" I cried out with my mind. She heard me, even though she was no longer strong enough to answer me, but what I had not reckoned with was that her father would also hear me. He did, and he must also have seen in my mind's eye a picture of the weapon I intended to use against him.

The Wind-Walker immediately turned to face me. He looked down upon me, and upon Whitey as he came rushing across the plateau's roof toward me. The monster's eyes slitted as they followed Whitey, then he lifted his free hand to the sky and thrust it into the lowering gray clouds.

"Whitey—look out!" I yelled, but my friend had also seen and knew what was going to happen. He knew, and on this occasion needed no precognition to tell him his fate.

Ithaqua moved closer, looming large over the roof as he hurled his ice-bomb. I saw it—saw Paul White's horrible but mercifully instant death beneath ten tons of ice that smashed down upon him like a meteorite—and I also saw his last heroic action in defiance of his destroyer. Not a second too soon, he slid the spear with its star-stone tip in my direction.

Skidding across the roof that weapon came, finally to slide to a halt at my feet. I stared at it for the merest moment, almost uncomprehendingly. Then, no longer fearing the stone sigil of Eld tied to the spear's blade—I was so numb with sick horror that I no longer felt or feared anything—I snatched it up. And as I felt the unevenly balanced shaft in my hand, so the sickness and the horror went out of me, *driven* out by murderous hate and a lusting for red revenge!

I drew back my arm and aimed the spear at the Wind-Walker, who seemed suddenly to lose coordination. As I hurled the spear, he began to bring his hands up to guard his face.

What happened then, is not an easy thing to tell. It seemed to me that the spear moved through the air in a sort of slow motion, and that Ithaqua's hand moved even slower, so that when the weapon shot in through the flinching slit of his left eye I could easily trace the disappearance of its length into his head. Then things began to speed up again. The dull roar that had been growing in my ears burst into a howl of approval from the warriors on the roof; the sky seemed to bend downward; the back of Ithaqua's head flew open and a stream of molten gold flooded out, through the midst of which the spear with its star-stone sigil continued its curving flight out over the plateau's rim.

It had passed through him just like the tracers we fired at him from the plane's machine gun (how many centuries ago?) during our first encounter, but with much more devastating effect! For while bullets were of no consequence to Ithaqua, the seal of the Elder Gods was very different.

The Wind-Walker reeled like a man struck in the forehead with a hammer. For a second I thought he would topple out of the sky as he fought wildly to regain his balance. Then something fell from his hand as he lurched erratically to and fro. It was Armandra, spiraling down like an autumn leaf, the dull pinkish flush emanating from her more dully yet as she slowly sank, until at a height of about twenty feet the glow blinked out and she fell like a stone.

As I ran toward her still form I saw Ithaqua throw up his hands to his swollen, pulsating head. I saw him striking his temples with the flat of his hands in a mad frenzy, while the stream of golden sparks continued to issue from his left eye and the wound at the back of his head, and then I "heard" a cry of what could only be described as purest alien anguish. It was his mental voice crying out against unbearable psychic stress, to which I automatically closed my mind lest I too feel his agony.

By the time I reached Armandra and knelt beside her, the Wind-Walker was lurching away down aerial paths, heading for the lonely sanctuary of his pyramid altar. But in contrast to his previous lordly stridings on the wings of the wind, now he moved with the spastic jerks and twitchings of a singed moth. He might well recover, but I knew that he would *never* forget.

IV

The Last Transmission

(Recorded through the Medium of Juanita Alvarez)

And for the present, Juanita, there is little more to tell. I believe I have already told you that Armandra may be crippled. There seems to be some injury to her spine; Jimmy and Tracy, however—they at least are safe. Jimmy received a few cuts from the ice-bomb that killed poor brave Whitey, but nothing serious.

When we left the roof, Jimmy and Tracy went off together to mourn in private while I returned to Armandra's chambers. Of course, she was not there; she had been taken to be examined by the plateau's greatest doctors. I stood on the high balcony looking out over the white waste and waited for news. I stayed there, in what must have been a state of delayed shock, for five or six hours.

When Oontawa came to me in tears I thought at first that she brought terrible news, but that wasn't it. She only wanted me to go with her to where her man, Kota'na, was lying in one of the plateau's hospitals. They had only just found him near the gates of the central snow-ship keep. He had been brought in with a pitiful handful of wounded men. His injuries were severe but not fatal; he needed rest but would not submit either to the physician's wishes or their drugs until he had seen me. I went with her, hurrying down into the bowels of the plateau.

Kota'na, who had a small room of his own befitting his rank and status, was hanging onto consciousness waiting for me. When he saw me a grim, tired smile creased his handsome Indian features. His arms were caked with blood and he bore terrible scars on various parts of his body, but he was in no way about to die. It was as Oontawa had told me; rest and recuperation were all he required to bring him back to complete recovery.

Now Oontawa translated as I bent over Kota'na's bed.

"Lord Sil-ber-hut-te, I beg your forgiveness."

"My forgiveness! For what, Kota'na? You fought for the plateau, for its princess, and for your woman, Oontawa. You fought well and commanded the bears and the men who handle them. You have no need to beg forgiveness of me."

Then he lifted up his hand from where it hung unseen on the far side of his raised pallet. His fingers were clenched in hair that was full of clotted blood, black hair rooted in the roughly severed head of Northan, which hung from Kota'na's fist and stared at me with wide, glassy eyes.

"Forgive me, Lord, for I knew that you would want him for yourself—and knowing it, I killed him. I tried to take him alive, but he would not let me. Take his head, it belongs to you."

"No." I shook my head at his offer. "The trophy is yours, Kota'na. Let it hang in your lodge so that your children will know of my debt to you, that their father killed Sil-ber-hut-te's great enemy, the traitor Northan. For this deed, I thank you."

Five minutes later, after accepting a drugged drink, Kota'na fell asleep and the physicians were able to begin washing him and cleaning his wounds. But it took them as long again to pry open his hand and remove Northan's head.

As for Ithaqua; he too appears to be resting. The monster crouches atop his pyramid altar and cradles his head in his hands. His left eye is half closed—yellow sparks drip from it like pus—and a dark spot is visible at the back of his head. Since his wounds were not fatal, I can only assume that he is recuperating. He has shrunk down into himself somewhat, though his size is still four or five times greater than that of a man. Even now I can see him as I gaze out across the white waste through my binoculars, and—

What was that?

Strange, I thought for a moment that—

But no, I must have been mistaken. Did you feel anything, Juanita? It seemed as though someone were listening in on our conversation. You didn't? Good. And yet I could have sworn that just for a moment I saw Ithaqua turn his head to peer evilly at the plateau out of his good eye . . .

A messenger has just arrived, sent by the physicians who attend Armandra. He seems to be quite delighted but I can't understand a word he says. It appears I am to accompany him.

I'll contact you again as soon as I have news.

NOTE:
The time was 5:50 p.m. on June 6 when Juanita Alvarez recorded that last hopeful message from Hank Silberhutte. His telepathic vibrations were then absent for some two hours, until, at 7:45 p.m., Juanita made the following, final, brief contact with him.

"Juanita, I'm back.

"*Everything is going to be all right!* I'm back on the balcony now, but I've just finished tidying up Armandra's—no, *our*—chambers, getting the place ready for her. She's conscious and they're carrying her up here right now. She's going to be fine, but she'll need a lot of rest and quiet. All she wanted when she awakened was to be with me.

God, Juanita, but you must be able to *feel* how happy I am! It's as if a terrible black cloud were suddenly lif—

"*Again!* And this time there can be no doubt about it. I was watching Ithaqua through the glasses while I talked to you. It was him, listening in, and suddenly he turned and looked at me—and he smiled in a terrible way!

"Juanita, I think he saw right through me—*to you!*

"But what in the . . . this? There seems . . . sort . . . interference. It's *him!* Ithaqua is scrambling my . . . losing you! And now . . . the altar and limping off across the sky. He looks back at me and . . . hideous laughter! . . . revenge? My God, it's you, Juanita. He can no longer hurt us, *so he's coming for you!*

"Tell Peaslee he has to look after you. Tell him—"

FINAL NOTE: For three long months, into the middle of September, Juanita stayed at Miskatonic and spent every minute of every day trying to reestablish contact with Hank. She never heard from him again, and having turned down my offer to take up a position with the Wilmarth Foundation, she left Arkham in the third week of the month.

When she went she took with her one of the star-stones of ancient Mnar, a genuine stone found with others by our African expeditions in 1959. We kept in contact until early the next year. When last I heard from her she was making wedding arrangements in Monterrey.

In March of the new year I learned how, along with her husband, she was killed in an automobile accident near Regina, Canada, where they were honeymooning. The car had been blown off the road and down a sheer drop in a "freak storm." I made inquiries and discovered that they had been returning to their hotel after a show. The gown Juanita was wearing had a plunging neckline—not the kind of gown she could wear her star-stone with.

As for Hank Silberhutte, his sister Tracy, and James Graywing Franklin: so far as I am aware they are still on Borea, a world at the edge of strange dimensions, somewhere out in remote regions of space and time.

My telepathic team at Miskatonic still occasionally try, without reward to date, to reestablish contact with Hank, and I personally will never give up hope.

—Wingate Peaslee.